LX

SKELMERS[...]

D1153184

FICTION RESERVE STOCK

LL 60

AUTHOR	CLASS
ALLEN, R.M.	F

TITLE
Farside cannon

ROGER MACBRIDE ALLEN

Farside Cannon

Futura

An Orbit Book

04091106

Copyright © 1988 by Roger MacBride Allen

First published in Great Britain in 1989 by
Futura Publications, a Division of
Macdonald & Co (Publishers) Ltd
London & Sydney

ISBN 0 7088 4305 0

Reproduced, printed and bound in Great Britain by
BPCC Hazell Books Ltd
Member of BPCC Ltd
Aylesbury, Bucks, England

Futura Publications
A Division of
Macdonald & Co (Publishers) Ltd
66–73 Shoe Lane
London EC4P 4AB
A member of Maxwell Pergamon Publishing Corporation plc

Dedication

**To Betsy Mitchell,
editor and friend,
without whom
all this
would not
have been possible**

FARSIDE
CANNON

Prelude

DEEP SPACE

In the bright light of the Sun lies the black of the void. It is the darkness not of night but of nothingness, darkness in the full roaring light of the raging Sun. Here there is nothing to see by that light, not the tiniest shard of matter that might catch the sunlight and reflect it back. The invisible photons of sunlight stream past into space, unhindered by anything larger than a microscopic dustmote.

Far off across space the stars shine, heroically distant and unimportant to this lonely place between the orbits of Earth and Venus. A few of the specks of light, the planets, are brighter, but none are so noticeable or important that one might assign them any special significance.

Even the double star of Earth and Moon, the closest and most brilliant points of light, seem unimportant against the field of distant stars.

Only the Sun seems of any power and importance—and it is so bright, so harsh, so intimidating that it must inspire fear, not familiarity. This is not the friendly Sun of Earth's sky, but a raging, dangerous star.

The Sun is over a hundred million kilometers away, its light several minutes old by the time it reaches this place, a remote neighbor by any human scale. Even so, fully a quarter of the sky is lost in its glare. But for the Sun, from here the Universe seems to be nothing but emptiness.

The Inner Solar System is thought of as being crowded with worlds—as indeed it is, compared to the far lonelier vastness of the Outer System, or the infinities of space beyond the last of the outer planets. But in reality, even the Inner System is mere emptiness, with only a handful of tiny worlds sprinkled niggardly across the darkness, easily lost in the trillions of cubic kilometers of nothingness.

Humans rarely come here—perhaps not just because there is little need, but because it is an unsettling place where comforting illusions fade away. Even here, in Earth's very backyard, space is clearly not the familiar and well-mastered domain humankind sanguinely imagines it to be—but an ultimately wild, lonely and desolate place.

Here, the idea that space is conquered, tamed, and civilized is given the lie. The truth is plain from here: Humanity's domains are merely tiny sphericules of settlement, minute volumes of space around a few of the planets; thin, wispy clouds of truly civilized space in the midst of emptiness. This spot, so close to mighty Earth's own orbit, is a wilderness.

But cruising, silently tumbling through the darkness here, barely visible to the naked eye from any distance at all—comes a sky mountain. Even against the gloom of space, and in the glare of the Sun, this dark worldlet of dim greys and blacks is hard to see. An oblong, carbonaceous-chrondite asteroid, an ancient burned-out comet long ago captured by the gravitic whirlpools of the Inner System, it is a treasure trove of the elements needed for life in space—carbon, hydrogen, nitrogen, oxygen—a treasure that has waited millions of years to be taken.

Coursing far above the plane of the Solar System, swinging through its lonely orbit, its form, size, probably composition and course have long been noted by humans. Robot surveyors venture to it several times and examine it close up, watching through robotic camera eyes as it tumbles end over end. The probes send their images back to engineers and planners, to men and women who have long had designs on this lump of rock.

The great-grandparents of these engineers found this nameless mass of stone over a hundred years ago, through telescopes that were old even then. But only now, a long century and more after this asteroid's discovery, has it become practical—or at least barely possible—to retrieve it.

Years after the robot probes finish their work, the ships come, shockingly small alongside even such a tiny planetesimal, like minnows seeking to capture a whale. Or, perhaps, the ships are more like piranha—for the long-term plan is to gnaw and tear at the asteroid, shred this worldlet into rubble, once it is captured and dragged back to Earth orbit.

For a long time, the tiny ships merely fly in formation alongside the asteroid, watching it, probing it gently with sampling lasers and robot surface probes. Finally, satisfied with their examinations, the mining ships prepare to take their quarry captive.

Spider-robots, ugly, metallic many-legged things that can cling tight to the tumbling world even as they scuttle across it, are landed on the asteroid. They crawl patiently across its surface, paying out line as they go, weaving a web formed of massive cables around the asteroid itself. They wrap the cables clear around the world, strapping it tight. The cables improve the worldlet's rigidity and load-bearing capacity, in effect forming into a tough, flexible exoskeleton for the fragile rock, ensuring that the asteroid will have the strength to endure the shocks yet to come.

Purpose—made fusion rocket engines, massive and powerful, land at carefully selected points on the asteroid's surface. The tiny controller ships retreat to a prudent distance. The engines begin to fire, slowly and carefully building up their thrust, firing not to move the world but to stabilize it, working to convert its erratic and awkward three-axis tumble into a slow, stately, orderly rotation straight through its poles. Bits of rock and dust are shaken loose and thrown gently into the orbit of the asteroid by the change in rotation. Most of the fragments reimpact back onto the asteroid's surface. A few are thrown altogether clear of the planetoid.

The huge engines shut down, and the asteroid, like a wild horse that has finally accepted her first rider, has begun to be tamed. Residual quakes and shudders ripple through the core of the worldlet as it settles into its new rotational equilibrium.

The controller ships return, now that the fusion flames of the stabilizing engines are gone. Their work done for the moment, the engines are removed from the asteroid's surface. A huge ball-shaped bagnet, woven of an enormously strong, thin, opaque material, is reeled out from the hold of one ship. The exterior of the bagnet is dazzlingly white, perfectly reflective, so bright in comparison to the asteroid that eyes adjusted to see the net cannot find the gloom-dark sky-mountain at all. The net's interior surface, however, is black as midnight. Massive cables unspool from the other ships and clamp onto the mouth of the net. The net, kilometers in diameter, is drawn open out across space, its open end pointed through the long end—and the new rotation axis—of the tiny planetoid.

With infinite care, the ships, with the net drawn up between them, begin to fire their maneuvering jets in perfect synchronization with each other, setting the whole ship-and-net construct spinning. After endless, worrisome hours, the net is spun up to exactly match the rotation of the asteroid. The ships move forward, pulling the spherical net around the worldlet, swallowing it whole.

The net surrounds the asteroid, but does not touch it yet, nor is the open end of the bagnet shut for a while. For long days, the net is simply left open, surrounding the asteroid. For the first time in its ancient history, the planetoid is wholly in shadow, without raw sunlight cooking half its surface while the other freezes in vacuum. For longer than humans have existed, it has maintained the same pattern of heating and cooling—but now the entire surface must cool at once. The asteroid radiates heat energy through the open end of the bagnet into the black shadows of space. The blackened interior of the bag absorbs heat as well. The interior heat conducts through the bagnet and is reflected away by the shadowed side of the net's exterior.

Again, the captive asteroid is wracked with quakelets as it cools, settling into a new and lower thermal equilibrium. The cooling causes the entire asteroid to contract, crumbling the surface. Contraction-shattered fragments of rock break loose from the main body of the spinning asteroid, flying into the fabric of the bagnet, caroming back and forth off the bag and the surface of the asteroid. The fresh impacts break off new fragments of rock, which join a gradually thickening cloud of rock and dust surrounding the asteroid. A few fragments escape through the open end of the net. One fragment strikes one of the control ships, causing minor damage.

When the cooling is complete, winches aboard the ships pull the bagnet shut, pinching closed the open end and furling the net tighter and tighter around the asteroid. The net becomes a form-fitting shroud for the captured planetoid. The once gloom-black world is now swathed in brilliant, reflective white, visible through simple binoculars from millions of kilometers away.

The spider-robots are landed again, to wrap another layer of cable over the net, at the same time checking the integrity of the bag.

The same engines that steadied the rotation of the asteroid are now set down again amidships, around the asteroid's "equator," at the asteroid's center of gravity. The engines are pointed aft and canted outward slightly. Smaller attitude control rockets are mounted here and there on the surface.

The control ships, all but one, back off for the last time. One ship is grounded at the forward end, the "North Pole" of the asteroid, to serve as a control station, the bridge of this enormous stone spacecraft. The fusion engines light once again, this time to burn for days and weeks as they shape the asteroid toward its new orbit— toward Earth.

At the aft end, the "South Pole," the spider-robots continue their task, heedless of the ragged edges of the fusion flames that surround them. They are hard at work, constructing the receptacle for the asteroid ship's braking system. The giant fusion engines must rage for weeks on end to accelerate this huge mass. At the other end of the journey, they will fire just as long to slow it. But the last maneuver, the final braking, must happen rapidly, precisely, violently, at exactly the right moment, exactly the right point in space. No rocket engine could provide enough power fast enough to do the job. Only one energy source can release enough power rapidly enough to do the job. The spider-robots are installing a hydrogen bomb.

When this lump of rock was first found, it was simply assigned a catalog number. Now, at last, it is christened: they name this world in motion Cornucopia.

At last, the massive engines shut down, their work done for the time being. The crew of the bridge ship grounded at the forward end of Cornucopia transfer to the others ships. The tiny fleet, which has done such huge work, turns for home. The robots and the telemetry transmitters aboard Cornucopia will be company enough for her in the two long years ahead, as she wends her circuitous way toward Earth. She can safely be left to her own devices, carefully watched and tracked from a distance. Only at the last, only at Earth-arrival, will there be need to board her again.

Wrenched from her ancient orbit, the captive planetoid charts a new course through the heavens. In a few months, she is already half-forgotten by the crews that wrested her from her old path, already busy as they are with new tasks.

But other eyes watch Cornucopia.

Eyes that do not forget: eyes that fear, and lust, and plan, and scheme.

Eyes that see their goals in view.

PART ONE

EXPEDITION

Chapter One

HAWAII

Shiro Ishida set the papers out on his desk, arranging them with an absolute precision. Each paper touched its neighbors edge to edge. No overlapping, no gaps between the pages—as orderly and exact as the squares on a chessboard. Or, better still, as precise as the grid for *Go*. *Go* was Japanese, after all.

Ishida bent over the desk, looking at each paper not merely by itself, but also in relation to all the others. Twice he rearranged the pages, then stood, unmoving, over the new arrangement while he contemplated the relationship of one set of facts to another.

The pages were an odd lot. Biographies, geology reports, a précis of a scientific paper from the last century, orbital plots, stock reports, business projections.

At length he seemed satisfied. The pieces were in place, the situation clear and sharp in his mind. He turned away from the desk and looked out the armored picture window at the cone of Kilauea Volcano.

The window, indeed the whole building, needed to be strong, for Ishida made his home dangerously close to the

11

volcano. Ash falls, clumps of rocks thrown out by the volcano, even occasional splashes of lava, reached this far.

One day, he knew, the lava would flow this way in earnest, and the building would have to be abandoned. But for now the danger was no price at all to pay for the great spectacle outside. A column of smoke rose from the caldera, and a jet of lava spurted up into the sky, only to splash down onto the barren surface. Hawaii continued to build herself. The earth trembled slightly.

Shiro regretted the necessity, still far off and yet inevitable, of leaving this place. But it would not be the lava that drove him out. Other forces, human and natural, would move him long before the volcano reached this far.

He returned to the papers on his desk. Yes, indeed, the pieces were in place. He had carefully studied the other players—or were the others merely pieces on his game board? He felt confident that he could predict their moves well in advance. There were great risks, but also great—incalculable—rewards. The situation called for subtlety, finesse, patience, but also great daring.

The game was ready to begin. Indeed, the first moves had already been made, halfway round the world, by people who did not even know they were playing—or that they were being played.

Outside, the volcano roared.

HRISEY, ICELAND

On a tiny island off the coast of northern Iceland, the short night of summer had finally arrived. The sun at last had sunk beneath the horizon, and deeds best left to the darkness could be committed in greater safety.

Under the dim glow of starlight, a single figure slipped out of one of the huts. It hurried over a frozen land that was less seen than sensed in the gloom of night. A moving shadow flitting across the darkness, it made its way quickly but cautiously across the rocky ground. It slid from shadow to shadow, through the quiet of the night, scuttled toward the supply hut. It opened the door of the little building, threw something inside, and then hurried away.

Behind it, a flickering orange glow blossomed in the open door of the supply hut. A fire was born in the land of ice.

The flames climbed higher, spread out—and reached for the drums of torchbit fuel. A violent explosion smashed the hut to rubble, and a leering orange light glowed malevolently over the landscape.

The camp awoke to shouts and cries, the crackling of flames, and the thudding explosions of more fuel drums. The fire lasted long enough to survive the night, and did its work well. By morning, there was nothing left of the storage hut.

It was full light, and Garrison Morrow had not gone to bed yet. Everything was wrecked. He kicked at a stone and looked out across the cold and sterile land. Miserable, desolate, the windswept island resembled the surface of the Moon. But Garrison had lived for a long time on the Moon, and even it had never been this bad.

A knot of smoke twisted and swirled overhead. Garrison turned and looked behind himself. The frigid wind caught him square in the face, a stinging cold that brought tears to his eyes. He winced just a bit as he turned. Even after six months back on Earth, his muscles still weren't entirely readapted to the home world. His own tired feet reminded him that this place was nothing like the surface of the Moon.

Fires couldn't start on the Moon, for example. Here, clearly enough, they could. The smoldering ruins of the supply hut lay in a blackened and worthless heap, a few embers still glowing here and there. One more piece of bad luck for the worlds' record bad luck expedition of all time. He kicked at some unidentifiable bit of ruined equipment. At least no one was hurt. That was something. And they had enough food and water stored in the prep/mess to last until more supplies could be brought in. As far as day-to-day needs, they could muddle through somehow, even if work came to a halt. It was the loss of the drilling equipment—and the torchbit fuel—that hurt the most.

The timing couldn't have been any worse either—a major cargo shipment had just arrived a few days before, and the storage shed was filled to bursting. Before the fresh supplies had arrived, there would have been nothing to burn but an empty hut.

Cathy Cleveland, the expedition's simulation specialist, slipped her heavily mittened hand into his arm. "I'm sorry," she said simply. Garrison didn't reply. Cathy was a good woman, a kind woman, the sort of person he had always dreamed of meeting and getting to know. But if the expedition collapsed—well, there wasn't much chance he'd ever see her again.

Ben Moscowitz came up behind Garrison and patted him on the shoulder. "Sorry, Garrison," he said, his voice muffled by his parka hood. "This is one hell of a mess."

"Yeah." Garrison couldn't think of anything more to say for a moment. "This could be it, Ben," he said at last. "This could pack us in."

"What?" Ben protested. "One lousy prefab hut and a few grand worth of equipment get torched and that shuts us down? We could replace the whole thing in the next cargo shipment."

"Quiet, Ben," Cathy said. "Garrison doesn't need a pep talk just now. And we can't make good the loss anyway."

"We could replace it all, if we could afford the next cargo shipment," Garrison agreed bitterly. "We were already just about out of money before this happened."

Ben looked surprised. "How could you be out of money? What about that new tax treaty?" The U.N., concerned about too much technology getting off-planet, had started requiring Earth-based companies to spend one dollar on Earthside research for every science dollar spent off-planet.

"Maybe Iceland isn't on Earth," Garrison growled. "We've barely been able to scrape up enough for the bare-bones operation we've been running. And now this accident happens."

Ben looked up sharply at the word "accident." He seemed about to say something and then think better of it. Garrison wasn't in the mood to hear from anyone. And Cathy looked ready to comfort him, for what that was worth. He patted Garrison on the arm again and walked away, looking for someplace warm.

Garrison gently stepped out of Cathy's embrace. "Listen, Cathy, I think I'd just like to be alone for a while."

Cathy looked up at him and nodded. There was something in her expression Garrison had never seen before, a sorrow and a sense of loss. "Okay. I'll see you later." She turned and walked away.

A gust of wind blew through the burned-out wreckage and threw up a cloud of ashes, shrouding Garrison in gloom and grey.

It was seven A.M. local before Garrison could bring himself to leave the wreckage and get inside out of the cold. He dragged himself to his office hut and sat down—that was as much as he was capable of. At last it occurred to him that he ought to let the museum back in New York know what was going on. He switched on the comm terminal and sent an urgent electronic mail message to Glenda Doyle. She was his contact back at the American Natural History, had raised the money that had gotten them this far. She deserved to know what was going on. The e-mail would reach her as soon as she got to work. With the time zones, that would be some hours from now.

He forced himself to get on with some of the routine chores that had been stacking up, and that kept him busy enough to avoid thinking for a while. But not for long. He tossed down his pen and gave up on his fifth effort at a list of things to do. He glared out of his office window down the length of the narrow fjord. A kilometer north, the cantankerous old *Glomar Surveyor* lay at anchor. Ben Moscowitz had scrounged up the floating hulk of an ocean-bed drilling platform from somewhere. The wind rattled past the hut, shaking the windows and setting the walls to creaking as the gale swept over the frozen shore of Hrisey. Hrisey. A great place to get into trouble. Nothing but a tiny spot of land in a narrow fjord called Eyjafjordurof, on the northern coast of Iceland, on the far end of nowhere.

Garrison shivered reflexively, though the frigid gale could not get to him through the well-insulated walls. It was *cold* out there.

In his mind's eye, he looked past the narrow inlet, past the drilling platform. On a line due north, past the *Surveyor*, there was nothing but cold water and colder ice as far as the North Pole and beyond. From here, the Arctic Circle lay fifty kilometers to the north. The frozen and useless coast of Greenland was about 400 kilometers to the northwest. It was a lonely view.

His thoughts returned to the job at hand. They were *close*, very close. And now they were about to fail.

Garrison paced mechanically to the southern end of the office hut. From the window here he could see nothing but the jumbled carcass of the island, the cliff walls which formed the surrounding fjord, and the shabby old lighthouse. The lighthouse keeper had been glad of the expedition's company at first, but Garrison had a feeling the old fellow would be glad to have his solitude back when the geologists cleared out.

Though southward was the less interesting direction to look at, Garrison spent more time at this window. South, ultimately, was where it all came from: food, drilling equipment, core tubes, money, communications. And now, if the money didn't come soon—they'd have to pack up and go home. If they could afford to do even that. *Definitely not a good place to get stranded,* Garrison thought.

There were other reasons to spend time at the south window: at times he could see his home from here. There she was, a waxing gibbous Moon peeking up over the southern horizon in the daytime. People who didn't think to look were always surprised at how often the Moon could be seen in daylight. Garrison always thought to look. There she was, a familiar face looking across the hundreds of thousands of kilometers to smile at him. It was cold and lonely in Iceland, and pleasant to think of the wheeling-dealing, boisterous, overbusy people of Central Colony buried warm and safe under the Moon's surface.

Garrison blinked and brought his thoughts back to Earth.

He walked to the middle of the trailer, flopped down in the blown-out old swivel chair, spun about to face the sideboard and poured himself a mug of coffee. Both the earthenware mug and the old-fashioned cast-iron coffeepot were heavy, substantial things, appropriate objects for a geologist to possess. Garrison liked to surround himself with solid, secure things, in part because a geologist in the field tends to find anything fragile broken when unpacked at arrival. Garrison's field work always seemed to be well past the end of a very bad road. This job was no exception.

Garrison Morrow, Ph.D., was the sort of man people labeled as "craggy." His hair was dark brown, a tousled mop he rarely bothered to get under control. His pale blue-grey eyes were nearly lost in wrinkled crows feet and bushy eyebrows. He sported a thick, reddish-brown beard at the moment; in this climate, anything that helped keep your face warm was eminently practical. And the beard helped hide the pallor that life in the subterranean world of Central Colony on the Moon had left him with.

His hands were hard, callused, and strong. His fingernails had been bashed by rock hammers in the field and stained by acids and chemicals in the labs endless times.

He fit the physical mold of the man who never worried or wavered. Both consciously and unconsciously, he *used* his appearance. People got out of the way of a broad-shouldered, stern-faced man, especially one almost two meters tall, because they assumed he'd win the argument anyway. That suited Garrison fine. He was a quiet man who hated to argue, and was perfectly satisfied if the fight could be avoided.

He forced himself to sit and try to think for a minute, but the results were still little better than free association. *Is it going to come off?* he wondered for the hundredth time. *If only there could be some sign one way or another in the upper strata, nearer the surface.* He fiddled with a pencil and again stared out the southern window. *Should I have told Glenda about Mjollnir? Every time I ask that, I come up with no. God, I hope this works.*

With a boom and a thud, the inner door to the hut sprang open, startling Garrison out of his reverie. Ben Moscowitz stomped into the hut. People tended to appear abruptly like that around here—with the super-insulated double doors on the huts, there was no hope of hearing a knock on the door. Besides, no one wanted to stay outside waiting for someone to *answer* a knock. It was too damn cold. And wrestling the outer doors open and shut in the howling wind was no fun either—though the noise did warn people inside of a visitor.

Ben getting out of his parka always reminded Garrison of a jack-in-the-box popping out. Ben zipped back the hood and pulled it down off his head. His hair was bright red, piled in tight curls on top of his head. He was a bit popeyed and sported a beaklike nose. His red beard suited him well and hid a slightly weak chin. His voice was high and pleasant to listen to, and he started talking the moment he came into the room. "Hey, Garrison. Ready to talk like a regular person, or you still brooding tragically?"

Garrison smiled in spite of himself. "Well, I suppose I could take a brooding break. What's on your mind?"

Ben sat down in the visitor's chair on the other side of the desk. "Something I wanted to tell you this morning, but I figured I'd better wait until you were in some kind of shape to talk. The money situation—is it really as bad as you were saying?"

"At least that bad."

Ben nodded. "Then let me suggest something. Call your funding people and have them get in touch with the Geological Research Fund."

"Who?" Garrison asked.

"The Geological Research Fund."

"Never heard of them," Garrison said.

Ben shrugged. "Their checkbook still works even so. They're a new startup, but they plan to do a lot of funding in this sort of research."

"How have you heard of them?"

Ben gestured vaguely. "Usual thing. Ran into someone at a party who knew someone who knew someone. They're out of New York."

Garrison grabbed a pen and jotted down the name. "Okay, I'll give it a try. What the hell."

Ben stood up to leave. "Do that. Like, right now. I've gotta get back and finish inventory on the last set of cores we drilled. See you at dinner." Ben pulled his parka hood back on and stood over the desk, as if there were something more, something important he needed to say. But at last he simply turned and left, making as much noise on the way out as he had on the way in.

Garrison watched him leave and sat there, staring at the door, for a moment. Strange that Ben would have heard of a new funder and not mentioned it before now. But this was no time to look gift horses in the mouth.

And so long as he was thinking in clichés, there *was* no time like the present. Garrison swung his seat around to face the comm console and punched the worldclock key. Glenda should be getting into the office in New York just about now. He told the terminal to call her office and signal him when the connection got through. In northern Iceland, even the most powerful comsat signal sometimes had trouble punching through atmospheric disturbance. But, for once, the signal dodged the static and got through on the first try.

The screen cleared as the connection was made, and Glenda's owlish visage appeared. "Garrison!" she said in surprise. "My terminal was blinking with an alert message from you guys when I got in ten minutes ago. What started it? Was anyone hurt in the fire?"

"Probably got touched off by some sort of short-circuit or something, but that's just a guess," Garrison said. "We don't exactly have a fire expert on the next corner. Whatever it was, it didn't need much encouragement once the winds started whipping up the flames. And everyone's okay—but we've got problems. The fire wiped out practically all our drilling supplies. We have maybe a week's worth of stuff already out on the drilling platform, but that's about it. After that we might as well pack up and go home."

"Jesus." Glenda frowned and chewed on a nail. She was a heavyset woman, round-faced and serious-looking, with long reddish-brown hair. If she had been a woman of less impressive presence, people would have called her fat. But as it was, no one dared do that, even behind her back. "Garrison, I'm sorry, but I don't know what I can do. I've shaken every money tree I know—and none of them want to back you. A lot of them tell me they don't understand what you're trying to do up there—and I can't blame them—your descriptions have all been a bit vague."

"Yeah, I know. Sorry. Listen, the reason I'm calling is that Ben Moscowitz suggested a potential angel."

"Anybody's worth a try, but I think I've tried everybody. What's the name?"

"The Geological Research Fund," Garrison replied.

"Never heard of them," Glenda said.

"That's what I told Ben. But he said they worked out of New York and they might be interested."

"I can't believe there's a New York foundation I haven't heard of," Glenda said flatly. "My sources are too good for that. But I just got through saying anything's worth a try. Let me work on it today and get back to you. I'll use e-mail if it gets too late your time. In the meantime take an inventory of what you need and wire it along, in case we hit pay dirt."

"Lots of luck, Glenda," Garrison said, dourly. "The way things are going, we're about due for some. And never mind sending e-mail. Go ahead and call whenever you know something. I doubt I'll be doing much sleeping anyway."

The rest of Garrison's day was pretty close to a dead loss. The one thing he managed to get done wasn't much of anything—just that inventory Glenda wanted. It wasn't hard to come up with it. All he did was copy over the bills of lading from the cargo shipment that had arrived the week before. The cupboard had been pretty bare before the shipment had arrived, close enough that they had nothing left without what had burned. He got the list into some sort of order and fired it off to Glenda over the e-mail network. She would receive it almost immediately, but Garrison couldn't see how much good that would do. What good was a shopping list without money?

Once that clear-cut task was out of the way, the rest of the afternoon just seemed to evaporate away. There were an endless number of small, unimportant tasks that sort of needed doing—reports to fill out, computer files to reorganize, stacks of old papers to go through. They made the hours slide by. It would have been more sensible to use that time planning on how to shut down the camp, or at least abandon it in an orderly fashion. But the comfortably numbing busy-work was a lot easier to face just then—even if the fire had made it all meaningless. The maze of small details drew him so far out of himself that he jumped a foot when the phone *bleep*ed at him. It was jarring to be drawn back into real life by machinery.

He hit the *accept* switch and Glenda's face popped up

on the screen. She had a funny expression on her face. "Garrison," she said. "We got it."

Garrison creased his forehead in puzzlement. "Got what?"

"The money. We got the money. This guy Brattleby was so eager to help I barely knew what to ask for. But a ship with everything on your buy list should be leaving Aberdeen within three days."

Garrison opened his mouth, shut it, opened it again, and finally managed to get some words out. "You mean we're okay?"

"*You're* okay," Glenda agreed. "But this situation is weird, and *I* don't feel so good."

"What do you mean?"

"I mean it's time you told me what the hell is going on up there."

Garrison's face turned expressionless. "I don't know what you're talking about," he said stonily.

Glenda glared into the screen. "Sure. Fine. Everything's peachy-keen normal. It's just that you're the one up there in the middle of nowhere doing God knows what with the vaguest research proposal I've ever seen. Then, just as you run out of money, there's a mysterious fire that couldn't have been timed better to do the maximum damage to your work. Then your second-in-command casually mentions this mystery foundation, and the foundation instantly gives an unknown geologist working on an obscure project six hundred klicks north of nowhere great pots of money in record time, no questions asked. Sound like the usual thing to you?"

"I suppose that it's all a bit strange," Garrison conceded. He hadn't thought of the fire as mysterious. It had never occurred to him that it could have been anything but an accident. But he was being naive. Glenda was right, the coincidence *was* too great. It took him a moment to realize Glenda was still talking.

"Strange is an understatement," she said. "This guy Brattleby said his foundation has heard about your work. Like, how? You haven't published anything yet. And he does a funds transfer to your working account while we're still on the phone."

"Any strings on the money?"

"Garrison, I don't even *know*. Both you and Brattleby put such a rush on things that I haven't had the chance to check. The money got credited before we got any paperwork. I *still* haven't gotten any papers. Nothing faxed over, no couriers, no e-mail, nothing in writing—and I've spent half the money already. I feel like I'm being railroaded by the tooth fairy. But you're so close to the edge I was forced to go along. Not very professional of me. Or them. So, I ask myself, why are they acting that way? I want to check into these people and find out."

"And you're sort of edging around to asking me if I mind, since they just saved my neck. Do we risk killing the goose that laid the golden egg?" Garrison considered for a moment. "How long can we keep operating on the money that's just come in?"

"Hard to say. I've had a little trouble before working with your expedition's accountant. I'm starting to get the feeling that there barely *is* such a person—"

"What's wrong with Cathy?" Garrison asked, just a trifle over-defensive.

Aha. Glenda recognized that tone of voice. So there *was* something going on between Garrison and Cathy. Glenda had suspected that for a while. In the gossipy world of science fundraising, knowing who was seeing whom could be vital data—and Glenda was very good at spotting the signs. Garrison had just told her a lot more than he had meant to. Glenda mentally filed away the information for later reference and went smoothly on with the conversation at hand. "Look, I'll take your word for her skills in other areas, but Miss Cleveland's idea of handling accounts is to look stern, shake her finger at the numbers and tell them to behave."

"Okay, she's a little offbeat, but she's good at what I actually hired her for, and no one else wanted to get near the books as a side job."

"After *she's* been near the books, neither do I. But that's beside the point. Her figures on your cash flow are a bit hard to follow, that's all. But if I had to guess, I'd say you should be able to operate for another . . . oh, maybe ninety days. Certainly sixty days."

"There's your answer. I figure to be done here by the end of next month at the latest."

"So you won't need to go begging to these people again anyway, and it doesn't matter if they get insulted by my snooping around a little," Glenda said.

"Exactly."

"Okay, good. If they're legit, they'll understand our need to know, anyway." Glenda put a sheet of paper to one side and seemed to relax a bit. But then she pounced. "So what *is* it you expect to come up with in a month or so?" she asked sharply.

Garrison squirmed in his seat, gestured elaborately and shook his head. The very picture of a bad amateur liar in action. "Nothing incredibly exciting. A better set of cores than anyone has done on Iceland's northern volcanic formations."

"Hrisey's not a *volcano*, is it?" Glenda asked.

"No, no, no. Hrisey's not much of anything, really. It's just an offshore island, geologically part of the main island, really. A hill sitting on a piece of flooded coastal area. It used to be connected to Iceland proper, but erosion has chewed the surrounding area down enough to allow the sea to flood in. We're drilling offshore here because that erosion has removed a lot of the upper strata and saved us the trouble of drilling through them. We'll get some good cores."

"And then what?"

"Then I publish and think of something else to do."

Glenda knew Garrison too well for him to get away with *that* evasion. Garrison was a person not given to vagueness: When he wasn't clear and concise, there was a reason for it. "Garrison, you could be toasty warm right now, burrowed underneath the lunar surface, raking in big bucks working for the Lunar Mining Authority up in Central Colony. Instead you quit your job there and schlepped back to Earth to go crawl around Iceland, of all places, getting a set of redundant cores. Why are you risking frostbite for something that dull, something you care so little about you won't tell me what it is?"

"Well . . ."

"In other words," she said firmly, "what is all this a

cover for? What is there you care so *much* about you won't even tell *me* about it?"

"Not much gets past you, does it?"

"Not even the fact that you still haven't answered my question."

"I know. Look, let me explain something." Garrison hesitated again.

"Go on," Glenda said carefully.

"Glenda, I'm going to give you good results. No one has ever drilled down this far into this sort of regolith. All this gear was developed for deep-drill mining on the Moon—I was part of the team that designed the Earthside adaptation of the gear. The equipment wasn't even *invented* three years ago. So we're looking at a part of the Earth no one has ever been able to get to before. I'm certain that I'll be able to give you good solid data on when and how fast the volcanic tuffs that form North Iceland were formed. At the very least, it will be a valuable cross check on the Surtsey data from the south of the main island."

"Fine, but all that is in your grant proposal."

"Right." Garrison paused one last time, as if he were working up the nerve to admit something. "But what *isn't* in my grant proposal is that I found an old theory that's *really* cockeyed, one I'm trying to confirm. It was even the orthodox view once, with lots of hints that it was true. Then it just sort of faded away maybe seventy-five years ago. No one could test the theory directly before, not until torchbit drilling was invented. Now, if I *can* prove that theory, you'll hear all about it. We'll all make the papers and get the Museum some good P.R. If I don't—"

"Neither of us will look like idiots for trying to prove the Earth is flat."

"Bingo."

"Okay, I can put up with that. *I* won't tell anyone. But you tell *me*. What are you looking for?"

"Microfragments of primordial cold-formed ores or rocks metamorphosed under extreme heat, pressure, and shock, possibly associated with palagonite tuffs."

"Oh, that. There was a big bin of it on sale at Macy's last week." Glenda decided to give up. She had done her best. If Garrison wouldn't confide in her willingly, she couldn't force him to do so. And she couldn't protect him, if it came to that. "You're not an easy man to deal with, Morrow," she said. "Just promise me one thing. When you do find something, or find out you won't, *please* tell me what it was all about?"

"Fair enough."

"Promise?"

"Promise."

"I'll be getting back to the paperwork here. Enjoy your rocks, Dr. Morrow."

"So long, Glenda." Garrison killed the connection.

NEW YORK

Glenda sighed at the blank screen. Strange to hear caution in that voice. She had worked with Garrison years ago, before he had emigrated to the Moon. She knew his style. In the old days, Garrison would chase after whatever it was he wanted and get it without regard to the consequences. He had wandered the Earth and the Moon in search of interesting rocks, and never had seemed to have much interest in anything else. His single-mindedness gave him a certain naive directness that Glenda found endearing. It was sort of pleasant to see him being careful for once.

But, she thought with sudden alarm—didn't it suggest that the stakes were pretty damn high when *Garrison* of all people felt the need to be cagey and careful?

Garrison's behavior was the first odd, inexplicable thing about this job—and Glenda didn't care for mysteries in her work. Money out of the blue was the second weird thing, of course. As to the third—there was so much grant money floating around it was peculiar that Garrison was unable to get *some* of it. Why hadn't any of her normal sources anted up—and then why did this white knight charge philanthropically up to save them at the last minute? She felt more sure than ever that she had better look into this Geological Research Foundation.

The fax machine buzzed and ejected a single sheet of paper. Glenda took the paper out of the hopper and looked it over. Well, that was progress. It was a letter from Leonard Brattleby, confirming the grant. It wasn't much, just a statement that GRF had deposited the money in the appropriate account. But at least it was a written record.

Glenda looked over the faxed copy. The original seemed to have been on foundation letterhead. As usual with such organizations, the letterhead included a list of important people in the outfit printed alongside the left-hand margin. You were supposed to see the list and be impressed. Glenda looked at the list and was confused. She had never heard of anyone on it. As the head of the museum's fundraising office, it was close to incredible that she wouldn't spot at least one name she knew. She decided to check her files.

Half an hour later, she was very much surprised and a little worried. *None* of the names on the GRF letterhead had ever been associated with science funding in any way. GRF might as well not exist, as far as its top personnel were concerned.

Which made *four* odd things. Five, if you included the well-timed fire.

Glenda looked up at her wall map and glared at Iceland. Six if you counted the fact that Glenda didn't know what the hell was going on up there.

Chapter Two

CENTRAL COLONY, HIPPARCHUS CRATER, THE MOON

The delegates hadn't arrived for the morning session yet. There were still a few minutes left. Governor Neruda put the time to use, checking over the arrangements one last time. All, it seemed, was in order. Or as close to order as could be expected. Neruda looked over the conference table in annoyance.

The table was long and narrow, measuring fifteen meters from end to end, four meters from side to side at its center point, tapering down a bit toward the two ends. Thus, the most junior pairs of opposing delegates, sitting at the remote ends of the table, sat closest to their opposite members. The leaders of the opposing factions, on either side of the table's center, were furthest apart from each other. The accidental symbolism was not lost on anyone.

While the unsuitability of the decor was not lost on the conference host. He winced now, as he did each time he saw it.

The tasteful sky-blue felt covering on the table could not disguise that it was a slab of aluminum underneath. Setting down on it even the smallest object would produce a muffled click or clank. A wood table would have been better, but wood was hideously expensive to import. The chairs, too, betrayed their domestic lunar origin. They were graceful, high-backed affairs, the frames of fiberglass tube, and the seats, backs and padding of fiberglass cloth stuffed with foam cushioning. To a terrestrial eye they were spindly, fragile things. On Earth, no sensible person would have risked sitting in one of them. They should have *looked* stronger. Neruda sighed. At least the flowers, the water pitchers and glasses, the notepacks at each delegate's place, were as they should have been.

Nothing else was—the windowless painted-metal wall panels, the too-rough texture of the carpet, the too-low ceiling. Every detail of the room revealed the same secret— this was a typically lunar rough-and-ready compartment, rudely and rapidly carved out of the living rock. The efforts to pretty it up and make it suitably elegant for high diplomacy were foredoomed to failure. They might as well have met in a grain storage compartment. There were more gracious chambers on the Moon, but the security people from both sides had insisted on a windowless deep-level compartment. It would be hard to put a bugging device—or a bomb—through the two-meter-thick rock behind the floors, ceilings, and walls of this room. Even the doors were blastproof steel and fiberglass.

Now those doors swung open, and his Excellency, Jose Neruda, Governor of the Lunar Colony, looked about the room in nervous embarrassment as the delegates filed in.

But, Neruda told himself, he need not have worried. The delegates were capable of ignoring all the uncouth appointments, and a great deal more—including Neruda himself. A fine state of affairs! The only head of government among the delegates, and both sides, Earth and Settlement Coalition alike, paid him no regard at all. When they wanted to hear something from the Moon, they asked the United Nations Lunar Administration Council representative—and the UNLAC rep had flown in from *Earth* for the meeting. It was galling.

At least, Neruda told himself, they had been forced to

give him a proper seat. The niceties of modern diplomacy might not cover courtesy to a head of state or a host, but they did dictate very clearly what the correct seating arrangements had to be. Besides, as host of the conference, Neruda had a certain influence in placing the nameplates. He waited until the rest of the delegates had found their places. Then, with as much of a gracious air as he could manage, he took his own seat, third from the center, on the right-hand side of U.N. Space Policy Director Suzuki himself. Perhaps his own team ignored him, but he hadn't gotten this far in his career without being a team player. He had to think not like the lunar governor, but like part of the Earth delegation.

Neruda set his face into an expression of dour righteousness and stared forthrightly at the delegates on the other side of the table. Damned Settlers! For all intents and purposes, they controlled the entire Solar System except for the Earth/Moon system—and *that* was not good enough for them. They wanted to horn in on Earth/Moon trade as well. Miserable upstarts.

Angela Hardin, head of the Settlement Coalition, was taking her turn in the chair today. She rapped the gavel (causing the aluminum table to give off a loud, undignified *clunk*, to Neruda's infinite embarrassment) and the meeting came to order.

In spite of himself, Neruda smiled. Today would be like yesterday, and tomorrow like today—hopeless, endless, pointless wrangling. Just the sort of thing suited to Neruda's temperament.

HRISEY, ICELAND

Bundled up in a parka, a ski mask, three layers of sweaters, and two sets of long johns, Dr. Cathy Cleveland hurried across the camp, bent double against the wind and certain that her body was about to freeze solid. The wind sliced through her cold-weather gear as if it wasn't even there. *Might as well be wearing a summer-weight tennis outfit*, she thought savagely. Cathy did not enjoy cold weather.

The photo hut came into the restricted view afforded by her ski mask and parka hood. With relief in sight, Cathy scuttled all the faster toward her goal. She reached the door and fumbled with the clumsy latch, cursing the cold, cursing her heavy gloves, cursing the wind and the god-damned weather, cursing Hrisey, cursing all of Iceland while she was at it. She gave a good hard yank on the latch, but it was frozen shut again.

She stepped back a bit and gave it a good swift kick with her oversized steel-toed boot. The latch popped free. Cathy pulled the door open with a bit more violence than called for and hobbled into the "porch"—the insulated chamber between the inner and outer doors. Once inside, limping on a brand-new sore toe that gave her something else to curse about, she slammed the outer door shut behind her, pulled the inner door open, tromped into the hut, and gave the inner door one last slam for good measure.

She yanked off her outer gloves, tossed them onto the desk, and, leaving her inner gloves on, began to undo the buttons and zippers and knots and velcro patches that kept her coat on. She had learned early on that the hard plastic of the buttons was just too damn cold to touch with her bare hands once it had been outside. She got the buttons undone and the hood down and wriggled out of the parka, hung up the coat and stepped in front of the mirror over the desk. She peeled off the ski mask and surveyed the damage done by the cold.

Her face was framed by a thick mass of luxuriant black hair. Just running her fingers through it once or twice tidied it up enough for present purposes. She took a good hard look at her face and grimaced at it. Thirty-one years old and she still looked like a teenager. Juvenile. Months of sub-zero temperatures had left no other mark than rosy cheeks. Her eyes were a clear, deep, blue, framed by dark, thick lashes. She had a pert little snub nose. Her ruby-lipped mouth fell easily into a happy smile, framing perfect white teeth. Her pale, clear, almost translucent skin was perfectly smooth and flawless. No wrinkle, no mark of maturity or experience, or wisdom. Life should have written them all there long ago. Cathy knew she was beautiful—but at times she would have traded beauty for a face with a bit more character.

She began peeling off the outer two or three layers of

sweaters and sweat shirts. Even the bulky clothing could not disguise the elegant, slender body, the generous but well-proportioned curves of her figure. She was forever unsure that she was being taken seriously, being respected for what she said and did, rather than how she looked or how she acted. She had always worried that people were making things easy for her, letting her slide because she was pretty.

Until she got to Iceland. Cathy dropped rather heavily into the chair in front of the desk and glanced into the mirror before sorting through her notes on the day's work. Here the ice and snow made it hard for everyone, including herself, and there wasn't any way a twinkle in her eye could smooth the way ahead. No one could read a disarming smile, or be charmed by beauty, if her face was hidden under a ski mask. Not even Garrison, damn it. Hrisey and the endless, bone-chilling wind made for a harsher world than the one she had known. At least here she knew she was being judged for herself, and for her work.

It sure wasn't simple work. She was supposed to integrate the facts and the data with the theories to predict the rock strata under the next drill point. It meant endless hours of grinding through the statistics and the geologic expert-system programs, creating the 3-D image simulations of the rock layers and how they related to each other.

The worst part of the job was in facing the rough-and-ready drill crew and telling *that* hard-bitten crowd what to expect next, talk to them as if *she* were sure of the facts—and even daring to tell them where to drill.

There weren't enough data points, she didn't know enough geology, she had to make too many guesses based on guesses. And this cash-poor expedition couldn't *afford* wrong guesses. There was a lot of pressure on her. Especially considering that she was doing a rather delicate task on the side at the same time.

Ben knew, she told herself again. Ben had to know. He had come very close to tipping his hand altogether. And what about Garrison? Would he understand?

She shoved the papers to one side, looked up at the mirror, and considered her divided loyalties, the propriety

of what she was doing. Her work wasn't *wrong*, exactly.
No one was getting hurt. At least not physically. But she
didn't feel exactly *honest* about it all, either. And if there
was one person in the world she didn't want to cause
trouble for, it was Garrison.

She sighed and decided the hell with it. She couldn't
work. No one in camp could, it seemed. The fire had
shaken everyone up. Time for a cup of cocoa. She stood
and started suiting up again.

Chapter Three

HRISEY, ICELAND

Garrison hit the *enter* key and sighed. Enough paperwork for now. He shut down the computer, shoved the keyboard to one side, and stood up. He began dressing for being outside on the North Iceland coast. He shrugged on his parka and lit a cigarette before he dealt with zippers, boots, and mittens. He tried to enjoy the vice of smoking whenever he was on Earth—back on the Moon it was just too damn expensive.

He looked out the window onto the frozen land. There was a purity, a sureness and precision to the weather here that Garrison admired: it was cold; the wind howled; it was either bright and clear or the storm was furious. No gloomy fogs, no misty overcasts, no middle ground. The weather was always extreme. It seemed to harbor no doubts. But then, people thought that of Garrison, too. Garrison idly wondered if the weather put up as false a front as he did.

He zipped up the parka hood all the way, so it formed a stovepipe-like snout, a cylinder that projected well past his face and gave him an opening about the size of his hand to see and breathe out of. He juggled the cigarette in his mouth, keeping it out of the way of the parka hood. He pulled on the huge, heavy mittens and clumped through the inner and outer doors of the office hut.

He took a long drag on the cigarette and clamped his mouth down hard on it so the wind wouldn't blow it away, holding the smoke in his lungs as long as he could. Having something recently on fire in his chest always gave him the illusion of being warmer.

He *needed* the illusion. As he stepped out of the lee of the building, he was hit by a ferocious gale coming off the landward side of the hut, hit hard enough so that he almost lost the cigarette anyway.

God, it was cold! The wind seemed to leach every erg of heat out of him. Garrison trudged carefully toward the prep/mess hut, a few hundred meters away. He spotted someone else heading toward prep/mess as well, coming from the boat landing. In a parka, everyone looked like a cross between a parrot and a periscope. The other walker stopped, swiveled his torso to bring Garrison clearly into his restricted field of view and waved enthusiastically. Garrison grinned to himself, recognizing the mannerisms. That had to be Ben Moscowitz. He waved and pointed to prep/mess.

Ben nodded and both men upped their pace to meet at the prep room door. Prep was where core samples went on their way to the labs stateside. Here the samples were carefully labeled as to depths, time of extraction, and which end was up. Cathy photographed them, the geologists gave them a brief initial examination, and then they were packed with exquisite care for shipment back to New York. Prep/mess was probably where you could be coldest while inside on Hrisey: it had the most frequently opened door. Since it was the largest hut in the camp, prep doubled as the mess tent as well, hence the name "prep/mess"—leading in turn to a lot of jokes about the quality of work that was done there.

The prep side of the room was a bustle of activity, with the cores awaiting processing stacked to the ceiling. The odor of coffee brewing mingled with the acrid scents of some chemical test the techs were running. As usual, there was a line-up waiting to use the rather beat-up scanning superconducting electron microscope Ben had bought used somewhere. Garrison waved hellos to a few of the people in the hut as he pulled off his gloves and undid his hood. Then he turned to Ben.

"Garrison, the layers are thinning down even faster than we hoped!" Ben announced as soon as Garrison's ears were clear of his hood. "Cathy's simulations are right on target. I was working here when I got a call from the workers on the rig that they probably had a perfect transition core! One tuff right into the next."

"That's great, Ben," Garrison said. At this point in the drilling, sample cores were being taken for a length of ten meters every fifty meters. The rest of the drilling was done with a torchbit, which simply melted the rocks and shoved it out of the way to form the sides of the drill hole. The torchbits were extremely fast, but destroyed the rock they went through—not much use in geology. The core-sectioning bits and sample tubes were much slower and much more expensive to use. Which bit you used depended on what you were after at the moment.

The drilling was proceeding through familiar strata just now, and saving time and money was worth more than redundant sampling. Ben and his workers had beaten the one-in-five odds and picked up the most interesting slice of core.

"The damn drill-rig workers said the wind was too high to get the core back here," Ben said. "I said the hell with that, I'd go out in our boat for it. They said I'd be a crazy fool to take the boat out, so I said the hell with *them*, too, and went out to the dock."

"So where's the sample?"

"Still sitting on the damn drilling platform. I got one look at the waves and I had to admit they had a point."

"Score one for the locals." Garrison had hired a dozen Icelanders from Akureyia, the town at the far southern end of the fjord.

"Big deal," Ben replied with a laugh. "Put 'em down in South Philadelphia and see how they do."

Garrison grinned back. It felt good to talk this way, to forget all about the outside world and get wrapped up in the excitement of the work. "Getting back to the core samples . . ." he said mildly.

"Ah. The core samples. There's no question about it; the volcanic layers are getting thinner. All the tuffs are only about half as thick as they were in the first core set we took 15 kilometers down the fjord from here. If Cathy's projections hold up—and they're going to—we'll break through the volcanic layers to the pre-eruption seabed if we drill another three kilometers north of here."

"Terrific." The pre-eruption seabed, the rock strata buried when the volcanoes of Iceland first erupted, was what they were after.

"If we can afford it, that is," Ben went on. "What about payday?"

Garrison grinned. "That reminds me. I ought to put up a notice on the bulletin board before people start packing and working on their resumes. I got the word from Glenda. We've got the funding to finish the job. Glenda put in a call to that GRF crowd you told me about, and they came up with a grant. There's a cargo ship loading in Scotland."

"Great! Nice work, Garrison," Ben said. "Well, if we're still drilling, then the question is, do we break off here and move the rig north immediately, or do we finish out the full length of this core?"

Garrison bit his lip and tugged at his beard. "Finish the core out. Full depth. Right now we're eager, but later we'll wish we had full documentation. Regular torch and sample, torch and sample, all the way down."

"Sounds right. I'll pass the word."

"Good. But, look, Ben—we got the money, and that's the main thing, and I'm glad for it—but how the hell did you know about GRF? Glenda had never heard of them—and it's her job to know."

Ben looked at Garrison for a long moment, his face unreadable. "I don't know. I'd just heard the name. Does it matter?"

"It might. Glenda seemed to think there was something funny going on."

"Sorry. I can't tell you anything more." Ben's voice was suddenly flat, expressionless. "Look, I gotta go. See you later." He rezipped his parka hood and hurried out of prep/mess, almost tripping over Cathy Cleveland as she came in.

Watching Ben rush out, Garrison barely noticed Cathy. He was thinking, worrying. It was hard to believe that Ben could have heard of the Geological Research Foundation legitimately. If *Glenda* had never heard of it, when finding sources of money was her job, then what were the odds on an obscure geologist knowing the name? And what about that damn fire? How *had* it started?

Cathy opened her parka. "Hey, Garrison. How's life?" She smiled up at him, and knew that it wasn't her usual charm-reflex that made her smile. Being next to Garrison made her happy.

He blinked and looked down at her, consciously noticing her presence for the first time. He smiled back, a bit shyly. Cathy was nice people. "Hi, Cathy. Things are looking up." He paused for a moment. "Cathy," Garrison said thoughtfully, "you know Ben pretty well, don't you?"

"More or less. Never knew him before this expedition, but we've talked a lot," she answered. "What's the matter. You two been fighting?"

Garrison ignored her question. "What sort of work did Ben do before he signed up with us?"

She shrugged. "I don't know," she said carelessly. "He did some work at the Smithsonian Space Science Center in D.C., he was a visiting fellow at some Cambridge study on Lunar vulcanism, and I think he did some consulting work for one of the orbital mining companies. Ground-based work, though, never went off-planet. He did a lot of work before that at Mount St. Helens and in Hawaii. Glenda Doyle picked him for us because the Hawaii expedition did some offshore drilling. Why? Didn't you read his resume?"

For someone who claimed not to know much, Cathy was pretty well informed, Garrison thought. "No, I left it up to the good old Natural History Museum personnel office, and I didn't even think to screen their recommendations."

"What's the problem? Isn't he qualified?"

"I think," Garrison said moodily, "that he may be a little *too* well qualified. Why would a hotshot with a resume like that want to sign onto a two-bit expedition like this?"

Garrison's secrets were giving him an unaccustomed

sense of paranoia, and, unbidden, his paranoia explained the puzzle for him. It was easy to put together a nasty little picture. The Foundation was a front put together by people who had heard about Garrison's trip, people who had figured out what he was really after, and maybe didn't want him to get it. Which would suggest that Ben had set the fire as sabotage. But then why was the GRF financing the operation? It didn't make sense.

Garrison hated secrets, and now he was remembering why. Openly telling the truth never tied things in knots. Damn it! If he hadn't been worried about making the Museum look foolish, if he had gone public with his theory, then the expedition would not have been vulnerable to this secret scheming. The fight would have been out in the open, and the very fact of there being controversy would have been some defense against conspiracy. Now it was too late for that.

Now he had to fight back, other ways. If the GRF was a front recently put together, Ben had probably been told about it after arriving in camp. If he was getting information *from* those people, then it was likely, in fact certain, that he was sending them information as well. Easy enough. The whole world was a few keystrokes away from either of the two comm consoles in camp. He'd have to do something about that. He needed to do a lot of things. He'd need help. He was going to have to trust someone. Garrison suddenly realized he was looking at his natural ally. Cathy.

Aside from her own simulation work, and photo-documentation, Cathy was the administrative head of the camp. When it was needed, the simulation work was intensive, but there was a lot of down time in between. So she wore another hat: buying the food, dickering with the locals over exchange rates, keeping the tug captain happy, keeping the drilling ops people from quitting. No one quite understood how she managed it all. Yet the food was the best any member of the expedition had ever had in the field, the mail was handed out to the homesick scientists almost before it was delivered to camp, and while no one could make sense of her account books, at the end of the month they balanced.

"Cathy, I think there's something pretty rotten going

on," Garrison said. "I might need you to help me be rotten right back and stop it."

"Now wait a minute . . ."

"Cathy, don't get stiff-necked. I *need* you. From the way he's acting, I don't think he's happy about it, but I'm not sure Ben is really working for this expedition. It's possible he's spying on us for someone else."

"Oh. Wow." Cathy swallowed hard. Great. Garrison had spotted something, misinterpreted it, *and* wrongly blamed Ben for it. Terrific.

"Let me tell you about it," he said. "C'mon, let's sit down so we can talk." He led her to the coffee urn and drew himself a cup of java. For everyone on Hrisey, getting something hot to drink whenever possible rapidly developed into a reflex action. Cathy made herself some cocoa and followed Garrison to an unoccupied bench at the back of the hut. Garrison sat down across from her, took a quick preliminary sip from his cup and winced. "Too hot to drink yet," he muttered, more or less at random. Cathy could see he was reluctant to speak. "The thing is this—you know better than anyone how short of money we were, even before the fire," Garrison started. Cathy nodded encouragingly. "Glenda called me today, and we've just gotten a very weird grant from an outfit we never approached, that Glenda knows exactly nothing about. And it was Ben, of all people, who told us who to ask for money. So what's going on when he knows more about fundraising than our fundraising expert? I think he's an amateur spy working for someone who doesn't like what I'm doing. I thin!: Ben's here trying to wreck the expedition."

Cathy listened, wide-eyed, and was silent for a long moment before she spoke. Garrison *hadn't* stumbled onto *her* snooping—but the competition was right here in camp! *That* bit of information by itself was worth the effort it had taken to get her placed on this expedition. It was certainly proof that the stakes were plenty high. But she had to be careful here. If Ben was an amateur, so was she. This called for a little misdirection, a little pumping for information. "Garrison, maybe it's paranoid, but let's say you're right, just for the sake of argument. Why would anyone want to bother wrecking this expedition?"

Garrison hesitated, and looked around him. No one was near enough to hear them. "It's Mjollnir," he said at last. "Mjollnir's Grave . . ."

"*Whose* grave?" Cathy asked. She held her breath. If she could get him to talk, her job would be an awful lot easier.

"The grave of Mjollnir, the hammer of Thor, which smote the Earth with a terrible fury," Garrison said, his eyes suddenly not looking at her anymore.

Bingo. Cathy looked at Garrison intently. This was the payoff. But he still needed a little tempting, and she didn't dare understand too quickly. "Garrison, what the hell are you talking about? What is it they don't want you to find?"

"The bones of Mjollnir."

"That's very pretty poetry, but *what the hell are you talking about?*"

"A killer beneath our feet."

Cathy whistled. "You may not be paranoid, but I'm getting ready to believe you're just plain crazy."

Garrison stood up and started to reseal his parka. "That's just the start of it all, and it gets a lot worse. Come back to my office, and I'll get some things out of my safe that might get you ready to believe me. I need to talk to someone I can trust."

Cathy, with a worried frown on her face, buttoned up her own parka and followed silently. She was starting to know what being a traitor felt like.

An hour later, she had seen enough. Her friends had been on the right track, when they had decided to keep an eye on Garrison.

Garrison took the last of the papers from her and put them away in his safe. "The stakes are what get me," he said. "They simply can't get any bigger." He looked Cathy right in the eye. "So—are you ready to help me on this? Help protect the project?"

"Yes, of course," Cathy said. But she felt dirty even as she spoke. This was the sort of information she had been sent here to get. But success didn't make her like herself much at the moment.

"I really, honestly, believe that Ben doesn't understand the danger," Garrison went on. "I think if I showed *him* what I've shown you, he'd come around. But we can't take the chance of talking to him, trusting him with the truth. In fact, we'll have to assume he'll sabotage the operation if he can." Garrison thought for a moment. "If he hasn't done it already, if that fire wasn't an accident."

Cathy didn't answer. Garrison reached over and touched her on the arm.

"Cathy, I may want to put you on overseeing drill operations as well as running admin and simulations. Could you handle it?" He picked up Cathy's parka and handed it to her.

Cathy looked again at Garrison. She had never seen him this frightened or serious about anything. "Yes. Yes, I could handle it," she replied, very soberly.

"Good," Garrison watched her, without seeing, as she put the parka back on. "I don't know if you'll have to take it on yet," he said at last. "Just read up on drilling procedure—quietly. I want you to know what sort of shape we're in and be ready to step into the job. Obviously don't say anything to Ben about this. I've got to go check on some things. See you later." He opened the inner door and Cathy stepped through it. She hesitated, tempted to turn back and tell him—but he had already shut the door behind her. Cathy stood there, between the two doors, for a long while.

Inside, Garrison paced back and forth along the length of the hut. One microscopic suspicion, one odd circumstance around a man he liked, a man he thought was on his side, and look what it could do. He hated distrust. What the hell was going on with Ben? And more to the point, what could he do about it?

Chapter Four

CENTRAL COLONY, THE MOON

"As I am to preside today, I hereby call this conference back into session," Hiroshi Suzuki said in his quiet, tired voice. He used his age well, Neruda thought. People instinctively paid deference to a man who appeared so frail. Suzuki tapped a few keys on his notepack and cleared his throat. "We have been in session for five days now, my friends, and have agreed on little more than to repeat this meeting one Earth year from now. I say the people of all worlds will condemn this conference as a failure if that is all we can agree to. Surely we can and must come to some sort of compromise."

Angela Hardin sniffed audibly and replied. "Mr. Chairman, with all due respect, I ask you not to speak of compromise when all you offer are terms that amount to outright surrender. Your idea of a 'compromise' is to flat-out ban imports to Earth from the Settlement Worlds."

"Once again, I must clarify," Suzuki said. "We seek only to rationalize our own economy. We seek a cessation of only redundant imports, those which duplicate items or materials mined or manufactured in cislunar space. If the product in question cannot be found within the orbit of the Moon, we welcome its importation."

"There *are*, as you know perfectly well, virtually no products or raw materials that are not available or manufactured in cislunar space," Hardin pointed out mechanically.

"Granting for the sake of argument that were true, why then should our people import from you what our domestic industry can sell them already?"

"Because 'your people' are the *other* ones you're gouging, pally," McGillicutty snapped. The other Settlement delegates shifted uncomfortably. The chief Mars delegate was not noted for his subtlety. "Ores, water and organics, fusion engines and fuel, spacecraft, even whole habitats—every damn one of them we could sell to 'your people' for half what your precious domestic industry crowds gets for them.

"But you exclude *us* to protect your industry from its own customers—because your industries are used to being monopolies. Your own people pay double prices, and we're forced to run a hemorrhaging trade deficit with Earth, because you sell us what we need at monopoly prices, but you refuse to buy from us." He pointed a meaty finger at Suzuki. "Talk smooth and gentle all you like, Suzuki, but your trade policy is a systematic effort to drain wealth from the Settlements back toward Earth. You want to convert us into a pack of miserable eunuch colonies like the bloody Moon."

Neruda started in shock and glared balefully at McGillicutty. "I must protest," he sputtered.

The Martian delegate shrugged indifferently. "Sorry, mate, but if the shoe fits. . . . Try calling anyone on Mars a 'colonist' and not a Settler. You'll get your face ripped off. Your poor sods don't even know 'colonist' is a dirty word." McGillicutty dismissed the outraged Neruda from his thoughts and continued. "So the question is, do the trade barriers come down, or do we all sit around on our arses yapping until the conference is over?"

Angela Hardin sat silent. Few around the table missed the noteworthy point of McGillicutty's outburst. Hardin had allowed it. Heretofore, she had restrained her second-in-command. That she was unleashing him today was significant. She was upping the stakes.

Suzuki pulled a paper out of his inside jacket pocket and unfolded it thoughtfully. "I am informed that the so-called 'trade barriers' you refer to are down already. There has always been a fair degree of smuggling, largely thanks to the difficulty of patrolling the vastness of space adequately. Until now there has at least been some honorable government-to-government effort to control the illegal traffic. I have before me what appears to be an authenticated copy of an order from the Settlement Confederation Assembly. It instructs Settlement custom agents to cease all efforts at interdiction of Earth/Settlement smuggling. How can we negotiate a trade agreement with governments who condone—indeed order—the violation of existing trade laws?"

"How can we cut deals with a mob of colonial monopolists who're ready to let our children die of malnutrition or disease rather than allow open trade?" McGillicutty snapped back. "We do not have the means, facilities, or raw materials to manufacture trace-element nutrition products. We don't have the medical labs or research capacity to manufacture anything but the most basic vaccines and drugs.

"Yes, we're forced to condone smuggling—or else watch our people die by the thousands in plagues. Disease spreads horribly fast in a closed-environment colony. But *you* tax the medicines and medical equipment straight through the ceiling. *That's* why we smuggle them. For what must be the first time in history, black market prices are cheaper than the official rate. Your taxes are so high the smugglers can make a bloodsucker's profits and *still* undercut the legal rates. They can sell *one* vitamin and trace-element tablet for the price of a whole bottle back on Earth. Plain old vitamins *you* can extract from natural sources cheaply and easily, while so far it's flat-out impossible for us to synthesize them in useful quantities. And you ask us to choose tight customs control over children with rickets and scurvy?"

McGillicutty gestured to the nervous faces on his side of the table. "My friends at this table didn't want me to bring all these things up, because they'd like to pretend it's all a grand secret. But your lot would have to be damned fools not to know it. Half of what we buy from you is health care in one way or another. But it's not just drugs and medicines you're keeping from us. It's people. Skilled, educated people.

"To this day, there isn't a medical school off Earth, because we've never been able to afford to hire a faculty or buy the equipment we'd need. We have to pay incredible wages to attract any doctors at all—and then your policies only make it worse.

"You've written laws and treaties that make all wages earned by a citizen of a U.N. country while off-planet liable to tax just as if the wage earner were back home— plus an additional twenty percent payable directly to the U.N.! Violators to be thrown in Tycho Penal should they ever return to the Earth/Moon system. We have to pay emigrants enough to compensate for the taxes *you've* forced *them* to pay *you*! It amounts to an indirect tax on the Settlement worlds, bribes we're forced to pay you if we're to attract the skilled people we need to survive.

"Not just doctors, but pilots, technicians, all sorts of specialists—anyone who might want to emigrate off-planet must hesitate under those circumstances. Those who *do* decide to emigrate and still want to visit Earth before they die must pay an unfair tax to a government a billion kilometers away. It's that or exile themselves from Earth for all time, never see their families or the home planet again. It's extortion."

"The twenty percent U.N. surtax is paid as recompense for the cost of our educating your specialists for you," Suzuki said smoothly.

"Learned that from old Soviets, nyet?" one of the Titan delegates sneered. The Titanians were virtually all of Russian extraction, Neruda reminded himself, and more paranoid for signs of imagined tyranny than most.

Suzuki ignored the interruption. "Each emigrant from the Earth represents a lost investment in education and other social services. We are within our rights to seek recompensation."

"And the medical taxes are there to recompense you for all the trouble of malnourishing our children?" McGillicutty shot back. "What's your excuse for that?"

"There are, as you know perfectly well, export taxes on many classes of merchandise and services. Medical supplies are taxed in accordance with the appropriate formulae for their classes of export."

"Double-talk. Bloody no-answer double-talk—" McGillicutty growled. Hardin reached out and touched him on the arm. He stopped in midsentence and the two of them leaned their heads toward each other to whisper together. After a moment, McGillicutty grunted and sat back in his chair.

"Tempers are growing hot," Hardin said. "I move we adjourn for the day and return to the issues at hand tomorrow."

Chairman Suzuki nodded regretfully. "I am forced to concur." He lifted the gavel. "Do I hear a second to the motion from the non-proposing delegation?"

That was Neruda's cue. He could tell when Suzuki *wanted* a second. "Mr. Chairman, I second the motion," he said promptly, not liking it for a moment. Why let the opposition get in such an insulting last word on the subject?

"Any objections or discussion?" Suzuki asked mechanically. "There being none voiced, I declare this conference adjourned until 0900 tomorrow, at which time Dr. Angela Hardin will be in the chair." He whacked down the gavel and the delegates began to shuffle their way out.

Hillary Wu, private assistant to the lunar governor, had been seated with the rest of the staff, in a row of chairs lining the edge of the room. Now she stood and caught up with her boss, Governor Neruda, as he left the room.

"Heartening, isn't it, Wu?" Neruda asked as she fell into step alongside him. "The Settlement delegation is clearly in disarray. Did you notice how far out of line McGillicutty stepped? Hardin won't be able to keep them together much longer. Once the Settlers split, then we can start negotiating more favorable agreements with each group, one at a time."

Hillary Wu sighed. She was past caring if Neruda was that stupid naturally, or if he had been forced to study. Once again he had managed to miss or misinterpret *every* important point of the day's session. McGillicutty's public admission of the Settlers' weaknesses was no outburst, but a carefully planned warning. It said very plainly that the Settlers were ready to go public with the medical story. There would be plenty of people back on Earth appalled by the medical shortages Earth seemed to be inflicting on the other worlds. Then Suzuki had come right back and revealed terrestrial knowledge of secret Settlement documents.

That had set hands to working over notepack keyboards on the Settler side of the table. No doubt half a dozen delegates had sent messages, and the Settler intelligence services were tracing the leak already.

The key point: Suzuki had willingly sacrificed a vital intel source to let the Settlers know he too was willing to go public. It would be highly embarrassing to Settler sensitivities to be branded as a bunch of bushwhacking smugglers. There was too much of that in the Settlers' past for them to be comfortable about a present-day accusation.

Hardin's delegation was under the strictest control, that was obvious. Even McGillicutty had fallen silent at her command. Now the stakes were raised, the gloves were off—and tomorrow Hardin was in the chair. She could control the discussion at a crucial juncture.

"All in all, quite a day, wasn't it?" Neruda asked.

"Yes sir, it certainly was," Hillary agreed. For once, she meant what she said to her boss.

HRISEY, ICELAND

There was a note posted in prep/mess the next morning; the main communications console in prep/mess had blown a fuse, a replacement had been installed and that had blown too. There was only one spare fuse left in stock, but it would not be put in the comm console until they could figure out why it was eating fuses. Until further notice, contact with the outside world would be limited to Garrison's unit, and limited to priority calls.

Meanwhile, the perfectly good fuse from the prep/mess comm unit, plus a large supply of spares, went into Garrison's safe. Garrison began to be careful to lock up his hut whenever he left it, and when he turned in for the night.

From New York, Glenda reported by e-mail that she had hit a brick wall. Leonard Brattleby was pretty good at hiding his traces. He was listed with the New York Bar Association as a member in good standing, and was listed as a member of the board of Lucifer Technologies, but he left no other traces behind. The only address they had was a private post office box—the same post office box as GRF, as a matter of fact. His phone was unlisted, there was no e-mail box under his name, nothing. The guy knew how to hide.

Garrison kept after Cathy to learn every detail of torch-bit drilling procedure perfectly, and as soon as possible. She was a quick study, but there was a lot of detail to go through. At least the drilling itself was proceeding well. They should be done with the present hole and into the final one, the clincher, in another few days.

There was an odd incident that got Garrison even more nervous, two days after GRF had made its funding grant. Garrison got a call from Lucifer Technologies. Cathy and Garrison were having a working lunch in his office when the call came in. Garrison hit the *accept call* button irritably. They were going over bit-changing procedure, and he was in no mood for interruptions. The screen came to life and revealed a fat, bald, bland-faced, popeyed man. He wore a meaningless grin on his thin-lipped face, and he was smoking a big black cigar.

Cathy peeked at him from outside camera range and wondered who this guy could be. He couldn't have looked like worse news if he had hung a sign on his neck that said DON'T TRUST ME.

"Good day," Garrison said carefully. Why should a stranger be calling here? he wondered. Almost on impulse, he hit the *record call* button.

"Hello," the stranger said with a saurian complacency. "My name's Lem Archer. I'm looking for a"—he paused to check a paper on his desk—"a Dr. Garrison Morrows."

"That's 'Morrow.' No 's' on the end. I'm the man you want."

"You certainly are!" Archer announced with a patently synthetic enthusiasm. "You're a hard man to get a hold of. Now then, Dr. Morrows—ah, Morrow, sorry. I'm with Lucifer Technologies, the orbital mining firm. We'd like to offer you a job."

A twitch of a smile escaped the side of Garrison's mouth. "I've got a job."

Archer gestured deprecatingly with one hand and blinked his eyes slowly. "I can offer you a better one. Exciting work. Good money. *Very* good money. A chance to work at the very cutting edge of science—"

"Doing what?" Garrison asked.

"Being a geologist. You know, *your* work," Archer replied, a bit vaguely. He shrugged. "Rocks."

"Wait a minute. LuTech is strictly orbital mining, right? No mining on Earth, or the Moon, right? So the work would all be on asteroids, right?"

"Yeah, we're strictly asteroidal." Archer said irritably. "But what's the difference? Rocks are rocks."

"But they aren't inner-planet crustal. Asteroids aren't formed the way Earth and the Moon and Mars were."

"So?"

"So I know nothing about asteroids. I work with planet-formed geology."

"Look, Gary, think it over before you . . ."

Hoo boy, Cathy thought. *That'll do it. He does not like to be called Gary.*

"The name is Garrison to my friends, and Dr. Morrow to everyone else," Garrison said testily, "and I'm rather busy just now."

"Now wait a minute! This is a good job I'm offering—"

"But it has nothing to do with my work. I'd suggest you contact some astrogeology specialists for the position. Good day to you." Garrison cut the connection.

"What the hell was all *that* about?" Cathy asked.

Garrison shook his head. "Maybe they figure hiring me away is one way to stop my research. They wanted to try bribing me with a swell job," he said sarcastically.

"Offer you a job?" Cathy objected. "That guy was just plain insulting. He couldn't tempt someone out of a burning building."

Garrison smiled, and then thought about it for a moment, and the smile faded. "You're right. They didn't want me to take that job."

"But they just offered it to you."

"And sent Quasimodo to charm me into it. They wanted

a record of a job offer as proof that they had no hard feelings toward me. And if I took it, great, that still accomplishes their goal. If I turn it down, as would be likely no matter who offered me the work, they can use it as proof later that my wild accusations against them are just the ravings of a disgruntled crank blowing off steam."

"Garrison, you are *not* making sense. What wild accusations?"

"The ones I'll make after they try and sabotage my work here again."

"Oh. Right." Cathy decided to change the subject. She didn't like the talk about paranoia, or sabotage. She stood up. "Look, I'm going to take off. The tug's scheduled to start moving the platform tomorrow morning. I want to talk with the tug captain and make sure everything's under control."

"Fine, but do me a favor on your way. Find Ben and tell him to come over, will you? Meantime, I'd better call Glenda and give her this latest tidbit."

Cathy bundled herself up and left, and Garrison turned toward the comm console. He had his finger over the autodial button for Glenda's office when he remembered the time difference. She would have left the office by now, and he didn't feel like chasing her down on her mobile phone, probably interrupting her dinner. He pulled out his keyboard and rattled off a quick e-mail note to her instead, using the habit of compressed spelling and syntax he had learned back when he couldn't afford long e-mail messages from the Moon.

> G—Just got strange and prob. bogus job offer from one Lem Archer of LuTech. Was legit? Any link Archer to Brattleby/GRF/LuTech? Have hunch job offer = LuTech doesn't want exped. to cont. What they try next? Advise soonest. Garrison.

Ben stepped into the trailer just as Garrison was sending the e-mail message on its way. The two of them hadn't really spoken, except for bland pleasantries, since the scene in the prep room—and the bland pleasantries had long since devolved into surly silence. Ben stood there for a moment, looking at Garrison, before he pulled off his gloves and got to work undoing his parka. "Cathy said you wanted to see me?" he asked. There was something nervous, something defiant in the way he stood, in his tone of voice.

"Yeah, Ben. Sit down. I want to know something," Garrison said. Ben sat down gingerly on the edge of the chair furthest from Garrison.

"Cathy and I have talked a lot about the whole situation, and I've been doing some thinking myself," Garrison said. "I've gotten as far as figuring out that you must be the link to LuTech. I also figure LuTech isn't working hard trying to do me favors. They won't like what I'm doing. I assume, therefore, your LuTech friends are trying to screw me up. Glenda has established that Brattleby is on LuTech's board. It had to be their money that paid for the supplies—and the ship carrying them. But since they don't want me to succeed, they can't allow me to be resupplied. That ship's not going to get here, is it?"

Ben forced himself to look Garrison in the eye. "I guess there's not much point in denying it anymore. You're right. The ship is being diverted."

"And without the supplies on that ship, we're dead," Garrison said. "Not only do I fail to collect my proof, but I'm made to look like a damn fool in the process, making it just about impossible for me to ever try again. The expedition will have been a failure, after all. But the thing I want to know is this—why did they bother with the charade of the ship at all?"

Ben bit his lip and squirmed uncomfortably. "Because they didn't want to take the chance of your finding another backer. With supplies on the way, and money in the bank, you're not even trying to find one—and you're not conserving supplies, either. Another week or ten days at the current rate of consumption, and you'll have to shut down and cease operations. When you shut down, that will be GRF's cue to cancel your grant. The ship will never come, you won't be able to pay anyone, and your people will quit and go home. And that'll be it."

Garrison looked closely at Ben, shook his head, and

sighed. "You're fired," he said at last. Garrison picked up
a piece of paper at random, looked at it without seeing it,
and tossed it back on the desk. "I'm putting Cathy Cleveland in charge of drilling.

Ben looked at Garrison strangely. "Cathy? After—"

"Cathy," Garrison said curtly. "Do you have any objections? She may not know everything you know, but at
least she won't be passing information to people who are
trying to wreck my work."

Ben snorted disdainfully. "It is wrecked. Even Cathy
couldn't do you any more harm. You've lost, Garrison.
What you were after was just too dangerous. It would start
a panic, turn the world upside down. It can't be allowed."

There was silence for a moment. Ben made no move to
leave. He just sat there.

Garrison spoke again. "Do you really believe that? Is
that what they told you? That I had to be stopped to avoid
hysteria?"

"They didn't have to tell me." Ben's voice was harsh and
annoyed. "It's obvious. What you're doing could frighten
millions, billions of people into believing the orbital asteroid mines could kill them. The miners don't want a lot of
panicky people out in the streets. The man in the street
just doesn't understand an asteroid in a high orbit can't
crash into the Earth any more than the Moon can. You'll
make him think it can."

"That's nonsense and you know it. The miners have
been whining about the ignorant public for decades now—
but the public just isn't ignorant anymore. None of the
orbiting rocks could possibly crash. Quite the contrary
from not understanding, *everyone* knows that's true. But
more important than they're *knowing* it's true, these days
people *believe* it, steadfastly and wholeheartedly, as an
article of faith. Why shouldn't they? The miners have
spent billions over the years hammering that point home.
And the asteroids have been up there in high Earth orbit
for nearly a century now with no significant problems—
they are an accepted presence by now, even taken for
granted. People are complacent about the orbital mines.
And my little project here couldn't even begin to make

a dent in the public's attitudes about the high-orbit mines.

"But the high-orbit mines aren't what's at stake. There's Cornucopia. And Cornucopia's what's dangerous."

"Cornucopia?" Ben asked.

Garrison gave Ben a wintry smile. "I wonder: have you truly never heard of it, or is this still part of the act?" Garrison went to his safe, spun the dials, opened it and pulled out a sheaf of papers.

Garrison dropped the papers on the desk in front of Ben. "A friend of mine who shall remain nameless used to work for LuTech. Left there rather abruptly. She got some of these papers for me. Once Cornucopia was just a rock with a number instead of a name. Then some engineers noticed it had an interesting orbit. LuTech came up with a very cheap trajectory for it, one that will drop it right into Earth orbit. The final braking maneuver is to be performed by a 'special nuclear energy device,' according to their plans. The less technical term being 'bomb,' of course. Cornucopia's already on its way here."

"So?" Ben asked.

"So the resultant orbit's perigee is only a thousand kilometers high. They need it that low in order to use the special gravity-assist orbit insertion technique. Besides, a lower orbit means cheaper transport of material to the Earth's surface."

"But a thousand klicks up?" Ben asked. "There's still atmospheric drag that low!"

"No kidding," Garrison said dryly. "But don't worry. According to the figures I've seen, the orbit won't decay for another three hundred, four hundred years. By which time LuTech confidently expects it to be mined down to nothing, or else that they'll be able to adjust the orbit. With today's technology, that adjustment would require setting off *more* nukes to move the asteroid—still only a thousand klicks over someone's head down here on Earth. Other than that, everything should be fine."

Garrison paused. "Unless something goes wrong on insertion into orbit. Say the braking bomb doesn't fire quite right. Or unless there's an unexpected variation in atmospheric drag at that altitude for some reason—and that's happened before.

"Or, unless later on, centuries from now, we decide we don't need orbital mines, or there's a bad war between now and then that clobbers civilization and we forget *how* to move asteroids. Do you read the news much? That big conference on the Moon that's not going so well? The way the U.N. and the Settlement Coalition are going at each other, I wouldn't say a war is outside the realm of possibility. I've thought up some other possibilities. Want to hear them?"

Ben didn't say anything. Instead he picked up the papers and started reading them, slowly, carefully.

Garrison kept talking. "Even if the main body of the asteroid never crashes, there are certainly going to be more meteorite impacts on Earth because of this thing. Tailing and debris from mining blasts will deorbit and re-enter—or else just float around up there until they punch a hole in some orbital facility. With the distant-orbit asteroids, the tailings are no big deal—but that's a crowded piece of space they want to put that rock in! The damnable thing is that they *know* it's going to come down! They admit it!"

Ben looked up at Garrison, waved the papers. "These are just copies. No authenticators, no proof that some backroom hacker didn't just cook these numbers up as a prank or to make LuTech look bad. How do I know—how do *you* know—they're on the level and not fakes or forgeries?"

"They're real," Garrison said. "And even without authenticator seals, I can prove it. Take a look in the back of the file folder. Read the clippings and newsprints. It's all open literature, if you know where to look."

Ben shuffled through the papers and found a series of news articles, from various specialized publications.

BOEING TO DEVELOP
SHORT-RANGE CARGO HAULER

Boeing Aerospace Group today announced plans
to develop a variant of its short-range Starlifter

77A7 personnel carrier as a bulk cargo lifter. By removing passenger equipment (life support, crash seats, galley systems, etc.) the cargo carrier will achieve an approximate doubling of surface-to-orbit and orbit-to-surface capacity. LuTech Industries has expressed an interest in the development of a shorthaul SOS (surface-orbit-surface) cargo vehicle. . . .

Someone had scrawled in the margin—*note interest in orbit-to-surface hauling*.

TRAJECTORY TECHNIQUES
EXTEND RANGE OF ORBITS

A Tokyo University study, sponsored by Lucifer Technologies, reports a new approach in gravitational assist or "slingshot" orbit insertions. By using a lunar gravitational assist, coupled with a near-retrograde velocity final approach, objects could be inserted in orbit around Earth in a far larger range of orbits, between five hundred and five hundred thousand kilometer perigees. The new technique would allow these insertions with a far lower expenditure of time, money and physical energy. The Near-Retrograde Velocity (NRV) technique is made possible by greater confidence in orbit insertion hardware, allowing for reduced safety margins. . . .

SIMULATED ASTEROID CAPTURE
USING NRV TECHNIQUE

May 15, 2114. As part of an ongoing theoretical study of new capture techniques, the capture of a specific asteroid was computer modeled at the Tokyo University Space Science Center. The simulation of the thirteen-month mission commenced with a June 23, 2115 launch date toward. . . .

"This is all pretty weak circumstantial evidence," Ben

said, a bit defensively. "So you've dug up some articles and some theoretical papers. So what?"

Garrison came over and shoved the computer keyboard across the desk to him. "You punch this up, so you *know* it's for real, that I didn't forge it somehow. Get onto one of the commercial data links and call up the electronic version of *Professional Astronautics*."

Ben glanced up at Garrison and ran the commands that linked the computer with the commlink and, through it, the datanode in Reykjavik. In ninety seconds, he was inside *Professional Astronautics*. "Okay, now what?"

"Key into the back-issues section. Call up the classified ads, under the heading *Crews Forming*. Get a sort by launch date, then by trip duration. Take a look at last June."

Ben ran the command, and watched the listings appear on the screen. And then he saw it. It seemed to jump off the page at him. A thirteen-month mission that had launched June 23, 2115—a year ago. Purpose and destination were unspecified—but Ben knew. The dates exactly matched the "simulation" they had run in Tokyo. There was no way that could be a coincidence.

"They captured the asteroid two months back," Garrison said. "They're on their way home now. The asteroid is coming slower. It won't arrive for another two years."

"Jesus." Ben was stunned. "This is incredible. You've sure as hell done your homework."

"Thanks," Garrison said wryly. "Nice to get recognition from someone else in the intelligence business. Do you believe me now?"

"Almost," Ben said. "Almost. But why haven't you gone public with this stuff, told the world about their plans?"

"Because the Moon has never crashed into the Earth," Garrison said bitterly, "and neither have the mining asteroids. Because they'll march out that old chestnut, and a dozen other slick, facile arguments that don't have anything to do with this situation. They've got some very slick P.R. flacks who could sandbag me in a second if I just wandered out with what I've got. It might be enough to convince you, to convince professionals—but it's not enough to make the public see the danger.

"The asteroid mining crowd is *powerful*, Ben, and they've done the world a hell of a lot of good. I'd be in the same position as someone warning that electricity is a bad thing. After centuries using it, who'd believe it? Who'd want to listen? Who *would* listen?" Garrison sat down in his creaking old desk chair and gestured helplessly. "Besides, it's all still years in the future. The P.R. boys would have all that time to get to work and make it sound okay. They would work real hard 'allaying needless public concern' or whatever." He took the file back from Ben and flipped through it. "What drives me nuts is that I sincerely believe these aren't bad people who want to do this crazy thing. Ignorant, dangerously powerful maybe, but not *evil*. They simply don't understand how high the stakes are in the game they're playing."

Ben shut off the computer terminal, took the folder from Garrison, tapped the cover, and handed it back. "Do me a favor. Hold off that firing for twelve hours. I need time to think, time to call some people. Let me check this out."

Garrison gave him a tired smile and took the file. He put it back in the safe and took one of the comm fuses out before he closed the door and spun the dial. He stood up and handed the fuse to Ben. "I was hoping you'd say that. It was a big chance, talking to you, but I wanted to take it. Call whomever you like. Take twenty-four hours."

Ben stood up and shook his head. "Garrison, I don't think you've *got* twenty-four hours." He turned and left, walked out into the dark.

Neither man spent a very restful night.

Garrison had just finally managed to nod off when he got a rude awakening. It was still dark out, in spite of the short Arctic winter, when Ben burst back in through the office trailer door, popping the lock right off the door, swearing and sputtering, scaring the living daylights out of Garrison.

Garrison practically jumped out of his sleeping bag, and

his cot teetered on the brink of collapse for a moment. He was about to protest the intrusion, but Ben was too upset to listen.

"Those dumb *bastards*! Those idiot *fools*!" Ben shouted. "I hate to admit it, Garrison, but you were right. Those maniacs actually think it's okay, that there's no risk!"

Garrison was not at his best first thing in the morning, let alone when wakened suddenly in the middle of the night. He blearily peeled himself out of his sleeping bag, half fell out of the cot, and staggered toward the coffee maker. "Then I take it you're convinced?" he asked as he fumbled with the grounds basket.

"I'm convinced," Ben answered, completely oblivious to Garrison's condition. "Thank God for time zones and workaholics. I caught people just coming in or just leaving the office all over the world—and on the Moon."

"So much for this month's long-distance bill," Garrison muttered grumpily. He blinked once or twice and made a conscious effort to force himself to wakefulness.

Ben sailed on, ignoring the wisecrack. "The real guys, the techs, the ones that *know* what they're doing—they're going *nuts*! No one will pay any attention to them. Larry Priory resigned in protest, and they just put a company stooge in his place. Joanne Mayron tried to go to the news media, but the public relations flacks absolutely smothered her, convinced all the reporters she was a nut."

"Whoa. Easy." The first trickling stream of the black, life-giving fluid was percolating into the pot. "Who are you talking about? Who are Larry and Joanne?"

"People I know at LuTech. I called around everywhere. Lots of engineering people know about this, but they can't *do* anything about it." Ben shook his head in wonderment. "The stupid bastards really are going to *do* it. They're going to hang an asteroid a thousand klicks up!"

"Does this mean you're willing to try and stop them?" Garrison asked.

Ben looked hard at Garrison. "Yes," he said. "Yes it does."

"Good. You're back on the payroll."

"Wait a second. You're willing to trust me? Just like that? Let bygones be bygones?"

"I don't really have a choice," Garrison said. "You're the only one who has the information to help me."

Ben grinned enthusiastically. "Just try me. Confession is good for the soul, even for a nice Jewish boy. It hasn't been any fun skulking around behind your back. Besides, those bastards *lied* to me. They told me you were a crackpot. I don't owe them anything. So what do you want to know?" he asked.

"For starters, tell me about the Geological Research Foundation. It's strictly a front for LuTech, right? Without any legitimate existence."

"Right. They put it together in a hell of a hurry. Fast enough that they might have made a few mistakes. Your friend Glenda might be able to trace them—though what good it would do you at this point I don't know."

"What more can you tell me about their plans?" Garrison yawned and ran a hand through his shaggy mop of hair. At least his brain was awake now. With luck, his body would catch up soon. The coffee finished brewing and he gratefully poured himself a cup.

"Not much," Ben said. "You figured out most of it. They plan to string you along, promise you support so you won't go looking for it elsewhere, and then not deliver."

"What about the ship?" Garrison dug his pants out from under the cot and pulled them on over his long johns. "Did it ever exist?"

"Oh, there's a ship all right," Ben said, helping himself to coffee. They wanted to look legitimate, remember. She's supposed to arrive forty-eight hours from now in Reykjavik—"

"*Reykjavik?* In the south? That's hundreds of kilometers from here! The ship was supposed to sail straight for Akureyia, just down the fjord."

"Exactly. But the ship will pull into Reykjavik, and the captain will sit there in port, wondering why you didn't show up to collect the supplies. We'll wonder why the ship never shows up in our neck of the woods—"

"And by the time it all gets straightened out, we'll have run out of drilling supplies and food, and be forced to give up. Cute."

Ben flopped back down into the trailer's beat-up old sofa. "It's good to get this off my chest. I didn't like being a sneak."

"Well, don't give up sneaking just yet. We need you to start sneaking around for our side," Garrison said. "We have to get out of this mess. We still have a job to do."

"Okay, fine. I can figure out what you're doing on Iceland, but what exactly are you planning?"

"I want to demonstrate how dangerous Cornucopia will be that close to Earth. Scare people enough that they not only prevent it from being moved, but stop *any* asteroid from getting that close," Garrison said.

"How do you feel about asteroid mining in general?" Ben asked abruptly. "Are you fanatical—uh—*rigidly* against it, or are you flexible? How do you feel about, say, the dangers of inserting an asteroid into, say, a geosynch orbit, 35,000 klicks high?"

"The danger from that is so low even I can live with it. Or at least the danger has been low up to now—until they dreamt up the NRV technique. All the asteroid orbit insertions have been fall-away orbits up to now—the change in direction in speed has always been *toward* Earth, forcing an asteroid that was going to drift off into space to get nearer us than it wanted to—so if the adjustment doesn't work or is too weak, it'll still miss the planet. Failure makes it fall away from Earth. With Cornucopia, they are planning to use a direct-intercept course and use a nuke to *brake* the rock, not accelerate it. If the nuke doesn't go off, and the backups fail—the asteroid is on a virtual collision course with the planet! So we've got to demonstrate the dangers." Garrison scratched at his beard for a moment. "But we were really talking about how to warn against Cornucopia—"

"Why not just show pictures of Meteor Crater in Arizona?" Ben asked.

"First off, the Meteor Crater impact was only about fifteen thousand years ago—and *it* didn't result in any mass—" Garrison was about to go on when Cathy came bursting in to the trailer. "Next expedition for me is in

Hawaii," she announced before she had even looked around. "Nice and warm. Plenty of volcanoes there . . ." She paused and noticed that Ben was in the room. "So you guys have made up?"

Ben laughed. "Yeah, we're friends."

Cathy shrugged and turned to Garrison. "Does that mean you want me to put the drilling rig back?"

"The drilling rig—you mean the *Surveyor*—" Ben ran to the north window and stood there, spluttering. The venerable old platform was sedately chuffing toward the north.

It was Garrison's turn to laugh. "I completely forgot. Last night I ordered Cathy to send her fifteen klicks north to begin the last hole as soon as possible."

Ben shook his head. "Figuring to steal a march on the company spy," he said, his expression caught between shock and amusement. "Well, whatever the motive, it was the right move to make. We have to work fast. LuTech is sure to try something to stop us."

Cathy gave Ben a funny look. "Lucifer Technologies? Again? *Now* what are they doing?"

Ben brought Cathy up to date as briefly as possible.

Cathy listened quietly, asking few questions. When Ben had finished, she said, "Well, the obvious thing to do is to call Reykjavik and get that ship rerouted up here pronto."

Ben shook his head. "No, that's no good. That would be the honest, straightforward way to get these supplies up here. But we need to get the cargo off the ship without letting LuTech know we know about them. If they found out we'd gotten the stuff, they'd think up some other way of stopping us. We've got to take the gear without getting caught."

"You mean, we have to steal the stuff off the ship," Cathy said.

Ben raised an eyebrow. "I suppose you could call it that."

"I don't care *how* we get the stuff as long as we do get it," Garrison said. "So what do we do?"

"We send someone to Reykjavik, and they play it by

ear—and make sure they're carrying a checkbook," Ben said.

Garrison thought for a moment. "Cathy and I will go," he decided. "Ben, you stay here. If we get any interesting phone calls from the bad guys, you'll be able to tell them what they want to hear. And get off a message to Glenda in New York. Cathy—go pack."

Chapter Five

CENTRAL COLONY, THE MOON

Hiroshi Suzuki stared, unseeingly out across the grim lunar landscape. He was a tall, lanky, man and age had settled a mantle of frailty upon his broad shoulders. His face was smooth and unwrinkled, his long years betrayed only by the delicate translucence of his skin and his snow-white hair. And yet, intangibly and unmistakably, he was *old*. The bloom and vitality of youth were long gone from him.

Usually, in spite of his years, he still could feel young and strong. Today, he felt *old*, tired, as ancient and worn as the lifeless craters that dotted the plain below.

The craters were a good metaphor for his own state of preservation. Even in the perfect vacuum of the Moon, nature had found ways—slow, subtle, insidious ways to wear down the landscape. The ceaseless rain of invisibly small micrometeoroids, the fierce heating and cooling cycles that expanded and compressed the surface until it finally shattered, a grain at a time. It was a slow process, but endless, relentless.

That was the sort of enemy he felt he was battling now. He was ninety-one years old, but that was the least of it.

The doctors could keep him alive, his body youthful, as long as he liked. It was history, not old age, that he was fighting, history that was grinding him down with excruciating slowness. History, and the obstinate shortsightedness of his compatriots, that would defeat him.

The door chimed and slid open. Angela Hardin stepped through and gave her old friend a tired smile. "Good evening, Hiroshi. Are they treating you well?"

He gestured about himself at the luxurious room. The President's Suite took up the entire top floor of Apollo Tower. There was no other place on this entire globe as sumptuously appointed as this complex. Only on Earth could it even be matched. "Adequately," he said in mock seriousness.

"For what comfort it is, my rooms are certainly pleasant, but nothing to compare with this," Hardin said.

"It would appear that our lunar friends know which side their bread is buttered on," Suzuki said with a smile. If there was one bedrock certainty to the morass of interplanetary politics, it was that the Earth, the U.N., *owned* the Moon. The Settlers would never dream of challenging that. It would never occur to them. Indeed, the two worlds were often thought of as one. "Come," he said, offering his arm and leading her toward a couch, "let us sit and find out what it is that the Colonists call sake."

Hardin let herself be escorted to a comfortable seat, and watched Suzuki go through the pleasant ritual of warming the rice wine and preparing it to be served. She was not as old as he, not quite, and her years sat somewhat more lightly upon her.

She too was a tall and slender person, but she had retained her suppleness, the grace and precision of a dancer in her movements. A smile flitted about her dark, round, solemn face as she watched her old friend go through one of the small ceremonies he so delighted in. He brought the sake from the serving board to the coffee table on a tray, the wine in a stoppered ceramic bottle. He poured it into the square wooden cups that always traveled with him.

She took her cup and waited for him to pour his own. "What shall we drink to?" she asked.

He thought for a moment. "To survival," he replied.

"Surely we can seek a richer success than mere survival," Hardin suggested, looking at his face. There was no humor there. He meant it. "But, very well, to survival." She raised her glass and then sipped her sake thoughtfully. "Is it that bad?" she asked at last.

Hiroshi Suzuki drank from his wine and leaned back into the couch. He allowed himself the luxury of *feeling* his tiredness, instead of once again thrusting it away. Here, with Angela Hardin, he could let his guard down. "It may be. You know the problem as well as I do. Earth's time is passing. We will always be more populous than your worlds, but the day is coming when we will no longer be richer or more powerful. It is not even that we are declining—but that you are advancing faster. Industries we now must defend with trade laws, we once *owned*. Twenty years ago, no one would buy a spacecraft built outside lunar orbit. Now, Mars is the leader in spacecraft production."

Hardin wanted to speak, but she held herself back. This was the real conference, where the deals would truly be struck. She had known Hiroshi for—how long?—nearly sixty years. All the endless conferences, the shifting assignments and ranks as they progressed up the career ladders of diplomacy. There were even rumors of a long-ago love affair between them.

In point of fact, the rumors were true. But that seemed a lifetime or more ago. Decades of life, and experience, the wielding of power had made both of them into wholly different people than the near-children who had shared a bed back when the worlds were young. She knew well enough when it was best to let him talk.

"I would try and guide Earth toward a graceful acceptance of this state of affairs," he said. "Sooner or later, we *must* come to know that the Settlements are neither our enemies or our underlings, but our partners. When that understanding comes, we can come to share our strengths, to everyone's betterment. Free trade would provide Earth with a most efficacious shock, and renewed contact with off-planet technology would stimulate us to new efforts. Perhaps in time we would again regain preeminence.

"But my views do not guide my delegation. There are terrestrials who regard you all as spoiled children to be taken to task, your will broken, your economies sapped, emigration stopped altogether. They know your birthrates, your infant mortality rates. Without emigration, your population would now be in *decline*. They see that as a weapon to be used, not as a tragedy to be avoided. They imagine Earth might somehow profit from your collapse. I do not share these ideas, even if I must tolerate them from my people."

"I know, Hiroshi. And McGillicutty does not speak for all the Settlements—though his views are growing more popular. His faction actively *hates* Earth. My extremists are just as extreme as yours. And I cannot control them for long."

There was silence for a long moment. The sheer emptiness of the vacuum beyond the picture windows seemed to draw all sound from the room. "Is there nothing we can agree on?" Hardin asked at last.

"Other than to meet again a year from now? I think not. If it were just you and me, Angela, just you and me, then we could leave this grim outpost with a secure future for all of us." He thought for a moment. "But your McGillicutty's performance today might be leaked," he suggested. "A bootleg recording of his words reaching Earth's media might be enough to sway public opinion, allow medical tariffs to be reduced or even eliminated."

Hardin's thin, stern face broke into a smile. "That had occurred to me, you know. And for some strange reason, my press people seem to have brought along some video images of sick children and primitive hospitals. But I was hesitant to use them. It might make Hiroshi Suzuki seem just a bit too heartless." Both of them knew who Suzuki's likely replacements were. None were likely to meet after hours with the opposition leader. "We might be able to edit around that problem, if you were willing."

"Can you stop the smuggling?" Suzuki asked.

"What? That blatant forgery?" Hardin asked playfully. "I'll deny ever signing it the moment you leak it. It's real, of course, more of McGillicutty's work. Foolish, too. That sort of broad general order was *bound* to leak sooner or later. I'll publicly urge all Customs officers to redouble their efforts against smuggling. They'll be confused about receiving contradictory orders, but they'll obey me."

"The real danger is people will see that smuggling order as a plant, disinformation planted by our agents," Suzuki said seriously. "Try and deflect any suggestions like that."

"But you had another reason for waving that paper around like that," Hardin said. It was not a question. "There hasn't been time for that order to get out to the Customs people and then leak back to you through the usual sort of intelligence channels. You were telling me that the Settlement Council has a serious comm leak somewhere. Where?"

Suzuki smiled. "You're sitting on it. The Moon. Half your long-haul communications come through the Lunar Communication Laser Array for relay. It's often the only powerful station in proper position for signal relay. Even when there's an alternative, the Settlement worlds often use the Moon. The rates are cheaper."

"But I thought our laser communication was supposed to be sealed. The hardware and the software are supposed to be blocked against any interference, with the same legal inviolability as a diplomatic bag. Technically and legally set up so no one could break into it."

"Quite true—on the Moon. But a lot of times the communications source and target aren't both visible from the lunar Nearside. Remember, Nearside can only 'see' half the sky at a time."

"What does that matter? The communications are relayed and get through anyway."

"Yes, but they are relayed through *Earth*-orbiting comsats which have none of the technical snoop-blocks on them. Legally, of course, communications channeled through them are supposed to be ultra-secured, handled as if they were top-secret U.N. material." He twisted his mouth up into a tight grimace. "And, in a way, they are. They receive highest priority for decoding and distribution at U.N. New York."

Hardin looked at him sharply. "Why are you telling me this?" she asked flatly. "Why compromise a first-rate intelligence source like that? We both play the game too well for you to think I'd think it was pure idealism."

"It's not pure—but there is some of that in it. Espionage against a clear target, a real enemy, with a real goal in sight, that I can accept. It's a necessary tool of diplomacy. It is part of the game. But indiscriminately and gleefully opening your neighbor's mail when you have specifically made solemn promises not to do any such thing is quite something else. It is dishonorable. Beyond that, I do not control the source. It is my rather intemperate rivals who control the tapping operation. It took some efforts for me to receive any information from it, and quite a bit of intriguing from my people to establish the source of the information. It would please me, and strengthen my hand, to leave my opposition in the dark as to Settlement actions. And it would be safer for us all. They are prone to rash acts."

"Besides, I have my own sources of intelligence—yourself for example," Suzuki said dryly, raising his glass to Hardin. "Head of the rival coalition you may be, but I do learn a great deal from you nonetheless."

Hardin smiled. "And I from you, Hiroshi. And I from you."

Suzuki set down his drink again. "I suggest that we propose a remedy to this problem—the construction of a laser array on the Farside, to complement the present Nearside array. With secure communications facilities on both sides of the Moon, your communications will be quite safe. Would the Settlement agree to assist in paying for it? As a sign of good will?"

"And to short-circuit your enemies?" Hardin laughed, a most youthful sound. "Of course we shall."

"I shall instruct UNLAC's engineers to begin planning tomorrow."

With that, the discussion of a Farside Array was over. Neither Suzuki nor Angela would even think of the matter again, for a long time.

And by then it would be too late.

HRISEY, ICELAND

Naturally, the moment it became imperative to hurry, it became impossible to do so. The expedition had been hamstrung right along by the lack of air transport, but any aircraft capable of operating safely and reliably in the temperatures, winds and terrain of North Iceland was prohibitively expensive to lease, let alone buy. Garrison's shoestring operation couldn't possibly afford any such thing. That left them relying instead on sea-surface transport—or, to put it less grandly, on one overage ocean-going tug.

At the moment even the tug was unavailable. It was at work moving the drilling platform, a job which should not have taken long. But the seas were high, and the tug didn't get the *Surveyor* into its new drilling position for another eight hours. Then it took her another three hours to steam back to the docks on Hrisey. Then it took an hour for the crew to refuel the tug and do other, unexplained nautical things before the crew was ready to let passengers aboard. To Garrison and Cathy, used to the high-speed, tightly scheduled world of air and spaceflight, sea travel seemed absurdly slow and haphazard. Things always seemed to take longer, for reasons that were never made clear.

This impression was not much changed when they finally got aboard the tug for the trip to Akureyia, the mainland port seventy kilometers south of the island of Hrisey. Even after Cathy and Garrison came aboard, the captain and crew found all sorts of mysterious things that needed doing before they could actually get underway. Most of these jobs seemed to involve one crew member vanishing belowdecks while the others leaned over the rails and puffed thoughtfully at their pipes. Even when they were all working at the same time, the seamen moved at an unhurried, even leisurely pace. After all these interminable delays without apparent causes, the tug finally cast off from the dock. The tug captain told them cheerfully that it would only take about three hours to cross the seventy kilometers of sea to Akureyia—four if the currents were strong.

NEW YORK CITY

Glenda felt like a fool. She was a fundraiser, a glorified file clerk who knew where the money was, two hundred pounds of grantsmanship talent and knowledge—not a private eye. Fundraisers didn't lie in wait in office lobbies, feeling faintly ridiculous and just waiting to be picked up for loitering. This was the sort of job a detective did, watching out for a sleaze-ball husband.

But she couldn't think of any other way to nail her man. She hadn't been able to find any way of catching up with Brattleby, and with every mysterious frustration of her efforts, she grew more and more certain that she *had* to talk with him, immediately. She had the distinct feeling that the museum might be in over its head. She *had* to know what the hell was worth all these strange goings-on. Garrison's cryptic love note about Lem Archer's job offer wasn't exactly reassuring, either.

Brattleby was on the LuTech board, and a few questions put to friends on Wall Street confirmed that he was one of the real powers behind the LuTech throne. A news archive service had come up with a few clippings and photos of him at this function or that. None of it was very informative. But Glenda was ready to make one guess: Brattleby was probably the only other person besides Garrison who knew what the hell was going on.

And Brattleby could no longer be reached at any office or home telephone number or address Glenda could locate. He was as thoroughly out of circulation as Garrison was, tucked away in Iceland.

The only way she could think of to get hold of Brattleby was by waiting in the lobby of the building where LuTech kept its offices. He was up there now, she was pretty certain.

She sighed, shifted her weight on the bench, and glanced at her wristaid. The tiny screen flashed angrily at her—she had missed three appointments this morning already. She tapped at the keypad to show the time. She had been here three hours already. She didn't like waiting around like this.

An hour later, a private elevator opened at the far end of the lobby and a rather fussy-looking man in a conservative business suit stepped out of it. Glenda, her mind dulled by sitting and staring into space too long, took a moment to register that her quarry had arrived.

She got to her feet and got a good look at him. She recognized him from the clipping service photos. She put a determined look on her face, stepped forward, and spoke. "Mr. Brattleby?"

He turned and looked at her. "Who are you?" he demanded irritably.

Glenda considered his face for a moment. She had grown adept long ago at reading the faces of the rich. He resembled his photo closely, but there was something more fussy and short-sighted to him in the flesh. Here was a man with no imagination, no ability to understand or be interested in anything that was not his immediate concern. He was bald-headed and pale, with a surviving fringe of black hair around his large bald spot, thick eyebrows, and a bushy mustache. Those, along with the charcoal-grey suit, made his skin seem almost translucently white. His eyes were a dark brown, bright and expressive. This was a guy who never gave anything away for free. "My name is Glenda Doyle."

"You're the woman from the museum," he said shortly.

"That's right, sir, and I've had a great deal of trouble tracking you down. There are some very serious questions I have to ask. The museum's legal department has been looking into the Iceland matter, and they are wondering whether to go ahead and file fraud charges," she lied. "They want my opinion before deciding whether or not to proceed. Shall I call and tell them what I think now—or should you and I talk first?"

Brattleby stared at her, his face a passive and calculating blank. Finally he cleared his throat and spoke. "I've got enough lawyer bills already. Come on, we'll talk in my car." Brattleby turned and led Glenda outside to where a long black limo waited at the curb.

Glenda was duly impressed. The last figures she had heard, the daytax to keep a private car in Manhattan was up over a thousand dollars. There were probably fewer than ten thousand private-license vehicles on the island these days. Hardly anyone could afford it. But then, hardly anyone could have afforded the sleek black Lincoln-Honda waiting for them.

The rear curbside door slid open automatically as Brattleby approached, without his making any sign or command Glenda could see. He gestured for her to enter, and Glenda stepped into a huge, opulent black leather-and-chrome interior that was a relic of the last century—or maybe the one before that. Chopin began to play from somewhere, hauntingly beautiful, as they sat back, facing each other, Glenda with her back to the front of the car. The opaqued windows suddenly went transparent, and the streets of the city were visible but unheard. The car pulled itself away and slid into traffic in ghostly silence, the gentle, sourceless music the only sound. In moments it was threading its way effortlessly through the flow of cabs and buses that streamed down the street. The robot car handled itself with a perfect, easy, daunting grace.

Glenda chalked up a few points to Brattleby. Why talk on the curbside when your own mobile piece of impressive turf was waiting outside? It would be a lot harder to browbeat Brattleby in here. Determined not to let it get to her, Glenda leaned forward and began to speak over the music. The moment she made her voice heard, the music faded courteously into the background, making her voice seen clumsily loud and uncouth. "You're at the center of something, Mr. Brattleby," she began, ignoring all the chips against her in this conversation. "You're taking risks, manipulating people, playing strange games. And I've very much concerned it'll be my museum who'll get caught up in the scandal when it all comes out. You'll fade away just as gracefully as your stereo does and leave others to clean up the mess."

Brattleby raised an eyebrow but didn't speak. *Tell me something I don't know*, his expression told her.

"At least that's the way you've *planned* it," Glenda continued. "Now you're very rich, very powerful—but you're not invulnerable, or infallible, even if you think you are. I've gotten some strange reports from Iceland," Glenda said. "I don't know what to make of them. Your front operation is paying for the research you're obviously trying to stop. You make phony job offers that sound more like bribes. A ship is deliberately sent to the wrong port. There are spies in camp. You're back at this end, apparently running your own little conspiracy, keeping it tightly held, inventing a phony foundation. Maybe you can get away with that—or maybe not.

"You can do a lot of things, but you can't control the news, or even influence the media all that much. If reports of these goings-on get to a reporter, you'll look as bad as the museum does. And in this sort of mess, sooner or later it's always in *somebody's* interest to call a reporter. My hunch at the moment is that somebody will be Garrison Morrow."

Brattleby's eyes flashed, and he spoke for the first time since they had stepped into the car. "What's your position relative to Morrow?" he asked sharply. His voice was stronger, more resonant than it had been in the office lobby. Maybe the acoustics in the car were good. Maybe the car robot was programmed to enhance its owner's voice with some sort of sonics trick. Didn't matter.

"Dr. Morrow is performing research in conjunction with the museum. We are serving as the coordinating center for his research, that is all. I view my relationship with him solely in terms of whether it aids or detracts from the mission of the museum."

"I see. Does the name Mjollnir mean anything to you?" he asked, abruptly changing the subject. "M-J-O-L-L-N-I-R?"

"No."

"Mmmmph. I don't think you're a good enough actor to keep a poker face if you were lying. It's a code name Morrow's been using. Look it up sometime." Brattleby was silent for a long moment, but at last he spoke. "Dr. Morrow needs to consider the consequences not only of his actions, but of his *knowledge*. He is boldly charging out after the golden, shining truth without any concern for what the results of what he learns might be. It would be in the best interests of the museum—and of everyone who wants to avoid food riots—to clip his wings. If I were you, I'd move heaven and earth to keep him away from the press." Brattleby thought for a moment and spoke again. "You've implied that my actions have been excessive. *I* think they are rather subdued and restrained, when the possibility exists that Dr. Morrow's new knowledge could serve to wreck Earth's economy—and therefore, that of the entire Solar System. People starve when economies fall. They die.

"And it could get worse than economic trouble. What Morrow is doing could set off a rash of anti-Settler xenophobia on Earth. Politicians who are already fulminating against the Settlement worlds wouldn't be able to resist the hysteria. There's already enough bad feeling thanks to that damn Martian McGillicutty. With the interplanetary situation as tense as it is, a panic like the one resulting from Garrison Morrow's work might touch off a war."

Glenda stared at Brattleby in astonishment, wondering if he were mad or merely paranoid. How could a bunch of rocks in Iceland start an interplanetary war? The car slid to a halt in front of the Central Park West entrance of the museum. It came to Glenda that Brattleby had spoken no instruction, tapped no keyboard, manipulated no control to tell the car where to drive. It had figured that out on its own. There were perhaps a hundred, hideously expensive computers in the world capable of making such a pseudo-intuitive leap. Most of them ran governments. This one drove a car. Brattleby was a very rich man indeed.

The door opened, but Glenda hesitated before stepping out onto the curb. "But what's it all about?" she asked. "What is so important and dangerous?"

Brattleby glanced at her through bored eyes that had already dismissed her, through eyes that were already looking a half dozen moves ahead. "You'll understand better if you learn it for yourself. You'll find it in the library of your precious museum. Look for the work of the Alvarezes, father and son. And that of the astronomer, Whipple." His eyes rose up to consider some far-off horizon of the mind's interior. "It was all a very long time ago," he said quietly, thoughtfully. "A hundred years ago. And sixty-five million. Good-bye, Miss Doyle."

She stepped out of the car, the door closed, the car pulled away. Glenda stood there, alone, for a long moment before she hurried inside to the proud safety of Theodore Roosevelt's museum.

Chapter Six

NEW YORK CITY

Glenda had neglected a great deal of work chasing after Brattleby. It was frustrating, but now that he was found, and had given her some rather cryptic leads, she was forced to give up the chase for a little while. No matter how urgent the cloudy struggle between Garrison and LuTech seemed, she had to spend some time on her other duties before she could get back to the search.

She endured an endless fund-raising party that began an hour after she was left on the curb by Brattleby, and an equally endless departmental meeting the next morning. It was almost noon of the day after she had talked to Brattleby before she could get back to her office, her terminal, and the search.

It was with a distinct sense of relief that she sat down behind her desk, pulled out a keyboard, flicked on a screen, and began to work. Nothing bothered her more than being forced to leave an urgent job unfinished.

The first question was easily answered, even if the answer didn't tell her much. Mjollnir turned out to be from Norse mythology, the name for Thor's hammer.

That was obscure, but at least easily traced. What was the rest of what Brattleby had said?

The Alvarezes, father and son, and the astronomer, Whipple . . . There were probably hundreds of Alvarezes listed in the reference databanks available to the museum's computers, and several dozen Whipples. But the library computer was smart enough to sift through the databanks at her direction. Finding the right ones wouldn't be a problem. But she didn't want to get ahead of herself.

A hundred years ago, and sixty-five million . . .

The number sixty-five million years reminded her of something. That date had some significance, somewhere. It was one of the eras in geology. . . .

She pulled down a well-thumbed volume from the shelf above her desk. She flipped through the pages until she found a table of the geologic eras. The book was one of a number of college and high school science texts she kept handy to look up a basic reference she wasn't quite clear on. She found the table of geologic ages and propped the book open next to the keyboard. The computer database could have shown her the same information just as quickly and easily, but she couldn't put a bookmark in a computer screen, or scribble in the margins. With the general book information in front of her, she was able to chase down the elusive specifics she was after.

She studied the table for a moment and nodded, the half-forgotten names and figures coming back to her.

The history of the Earth was divided up into five eras, from oldest to youngest: Archeozoic, Proterozoic, Paleozoic, Mesozoic, and Cenozoic. The eras were further divided up into periods. The convoluted old names were laid out neatly on the page, and Glenda smiled to herself, remembering how she had memorized them back in high school science class. She read them now, chanting them to herself the way she had so long ago. "Paleozoic: *Cam*brian, *Ordo*vician, *Si*lurian, *Devo*nian, *Mis*sissippian, *Pennsyl*vanian, *Permian.* Mesozoic: *Tri*assic, *Ju*rassic, *Lower* Cretaceous, *Upper* Cretaceous. Cenozoic: *Terti*ary, *Quater*nary, *Recent, Present!*"

She remembered how silly the names had seemed, how she and her friends had giggled and made up pretend

names—"Obnoxious: *Contentious*, *Portentous*, *Pretentious*.
Cinematic: *Photographic*, *Pornographic*, *Video*, *Tridimen-
sional*. Bulemic: *Early* Devouring, *Late* Devouring, *Retro-
peristalsic*."

Mr. Stemegna, the science teacher, had done his best,
tried to explain that the names weren't empty and pomp-
ous, that the periods weren't meaningless labels stamped
arbitrarily across the map of time. She could hear his
earnest, reedy voice, trying to get his message across to a
fidgety class long ago succumbed to spring fever.

"Cross the border between Cambrian and Ordovician,
and the rocks change, the fossils change," he would tell
them. "And the rocks are the written history of life. That's
what the names mean—Paleozoic, Mesozoic, Cenozoic.
Long-ago life, Middle life, Recent life. It is life it*self* that
has made those rocks meaningful.

"The old scientists didn't just decide to divide time up
into hunks and give them funny names. They found the
rocks *changed* in certain places, in consistent ways, all
over the world, and named the geologic periods, usually
after the first place they noticed the changes."

Glenda blinked and brought herself back to the present.
Alongside the table of geologic periods was a column marked
MYA—millions of years ago, marking out larger and larger
units as it stretched further back in time. She traced her
finger along the line and stopped at 65. She found her
finger was right alongside the Mesozoic/Cenozoic divide,
the border between the end of the Cretaceous period,
closing out the era of Middle life and the beginning of the
Tertiary period at the start of the era of Recent life.

But Mr. Stemegna told us those were special names, she
thought. They told you something about the life in those
periods, and sixty-five million years ago was a moment so
important it not only divided two periods, but two *eras*.
Sixty-five MYA marked the frontier between two of the
largest units of geologic time.

Sixty-five MYA there had been a change in the fossil
record so drastic it could be demarcated only on the
largest scale. So what was different between Mesozoic and
Cenozoic? She flipped over to the next page of her geology
book. Another chart, more detailed, marking out the key

events of geologic time. There it was, just at the Mesozoic/
Cenozoic split. *Dinosaurs Become Extinct*, it said simply.
Age of Mammals Begins.

She sat and thought a long time, then turned to her
keyboard.

Open biography files, she typed. *List father-son pairs of
scientists, last name Alvarez, in last 150 years, particularly late twentieth century.* It was a fairly complicated
and vague command, but the mainframe's parser was able
to handle it easily. She breathed a sigh of relief when only
one pair of names came up.

From era 1960–1990: the computer announced, *Dr. Luis
W. Alvarez, Nobel Prize for Physics, 1968. Professor Emeritus of Physics, Lawrence Berkeley Laboratory, University
of California, Berkeley. His son, Dr. Walter Alvarez, Department of Geology and Geophysics, University of California, Berkeley.*

A moment later she had added another name from the
hints Brattleby had given her.

*Dr. Fred Whipple, Professor Emeritus, Smithsonian As-
trophysical Observatory, Cambridge, Massachusetts, same
era.*

She frowned and stared at the names. These were the
names that frightened Brattleby a century later? So how
the hell did an astronomer, a physicist, and a geologist
from a hundred years ago threaten asteroid mining?

Now she was ready for the big-time question, the sort of
question that made library computers better than rubies to
a researcher. The computer could search at heroic speed
through virtually all recorded human knowledge, linking
with other computers elsewhere as it saw fit, weaving the
scattered threads of information into a new and perfect
tapestry. Only human beings could think of the questions,
but only with computers did humans have any hope of
tracking down the answers in the boundless, tractless wilderness of knowledge.

*Relate above name citations, Mesozoic/Cenozoic bound-
ary and other events circa 65 million years ago, and
Iceland. Check all appropriate sources and databanks to
credit limit of this account. Print out a hard copy at this
terminal,* Glenda typed in. Even for the fastest of rela-

tional systems, it would be a difficult, time-consuming job, as she had told the system to perform a virtually unlimited search. It would check the most likely places first, then work its way down through all levels of probability. After all, the link might be *anywhere*. She had placed no limits on the command, and the machine would search tirelessly through every index and cross-referencer, sifting through all knowledge until it found something, until Glenda told it to quit—or until her computer-credit account ran out. Left to its own devices, the library computer had been known to take hours on such relational problems. Even so, that was preferable to the months, or years—or centuries—a hand search could potentially take.

Glenda nodded and shoved the keyboard away. Time for lunch. With any luck, the library would find some tenuous link that she could track down in less than an hour. She expected to come back to see a line or two of text in the printer, or perhaps not receive any answer before quitting time.

Five minutes after she left, the printer came to life, and began spewing out page after page, until the hopper was overflowing.

ICELAND

Garrison stared up the fjord as he listened to Ben's voice over the radio. The news was not good.

"Half the locals bugged out, which works out to a third of the crew, overall. They're gone. Quit. No more. Over." Ben's voice came to them scratchily over the decrepit ship-to-shore radio as they rode the cargo tug back up the fjord. The truck ride back from the capital had been another bone-crushing nightmare, and another disaster was not what Garrison and Cathy needed just now.

"Oh, for God's sake, Ben. Have they started slaughtering the first born yet?" Garrison asked. "Over."

"I'll pass over that remark. Over."

"Bad joke, Ben," Garrison said. "If I laugh, tell me you're glad I still have my sense of humor. Over."

"If you've got yours, then go out and look for mine," Ben muttered. "Listen, I had to do a few things to hang onto the rest of them. I'll explain when you get here. Oh,

and you might as well save some time. Skip landing on the
island—we're all out here on the drilling rig anyway. Head
straight for it. We'll have a candle in the window for you.
Over. Out."

"Right. Morrow out." Garrison put down the mike,
shrugged at the tug captain and stepped out of the cabin
onto the tug's deck. He trudged back to Cathy at the
stern, joining her as she stared out into the roaring water
that swept past the boat.

Empty. The damned cargo ship at Reykjavik had been
empty, or near enough. A token cargo, to add verisimili-
tude to the scam. The captain had let them have what
there was—some spare parts and torchbit fuel—and the
crew had helped load the stuff onto a truck. One truck.
With lots of room left over.

"LuTech bribed half the Icelanders off the crew," Garrison announced to Cathy, shouting to make himself heard
over the rushing water and the growl of the engine. "A
guy simply came onto Hrisey one night and said he'd be
pay them twice what we gave them *not* to work for us.
Plus, he spread some rumors that we're drilling so deep
because we want to set off an artificial volcano. We lost six
of the twelve locals."

"What about the other six?" Cathy asked woodenly. She
was beaten enough, dragged down enough, even without
this news.

Garrison shrugged. "They stayed. I don't know why.
Maybe a combination of things. Maybe they're really interested in the research, curious. Maybe they have pride
in their work. Or else maybe they know the do-it-yourself
volcano story is a damn lie and being lied to got them
mad. Or maybe they just like us. I dunno. I'm too tired to
be mad or upset or surprised anymore. I'm just glad some
of them stayed. I'm going to go below and grab some sack
time. Why don't you find a bunk yourself?"

"I can't sleep. I wish I could. I'll hang out here, I guess.
I'll wake you up when we get there."

Garrison shook his head. "If you can't sleep, take a pill,
sister. We're going to need you alive and alert at the other
end."

Cathy's mouth flickered at the edge of a smile, invisible inside the parka. "Okay. In a minute. *Christ*, it's cold." Garrison patted her on the back and left her to stare at the sea a while longer.

The welcome back was not a very joyous one. Ben met them at the landing stage of the *Surveyor*. Even with his face hidden inside his parka hood, they could see the tiredness, the exhaustion that expressed itself in his every movement. He led them inside to the cold, barren room that served as office space aboard the *Surveyor*. At least it was above freezing inside, and they unzipped their outer gear.

Garrison looked at Ben and shook his head. Ben looked like hell. Garrison wondered if he had slept at all since they had last seen him. "How's the drilling going, Ben?" he asked.

"We're moving, we're getting deeper, but it's not going so well. God, I can't even *think* straight even more. Everyone here knows this is our last shot. I pulled everyone off the other jobs—analysis, core storage, cap maintenance, everything. Everyone is doing all they can. We've been setting records shifting bits, refueling bits, stripping and repairing bits—we've cut our old man-hours-per-meter-drilled rate in half—but there's not enough people left to keep going. Ten people can't do the work of eighteen. You two are back, so that'll help, some. But we don't have much time. Sooner or later—probably sooner—LuTech or GRF is going to try some other stunt to stop us cold. What, I don't know. Maybe a strafing run. So far, you sure as hell can't fault them for lack of imagination."

Ben looked up at Garrison and blinked sleepily. "Look, I had to do something to hold the others here—and make them work as hard as we'll need them to. So I spilled the beans. I explained what we're *really* doing here—and explained why you couldn't tell them everything early on. They're all with you."

Garrison nodded. "Yeah, I thought you might have to do that. It's okay. It's not important any more. But what you're telling us is that it's not just a supply shortage we're up against—it's time."

"Yeah, but without drilling supplies, time isn't going to matter," Ben said. "Lemme see the paperwork on what you've brought." Garrison dug the papers out of his pocket and handed them over. Ben read them over slowly.

"Is it enough?" Cathy asked. "Is what you've got left and what we brought enough so we can get deep enough?"

Ben scratched his beard moodily. "No problem—if. If, if, if," he said absently, reading the shipping list. "*If* the fresh bits hold up under the sort of abuse this bunch has gone through. *If* the torch fuel is of good quality. *If* the lower rock strata doesn't turn into stainless steel on us. In fact, we'd better hope for some nice, soft rock down there. Sandstone we could handle," he said sourly, "but you don't run into much of that in volcanic strata. Oh, and of course *if* the pre-eruption strata doesn't decide to be a kilometer further down than your simulations say it should be, Cathy. If we hit all those ifs, sure, we'll make it." He looked up at Garrison. "Otherwise, we're screwed. No sample core collectors in the shipment, were there?"

"Nope."

"Then we'd better add another if—*if* we're good guessers. I checked our stock of collectors here. We had twenty. Eight of them were no damn good."

"Christ!" Garrison pounded his right fist into his left palm in frustration. Without sample cores, they would have no idea what they were drilling through. They'd be working totally blind. They could drill right through the center of the Earth and it wouldn't do them any good. "Okay, Ben. That's enough good news for right now. Show us some kind of status report and then get yourself to bed. Cathy, let's you and me get to work in there." Garrison wasn't quite willing to give in yet—but he was giving it active consideration.

NEW YORK CITY

"Oh my God!" Glenda came into her office to find an ocean of paper on the floor. She had left the window open, and the printout had blown everywhere. There had to be five hundred pages of copy, diagrams, charts, and photos strewn around the room, as if the Sorcerer's Apprentice had given up hauling water and gone into the data retrieval business. It could have been worse, she realized, looking at the message flashing on the printer's status screen. *OUT OF PAPER PLEASE RELOAD.* "The hell I will," she muttered, stepping carefully into the office, picking her away around the blizzard of paper. She brushed enough pages off the desk so she could find the keyboard. *Cancel last search command, clear printer buffer,* she instructed the machine. She glanced at the wall clock. Four o'clock. Damn Fogarty for button-holing her into that meeting! She had thought she'd never escape. She dropped her handbag onto her desk, got down on her knees and started gathering up the paper. At least the pages were numbered. It shouldn't be too tough to get them in order.

Ten minutes later she had the last of the printout recaptured and in a single, if rather rumpled, stack on her desk, her oversize handbag serving as an industrial-strength paperweight. She started sorting the pages out, then thought better of it and went for coffee first. This was likely to be a long job.

ICELAND

Garrison ratcheted the last bolt down onto a new torchbit and signaled the team to hoist the drill and lower away. He stood up and felt the dull throb of pain in his back. He glanced at his watch, tried to decide if it was three a.m. or p.m. He shrugged and decided it didn't much matter. The units of time had stopped meaning much of anything around here a long time ago. The weather made day and night almost indistinguishable, and no one could go outside anyway. Another storm had closed in, darkening the sky, making the old platform creak and moan in the fierce wind and waves. No one could sleep. The off-duty crew members would wander in after spending a restless hour or two in their bunks and pitch in with the duty crew until exhaustion or hunger stopped them. They'd gnaw at a few bites of bland food, collapse back into bunks for an hour or two that rested them not at all, then stagger back to the job again.

Food didn't taste like anything when it went over tongues that had been scalded by ancient overcooked coffee. The smells of torchbit fuel, of unwashed bodies, of too much cigarette smoke, of a toilet whose outlet tube was frozen shut, of uneaten and uneatable food, all congealed down into a sullen miasma that insulted the nose.

Everything settled into greyness.

Drop a loaded bit down, hoping the damn thing won't break the moment you reach the drill face. Hit some buttons, watch the instruments, make sure that the torchbit flame lights up, track the meters to see that the thing actually moves downward. Watch the stress gauges, the temperature gauges, wonder how long until something down there craps out. Mark the tediously slow progress on a chart made almost unreadable by coffee stains. Swear at the machines when something goes wrong, when the fuel load sputters down to empty, when the cable kinks. Feel your insides go to jello when you think the cable might have snapped, and the bit is at the bottom for all time and the drill hole is blocked and useless. Breathe again when the strain gauges twitch and show the bit is still there. Listen to the nerve-gnawing whine of the power winches as they drag the dead bit up, wait for something to give as the kilometers of cable snake up out of the drill hole, wait for some piece of the machinery somewhere to seize up and stop you dead in your tracks. Join the others in hosing down the red-hot bit when it finally emerges. Lose the universe in a cloud of greasy steam as the jets of water play on the bit. Hoist the bit clear of the drill head, grapple a fresh bit into place. Drop the loaded bit down, hoping the damn thing won't break . . .

The progress chart moved slowly, slowly. Garrison was unconscious of doing anything besides watching the marks on the paper get just a little longer, a little longer. He had no real idea how long they had been at it. A day? Two? Ten? It didn't matter. They weren't down deep enough yet, but they were still moving.

Somewhere along the way it had all changed. It wasn't just a quest for knowledge anymore, it was a fight. A desperate battle against unseen opponents, for a jewel beyond price, a jewel made of crumbled rock, a jewel made of knowledge with the power to change the world. How had that happened? How had the character of the struggle changed so radically? He shook his head. It didn't matter. The next bit was being dragged up, emerging hell-red from the stygian blackness. His worries were lost in another cloud of cloying, sickly steam as they hosed the bit down.

Finally, painfully, slowly, the marks on the progress chart crawled under a thin, doubtful-looking dotted line— the guessed-at depth where they should be under the strata thrown up by Iceland's vulcanism. Soon after, the readings on the strain and motion gauges started to quiver downward at a fractionally higher rate—they had hit a softer vein of rock and the bit was moving faster.

They had cut through to the shattered remains of the old sea-bed floor, the breed of rock that had laid highest up, on the surface, before Iceland was born. If what they were looking for was anywhere, this was where it would be. If Mjollnir had ever existed, this was its grave, its bones were here—microscopic fragments and shards jumbled and tangled into the old seabed.

A buzzer went off, and Garrison looked with sudden eagerness at the indicator board. The bit had run out of fuel. They hauled it out. Ben, his face lost behind a mask of dirt, sweat, rock powder, grease and exhaustion, looked to Garrison. Garrison nodded, once, very slightly, his face a blank, abstract, his mind far off from the drill room, lost inside himself.

Ben called for a sample core. The crew attached it to the drilling line and positioned it over the drilling rig. The winches lurched into life and the sample core fell, slid long kilometers downward under precise control toward the drill face. It slowed and stopped a few meters above the face, waiting for the commands from the drill room kilometers overhead.

Garrison reached out a begrimed finger and pressed the *start* button. The signal flickered down to the core tube and the extractor system came to life. Twin tiny, powerful lasers, small enough to be set into the lip of the sample extractor, flashed into brightness. The extractor started to spin. Centimeter by centimeter, the lasers cut down through the rock, forming a perfect cylinder fifty centimeters wide. The extractor slid a brass sleeve of precisely the rock cylinder's diameter down along the sample's length as the lasers sliced it away from the surrounding rock.

When the sample core filled the entire length of the brass cylinder, the lasers redirected themselves inward. As the extractor sleeve continued to spin, they sliced away the base of the core sample. A special directionalized sealant flowed out of the lower edge of the sample tube. The sealant adhered laterally, but not vertically, and so sealed the bottom of the tube without bonding it to the bottom of the drill hole. The extractor sent a signal to the surface. Slowly, carefully, the winches spun up, gently lifting the hard-won prize to the surface.

Long minutes later, the core tube came clattering up through the surface of the planet. The winches dragged the eight-meter tube clear of the drill hole and held it by a cable over the heads of the expedition members. Black with burnt stone, dented and dinged by the rough rock walls of the drill hole, the core tube seemed a defiant mechanical refuge from some earlier underworld, the clock-work servant of one of the older Gods of Hell.

They shifted the core to another cable so as to let the winches get back to work with the next bit, and they left the core hanging in mid air, cooling, shedding the heat of the planet's interior slowly. Garrison didn't want to risk shattering the rock inside with the cooling force of frigid seawater jets. Finally, the brazen rock-filled pillar was laid gently on its side for later examination.

The next torchbit was already on its way down. Two hours after the first sample core had been drawn, its twin was hanging over the crew. Then another, and another, until they had used all the operational core extractors.

Garrison watched the last of the cores as it was drawn up. That was it. It was over. Either they had found some-thing or they hadn't. All around him, crewmen were virtu-ally collapsing where they stood, exhaustion finally over-taking the frantic urgency of finishing before something *else* could happen to stop them.

He saluted the core feebly and staggered out onto the deck. He gradually noticed it was night, and that there was another storm raging over the rig. There was no chance of return to the base camp tonight. He turned and went back inside to find a cot somewhere.

It was not until the next morning, when the cores were laboriously and gently trundled back to prep/mess on the island, not until the cores were opened, that they found something. There, nestled deep inside the last few cores, they found something they had long since stopped hoping for.

They found victory.

NEW YORK CITY

The night was old in Iceland as twilight still lingered in Manhattan. Glenda sipped at the tepid dregs of her coffee and continued her reading. The story was tangled, confused, hidden in the mass of references, but gradually she was beginning to understand.

It had started out, a hundred years ago, with a thin layer of clay found in a limestone cliff face, part of an Italian hillside outside the town of Gubbio. The fossils in the stone above and below the clay layer demonstrated that it precisely marked the Mesozoic/Cenozoic boundary.

The limestone layers had formed at the bottom of a vanished sea, later thrust up by the movements of the Earth's crust. The stone was made primarily out of the endless trillions of corpses of plankton. The calcium from their shells dissolved as their single-celled bodies decayed, and then settled out into calcium carbonate—limestone. The infinite generations of plankton built up the limestone millimeter by millimeter, meter by meter, over millions of years.

The clay layer in question interrupted the limestone part way up the cliff. Wanting to find out how long it had taken for the clay layer to be deposited, the Alvarez team tried to measure the amount of iridium in the clay. Any iridium there in the clay could only come from one source: cosmic dust, sifting down from space to the surface of the Earth at a fairly constant rate. While the clay layer was forming under the sea, the cosmic dust was landing on the water, sinking down to the bottom and being absorbed into the clay.

If the clay had deposited quickly, it would not have

been exposed to open water long enough to accumulate much dust. If it had accreted over a longer period, it would be richer in iridium.

The clay had contained iridium, all right—incredible amounts of it. Measured in parts per billion, undetectable by any but the most sensitive means, there was still thirty times more iridium than the maximum amount predicted. Many other elements that could not have come from terrestrial sources were also found in the clay.

Something had injected massive amounts of platinum group elements into that clay layer. Other Mesozoic/ Cenozoic boundary layers in Denmark and New Zealand and America were found to have similar concentrations of the foreign elements.

Directly below the Gubbio boundary clay were limestone layers filled with the fossils of many species of small one-celled creatures, *foraminifera*, dozens of types. There were no forams in the clay itself—and in the limestone directly above it, all but one of the foraminifera species had vanished.

Something had wiped out the plankton, the foraminifera, so they were not there to provide the calcium needed to form the limestone layers. Only fine sediment devoid of animal matter settled down alone, forming the clay layer instead. Only when life returned to the sea above it did the limestone begin forming anew. And when it returned, there were fewer forms of life. Thus, the clay layer marked a time when the sea was dead, lifeless. And not just foraminifera had vanished then, Glenda remembered. The dinosaurs picked that moment to die off as well. Glenda tapped a query into her keyboard, looked at the screen, and whistled. According to one estimate in the library computer, seventy percent of all living things had died. Other sources said those numbers were too high—but all of them agreed that there had been a great dying, indeed.

Something had dusted the entire world with iridium at just the moment of the mass extinction. That could not be coincidence. But what possible link could the two events have? It couldn't be the iridium itself that did the killing. Thirty parts per billion of iridium couldn't wipe out that many critters. It wasn't even poisonous, was it?

Glenda turned over to the next page and sucked in her breath in shock. There was the answer to all her questions, in plain terms.

An asteroid. A carbonaceous chrondite asteroid, six or seven kilometers in diameter, impacting on the Earth would contain enough iridium to account for the high values—and raise enough hell to kill off a lot of animals.

But wait a second. Something that big would leave a big, obvious crater, wouldn't it? So where was the crater? And what the hell did all this have to do with Iceland?

She flipped through the pages, skimming until she spotted the word *Iceland*, then went back and read the passage. Whipple. Ah. This was where he came in. It was Whipple who suggested that *Iceland* might have been the impact point, a super volcano smashed open by the asteroid.

And the appropriateness of the name *Mjollnir* came to her. Sweet Jesus God. Garrison was trying to dig out an *asteroid* up there. A sixty-five-million-year-old asteroid named Mjollnir, named after Thor's hammer which smote the ground with incredible fury. Garrison wanted not just a hoary old theory, not just wild conjecture, but proof, truth, reality.

She rubbed her hand across her forehead and it came away damp with sweat. *No wonder LuTech is scared of Garrison*, she thought. *If this gets out, it could turn the whole world anti-space. It would scare the world's governments into a treaty banning asteroid mining altogether, and too bad if that wrecks the economy.* She turned and looked out her window, and chanced to see a bright star she knew to be Lucifer hanging low in the sky.

The sight of it had never frightened her before. She swallowed hard and forced herself to look at it. Mjollnir would have been about that size.

Chapter Seven

ICELAND

There should have been ceremony, and triumphant drama, for such a grand discovery. But core samples do not lend themselves to theatrics. They are big, unwieldy, fragile things that do not give up their secrets at a glance. No one could possibly know what was in the cores until they got them back to prep/mess and opened them up. Even then, rocks would look like rocks. No one could know for certain that they had found anything until after a long study—perhaps weeks or months.

Garrison *felt* as if he had something when he woke up the morning after the last core was extracted, but he knew how much and how little feelings and hunches could be worth. It was a bright, crisp, clear morning, with the gale-force wind of last night reduced to a freshening salt-tanged breeze. The sky was an impossible cobalt blue. People were waking up slowly to the fresh-scrubbed day, after the longest and best rests some of them had had in weeks. Every one of them had the clear conscience that came from having done his or her best. It would be difficult to feel anything *but* optimistic on such a morning.

They all wanted to get off the platform as soon as possible, having had enough of its uncertain amenities, with the result that *everyone* wanted to ride the tug back to camp, escorting the sample cores on their trip to the base.

Two hours later, the mess tent side of prep/mess was serving the first hot food anyone had seen in days, there was a carefully negotiated schedule for the showers, and the eager core technicians were cautiously cracking open the first of the cores.

The brass sleeve was drawn back, and a few crumpled bits of dust and rock chips fell away from the dirty, mottled grey cylinder of stone, a piece of the Earth's interior as wide across as a good-sized tree stump. Lying on its side, the core sample looked like a toppled, fire-blackened column, sole remnant of a temple destroyed by fire long ago. It was a massive thing, far larger than any cores made by traditional methods. Torchbit drilling gave you a nice big sample, Garrison thought.

Cathy carefully recorded every moment of the procedure, got 3D stills and moving photos of every square millimeter of the core's surface, even made the core technicians roll the core over so she could get images of the other side. It was obvious at first glance that this stone was born of violence. There were no gentle layers, no strata piled sedately one atop the other in the stately processes of sedimentation, or even any sort of orderly volcanic process. This rock had been shattered, tortured, crushed down to rubble and then recompressed down into solid stone.

Garrison screwed a jeweler's loupe into his eye, took a powerful portable lamp in his hand, and squatted down next to the core. With infinite gentleness, he ran his hand down its surface, and peered closely at it.

"Yes, yes," he said to himself. He stepped back, removed the loupe, and took a rock shaver from the tool bench. He set the specialized power cutter down on the column and ran it over a short strip of the surface. There was a high-pitched buzzing, and a thin strip of rock slithered out the back of the shaver. Garrison let it crumple and fall to the ground. The chemistry of the exterior rock might have been altered by the cutting lasers during the extraction of the core. He didn't want to risk a contaminated sample.

He clipped the sample holder to the shaver and ran a second pass over the same piece of surface. He unclipped the sample holder from the shaver and carried it to the scanning superconducting electron microscope. Clamping the sample holder securely into the stage chamber, he sealed the chamber's hatch, and kicked in the vacuum pump, then reset the select switch from "Microscope" to "Electron Bombardment Spectrograph" and activated the analyzer.

It took five long minutes for the EBS system to finish its work. Finally, the printer woke up and the results scrolled out, three pages worth.

Garrison grabbed the printout and read down the elements column eagerly. He found the *Iridium* line and felt all the tension run out of his entire body, tears welling up in his eyes. He had won.

He stood up and turned to face the waiting people. "Iridium," he read aloud. "Twenty-eight thousand parts per million. Nearly ten thousand times normal terrestrial background. Some of this rock is former asteroid. It buried itself here—and we've dug up Mjollnir's grave."

The room erupted into cheers. Ben walked over and shook Garrison by the hand. "Nice going, boss. You've proved it. Now all you have to do is convince the world."

One of the rules of science is repeatability—which can be pretty dull. Repeatability doesn't just mean the experiment, the measurement, the test must work again and again. It means it must work with double-blind procedures and control samples, so that the scientist cannot know which is the test sample. This prevents any bias (unintentional or otherwise) from affecting the measurement.

Garrison had broken every one of those rules with his quick-and-dirty test. He had proven to his own satisfaction that an asteroid had made Iceland, but one sloppy field test would not be enough support if he wanted to set the world on its ear. He needed to reconfirm the results, make them fireproof.

Over the next few days, he and his staff repeated the

sampling over and over, with all the proper controls and documentation. Some samples from the cores contained even more iridium—others, taken right alongside, almost none at all. In a way even that was a confirmation. It would require an incredibly energetic event to inject one rock form into another that way.

Garrison was astonished to find several rather large chunks—four or five centimeters across—of what appeared to be unaltered asteroidal ore intruded into the surrounding strata. They were in every way identical with asteroid rocks, utterly unlike any stone formed on Earth. He couldn't understand how macroscopic fragments had survived the impact—but he wasn't going to argue with such a spectacular proof.

But even that wasn't enough. What works for *you* must also work for everyone else who tries it. Garrison rattled off a feverishly rushed preliminary letter, enclosed certified samples of the core, and express-shipped them off to labs all over Earth and even one or two on the Moon—after all, if anyone understood impact-formed rocks, it was his former lab partners dug in under the lunar crater fields.

The core samples had to be subjected to many other tests beside EBS, cross-checked in case there was some other reason for the absurdly high iridium test. More chips of the ore and the pure intrusions were likewise shipped out, to be subjected to whatever fiendish tests Garrison's fellow geologists could dream up. Stress tests, structure tests, chemical tests, computer back-simulations of possible modes of formation—all of them came back, confirming the incredible truth—Mjollnir was real.

Another rule of science, almost always honored in the breach, was that it must move with ponderous slowness. Only in the rarest of circumstances would there be less than six months or a year between a discovery and its initial announcement and publication—and months or years more before other scientists could examine the evidence and respond with their own tests.

It was a sign of Mjollnir's importance that the whole process took only weeks.

All the work and correspondence was private. Garrison

did not want the news to reach the general public yet—not until the proof was irrefutable. Not until he was ready, not until he could be certain it would reach a wide enough audience to do some good.

Even as the flurry of scientific activity continued, more mundane problems distracted everyone. The camp had to be struck, all the gear and tents and samples packed up and out. The team started melting away as the workers went on to their next jobs. The work at Hrisey was at an end, the project complete. Like so many research groups in science, the Hrisey group was an ad hoc collection of whoever happened to be (a) qualified and (b) between commitments when Garrison and Glenda had put the team together. The local workers left, and the science team started heading for home, or for the next job.

That left a rapidly shrinking skeleton crew to handle the final details. The logistics of shutting down were at least as complex as putting the operation together in the first place, but Ben and Cathy managed the job without really even noticing they were doing it. Even arranging for the *Surveyor*'s owners to come and collect her seemed a minor detail. There was too much exciting news about Mjollnir to bother much about anything else.

One of the best things, for Garrison and Cathy, was the slowly dawning realization that *now* was the moment when they had time enough, privacy enough, to discover that their shy, unspoken affection for each other could blossom into something much more.

The press of work—and the constant presence of others in the highly unprivate camp—had dissipated now. There was time enough, and chance enough for the two of them to be alone.

Everyone but Ben, Cathy and Garrison had left for home, and there were only two huts left in the camp. There was just Garrison's office and one other general purpose structure. Ben managed to find logical reasons for Garrison and Cathy to stay in Garrison's hut while he slept in the other.

The first night that Garrison and Cathy spent together alone was a delight, a revelation. Even the unromantic setting seemed *right*, the way it should be. The second night, and the next, and the next, were just as good.

But there was also something sad and foredoomed about their time together. The moment was possible only because their work, their lives, had come to a stopping point, a pause and respite, at the same time and place. All too soon, the hut Ben was using would have to come down, and somehow the three of them would have to be shoehorned in under one roof. That would be the end of their privacy for now—and perhaps forever. Garrison and Cathy sensed that events would engulf their lives once again, and soon. There was to be little more peace for either of them for a long time to come.

So they clung to each other in thus few nights, as if they feared their next night together might be their last. All too soon that would be true.

After a few more days' disassembly work, there was nothing left of the camp but Garrison's hut—which would be left behind as a gift to the lighthouse keeper. Everything else had been taken apart and carried down to the docks to be packed aboard a freighter/hovercraft that was due in the next morning. The only thing to get rid of was the leftover food.

"We've won the battle," Garrison announced, as the three of them dined on freeze-dried chicken and the last of the camp's beer supply. "Now we have to win the war. How do we get the word out about Mjollnir?"

Ben shrugged his shoulders. "We write a paper and submit it to *Nature* or *Science,* what else?"

Garrison smiled and tossed a denuded chicken bone back onto his plate. "Ben, I'm lucky the opposition picked you as a spy. It would take four or five months *minimum* for the paper to get written, edited, juried, and published. We *have* to do something else *fast*, or else the department of practical jokes at LuTech is going to have all that time to discredit us. We have to announce before they can sandbag us. Later, yeah, we do the formal paper—but we have to worry about getting the news to the public first."

"That means a news conference," Cathy suggested. "Invite everyone from the press, on- and off-planet."

"Not good enough," Ben objected. "What if we gave a news conference and nobody came? Why send a reporter to listen to a bunch of frostbitten nuts who've been playing with rocks on the back end of Iceland? Besides, we don't *know* anybody. Who do you actually call when you 'call' a news conference? I don't know. Do you? We need to talk to a good packager."

"You're talking money all of a sudden," Garrison objected. "Real money."

"Yup," Ben agreed as he reached for more chicken. "But I don't see any other way around it. You're saying that we have to make a big noise to get enough attention. That means we have to hit all the media all at once, right across the board. And that calls for more organization than we know how to do. And the people who *do* know how charge plenty."

"Dammit!" Garrison shoved his chair back from the table, grabbed his beer, and started pacing the hut. "Every time I turn around, it comes back to money. And if it was tough to get financing *before* we found Mjollnir—think how bad it's going to be now."

Cathy cleared her throat. "If I could make a suggestion . . ."

"Yeah, Cath, what?" Ben asked.

"There's some friends of mine that might be able to help. Have you guys ever heard of an outfit called CRATER?"

"*CRATER?*" Ben said, sounding startled. "I thought that you were—" He stopped himself and looked from Cathy to Garrison. "Never mind. Not important."

"Wait a second," Garrison objected. "What's CRATER?"

" 'Citizens for the Removal of Asteroids from Technological Enterprise Regions.' " Ben said promptly. "Terrible name. Stay the hell away from them. They're a major bunch of nuts. They're sort of a Neo-Luddite group that wants *all* asteroid and large-artifact operations shut down. They're afraid of the dangers to Mother Earth from meteor strikes, and the dangers of the ecology getting zapped by microwave powerbeams. There's evidence of about a one percent increase in meteor strikes, and about eight people have been hurt or injured in the history of powerbeaming. They feel the dangers are great enough that the whole shebang must be shut down. Never mind that such a move would wreck the economy and people would starve."

Cathy looked at Ben in annoyance. "Anyway, they've been monitoring the expedition for a while."

"Wait a second—" Garrison protested. "Cathy, do you mean to say that *you've* been spying—" Garrison shook his head. "Oh my God. Not you too."

Cathy frowned. There was no way to answer Garrison. "For a while we—*they* thought that Garrison was working for the mining people." Cathy looked up at Garrison. "They thought you were planning to fake results, and 'prove' that Iceland *wasn't* formed by an impact. They were glad to find out you were legitimate. But all I want to suggest is that CRATER might have the resources to help you get some publicity."

"If they have the money to help with PR, and they decided that they believed in Garrison, why didn't they have the money to finance the drilling here?" Ben demanded. Garrison noticed a strange, suspicious edge to his voice.

"I didn't say they had *money*," Cathy said. "I said they had *resources*. They're a pressure group, trying to influence public opinion, so naturally they have a press office and a video lab. That's how I know them—I used to do some freelance video work for them." She looked up at Garrison. "They'd help. The boss over there is a Japanese man, Shiro Ishida. One call and we'd be in business."

Garrison thought for a long moment. Ben as a confessed spy he could just about handle, but Cathy? He had slept with her last night, made love with her. He forced himself to forget all that. Personal questions couldn't enter into this. "No," he said at last. "Not yet. They may be just what we need, but we can't afford to risk lining up with a fringe group just yet. We're skating on thin enough ice as it is."

Cathy shrugged unhappily. She had blown her cover, risked everything she had, and Garrison barely reacted—at least out loud. "Well, okay, but keep them in mind. We might need them." She sat quietly, for a long moment. Garrison looked at her, hurt and bafflement in his eyes. "I'm going to bed," she said at last. "I'll be back in a moment—and I hope no one has shut off the heater in the latrine."

Ben watched her leave, and began to speak the moment she was out the door. "There is something strange going on here, Garrison. Damn strange. All this time, I thought Cathy was working for LuTech. Now she as much as comes out and admits she's been spying on you for *CRATER*. I don't know how far we should trust her."

Garrison, stunned, looked at Ben, so astonished that he didn't really realize what Ben was saying about the woman he was falling in love with. "*LuTech*? What the hell made you think she was working for LuTech?"

"Because of the fire," Ben said

Garrison was starting to get angry. He had resolved to let sleeping dogs lie, and never bring up the fire. Ben was too useful a partner even to let arson interfere. But now *Ben* had the gall to mention it casually. "What does your setting a fire in camp have to do with Cathy?"

"Huh?" It was Ben's turn to be shocked. "*Me*? Hell no. *Cathy* set the fire, not me. I thought you knew."

Chapter Eight

Garrison just sat there, open-mouthed, unable to respond. *Cathy* had set the fire? He couldn't believe it.

Ben didn't notice Garrison's reaction, but just kept talking. "But to get back to what I was worried about. If she's working for CRATER, why did she sabotage your work?"

"Wait a second. How do you know she set the fire?"

"I saw her. Cathy and I were working late in prep/mess that night. She left first, and I noticed she had left her video camera behind. I knew she'd want it the next morning when she went to the rig, and I decided to bring it to her at her tent. When I came outside after her, she wasn't headed for her tent. She was headed for the far end of camp. I went after her. I was just about to call to her when I saw her throw something into the storage hut. Ten seconds later, up goes the hut."

"And you're sure it was Cathy?" Garrison demanded.

"Saw her face by the firelight."

"I can't believe it. I *don't* believe it."

"You want proof?" Ben asked. "Hold on a minute. My backpack is around here somewhere." He stood up and scrabbled around in the crowded hut. He came back a minute later and stood over Garrison, holding out a one-shot record block in his hand. "It's recorded in there. I had the camera with me. When I saw what was happening—well, using it seemed the obvious thing to do."

Garrison looked up at Ben for a long minute, and then down at the small block of plastic. He did not want to be confronted with anything like this.

Cathy picked that moment to return. They heard her coming in the outer door. Garrison snatched furtively at the record block and shoved it in his pocket before she got through the inner door. "Thanks, Ben. I'll look at it later," Garrison said.

Cathy came in and instantly noticed there was something wrong. "What's going on?" she asked.

"Nothing, Cath," Garrison said. "Nothing at all."

Garrison lay awake for a long time that night, staring into the darkness, a thousand strange and conflicting thoughts running through his mind. Ben *had* to be lying. He had set the fire, not Cathy. But Ben had handed him the proof of Cathy's guilt. He could feel the record block jabbing into his side just a bit. But *Cathy*? Why? He needed to talk further with Ben. And dammit, he needed to see that video record.

Finally he couldn't take it anymore. He fumbled his way out of his sleeping bag and got up as quietly as he could. There was a playback unit on the comm console at his desk. He sat down at the desk and made sure to turn the monitor away from Cathy's sleeping figure on the floor.

He turned the sound volume down to zero, slid the block into the slot and punched the *play* button. The view was a little jerky at first, and the camera had a little trouble handling the low light, but the image was clear enough. Ben, it seemed, had started recording just a moment too late to catch the actual act of arson, but the recording told the story anyway. The flames were already spreading inside the hut, and a lone figure was silhouetted by the flames, standing there calmly watching the fire grow. The figure looked behind itself, as if it heard a noise, and Cathy's face was plainly recognizable, just before she turned and ran into the night.

Garrison thought back to that dreadful night—and distinctly remembered Cathy being one of the last to appear on the scene. He shut off the console and swallowed hard. His stomach was twisted into a knot, and his eyes were stinging. He felt a hand grasp his shoulder.

"I'm sorry," Ben said in a whisper. "I thought you knew. I thought you knew and you were keeping it quiet for some reason—because—because you two were . . ." Ben didn't finish the sentence.

"We have to talk," Garrison managed to say at last. His voice wasn't working right.

"Put on your parka. We'll talk on the porch, between the inner and outer doors. Cathy won't hear us if we keep our voices down."

The two of them got out to the porch without waking Cathy.

"Lucky she's a heavy sleeper," Garrison whispered as Ben shut the inner door. It was bitterly cold in the space between the two doors, and a bit too small for two men to stand in comfortably. They leaned in toward each other, their steaming breath mingling in the cold and the dark.

Ben's face was only a handsbreadth away from Garrison's, but he could barely see him at all in the almost perfect blackness. Garrison was tempted to switch on the light, but he thought better of it. Cathy might see.

Garrison stood there in indecision for a long moment. "I barely know where to start," he said. "Why the hell did you think Cathy was working for LuTech when *you* were working for them? Wouldn't they have told you?"

"Rule number one of industrial espionage—you can't tell what you don't know," Ben replied. "*My* job was to pass information back, nothing more. They never told me much, but it seemed to me that they intended you to fail through screw-ups. Look at the gags LuTech did pull—they saw to it you got no funding, that half your staff would suddenly up and quit, that your supplies would get sent to the wrong port. All nasty—but all a lot more subtle than setting a fire. The idea was to make you look like a loser, a bumbler. It was a smart move. It avoids the main problem with overt sabotage—bumblers don't get the sympathy martyrs get."

Garrison nodded. "If I seemed to fail on my own, I'm a loser. If the big guys go after me, it's my David against their Goliath, and I can't help but look good. But what would they have done if the fire hadn't happened?"

Ben shrugged. "I don't know. A few cubic centimeters of hydrochloric acid in the torchbit fuel would cut its efficiency by ninety percent. Your comm service might have been cut for nonpayment. All the tugs in the area might have been hired away, and you'd have been left with no way to get out to the drilling rig. That would be LuTech's style.

"It never occurred to me that someone else *besides* LuTech might be watching you, so naturally I assumed Cathy was working for LuTech. But torching the place was not their way of doing business. That should have warned me. But CRATER ought to be *supporting* your work— why would they sabotage your operation?"

"To force LuTech's hand," Garrison said suddenly. "If my work had been wrecked by a fire of suspicious origin, LuTech would have had the martyr they'd been worrying about. So they had to improvise, and they were clumsy. And it was that clumsy improvisation that let us spot them. They put together that phony GRF operation solely for the purpose of resupplying me—or, more accurately, for the purpose of *seeming* to resupply me, right? And they must have done it real fast, after the fire."

"You're right. I got called back with instructions to feed you the suggestion about GRF an hour after I phoned in my report of the fire. They barely had the name made up. But I can think of easier ways for CRATER to warn you about LuTech. And safer ones."

"But suppose CRATER *didn't* know who was screwing us up. There are plenty of outfits besides LuTech who won't like what I've found out about Mjollnir. Starting the fire not only warned us—it let *CRATER* find out for sure who they were up against. It was risky. It was pretty rotten. But it worked."

"I suppose," Ben agreed. "Even so, whoever thought of it has a mind like a pretzel. That guy Cathy mentioned, Shiro Ishida. It must have been him. Sneaky bastard."

"And he would appear to be on our side," Garrison said sourly. "Not my first choice in allies."

"Allies? You're still thinking of working with him?"

"He might end up being the only game in town," Garrison said. He shut his eyes, and thought of Cathy, thought of her eyes, her smile, her touch, her joyous approach to life—her betrayal of him. None of that, none of those daggers in his heart, could be permitted to interfere with the project. "We have to keep that door open," he said. "We can't let Cathy know we know she set the fire. If she relayed that news back to Ishida—God knows what he would do. We have to pretend everything is fine."

Ben wanted to disagree—but he looked at his friend, looked hard at the pain in his face, and knew what the words cost him. If Garrison was willing to hurt himself that much for the cause, then Ben knew he had no right to argue.

Garrison was the last to leave the Hrisey site the next morning. Cathy and Ben had already boarded the hovercraft, but Garrison felt the need for one last walk around.

Both of his chief deputies, Ben and Cathy, had betrayed him. And yet somehow Ben's betrayal was the more acceptable, forgivable. Because Ben had admitted it already? Because Ben had done some sort of penance, made amends? Or because it was Cathy that Garrison was in love with?

Hrisey was a strange and especially gloomy place that last day. The clouds hung low and battleship-grey. The winds had died for the moment, as if waiting for the last of the intruders to leave before roaring back over the island. Garrison looked about himself. Here lay the grave not only of Mjollnir, but of half a world's life. What would the world be like today if the slates had not been wiped clean sixty-five million years ago? What manner of creature would be walking the Earth in humanity's place? He shivered as the first gusts of an approaching storm caught at his parka. A cold, bleak, barren place.

The entire Earth must have looked like this, after the impact. It must have been so *lonely* after the asteroid strike. One day, a whole world teeming not just with life, but with giants. The next, the skies blanketed in a funereal pall, the dying surrounded by the dead.

He blinked and came back to himself. He would be glad to leave this place. Garrison trudged about the deserted site one last time, collecting whatever bits of trash had managed to lodge themselves between the rocks. He paid a last visit to the lighthouse keeper, and hoisted a drink with him as official recognition that the keeper was finally getting his island—and his solitude—back.

Then it was down to the pier to climb aboard the hovercraft. Garrison looked out across the barren isle. Not for the first time, he thought of Robert Frost's two roads divided in the yellow wood. Again and again in his life, Garrison had taken the one less travelled by.

If he had ignored that ancient work by the Alvarez team, had let the forgotten idea lie fallow, if he had never come to Hrisey and dug up the bones of a world-killer—then he could have gone on with a quiet life in his lab on the Moon, troubling no one, with a secure future. If he had merely given up once he had started, given up when the odds were so great that there seemed no point in continuing, he could have returned to his former life.

But none of that was possible now. There was no turning back once he had chosen his road—and so there was no point in looking back. Hrisey was the place the road had branched. There was no sense in looking down the ways he had not gone. He turned his back on the ruined land as the hovercraft reached the shore, and never looked upon it again.

NEW YORK CITY

Hope had evaporated quickly back home in the States. Two days of searching for support had gotten them nowhere. No one wanted to get near them anymore—especially Glenda and the museum.

The GRF had seen to that by slapping a lawsuit against Garrison's expedition, filing criminal and civil charges, accusing Garrison and company with fraud in the diversion of material from a GRF cargo sent to Iceland. The suit was ludicrous, of course, but whatever its merits, it had the intended effect of making Garrison as popular as typhoid. Say what you would about LuTech and GRF, Ben thought. You had to give them credit for gall, if nothing else.

After a second fruitless day of looking for help, they were meeting again. Ben looked from Garrison to Cathy and shook his head sorrowfully. "I talked to all the people I knew who might be able to help, worked the phones like crazy—but nobody wants to fund a nut group. I mention asteroid impact and get a dial tone. They all assume we're friends of CRATER." The three of them were sitting in Garrison's room at the robotel, practically knee-to-knee in the cramped quarters. All of them had had a long day of pounding the pavement.

"We could *use* friends like CRATER right now," Cathy said. "I talked to Mr. Ishida over there again," she said casually.

Garrison looked at her carefully. Was there something over-ingenuous in her voice, or was he finding what he expected to find, detecting proof of her guiltiness in everything she did, in every fancied nervous gesture and imagined tone of voice?

"They offered use of their entire video and simulator complex," Cathy went on. "They want us to do a complete show on Mjollnir, and Mr. Ishida promised worldwide and system-wide distribution of the recording."

Garrison shifted his legs in search of a bit more room and stroked his beard thoughtfully. This was too big to let his own personal feelings—or even safety—get in the way. They *needed* help, and there might be only one source offering it, no matter how much he distrusted them. "Do they guarantee us control over program content?"

Ben looked up in alarm. "Garrison, you're not thinking of accepting the offer, are you?"

Garrison looked up at Ben, his eyes tired and unhappy. "We're running out of time, Ben. GRF and LuTech are trying to throw our asses in *jail*—or did you miss that part?"

Ben gestured pleadingly. "Garrison, *think* about this. The thing you don't understand about these people is how far off into the fringes they are—which you ought to realize by now. No offense, Cathy, but I just don't think we can afford to treat your friends like a responsible political group. You can't do a deal with them, reach a compromise halfway between your view and theirs. You're completely with them, or you're the ultimate enemy. Politics is the art of compromise—and CRATER is made up of absolutists, not politicians."

"Hell, Ben, I don't even belong to CRATER," Cathy said. "I barely know anyone over there." Ben and Garrison exchanged glances. Neither of them told her they knew that was a lie.

Ben spoke sharply, his tone of voice as accusing as the words he did not say. "No, Cathy. Not CRATER. We can't afford to get mixed up with crazies."

Garrison turned toward Cathy. It was a delicate and fragile alliance between the three of them. Navigating between Cathy's defensiveness and half-lies on the one hand and Ben's suspicions on the other was tricky. But they all *needed* each other. That was what held them together. "You got anything to say to that, Cath?" he asked quietly.

Cathy reached up for a strand of her hair and twisted it around her finger. "Ben's right, in a way," she admitted reluctantly. "They're a bit radical, a little strident—but they're not *crazy*. And some of them are even a little concerned about the direction the movement is taking. But right now *we* offer *them* the best political weapon they've ever had—and I don't think they're going to let that slip through their fingers."

"So you think that they'll play it straight with the broadcast, be willing to let me do the straight presentation of a simulation without going overboard?" Garrison asked.

Cathy untwirled the length of hair and it bounced back into place in the mass of curls that framed her face. "Ye-esss, I think so. But let's not forget that they know *we* need *them*."

Ben shook his head vehemently. "We don't need them as much as you might think. Give me a few days, and I can come up with someone else willing to buy the air time and rent the studio."

"But we don't *have* a few days," Cathy reminded him wearily. They had been over this ground a half-doz times. She didn't have enough energy to get impassioned about it again. "You can bet our PR pals at LuTech are busily planting false stories about us, dusting off experts who'll tell the world what we've found is a hoax and a fraud. Every day that passes, people will be less willing to believe us—and the quote responsible unquote people with money will be less and less willing to help us. CRATER's got the only checkbook that's out right now, and they're willing to spend every dime they've got to promote our message. They care about it, passionately. They'll give it their all. I don't see how we've got a choice but to accept their help." She looked hard at Ben. "Tell me, straight off, who else we could go to—a specific name of a person or organization, not some vague 'someone else.' Tell me, and I'll shut up about CRATER. Who, exactly, would the alternative be?"

Garrison didn't speak. If Ben would concede this point, and accept the inevitable without prompting, then all the better. People handle unpleasant realities better when they arrive at them on their own.

"I can't think of anyone," Ben admitted at last. He was silent for a long moment. "And I can't think of anything else to do." He leaned back in his chair and set his hands on his knees. "Okay, we go with CRATER. But we go in with our eyes open. Call Mr. Ishida and let's get it over with."

Ben stood up and crossed to the window. Garrison was playing a dangerous game, to put it mildly. Ben stared out across the wilderness of skyscrapers. They made for a strange change from the windswept wastelands of Hrisey. He almost *missed* Hrisey for a moment. At least there, you knew where you stood.

Chapter Nine

NEW YORK CITY

Garrison was uncomfortable in front of the empty auditorium. The blank rows of seats seem to stare back at him, a mute reproach at his inability to get it right the first time. They were *assuming* he'd blow it, that they'd have to make it pretty.

Garrison had wanted to do it on a live feed, but Cathy had convinced him that an amateur such as himself needed the help professional editing could afford, and besides, the complexities of time zones would give a live broadcast a much smaller potential audience. It was much easier to place a recording in the various media. They'd make the video here, edit it, clean it up, and ship it all over the world to the various news services, both free press and controlled.

Garrison had talked to plenty of audiences in the endless pursuit of funding scientists were forced to undertake. He knew he *could* have done it live, *should* have—but there was never any arguing with self-appointed experts. Ben and Cathy were back there in the control room, with that Ishida guy watching over their shoulders. A few other technicians watched their dials behind the soundproof glass.

Garrison didn't like it. He felt like he had lost control of what should have been his operation. And he was impatient to get started.

Now, at last the red camera light went on. Garrison cleared his throat and began. "Hello. I am Dr. Garrison Morrow, and I am an astrogeologist, a scientist who studies the geology of worlds beyond the Earth. Recently, my team completed a study right here on Earth that I would like to tell you about. Before I tell you why a scientist concerned with extraterrestrial worlds was digging here on Earth, before I tell you the importance of what we were working on, let me tell you what we found.

"We used some very highly sophisticated drilling equipment, developed on the Moon, and drilled through the seabed just off the coast of Iceland, going far deeper than anyone has ever gone before. Once we had drilled far enough, we extracted core samples from the seabed, and the samples were opened and examined back at the laboratory. What we found was this." Garrison picked up a small, blackened, nondescript chip of rock, and the cameras zoomed in on his hand. "This is by far the largest fragment we found. Most of the pieces were microscopic. But the smaller microfrags contain this identical material. I know it looks like a plain old rock, but this is a very special type of stone.

"Samples of it were subjected to a battery of tests of various sorts, at a number of labs around the world, and on the Moon. Physicists, astrogeologists, specialists in metamorphology—all have come to the same conclusion. This lump of rock that I hold in my hand, and the fragments like it, taken from rock strata many kilometers below the surface of Iceland—*came from outer space*. Furthermore, this type of rock is effectively identical to what has been found in a number of asteroids. This type of rock could *only* have been created in outer space, cold-formed by processes totally unlike anything found on Earth."

Garrison held up his open hand, the nondescript bit of rock nestled in his palm. "This is a piece of an ancient asteroid, a meteorite of tremendous size, a lump of rock from another world. We have given this asteroid the infor-

mal name *Mjollnir*, for Thor's hammer, a hammer that
struck the ground with the full power of a God's wrath.

"Now, obviously, there is only one way an asteroid could
come to be eighteen kilometers below the surface of our
planet. It smashed its way down there.

"If I can digress for a moment, I'd like to mention
another asteroid, one which has been named *Cornucopia*.
Like Mjollnir, Cornucopia is a carbonaceous chrondite
body. Lucifer Technologies plans to move Cornucopia into
a very close orbit of the Earth—only one thousand kilometers up. Indeed, Cornucopia is already on its way here.
You have not heard about any of this because LuTech has
done its best to keep the project quiet.

"They've kept it quiet for a good reason. Once Cornucopia is in that orbit, it will eventually, inevitably, *come
down*—unless something is done to stop it. Atmospheric
drag will degrade that orbit until it fails altogether, and
about four to six hundred years from now, Cornucopia will
strike the Earth with approximately the same force as
Mjollnir. Once that degradation begins, it will require a
heroic effort to keep the asteroid safely in orbit.

"The only currently known means powerful enough to
move it to a higher, safer orbit would be a nuclear charge—
ignited within a thousand kilometers of Earth. If that
sounds like an unlikely and risky thing to try, I should tell
you that it is precisely the means they intend to use in the
final braking maneuver when the asteroid *arrives* in Earth
orbit two years from now.

"LuTech is betting that their engineers will be able to
place the asteroid precisely enough so that it will be safe
in orbit for five hundred years or more. They are gambling
not only that their insertion two years from now will be
precise, but that our ancestors, five centuries from now,
will be willing and able to pull Cornucopia safely away
from the planet in time.

"But what if civilization should for some reason fall?
Even if civilization should survive, as we all hope and
expect it to do, what if our ancestors no longer use our
forms of space travel—or merely lose the highly specialized art of moving asteroids? *We* assume they will track
such a large object carefully, to watch against any threat-

ening degradation of the orbit. But isn't it more like human nature to take a moon in the sky for granted—especially after it has been harmlessly there for five centuries? What if they forget? Even if we decide we *can* trust them to prevent the crisis, what is our right to set such a disaster in motion today, leaving a potential planetary catastrophe as our legacy to the future?

"If Cornucopia does impact, it will be moving slower at impact than Mjollnir did. However, it is a larger body than we think Mjollnir was, and so will have about the same energy behind it. Thus, the fall of Cornucopia will be a close parallel to the fall of Mjollnir, and will yield about the same results. So let me return to Mjollnir, and tell you what happened when *it* struck the Earth. Let me show what Mjollnir did to Earth, what happened when the hammer of Thor smote the Earth."

A large video screen popped up behind Garrison, and Cathy's accurate—if somewhat lurid—computer simulation began. At first, it showed only an empty starfield. Garrison watched it from a small pocket screen sitting on the podium, his hands on a control panel, ready to stop the simulation, start it, highlight and emphasize this or that image as needed. Garrison wasn't really familiar with the equipment, but they had told him not to worry about that. He was to control the image for his own reference and to cue his own remarks. The video techs would take the result back into the lab and smooth out any clumsy words later on.

The Earth, achingly beautiful as seen from space, appeared on the screen. A tiny grey blob crawled onto the screen from the outer edges of the view. The image zoomed in on the blob, which resolved itself into a typical asteroid shape, a cratered, oblong shape. The huge, vaguely threatening potato-shaped rock tumbled through space.

"Imagine, as we have here, a mass about ten kilometers across approaching the Earth. Most likely, its orbit has been wrenched around over the course of thousands of years, by repeated close approaches to Jupiter, Earth, Mars, and Venus. Finally, it is about to intercept not only Earth's orbit, but Earth herself.

"Attracted by Earth's gravity, it steadily accelerates as it comes closer. As Mjollnir reaches the fringes of the atmosphere, it is moving at least fifteen kilometers a second, probably much faster. In reality, Mjollnir's journey from the top of the sensible atmosphere to impact took fewer than ten seconds. In this simulation we must slow events down, and stop them from time to time, to be able to see and understand them."

The image of the asteroid began to glow and glimmer in places as it reached the upper boundary of the atmosphere. "The asteroid is so big and so heavy that air drag barely slows it. It brushes away the megatons of atmosphere as if they weren't there." The view on the simulation rode the potato-shape in toward impact, watching the planet leap closer, watching the surface of the asteroid suddenly brighten and glow fiercely.

A hunk of the asteroid split off and careened away, splitting off smaller fragments that vaporized immediately. The largest fragment survived and spun toward the edge of the view. "We believe that the stress of impact with the atmosphere caused the asteroid to 'calve,' that is, to split up into two or more bodies," Garrison said.

He stopped the simulation and hit a key that highlighted the large fragment. "Over a century ago, scientists discovered microfragments of shock-formed quartz in certain rock layers, all exactly the same age, all over the world. Such quartzes could only be formed by the impact of a large body on a landmass. No other event would have the energy needed to produce such forms. Seabed rocks are entirely different from continental rock types and would not produce such quartzes. But we have determined that the shock-quartz is exactly the same age as Mjollnir, and we know Mjollnir struck the water. Therefore, we believe that Mjollnir calved, and a smaller fragment struck elsewhere, perhaps in Greenland. We will concentrate on the large portion of Mjollnir." The image unfroze and the large fragment spiraled away, out of view. "This calving would not in any event significantly change the outcome. We will follow the main asteroid body in. Air drag heats the crust of the asteroid, raising it to red-hot in a few seconds."

Garrison let the image of the plummeting asteroid continue a moment longer and froze it again. "The sonic boom and shock wave formed by Mjollnir hitting the atmosphere have major results on Earth all by themselves. The shock wave sweeps out like an aerial tidal wave at supersonic speeds, killing every living thing in the air and on the land, by the sheer force of impact, for hundreds of kilometers in all directions. It deafens any creature with hearing throughout perhaps half the globe. At the same time, a small fraction of the Earth's atmosphere—perhaps as much as half a percent—is ejected into space. This alone could distort weather patterns for decades, but as we shall see, other calamities will mask those changes.

"In a few seconds, Mjollnir has already killed millions or billions of animals, and done major damage to the ecostructure. And it hasn't even hit the ground yet." Garrison restarted the frozen image and the simulated asteroid plunged groundward.

"Moving at between one-and-one-half to three times escape velocity—that is, between about sixteen to thirty-three kilometers per second—Mjollnir slashes down from the top of the sensible atmosphere to the surface of the Atlantic Ocean in ten seconds at most, already furnace hot from the speed of its passage." The asteroid on the screen dove down, ramming the air before it out of the way. The view pulled back to reveal massive toroidal clouds abruptly forming around the path of the asteroid, a bull's-eye painted around the planetoid as it struck its target, created by the shock wave slamming through the atmosphere, forcing the ambient water vapor to condense out. Garrison halted the motion of the asteroid on the screen and zoomed in on it, diving through the cloud cover to hang over the crash site. Garrison picked up the narrative and unfroze the image.

"Mjollnir reaches sea level and crashes through the kilometers-deep waters, again without being noticeably slowed. Indeed, the asteroid may never actually strike the water. The compressed column of air driven ahead of it might, in its turn, force the water out of *its* way, throwing up huge supersonic tsunami, tidal waves more powerful than any in the modern age, clearing the water out of the way in the split second before the asteroid hits." As he spoke, huge waves leapt into existence on the screen.

"In either event, the shock of impact exposes a large

portion of sea floor for a brief time. But before viewing the impact, let us first examine other results, caused by these pre-impact effects on the water." The video image turned away from the impact and watched the kilometer-high waves racing across the sea. Massive waves raced away from the epicenter, streaking across the ocean. Garrison stopped the image and called up another sequence. A green and pleasant coastline appeared on the screen. A herd of triceratops grazed in the foreground, a stand of giant ferns rustled in the breeze.

"Here are some of the effects on the oceans and coasts so far, before the effects of the impact itself can reach the distant land. The tidal waves crash into Northern Europe and the lands that will one day be the British Isles." On the screen, the mountain of water crashed down on the coast, inundating everything, tossing the huge animals about like match sticks, flattening everything, crushing the green land beneath the seething grey cauldron of the enraged waters. "The waves strike Greenland, and, soon after, North America. The Atlantic was far narrower in those days, so the energy of the wave fronts would have less time and distance to dissipate. Other tidal waves reach north over the Pole to strike the north of Asia. A great deal of coastline would be directly in the line of fire.

"Of course, it is not just the land animals that suffer. Probably all macroscopic life in the North Atlantic and Arctic Oceans for fifteen hundred kilometers around the impact is killed outright as the shock front moves through. Large areas of coastland—including the delicate wetlands many species rely on for nesting grounds—are destroyed.

"Inland areas are flooded with saltwater, killing more plants and animals. Residual saltwater poisons groundwater for years to come. All this, merely the result of the tidal waves thrown up just before the impact." The image flicked away from the ruined coast and returned to the frozen image of the impact site.

"But now, Mjollnir slams through—not into, but *through* the sea floor. The Earth's crust is thin in the North Atlantic; Mjollnir cracks it open, like a bullet going through an eggshell."

Garrison stopped talking, and let the images move forward, in horribly compelling slow motion. The asteroid, now glowing white-hot from atmospheric heating, smashed into the sea floor in an explosion of light, brighter than any lightning strike. The rock of the sea floor rippled, bent, twisted, broke, flew off into the sky. Like gore from a ghastly, bloody wound, the raw molten magma of the Earth's mantle spewed up into the sky.

"The shock wave has forced aside a column of atmosphere and ocean—as the asteroid strikes, the ruined sea floor is exposed directly to the vacuum of space, and a vacuum sucked in behind the asteroid.

"The impact pulverizes the sea floor and the asteroid. Huge amounts of material are thrown up. Mountain-sized chunks of ocean bed, boulders, megatons of still-liquid magma, rocks, stones, steam, particulate matter formed from both asteroid and seabed; all of it is ejected into this column of vacuum. The larger fragments fall away and reimpact, some half a world away. A few may actually reach orbital speed and circle the Earth for a time before their orbits decay and they reenter. Some fragments may even reach escape velocity. As to the smaller ejecta, the partial vacuum serves to suck up a tremendous amount of dust and smoke, injecting it directly into the upper atmosphere.

"Back on the ground, the shock of the asteroid's progress past the crust and through the mantle has uplifted a huge area of sea floor, possibly forcing it above the local sea level. Atop this mount, of course, the impact forms a crater, perhaps half the size of Iceland, a blood-red wound of scarlet magma visible from space, a horrible scar many tens of kilometers in diameter. Immediately, molten rock, until this moment held under enormous pressure by the weight of the crust above it, rushes up through this hole in the planetary crust. A massive volcano is born."

On the screen, a blood-red fountain of flaming rock, kilometers high, surged out of the hole punched in the planet's surface. The lava began to fall back, splattering down on the exposed seabed and the roiling waters that surrounded it. "The magma, the raw molten rock of the Earth's mantle, roars up from the planet's interior. Perhaps tidal waves, reflected back from coastlines, or having ringed the Earth completely, crash in to inundate the crater. Or perhaps, as we have shown here, the lip of the newly forming crater is high enough to hold the waters out. In either event, the volcanic vent begins to build itself into a mountain, sooner or later forcing itself up above the waters.

"But the seismic effects of the impact are not merely local. The impact touches off a sudden, planet-wide increase in seismic activity. Probably it sets off eruptions of every active volcano on Earth. Quakes shake the ground everywhere as the shock waves overwhelm any resistance to built-up stress in local fault lines.

"Bear in mind, it is still only a few minutes since the impact. In the North Atlantic, the ocean's surface is a roiling, seething cauldron of megatons of water heated beyond the boiling point. Tremendous amounts of water vapor are released into the air, along with other gases. The massive heat of the volcano, and the uprushing gases from it, reinforce the column of low pressure formed behind the incoming asteroid. The air that has been forced aside by the asteroid now rushes violently back in to fill the vacuum, twisted in its path by the Coriolis effect of Earth's rotation.

"The water vapor condenses abruptly and a huge, perhaps semipermanent, hurricane is formed, tens of times larger than any we have ever seen, possibly spanning the entire Atlantic. At or near the eye of the storm, a proto-island of molten lava has welled up through the sea-floor, perhaps hot enough to remelt the initial crater. Not yet solidified, the heat of the semi-liquid volcano holds the sea back. The lava continues to flow, the solid land gradually forms, and Iceland is born of flame."

Garrison let the images dwell on the hurricane and the nightmare island growing below it, and then let the screen fade to black. He hit another button, and a view of the whole planet appeared behind him, the massive storm with the hideous red eye for the volcano at its center shrunk to seeming unimportance.

A red-black plume hung over the calved fragment's impact site in Greenland. Other, smaller, spots of red betrayed the volcanoes touched off worldwide by the seismic shock of impact. Even so, the cloud cover hid the flooded coastlines, and the planet seemed almost at peace. "We have shown events up to now in real time, or in slow motion. Now let us make time move faster." The clouds hanging over the world began to grown, began to turn darker, greyer. The whole world began to get dimmer, harder to see.

"We have thus far seen only the beginning of the disaster. For months, perhaps years or decades, the new volcano continues to erupt, not merely adding land area to Iceland, but pumping megaton after megaton of smoke and ash into the air. All that dark particulate matter is added to the huge volume of sun-blocking dust and soot thrown into the atmosphere during the initial impact."

Garrison spoke on as the planet darkened behind him. "Million and billions of plants and animals have been killed in the initial asteroid strike. No doubt many whole species have been made extinct in that single moment. Oceanic and terrestrial ecosystems for thousands of kilometers in all directions have been damaged or destroyed. But all this is as nothing to the injuries yet to be inflicted." On the screen, the volcano finally sputtered out, the hurricanes dissipated, and more familiar weather patterns gradually formed up.

"For there is still the dust and smoke and soot. Even after the last of the volcanoes stop erupting, the dust hangs in the air, hovering like a dark sepulchral shroud in the upper atmosphere. It blocks the sunlight, dimming the skies by as much as ninety percent, perhaps even more. At high noon, perhaps the sun provides only as much illumination as a full moon. Starved of sunlight, the plants everywhere begin to die. Animals that lived on the plants starve and die, as do the animals that lived on the plant-eaters. The whole Earth, deprived of warming sunlight, begins to cool."

The upper latitudes of the darkened planet begin to brighten in patches, a sign of false light and hope on the face of the tortured world. "Snow falls where it has never fallen before. The northern and southern oceans begin to cool and freeze. If the cooling is severe enough, and if the ice and snow blanket enough of the ground to reflect too much sunlight back into space—then the ice begins to feed on itself, cooling the planet, causing more ice to form, cooling the world still more. An ice age may start, one that might last ten years, or a thousand—or a hundred thousand.

"But even if the ice does not stay for long, the darkened skies kill. Within a few years, fifty percent of all genera are extinct. Far more than fifty percent of all families of species living things have died. It will take millions of years for the planet to recover fully—and much has been lost forever."

The wrecked Earth of the past faded into darkness on the screen, and the green and lovely world of the present appeared.

Garrison held up the small lump of rock and gestured with it. Not by chance, the lump of rock was about the shape and color of the image of Mjollnir shown in the first moments of the video simulation.

"None of this is conjecture," he said. "The proof is here in my hand. Mjollnir existed. We have dated the fall carefully, through various radiometric measurements, through examination of the rocks surrounding the asteroid particles, and through other means.

"Mjollnir struck the Earth 63.5 million years ago. It has been known for many years that virtually all the dinosaurs, along with many of the other animals on Earth, suddenly became extinct approximately 65 million years ago. Now, definitely and unequivocally, we know how they died.

"Mjollnir wiped the slate clean, made room on the Earth for the mammals, for ourselves, when it destroyed the world of the dinosaurs. Our kind could not have arisen if Mjollnir had not emptied the world stage of life. There can be no doubt of this basic chain of events. All the pieces fit the puzzle.

"We are the children of a vast cosmic accident. Let us not cause another. Let us consider carefully before we bring a disaster waiting to happen, a disaster called Cornucopia, to our world."

The screen behind Garrison went blank, the video lights faded, leaving the room in a ghostly gloom. A muffled voice from the control room gave Garrison its congratulations, but he didn't hear it. He felt the hand that held that rock tremble, felt the sweat stream down his body and bead up on his forehead. He looked down at the rock, and marveled at it. It struck him fully for the first time just how *real* the catastrophe he had just described was. This was no interesting intellectual puzzle. This was the fate of worlds. He closed his hand around the precious sample from the scarred depths of the Earth and flung it away, into the darkness of the auditorium. Ben, watching from the control room, popped the record block out of the recorder and slipped it into his pocket. Later, he knew, the pros would tidy the show up, but he knew Garrison would want to get a look at his own, unprettified performance.

Ben made a mental note to recover the rock sample later. It was a priceless thing, the fruit of all their work. But best not to go get it just now. With those hideous images of a shattered Earth still fresh in his mind, he could not blame Garrison for despising the unclean shard, the remnant of the Thing that had smashed the life out of a hundred million years' evolution. "It's all yours, Cath," Ben said, and went to take his friend home.

"Your friend has acquitted himself well, Miss Cleveland," Shiro Ishida announced after Ben had left. "It will require only slight changes to adjust his statement to suit our purposes."

Cathy had long ago decided that Mr. Ishida was not a nice man. He *said* all the right things, was most polite and courteous, very kind. He never spoke a cruel word. He was even handsome. And yet, on the purest gut level, Cathy didn't like him. Maybe she was just over-sensitized these days, so she was finding imagined invective everywhere —but to her, Ishida seemed to have a talent for the hidden insult, for jabbing at people, for maneuvering them into doing things they didn't want to do.

He had just put both of those talents on display. How dare he talk about Garrison as if he were a clever dog who had done all his tricks properly—and how had he maneuvered Cathy into betraying Garrison even further in the next breath? She glanced over at Ishida, then looked away. She was, in point of fact, afraid of him.

He was a young man, tall, dark-haired and olive-complexioned, of pure Japanese descent—a fact he made sure you knew the moment you met him. There was about him the sort of grace and confident poise that only generations of wealth and position could afford.

His family had settled in Hawaii four generations ago, but still they did not regard themselves as Americans, or as Hawaiians, but as Japanese. Rich and powerful, owning vast tracts of real estate in the islands, to this day his people acted not as settlers or immigrants, but more like the colonial plantation owners of the nineteenth century. He had followed in the tradition of his family and rejected U.S. citizenship at age eighteen. He held a Japanese passport, a resident alien in his native land.

The unassimilated Japanese were a sticky issue not only in Hawaii and the west coast of the United States, but throughout the Pacific region, and Shiro Ishida was an archetypal product of the tradition. Respectful, law-abiding, and yet alarmingly powerful, intimidatingly confident and assertive. Even the Japanese government was unnerved by them. Home-island Japanese regarded them as an embarrassing reminder of the arrogant Imperialist past.

Cathy felt big, clumsy, obvious, crude, overbearing around Ishida. She felt herself cast as the clumsy barbarian in the presence of a sophisticated member of a culture far older than her own. She had been born in New York City—and in a few words he could make it clear he knew the city, its geography and history far better than she ever could. Cathy had always been proud of her French—and she was dismayed to learn in five sentences that he spoke it better than she did, as well as German and Russian and who knows what else.

"Do we really have to do the cuts and changes, Mr. Ishida?" she asked. "I think what Garrison said was fine the way it is. Very powerful. The reality is good enough without being 'adjusted,' and we're exposing ourselves to a lot of legal problems if we tinker with it too much."

"We are seeking to secure the future safety of the planet, Dr. Cleveland," Ishida said evenly. Clearly, he already knew who would win this argument. "Can 'good enough' ever be sufficient for that? If we must alter a mere word or two, enhance an image or two in order to prevent the ultimate disaster, I regard that as not a choice, but a duty. We will adjust the recording as planned."

"But how can you do this to Garrison, when he is providing you with such a great prize?" Cathy asked. She felt trapped, cornered. She did not want to hurt Garrison. Right now, at this moment, she would have let the damned asteroid fall wherever it might, if it would take the guilt of betraying Garrison off her hands.

"That is a question you should have asked before you agreed to be our representative to Dr. Morrow."

"But we're breaking the law!" Cathy protested, knowing how weak that argument had to be.

"Rest assured that we will be well beyond the reach of the law long before there can be any move made against us. You have cooperated in the arrangements for that departure. You must journey with us, as we have arranged." He paused for a moment and looked at one of the monitors. "It is an axiom that sacrifices must be made in a great cause. Silence now, there is much to do."

Already, one of the technicians was working. A perfect 3D image of Garrison appeared on the stage, frozen in time. "We're picking it up a few pages into the script, Mr. Ishida," one of the technicians announced.

The image flickered once or twice, then settled down and began to move. It shuffled through its notes for a moment and spoke. ". . . indeed, Cornucopia is already on its way here. You have not heard about any of this because LuTech has done its best to keep the project quiet."

Garrison's image blinked out of existence for a moment. Cathy felt a little sick when the revised version appeared on the stage. They had changed the color of his shirt, his hair was a bit shorter, his beard a bit more neatly trimmed. He seemed to stand up straighter. She knew they were going to do this, but she still felt it to be wrong.

In spite of herself, Cathy was impressed with the technical skill of the adjustments. She told herself she shouldn't have been surprised by the quality. She knew how good this team, this equipment was—and she had done some of the programming herself. If this group could simulate the wreck of an entire world, giving a recording a haircut was trivial.

The recording spoke in Garrison's voice—but the voice was changed as well. It was Garrison's voice, but made deeper, stronger, more expressive than the greatest actor's voice had ever been. And the words themselves were "adjusted" as well.

". . . indeed, Cornucopia is already on its way here. You have not heard about it because LuTech has done its best to keep the project quiet.

"They've kept it quiet for a good reason. Once Cornucopia is in that orbit, atmospheric drag will degrade the orbit. The orbit will degrade rapidly, and Cornucopia will strike the Earth with approximately the same force as Mjollnir within six years. The only means powerful enough to move it to a higher, safer orbit would be a nuclear charge—ignited within a hundred kilometers of Earth." The reconstituted Garrison looked up, a blazing passion in its simulated eyes. "But the fate of the Earth is no concern of the orbital civilization. Let me show you what LuTech has planned for Eart—."

The image vanished in a crackle of static. "Ah, software glitch there. Might take some time to clean it up. That's as far as we can get with the preprogrammed stuff, Mr. Ishida," a technician announced. "Then we cut right into the impact presentation, more or less as it stands—we'll just make it a bit more vivid, that's all. What do you think?"

Ishida smiled. "Most satisfactory. Does it meet with your approval, Dr. Cleveland?"

Cathy shivered. This was not what she had written. She had set up a pretty standard appearance-enhancement program to make Garrison look better, maybe even clean up his grammar and usage a bit. Every public speaker used such enhancement programming these days. But these were outright lies, put in Garrison's mouth!

This was craziness, wild fanaticism. Only a lunatic would do this. She looked up at Ishida, and did not find what she expected. She searched for the look of madness, but it was not there. She remembered what Ben had said about CRATER's fanatics and absolutists. They were exactly the sort of people who might produce such a recording out of passion. But Ishida's expression was smooth, calm, calculating. Calmly, needlessly, risking everything. Wrecking everything. This effort could only lead to disaster.

Why? she wondered.

The recording he planned to release systemwide would be needlessly inflammatory, as damaging to Ishida's friends as to his enemies. When the truth came out, it could destroy CRATER.

But CRATER was not important. Stopping Cornucopia was all that mattered. And a recording like this, scaring the hell out of everyone, might very well do the trick.

She wanted to run, to hide, to wash her hands of it all—but how could she *not* fight to save Earth? What did it matter who her allies were? Ishida was running the show. They needed him. And he had asked her a question.

"The recording seems quite effective, sir," she replied.

Chapter Ten

NEW YORK CITY

The headlines weren't pretty to start with. They got worse as the days went by.

SCIENTIST WARNS OF ASTEROID CRASH
WITHIN DECADE

LUTECH, ORBITAL MINING CO. OFFICES
WRECKED BY RIOTERS

LUTECH FILES LIBEL SUIT AGAINST MORROW

SPACE-BASED STOCKS TAKE BEATING,
OFF-PLANET ECONOMIES FEAR RECESSION

MORROW ARRESTED, INCITEMENT
TO RIOT CHARGED

The electronic media were even worse, of course. They could show the bogus video, complete with raving lunatic Garrison and a tarted-up destruction of Earth, over and over again. And they did. Worldwide.

It scared people silly. People got frightened not just of the asteroid miners, but of all activity in space. Rumors started flying that one of the larger space habs was going to spiral in and impact, and even that large impacts had taken place and been hushed up, that some hardliners among the Settler leadership were plotting deliberate asteroid attacks on Earth.

So the video crews got to show the anti-space riots as well.

It all hit Garrison hard. More betrayal, another victory yanked away from him by someone he trusted, by someone he loved. Worst of all, his warnings against the coming real disaster were lost in the general clamor of the riots and panic over a phony catastrophe.

And then the cops busted into Garrison's robotel room and hauled him away on incitement to riot charges. It was probably just as well they did pick him up. There were already mobs howling for his blood. At least in jail he'd be safe.

Ben worked like the devil to meet with the judge on the case, thanking whatever gods there were that he had decided to save a few bucks by recording Garrison's presentation on one of the cheaper read-only-memory record blocks. Once recorded into, a ROM block could not be altered, and Ben was able to show the judge a true version of the presentation in a preliminary hearing, and back it up with documentation from half a dozen sources and confirming statements from dozens of aerospace scientists.

That got Garrison sprung, and severely damaged LuTech's libel case against him—and got the judge plenty mad as well. Fraudulent information manipulation was regarded as a very serious crime. Acting on a court order, a data-retrieval specialist was able to recover the original recording, along with three or four interim versions, from the video lab's computers, confirming Garrison's innocence, so at least the legal problems were cleared up quickly. The judge even ordered the U.S. Marshall's office to provide Garrison with protection—there were still a lot of people out there who might wish him harm.

On the down side, Cathy, Ishida, and CRATER's video team had vanished altogether. Warrants for their arrest on data fraud charges were sworn out, but no one could find a trace of them. By the time the warrants were sworn, they could have been anywhere on Earth, or en route to a half-dozen points off Earth.

The public was not going to be put off blaming the

messenger for bad news just because his innocence had been proved. The American Museum of Natural History disavowed all connection with Dr. Morrow when Garrison was arrested—and they did not reinstate their support when he was exonerated and released. Garrison could hardly blame them, of course. Who wanted to hop back into bed with a serious case of bad luck? The same would hold true with every other scientific organization. It was going to be hard to find work.

But by far, the worst of it was the damage done to their cause. Even with their libel suit dead, LuTech was able to leap into the fray, and prove that the exaggerated claims that Cornucopia was going to impact soon were false. That was enough to make most people forget the threat to future generations—or make them think the warning of an impact five hundred years from now was also false. All Garrison's work—even, for that matter, all of CRATER's work, was made useless. Nobody believed the boy who cried wolf.

PORT VIKING, MARS

Angela Hardin cleared her monitor and swore under her breath. As if there hadn't been enough trouble already. As if an anti-space feeling on Earth hadn't been running high enough! Just when there was some real help on a deal for cutting tariffs on medical supplies, this had to happen.

She drummed her fingers on her desk and fumed. The damnable thing—one of *many* damnable things—was that the Settlers were getting bad publicity because of an *Earthside* operation. Lucifer Technologies, the one causing all the trouble, was strictly an Earth/Moon system operation.

LuTech had nothing to do with the Settlement worlds, and it was LuTech moving this asteroid in—yet somehow LuTech was perceived as the injured party. A few video shots of their burned and ransacked offices, one or two printed reports of the pummeling their stock had taken in the markets—and people were already forgetting who was ultimately to blame for this whole situation. Morrow hadn't dragged that asteroid out of its orbit. The Settlers hadn't.

But LuTech *had*—and LuTech was managing to cast itself in the role of the victim even as Morrow and the Settlement Worlds took the heat.

There were more subtle things going on in the press campaign. This man Morrow was being castigated for irresponsibly spreading word of the danger. By focusing on that alleged irresponsibility, the LuTech people were making it seem as if the danger did not exist. The blatant data forgery by those CRATER fools was playing directly into LuTech's hand.

All in all, a masterful PR operation, Angela admitted. It was hard not to admire the bastards, in a way. But she was willing to make the effort. After all, LuTech was making life very hard for her people.

And they were doing it while leaving the Settlers nothing to fight back against. Neither LuTech nor anyone else had actually accused the Settlers of anything in the Cornucopia affair. There was nothing tangible or specific for Hardin or her people to respond to, just a vague perception that it had to do with space, with space outside the Moon's orbit—so it had to be that the Settlers were involved.

The people—and politicians—of Earth had been in no mood to think kindly of their kindred on the other worlds even before Cornucopia. Things could only get worse now.

Angela Hardin got up from her desk and stared out her office window at the domed city. A small town, really, dusty and a bit drab, a utilitarian settlement that had not yet considered the fact that it was supposed to be the capital of a planet and the headquarters of a system-wide confederation.

Her eyes shifted from the slightly shabby buildings and streets to the twilit landscape beyond the city limits, seen but dimly through the tough insulating plastic of the dome. Night was coming on, and the dome was being slowly darkened down into opacity so as to retain heat during the frigid hours of night. They opaqued the dome every night as part of the heat-management operation, and thus you could never see the night sky from inside the dome.

Angela, though born on Earth, had spent most of her adult life in the asteroid belt and in the free-flier habitats. The chance to see the stars was important to Belters and habitants in their closed-in worldlets. Even when it was structurally awkward, they built ports and windows—not video monitors hooked up to cameras, but real *windows* with nothing but a thickness of quartz between you and outer space. Seeing, actually *seeing*, the outside world, was an important part of Belter psychology.

But not for the Martians. They never seemed much interested in the sky. They could, with a minimum of fuss, put on a pressure suit and step outside their domes whenever they wanted to get a look at the sky—a look unfettered by viewports, with no one crowded up behind you to get their turn. To a Belter, that was luxury undreamed of. But few Martians ever thought to go outside if they could avoid it. They seemed to turn their backs on the outside universe, down here on their dusty planet. They were a strangely insular people for a bunch of pioneers on the edge of space.

Perhaps it was because Mars was *nearly* habitable. No one could ever imagine living on any of the other Settlement worlds without massive and constant effort to maintain the artificial environment. On Mars, it was just barely possible for people to survive on their own, without a tremendous investment in technology. The dust rats did all right, out in their caves and dug-in shelters, pulling power from home built wind farms and solar power arrays. You could *almost* survive here without technology, without civilization. The Martians *almost* didn't need anyone else. Maybe that was what made them resent the help they did need.

Angela did not pretend to understand the Martians—or even like them very much. But Mars was far and away the richest, most populous, and most powerful world of the poor, underpopulated and weak Settlement Worlds. It was inevitable that the Council Headquarters should be established here.

The trouble was, having Settlement Council HQ on Mars made it all the easier for the man in the street on

Earth to think that Mars and the Settlers were one and the same. And the Martian leaders, typified by that Neanderthal McGillicutty, were among the most radical and confrontational the Settlers had to offer.

It was damned frustrating.

JERSEY CITY, NEW JERSEY

They couldn't afford to stay here much longer. Even here across the river, prices were too high. It was time to move on, time to go somewhere. Garrison sat in a little park not far from the robotel thinking it all over one last time. The asteroid would not reach Earth for another two years—and if it was safely injected into orbit, would pose no danger for perhaps another five hundred.

Two years, or five hundred. He had that long to stop it.

But he couldn't do it from New Jersey. And publicity couldn't solve things—not when the opposition was calling all the shots. He had to fight with other weapons; and he wouldn't find those weapons here. He needed work, he needed a place where he knew the score, a place where he had contacts, where he could hear things, where he could talk to people who understood space, where the scandals of Earth didn't make any difference.

Garrison noticed Ben coming up behind him. Garrison didn't speak, but let him approach quietly. Ben sat down next to him on the bench, and the two of them were silent for a long time, staring up at the sky, at the big bright full Moon that hung high in the firmament.

"I brought you a beer," Ben said after a while. "And one for me, too."

"Thanks." Garrison took his beer and opened it. He sat, sipping it, for a while. He thought of Cathy, and the hurt she had given him. Had she ever cared for him at all, or was going to bed with him on orders from CRATER, from Ishida, as well? The question hurt. And that pain decided him. He wanted to get further away from that memory. "There's nothing here for me anymore," Garrison announced at last.

"Me neither," Ben replied. He had been thinking too. Maybe he'd be able to work his way back from the scandal—

but there would always be whispers. He didn't want to live that way. "Me neither."

Garrison raised up his beer carton and toasted the sky. "I'm going home," he said quietly. "To the Moon."

Ben sat silent for a long moment. "Can I come too?" he asked at last.

PART TWO

EXILES

The Moon does not make sense.

In the affairs of cosmology, and in the affairs of human-ity, it does not fit in with the rest of the universe. In both these wildly different fields, the Moon is an anomaly for the same reason: it is too big, and too close to another world.

Nowhere else is there a satellite so huge in comparison to the planet it circles, or one that so profoundly affects its planet. No other satellite can raise the powerful tides or provide the periodic night time illumination, two effects that have left their mark on all terrestrial life.

In the long centuries it has been studied, no one has ever explained with complete satisfaction how the Moon came to be there. Dozens of theories have been put for-ward. Some have been flat-out bizarre, some have been compellingly satisfying—and some have even managed to be both. But astronomers, cosmologists and geologists have found the evidence to refute them all.

It should not be there. But it is.

So too in the affairs of politics. Had it been further away, harder to reach, or perhaps if it had been a smaller, less tempting prize, Earthlings would not have landed on it so soon, colonized it so soon, before law and precedent could catch up with a new reality.

Long before the Settlers landed in the asteroid belt, on Mars, on the moons of the gas-giants, the rules of the settlement game had been set down in an orderly, tidy way. It was simple to establish who owned what, or who had what rights. But it was far too late for the Moon. Even though no one knew who owned it, everyone landed on it. By the time the United Nations Lunar Administrative Council established—and enforced—its claim to the Moon and settled down to govern the satellite in the name of the people of Earth, the satellite was ungovernable. UNLAC quickly found it could do little more than restrict the chaos—in large part by restricting the people. It gave up any attempt at equitable government, and concentrated all efforts toward two goals: establishing order and retaining its own possession of the Moon.

But the Moon is no frontier anymore. UNLAC's repressions continue long after there is no need for it or them.

No one who lives on the Moon thinks UNLAC has any real reasons to exist anymore. Given the chance, the colonists could govern themselves. But the Conners don't get the chance.

Indeed, cosmologists on the Moon tell a joke about UNLAC, saying it is a lot like the Moon itself.

It should not be there. But it is.

Chapter Eleven

CENTRAL COLONY, THE MOON

Ben wasn't really ready for debarkation on the Moon. No one was, the first time. The transit from Earth in and of itself was straightforward enough. Launch from Kourou in French Guinea in a big horizontal launch passenger job, transfer to the cheapest berth on a strictly no-frills interorbit ship, then yet another transfer to a lander at the L-5 station. One set of airlocks and crash couches was much like another, and the key feature of all the rides (aside from the excitement of Earth launch) was boredom—a tradition of many years standing on long trips. There wasn't anything to see, either—portholes or viewscreens were too expensive to waste on economy class.

The landing itself should have been exciting—but all there was to show movement were occasional shifts in and out of zero-gravity and a few bumps and clumps and subdued roaring noises as the engines cut in and out.

Ben wasn't even sure they were down and landed until his ears popped. It took him a moment to realize that a hurried airlock operator must have thrown the hatch open even though the pressure wasn't quite equalized yet.

Ben later thought back on that first act upon arrival as a

perfect analogy for the way the whole Moon was run. A little sloppy, cut a little close, a little bit dangerous, a bit too impatient, a trifle too uncaring about pride or care in the job.

In any event, an open hatch was the cue for everyone around him to pull their luggage out from beneath their seats and shuffle toward the airlock door with the other hundred or so passengers. Ben stood up carefully, opened the luggage bin under his crash couch, pulled out his duffel bag, and followed Garrison.

They made their way out through the lock, and into a windowless accessway that must have docked itself to the lander almost before the engines had shut down. The accessway led toward a pressurized tunnel. The tunnel was square in cross-section and made out of some flexible grey material, barely stiffened enough to keep it from falling down. Ben noticed footprints on the walls and ceiling of the thing, as if they sometimes served as the floor, depending on where the ship landed. Apparently the tunnel was twisted and pointed into whatever direction and position was needed to dock with a ship and then pumped full of air. Pressurization served to rigidify the tunnel walls—giving the passengers something to breathe was almost incidental.

The whole tunnel wriggled with every step the passengers took. It led downward on a steep grade—far steeper than anyone could have walked without falling backwards on Earth. Even here, one or two people stumbled, but caught themselves before they fell. Ben followed Garrison down the tunnel. They crossed over a complicated articulated joint, and the floor suddenly stopped shaking around beneath their feet. The tunnel, which had been a straight down-ramp, suddenly turned into a broad, downward spiraling corridor, carved out of solid rock. It suddenly dawned on Ben that they must be underground already. He had arrived on—and in—the Moon without ever *seeing* it. His last view of the surface of the Moon had been from Earth—and now here he was *inside* this world.

The wide curving down-ramp abruptly decanted them out into a horizontal tunnel carved out of the raw, unhidden rock.

The tunnel was a cold, bare, unwelcoming place. Power cables and ventilation ducts leading back from the other end of the tunnel were simply bolted to the ceiling without any attempt to hide them. A sharp, chilling wind blew down the echoing tunnel and slapped their faces. *Welcome to the Moon,* Ben thought.

The tunnel had all the hospitable ambience of a mine shaft, with no attempt to smooth over or pretty up the reality. Bright lights were bolted to the ceiling at infrequent intervals, so the tunnel led off through alternate patches of glare and gloom, pools of light between half-lit islands of near-darkness. An elderly moving walkway clattered its way through the dust-hazed tunnel, the noise of its operation doubled and redoubled by the echoes. The walkway, leading from the lighted base of the ramp into the shadowy tunnel, looked more than a little decrepit.

"I thought you said this landing complex had been here for decades," Ben asked Garrison. "Why haven't they finished the tunnel yet?"

Garrison grinned. "Oh, it's finished all right. Been like this for years. It's just that UNLAC didn't see much point in making it beautiful when a lander's engines could go out too soon, crash right through the surface, and wreck the tunnel anyway. It's happened."

Garrison laughed, and Ben looked at him oddly. Being back on the Moon seemed to have done something to Garrison. He seemed more chipper, more self-assured than he had in a long time. There was a twinkle in his eye, and he seemed to be standing a bit straighter, as if he felt surer of where he was, who he was, what the rules were.

"Even the vibration caused by a normal lift or land can open a crack and vent a tunnel," Garrison went on. "So, since these tunnels are expendable—they make them cheap. There's a safety rule that no one is to be in a landing field tunnel when a ship is landing or lifting, just in case." Just then a low-pitched clamor rattled the passage, kicking up new clouds of dust. Garrison grinned evilly. "Obviously, they don't follow that rule to the letter."

Ben noticed that the passengers were about evenly divided into those who confidently stepped forward onto the moveway, and those who hung back, a little uncertain about where to go. Veterans and newcomers, obviously.

It was easy to see why the newies were uncertain. Ben hadn't seen a single sign telling you where the tunnel led, or where anything was. There was no guide or attendant pointing the way, no attempt to explain anything. Another subtle, subconscious message about exactly how little of a damn the Moon gave.

Ben had gotten a lot of warnings about the Moon from Garrison. The chief theme was not to try and fit it in as a variant of *American* culture. Many, perhaps even the majority of the colonists, were American or American-descended, and they had left their stamp on the place—but so had the Russians, the Europeans, the Indians, the Japanese, the Brazilians and the Settlement worlds. UNLAC was the law here—and, and Garrison warned, that meant that the place was run with a hodge-podge of rules and laws and contradictions inherited from every nation on Earth.

Ben shook his head, got onto the moving walkway and rode it without speaking further. Another rattling shiver ran through the tunnel, announcing a lift-off a bit too close, and Ben started to wonder about the incidence of claustrophobia on the Moon.

At the far end of the tunnel was a large airlock, capable of handling about thirty people at a time. They cycled through it without incident and stepped out into a large, crowded compartment, about a hundred meters from end to end, and about twenty meters across.

"Now stick close and we'll get through this mess fast," Garrison said. "And if we get separated, *stay put*. I'll find *you*. And for God's sake, don't *buy* anything. Not food, not supplies, not information. Things cost different here." He led Ben from the lock area, physically holding him down to keep Ben's Earth-acclimated muscles from literally throwing him through the ceiling. The ceilings in Customs Rights and Naturalization Zones were padded to protect Earthlubbers against just such hazards, but it would be embarrassing for Ben nonetheless. A few unescorted first-timers had already slammed themselves into the padding just behind them.

Garrison smiled to himself and made sure of his grip on Ben. Nice to be home, he thought, where he understood the rules.

He looked around the big, dismal chamber. CuRiNa Zone (as it was called under the unfortunate style of abbreviation the colonists used) was packed to the gills. The room was lit with a gloomy grey light, the air was close, hot, and stuffy. Dust motes swirled about, drawing the eye to the too-low ceiling. It was too warm and too noisy for comfort. CuRiNa was designed that way deliberately, of course. A lot of effort and imagination went into encouraging the hesitant to buy their air rights immediately. He looked up and searched for the warning he knew would be there.

YOU HAVE NO AIR RIGHTS
BEYOND THIS COMPARTMENT

the big sign warned in bright red letters.

FAILURE TO OBTAIN AIR AND RESIDENCY RIGHTS
WILL SUBJECT YOU TO POSSIBLE REVOCATION
OF BREATHING OR OTHER PRIVILEGES.

The claustrophobic room and the stuffy atmosphere, teamed up with the signs, was very good for sales. It was all a fraud, of course. The International Court at the Hague (granted ultimate appellate jurisdiction over the Lunar Colony in the Azores Treaty) had found years before that air production was self-financing through the photosynthesis of food production and as a surplus of various mining processes—and indeed the colonies were more likely to be subjected to oversupplies of oxygen as an unavoidable by-product of industry, rather than faced with a shortage. Further, it was found that there was no equitable way to assess charges for air. The Court therefore held that no person could be compelled to pay for air, or subjected to civil or criminal liability for failure to pay any such fee.

But this was the Moon, and what the rules *said* and how they were *interpreted* were two very different things.

True, the local entrepreneurs and revenue agents agreed, the Hague had held no one could be *compelled* to pay for air rights. But the law didn't say people couldn't be *invited* to do so of their own free will. The actual regulation requiring that the warning signs be posted and the rights brokers be present in all CuRiNa Zones were never specifically struck down by the Hague. So the CuRiNa Zone compartment stayed stuffy and claustrophobic and the brokers skinned the suckers. It was rackets like air sales, and not a derivation of the word "Colonist" that caused residents of the Moon to be called Conners. Everybody had an angle.

Garrison steered his friend past the throngs of frightened and nervous air buyers.

"Don't we have to buy—" Ben began anxiously.

"Nope. Air's on the house."

Ben looked back nervously. "Garrison, you *sure* that I'm safe without—"

Garrison smiled. "Relax. Faithful native guide here, remember?"

"I thought you born in Denver."

"Okay, semi-native. Hold up, this is the line we really want to be in."

Garrison stopped them in front of a smaller and more discreet sign labeled *Citizenship Rights*. There was no one ahead of them in line, unusual in such a large and crowded room. It occurred to Ben that the government was less eager to sell civil rights than air. A bored looking middle-aged woman in a baggy grey uniform smiled up at him. "Buying or selling?" she asked as she put down the paperback she had been reading.

"Buying, full package, if the official rate is right. And where are the independent brokers?"

"Oh, they're working the other airlock. They have a deal with CuRiNa to dump most of the tourists out that side where they can get at them all at one time."

"You on commission?" Garrison asked. Ben was having a harder and harder time following the conversation.

The rights broker seemed to understand what he meant. "No, some do-gooder higher-up shut that down. No civil servants to work on commission. Me, I'm not even hourly wage," she said in a tone of voice that suggested the fact was a sales point in her favor. "I bought up a straight salary job. Better pension deal that way. So I got no stake at all in the price—or in making you wait around. What currencies you in?"

"U.S. dollars or pounds sterling. In notes, no electronic transfers or scrip."

She nodded respectfully. "Go first class if you can afford it. We've get a lot of drachma and pesos at the moment. Both worth nothing, less ten percent exchange fee." She reached for clipboard. "You want to swing a full set, right? Good plan. Play it safe, that's what I do. Okay, the population quota just went up again, so it's a buyers market at the moment. The independents are buying at four hundred U.S., 60 sterling, selling at five hundred or 75. We're selling at five-twenty-five or 80, your choice."

"So we go to the independents?" Ben asked.

Garrison and the clerk grinned at each other. "No, Ben I think I'll spend the extra twenty-five on your rights card here and know it's genuine," Garrison said.

The clerk winked conspiratorially. "You might be making a mistake. Some of the forgeries look better than our stuff."

"It's a chance I'll take," Garrison said cheerfully as he handed her the money.

"Only one set?" the clerk asked as she counted out the money.

Garrison nodded toward Ben. "He's the newie. I kept my set when I went off-planet. Wanted to be sure of a place to come home to."

"Smart boy," the clerk said approvingly.

"Come back here and sit on the chair in front of the background curtain," the clerk told Ben. "We'll get you photographed, fingerprinted, and registered in no time," she said, scooping up the bills. "I even have some laminating plastic for you. Seal the card by hand for five bucks extra."

"Sold," Garrison said, throwing down another bill. This clerk might not be on commission, but there wasn't a soul on the Moon without a side angle. And it was never worth saving the few bucks to annoy a government clerk. She pulled a camera, the laminate, and some paperwork out of a drawer.

Ben looked at the banged-up camera and the other gear doubtfully. This didn't seem like the sleek sort of high-techery he was used to. Not like the government back home. Back there it was all robots and artificial intelligence for this sort of thing. This seemed awfully slipshod. "You do all this by hand?" he asked. "Why not an automatic photo ID booth to handle it?"

The clerk looked offended for a moment. Garrison grabbed Ben by the arm and pulled him close to whisper in his ear. "Don't *ever* say things like that here, kiddo. This is the Moon. People are *cheaper* than machines here. And they don't like to be reminded of it." Ben looked flustered and meekly stepped behind the desk. He sat down to have his picture taken.

Five minutes later they were on line for Sanitation and Quarantine, and Ben was studying his Lunar Citizenship ID. "Carry that if you feel like it," Garrison told him, "but don't worry about it or get paranoid if you lose it. The important thing is that you and your rights are on file in the police and civil computer banks."

"Great, so I'm an instant citizen. But what the hell does it mean?" Ben asked warily.

"I'll explain later," Garrison said.

On Earth, on Mars, on all the other worlds and habitats, they had different ideas about human rights. Governments might be more or less restrictive, or perhaps recognize differing sets of rights, but no one had ever seen rights as saleable commodities.

But this was the Moon. Rights, complete sets and discrete privileges, temporary rights packages, rights futures, options on freedom-of-the-press packages, jury trial rights, freedom from surveillance certificates, rights-based loan collateral and rights-purchase bond issues were bought, sold, leased, gambled, hocked, borrowed, stolen, placed in trust, inherited, sublet, repossessed and bartered just like anything else. Blue Cross/Blue Shield even offered group rates on rights packages.

It was no joke, no game. The UNLAC cops would never dare touch Ben without demonstrated cause once he held his due process rights. Without that rights card, he could quite legally be thrown in Tycho Penal if an UNLAC cop thought Ben was looking at him funny. Many a Tycho inmate had ended up there after "temporarily" selling his due process or trial rights when times were hard.

Garrison was in no mood to explain it all just then. His mind was already on the probes and needles and assembly line doctors of SaniQuar. Maybe it wasn't all *that* nice to be back.

NEW GODDARD STATION, EARTH ORBIT

Oh my God, this one's spotted me, Cathy thought in a panic.

Dr. Catherine Cleveland, traveling under false papers and false pretenses, stared pop-eyed at the customs clerk as he examined her phony passport. She imagined alarm buttons about to be pressed and guards about to appear as he carefully compared her face to the photograph. Sweat was beading up on her brow, and she could feel her nails digging into the palms of her hands. It was a very strange feeling to be a wanted criminal.

Suddenly, she was aware of the weight of the wedding ring on her finger. The ring was part of her false persona— but she wasn't used to it, it didn't fit quite right, it made her hand awkward. She didn't feel married. She didn't *look* the least bit married. Surely the customs man would notice. She swallowed hard and had the mad feeling that if anyone looked at her hand right *now*, they'd be able to tell she wasn't really married.

She forced herself to calm down. She had gotten through four ID checks already, she reminded herself—two at the spaceport, one upon boarding the shuttle craft, and one to board the space station. *Oughta be used to it by now,* she chided herself. She'd get through this checkpoint just as easily, Cathy promised herself.

She told herself, as she had at each other checkpoint, that if the customs officer was looking at the *photo*, and not the passport itself, or the bogus visa stamps and endorsements, she was probably all right. After all, the photo *was* of her. That part was genuine. If he had started holding the paper up to the light, or feeling the texture of the cover—then she would have problems.

She forced herself to smile at the clerk. After all, she was smiling in the photo, and she might as well resemble it as much as possible. On top of which, she knew she was pretty—and just at the moment, she wasn't going to worry about using her looks unfairly. Anything to get the hell out of here.

The clerk smiled back at her, and handed her the passport. "Have a nice trip, Mrs. Wilson," he said. Cathy managed to force out a strangled "Thank you" without her voice cracking and made her way down the access tunnel. She shouldn't have worried about the false papers, she told herself. After all, Ishida's people had proved they were experts at flawless simulations.

The access tunnel led from the outer rim of the station in toward the zero-gee section at the station's center. Almost as soon as Cathy entered it, it began to slope gently upward. The grade got steeper and steeper, but with each step Cathy was getting lighter and lighter. Finally, toward the end, walking was altogether impractical, and Cathy started using the handrails to haul herself along. At last she came to the liner's hatchway.

She still had trouble believing in what was happening. They had to hide out; that she could cope with. Given all the nasty publicity their forgery had gotten, it suited her just fine. But fleeing off-planet was just a trifle extreme.

She shoved herself through the hatch and into the *Dawn Treader*.

There was no one there to greet or direct her. Good. She could do with a few moments to herself.

Just inside the airlock was a large viewscreen, slaved toward an external camera looking down on the blue and white globe far below. *So long, Earth*, she thought to herself. She stared down at the lovely blue planet, missing it already. Running all the way to Mars was going a bit far, she thought—in more ways than one.

But Ishida had decreed Mars, and Ishida was in control. That much was clear, certain, and unarguable. It was his power, his influence, and above all, his money, that had shielded them all from the law so far. Cathy knew for certain that she would have been in jail long ago if she had been on her own. Of course, she reminded herself sourly, if she had been on her own to start with, she never would have broken the law in the first place. She would never have betrayed Garrison. She found herself wondering once again if that had been one of the goals of the video data fraud—to create a whole crew of people who had no choice but to stick by Ishida.

Too late for that. She had cooperated with Ishida, and now her fate was tied up with his. At least he had stuck by them, whatever his motives. He had put together the phony IDs. He had organized the careful travel plans, so that his entire team got onto this liner, each having arrived by a different route. He had purchased eight one-way tickets to Mars. Certainly no one else could have afforded to do *that*.

Still, it seemed extreme to run so far. More so when it was all so obviously planned long *before* the fraudulent broadcast was even made. Surely, a man of Ishida's resources could have hidden them all well enough on Earth. What possible reason could there be for taking them to Mars?

Cathy glanced up and noticed another passenger coming down the accessway toward her at a pretty fair clip. She drew herself in toward the wall (or was it called a bulkhead on a ship?) and let him pass. He was a big, smiling, round-shaped person, wearing a bright-blue suit and moving at an impressive clip for a man of his considerable size. She had never seen him before. He maneuvered himself through the hatch with great agility, smiled and said "excuse me" to Cathy, then grabbed at a stanchion and heaved himself down the passageway, obviously a man who knew exactly where he was going. Cathy noticed a slight scent of bay rum. Wishing to hell *she* knew where she was going, headed down the same corridor her new acquaintance had taken. She had to go find her cabin. *That*, at least, was a clear-cut, discernible goal.

Shiro Ishida checked his wristaid and allowed himself a small smile. The last of his team should be boarding by now. Legally, the ship was Martian territory. Even if the security forces aboard the station now realized who they were, it was too late. They had no right to board the ship. Not that any such thing was remotely likely to happen, but it was pleasant to mark the moment when even this last and small danger was passed. All had gone smoothly, each detail of his plan occurring precisely as expected.

By far the greatest danger had been in controlling his fellow fugitives in these past weeks, keeping them busy and off-balance enough that they would not have time to think through the next step for themselves.

But there were more of Ishida's people aboard than just the video techs. Quite a number more. The entire crew, Captain Broadmoor, even the ship itself, were Ishida's own. No need for cover stories now. Ishida glanced again at his wristaid, and then caught himself. To needlessly check it a second time in under a minute was a rare sign of nervousness for him. He must keep himself under the strictest control as well.

GOVERNMENT HOUSE, CENTRAL COLONY, THE MOON

Hillary Wu tossed another paper into the governor's in-box and noted the time. The governor was late for work, again. Just as well. That way, he'd have less time to do any harm. Of course, she thought, he rarely *needed* much time. *Or much brain,* she noted sourly, *if you consider the meager supply he had laid in.*

In point of fact, the lunar governor was not a very intelligent man. It didn't matter: there was no need for the governor to be smart. In fact, a certain dullness of wit was an absolute boon in the job.

After all, the lunar governor did not govern, and a person of greater wit than Neruda might be bothered by that fact. As she shuffled through the paperwork, Hillary imagined him, as she often did, as a sort of human rubber stamp, bouncing up and down to the tune played by the U.N. Lunar Administration Council, stamping his approval wherever they told him to land. And even UNLAC wasn't in ultimate charge. The Council took *its* orders directly from the major space powers back on Earth.

But, for the most part, it was UNLAC technocrats—on

Earth and on the Moon—who actually ran things. They had the manpower, they had the budget, they had the hardware and the political connections and the clout.

Even so, they needed a governor for all sorts of political and ceremonial purposes. Who else could preside at the ground-breaking ceremonies, swinging an old-fashioned pickax to chip out the first chuck of rock for a new tunnel—before the UNLAC tunneling machines tore into the rock for real?

Since UNLAC was the real government, the job of governor required a person capable of being a mere figurehead, that was clear. And, in Jose Neruda, they had just such a person in place; that was clear, too.

The trouble was, there was exactly one person on the Moon who *didn't* know the governor was a powerless puppet—and that was the man who looked back out from the mirror when the governor looked in.

Unfortunately, while the governor was powerless to *accomplish* anything positive or worthwhile on his own, he was perfectly capable of gumming up the works, causing endless trouble with just a wave of his hand. And when he was this late in the morning, it usually meant he had spent the morning fuming over some imagined crisis and all hell would break loose when he finally did come in. Hillary found herself glancing anxiously up at the elevator door again and again, waiting for his arrival.

As the governor's private aide, Hillary Wu saw her primary job as one of damage control. She had to spot the disasters Governor Neruda was about to cause and head them off—or at least mitigate them—before they had a chance to happen.

It was not very rewarding work. The best days were when nothing much happened—a frustrating idea of "best" for an ambitious and energetic woman like Hillary.

She was a short, middle-aged woman, wiry, thin and tense, with strong hands—far different from the slightly chunky, under-exercised person that the Moon's gentle gravity usually bred.

The elevator pinged in its understated way and its doors slid silently open to reveal Governor Jose Neruda in all his glory. Hillary took a quick, silent inventory of his appearance. His silver mane of hair was perfectly combed as usual, but his tie was knotted not merely tight, as usual, but so tight as to threaten breathing. (He was widely suspected of being the only person on the Moon who wore a tie in the first place.) His boutonniere this morning was an alarmingly red carnation, and both his fine patrician nose and elegant snow-white moustache were quivering with indignation. Hillary swore to herself. It was going to be a bad day. At a guess, and judging from the fact that he did not bark at Hillary demanding that this person or that be in his office in two minutes, at least no one in the department was to blame this time. Probably something in the news then. Hillary watched the news carefully, for the express purpose of keeping ahead of the curse on Neruda's crusades. Apparently, something had slipped past her. Neruda stalked past her desk and gestured brusquely for her to join him in his private office.

With a sigh that she hoped was philosophical, Hillary switched the phones to ring on her belt unit, scooped up her notepack and followed the governor into his inner sanctum. He was already seated at his desk, glowering irritably, when she came in. "Have you seen these, Wu?" he demanded, tossing a hardcopy of the morning news down on his desk.

Better tread carefully here, she reminded herself. No telling what it was that had infuriated him. "Well, yes sir, I did read the paper this morning. Was there something that particularly caught your attention?"

Neruda glared even more venomously at her. "Good God, am I the only one with any political awareness around here? There, in the middle of page five, the passenger lists. I've circled the ones that 'particularly caught my attention,'" he growled sarcastically.

Hillary Wu cursed silently to herself. Now he was taking to reading the daily in-and-out *passenger* lists from the spaceports. Lots of people checked them, watching for old friends returning—or for friends packing it in and giving up. The rights brokers watched them too, comparing incoming to outgoing as a key to gauging their rates. But the *governor* watching them for political reasons? Did this mean *she* would have to watch them from now on, try and keep one step ahead of him there as well? What was next? Graffiti on the bathroom walls? Good luck she'd have trying to monitor the things scribbled *there*.

She picked up the paper and looked at the names. "Garrison Morrow and Benjamin Moscowitz?" she asked. "I'm afraid those names don't mean much to me. Sir." She typed the names into her notepack to see what the government computers had.

The veins in Neruda's forehead began to throb menacingly. "These are the two who caused the unholy row against orbital mines back on Earth!" he shouted. "Do you have any *idea* how much of the Lunar economy is tied, directly or indirectly, to orbital mining activity?"

"Eighteen percent," Hillary promptly blurted out, immediately wishing she hadn't.

Neruda's face threatened to turn purple, but he forced himself to calm down and speak in normal tones. "If you are so conversant with our economic situation, then I suggest you learn more about the people who threaten it. This fool Morrow and his group caused riots with a video program that claimed there'd be an asteroid impact on Earth within ten years. All lies, of course but the *damage* they caused! Mining stocks have dropped. There could be layoffs here, on the Moon. And now they come strolling in *our* front door, as if they had done nothing, as if they were normal immigrants. I insist that we do something about it!"

Hillary's notepack had scrolled out information digests on both men by now. "Sir, I'm not entirely clear what *can* be done. As of yesterday, they are both fully rights-endowed lunar citizens, with no current criminal or civil violation records on file here or elsewhere."

"Weren't there charges brought for the false video?"

Hillary keyed up a cross-reference on the subject of the trial itself and skimmed the report that scrolled out of the hardcopy printer. "Nooo—not that I can see. The video we all saw, and we know about the riots, of course. But we don't have much information on the trial itself— our news monitoring program didn't skim more than a brief summary of the trial. All charges against them were thrown out for some reason. The video was released in the

United States, and that might explain it. They're pretty slack on that sort of thing in the States. And there was some sort of confusion about who controlled the final version of the show, apparently."

Neruda shook his head in disgust. "Well, maybe *they* can't deal with such irresponsible behavior back on Earth—but *I* don't intend to sit idly by and let that sort of person avoid punishment. Not while they're on my territory."

Hillary looked up in alarm. "Ah, sir, we *can't* punish them. They have full rights, and they haven't done anything. No charges pending. Sir."

Neruda's upper lip twitched slightly in an attempt at a smile. "I'm surprised at you, Wu. Surely you know there are other ways than the criminal law to deal with this sort of person. What do you think bureaucracies are for?"

Chapter Twelve

CENTRAL COLONY, THE MOON

With a vast sense of relief, Ben staggered to the door of room 232 of the Perimeter Hotel. A bit of juggling with the keycard, and then he slumped into the tiny cubicle, joggled the light switch on with his elbow, and dumped his luggage on the floor. It was amazing how *heavy* things could feel, even in this low gravity. His duffel bag had all the mass—and inertia—it had ever had, and it took a whole new set of muscles to control it and keep from falling over every time he changed direction carrying the thing. Even just walking *without* carrying things was tiring. It required energy to hold muscles *back* from their accustomed motions.

Ben looked around the compartment and sniffed. The air was musty, and a faint haze of dust sifted through the air. The ventilation system had just been turned on from the front desk as they came in, and hadn't had a chance to flush out the stale air yet. That first sniff of musty air probably also served to remind guests to keep their hotel account current unless they wanted the vents shut back off. *Welcome to the Moon*, Ben thought.

It was a bit of a reverse shock to step into such a sterile

room. Stepping out of CuRiNa and SaniQuar through the main hatchway into Central Colony had been startling enough. Out of the bureaucratic greyness and the dismal, musty air of the immigration section, they had stepped into the world of green, all polished shiny-bright in the gleaming clear light. The huge New Subbubble of Central Colony stretched out below them, an underground city that looked more like a forest. Plant life of all description grew everywhere, between the buildings, on the buildings, even on the walls of the subbubble itself. Huge mats of some dark green broad-leafed ivy climbed upward toward the blue-painted upper dome.

The air smelled of spring in the country, of the sharp tang of fresh-cut lawns mingled with a subdued and strangely pleasant mustiness of last year's cutting moldering in some mulch pile. There were flowerbeds everywhere, and the air of the artificial sky was alive with birds—and even, if Ben wasn't imagining things—with a few flying squirrels flitting past, performing acrobatics their ancestors had never dreamed of on Earth.

Ben learned his first important lesson about the colonists in that first moment. Perhaps because they lived in a dead world, they loved life, and living things, and delighted in making things grow.

Except, apparently, in their hotel rooms. This one was certainly institutionally grey and sterile. Ben found a handle marked *CHAIR* and pulled it down. A fairly comfortable-looking armchair clunked out of its niche and he flopped back into it gratefully.

Garrison grinned at him, pulled open a drawer that was set into the wall, and started unpacking his own duffel bag.

Ben looked about himself. "Is it my imagination, or is this the same robotel room we had in New Jersey?"

"Close enough so it doesn't matter," Garrison said cheerfully. "It's not much, but it's cheap and it'll hold the vacuum out until we get settled."

"So, what's the next step toward *that*?" Ben asked. "Maybe we should change our money into the local currency?"

Garrison looked at him a little strangely. "You *sure* you read up on the Moon? There *is* no local currency. People use the various Earthside and Settlement currencies, or else they barter."

Ben knit his brow in bafflement. "But how do you run an economy without having your own money? How do you know what anything is *worth*?"

"You don't, mostly, to answer both questions at once," Garrison said evenly. "Everyone here is an expert at exchange rates and currency values. Right now there's a shortage of U.S. and U.K. money up here, which is why I bought those currencies Earthside. Two years ago, it would have been Japanese yen and Czarist rubles."

"But why doesn't the local government print its own money?" Ben asked.

Garrison sighed with the patient resignation of someone who knew he was going to have to explain something many times before he was understood, or believed.

People compared the lunar economy—and lunar society —to baseball. Understanding either subject required such an intimate, gut-level familiarity with the rules and the players and the history that the understanding became reflexive, making explanations tricky. Who can explain why they know something out of reflex?

It was no easier on the other side of the coin. By the time someone had learned enough to *understand* an explanation of how the Moon—or baseball—worked, the explanation itself was superfluous.

But Garrison knew he would have to start at the beginning. "Because," he said slowly, "the real 'local' government is back in New York, at U.N. headquarters, and from their point of view, the Moon is just another U.N. operations site, no more needing or deserving of its own currency than a space station or an oil rig or the Antarctic research stations."

Ben shook his head. "I can see I'm going to have to get this in small doses. Okay, if we can't change our money, what do we do next?"

Garrison glanced at this wristaid, glad of the reprieve. "We bag some zees. It's getting late, local time. We might as well start getting acclimated to the time shift, get some rest and start tomorrow. Then I see about getting my old job at the lab back—and we see if they could use you as well. I bet they can. If there's one thing the Moon needs, it's geologists."

Genia Lumbroska scooted under the counter and popped up on the other side of the Perimeter Hotel's front desk. She unlocked the door to the main office, directly behind the desk, tossed her keys onto the counter, settled herself back on her high-backed swivel chair and sighed happily. Life was good and the morning was bright.

She spun around in the chair to look out the plate-glass window set into the far wall of the lobby. Every morning of her life she blessed the day she got talked into putting that window in. It was worth letting that skinny girl who did the job stay here free a month in exchange, just for the view from that window.

Outside it, the wide expanse of the New Subbubble stretched out below her. The new Subsurface Bubble was a massive lens-shaped hollow twenty kilometers in diameter, three kilometers high at the center, the highest point being a hundred meters below the surface of the Moon. Genia knew vaguely that it had been built by doming over a big crater and burying the dome but she never bothered that much with technical stuff. The main point was it made for a wonderful view of the green vistas below. Genia smiled proudly. The Perimeter Hotel, nestled right into the corner formed by the upper and lower faces of the hollow, might not be the fanciest place, but it certainly had one of the nicest views—from the rooms that had windows, that is.

Genia dug her cigarettes and lighter out of her handbag with the clink and clatter that followed all of her movements, thanks to the mountains of clashing costume jewelry bracelets and necklaces she wore. She lit up and dumped the cigs and lighter on the counter for later reference. She should really cut down, she told herself. Filthy habit, and too damned expensive on the Moon. Reopening the capacious bag, she removed her compact and checked out the situation, facewise.

Her rather heavy make-up job still was hiding her typical Lunar pallor; but hide it or not, the pallor was there. *Get under a sunlamp soon if you don't want rickets,* she warned herself. Sunlamps cost, but they were cheaper than doctors. She confirmed that her even heavier dye-and-perm beehive hairdo was still held rigidly in place with a judicious poke here and there. She blinked violently several times and nodded with satisfaction. Eyelashes firmly attached as well. Finding that all was to her satisfaction, she stuffed the compact back into her handbag. Her day had begun, and she was feeling right pleased with herself.

Genia was a sharp cookie when it came to turning a profit—that was why she bought a prime piece of cliffwall right next to the main transit point from the spaceport and put up a low-price hotel right there. She caught all the new fish who were feeling a bit strapped for cash—and after spending on spaceliner tickets, there were a lot of those. The Perimeter was spare, simple, clean, and priced right. Result: Genia made a nice piece of change on her guests, and she appreciated it. She liked to think she took care of them, returned their patronage with good service.

Most visitors to the Moon expected everything to be glowing cybernetics and smooth, impersonal efficiency, and maybe Genia could have put in an artificial intelligence system to run the front desk, hooked it up to maintenance remotes, and made the place into a real robotel—but *then* what would she do with her days?

And what kind of robot could not only track the currency fluxes, but judge the value of payment-in-kind, the quality of info-tips, or even state of the rumor and info-trade as a whole? Plenty of times a newie had given her an investment tip or a political rumor well worth the price of a room. Practically all the maintenance on the place was done by a loose network of itinerant laborers, drifters who traded everything from computer programming to cleaning the pool in exchange for a room and maybe a meal. What kind of robot could look all of *them* in the eye and decide which were the bad news crumbs, which were the nice boys and girls with itchy feet, or maybe just a little down on their luck? No, an AI setup couldn't do this job, Genia thought comfortably. Besides, she couldn't afford an AI system.

Anyway, what robot could *enjoy* the job? Meeting all the folks coming through, having a nice chat with a tourist over a map of Central Colony, telling them where to visit, what neighborhoods to stay out of, listening to them tell about far-off places. And she loved the nice little thrill she got whenever a guest got good news.

Like this morning. Those two nice young boys hadn't been here a whole day, and here through the mail chute came a letter for each of them—and to Genia's practiced eye, an official government check in each envelope! Genia debated with herself for a minute or two about walking down to 232, knocking on the door, and hand delivering the letters herself right this minute, but she thought better of it. In all probability she'd manage to embarrass them, catch them in their underwear or something. Besides, they'd have to pass the office on their way out—she could catch them then.

She switched on the hotplate and waited for it to heat up the water for her morning tea. The printer purred to life and kicked out a copy of the morning paper. She pulled it out and checked her horoscope, which only confirmed what she already knew this morning. Life was good.

Garrison and Ben felt much the same way when they got up that morning after a good night's rest—their best in some time. It was a pleasant sort of morning for Ben; he knew exactly what the marching orders were. A necessarily quick cleanup in the water-rationed shower, a quick spot of breakfast somewhere, and then it was on to Step One: find a public payphone so Garrison could contact the Lunar Mining Authority. He gave Garrison (who was far less of a morning person than Ben was) a quick poke to get him moving and then beat him into the shower. In short order they were both up and dressed. They made their way out into the lobby of the hotel.

"There's some mail for you two fellas!" a friendly voice shouted from the front desk. Ben turned to see the same cheerful gargoyle who had checked them in the night before, waving a pair of envelopes at them.

"Uh-oh," Garrison said, almost to himself. "What've you got for us, Mrs. Lumbroska?" You made sure to learn people's names fast on the Moon. And use them.

"Looks like a nice, friendly pair of government checks from what I can tell. Here you are, one each." She grinned at them, happy to be the bearer of good news.

Ben looked at the letter. Addressed to him, all right, from Government House. He fumbled with the envelope, unaccustomed to the reusable plastic ones used on the paper-short Moon. Even so, he still got his open before Garrison did. There was a check inside, all right, drawn for nine U.S. dollars against Riggs Bank (Luna). Along with it, a form letter.

Dear Dr. Moscowitz:

As per your request of yesterday, the UNLAC Bureau of Human Rights, Brokerage Office, has found a buyer for the right(s) held by you and listed below. This/these rights have been sold and your official citizenship files, stored in this office, adjusted to reflect this change. Your payment for this/these rights, less the standard ten percent seller's commission fee, deducted by this office, is enclosed.

RIGHT(S) SOLD:

Right to free choice of employment

Sale Price:	$10.00 U.S.
Payment to you (sale price less 10% seller's commission):	$9.00 U.S.

"Oh my God," Garrison moaned. "We've gotta move fast before this hits the databank."

"But what does it mean?" Ben demanded. "We didn't ask anyone to sell off these rights."

"No, but someone diddled the computer to make it look that way. So they sold our job rights, and now we're exposed to the labor draft. And you can bet for damn sure our numbers come up in the draft *fast*. If we're unemployed—or even just *under*employed when that happens—they can drop us in whatever damn jobs they want, and we're not allowed to quit for five years."

"Can't we just go down to the Rights Office and tell them it was a mistake?" Ben asked.

Garrison restrained himself. The guy was new around here. He wouldn't, *couldn't* understand. "There *wasn't* any mistake. They did this on purpose. Someone who wants to score points with the orbital mining crowd, probably. C'mon, we've gotta move fast. Never mind the phone, we gotta get straight to Ken Beasely's office and talk to him in person. Let's *move* it!"

Genia Lumbroska watched the two young men rush out, not even blaming them for leaving without a goodbye. You understand a person forgetting their manners at such a time, even such nice boys. *Someone* had it in for them to play a rotten trick like that. She shook her head—and noticed they had both dropped their empty envelopes. She came out from behind the counter and picked them up. She might as well collect the deposit on them before someone else did.

Ken Beasely was a nice guy. The head of the Lunar Mining Authority, he was in charge of finding better ways to manipulate and refine dirt and rock on the Moon. Earthside, that might not sound like a particularly vital function. But as virtually all Lunar habitations were underground, most of the intra-city transport was by tunnel, and the living rock itself was the only material natural resource the Moon had, it was a more important job than it sounded. Ken had always liked Garrison, had admired his work, had been proud to have him as an employee. Ken was a pudgy, soft-looking, dark-complexioned black man whose complexion nonetheless betrayed the inevitable sallowness that life on the Moon produced. His skin had not felt the sun in a long time. He was totally bald, and his bullet-shaped head gleamed in the overhead lights.

Ken took it as a high compliment that Garrison explained the situation frankly, rather than hemming and hawing about why they needed work *now*, immediately. But all that just made it more frustrating—because Ken couldn't help. "There's nothing," he said flatly. "No jobs at all. Absolutely nothing. The word came down this morning—budget freeze on scientific personnel throughout the government. No hiring until further notice. *I* get fired if I hire anyone."

"And I'll bet anything the freeze is off the minute we're drafted," Garrison muttered sourly.

Ben looked at Garrison oddly. "Come on, they wouldn't shut down a whole category of a planetary government's hiring system just to freeze us out."

Garrison shook his head. "Wrong again, Ben. It's a mighty small planet. Population is one and a half, maybe two million. Probably only five, ten thousand positions in the whole government to start with. Maybe four or five hundred government scientists. Maybe two percent of science jobs vacant at any one time. So they delay hiring on eight or ten existing jobs, tops—and also keep Ken here from inventing any new positions where he could use us. They could keep that freeze in place for a long, long time if they had to. And they *won't* have to. We'll be drafted pronto."

Ken nodded glumly. "The one thing I don't get is what you guys *did* to tee anyone off this much. There was just digging up the asteroid, and that video presentation, right? It didn't get much play up here."

"And we didn't even do the video," Ben muttered. "That was a friend of ours' idea of a joke."

"Great friend you've got there," Ken said ruefully. He reached up and stroked the top of his billiard-ball head with the palm of his hand—Garrison recognized it as a sign of Ken thinking hard. "I'm just trying to work this out," Ken said slowly. "I still can't see who'd bother doing this. You need someone who's got the pull, not just to place the freeze order—any flunky in personnel could do that and make it stick for a day or so. You're talking about someone who has enough power to lie to the government *rights* computers and make it stick. In theory, no one but *you* could register a request to sell rights—and you'd have to show plenty of ID to get it approved. Lots of safeguards to protect against just this sort of thing. So it's either a very good hacker, or else someone who knows how to lean on a very good hacker." Ken thought again for a minute, and his eyebrows shot up. "*And* you need someone stupid and petty enough to want to bother with a pair of small potatoes like you guys," he added, in a tone of voice that made his words the answer to the puzzle and not part of the question.

Garrison's eyes lit up. "Oh my God. The Governor."

"Who else?" Ken asked rhetorically. He pulled up a keyboard and rattled a few commands off. "Bingo. The freeze order shows origination in the Guv's office. Garrison, lemme see that notice-of-rights-sale." Garrison handed the paper over, and Ken compared it to the information on his computer screen. "This doesn't show an office of origination—but the time stamp is for two minutes after the freeze went through."

"But why would the Governor get that steamed?" Ben asked. "So we were mixed up in a mess on Earth. So what? I thought half the colonists on the Moon were some sort of exiles. So why does he bother?"

Ken chortled humorlessly. "Man, ask me a tough one. Neruda has his fingers in so many mining companies it's not even funny. Everyone in LuMiAu knows that. He's on about half a dozen orbital mining company boards—including the board of directors at your old friends, LuTech. Ain't that sweet?"

"What about conflict of interest? Aren't there laws against"—Ben noticed that Ken and Garrison were looking at each other with a certain world-weary expression he was beginning to recognize. "Okay, okay," he said. "I'm starting to get it. This is the Moon."

They left Ken's office and found a public data terminal at the Armstrong Library. Garrison started working the want ads—after checking with the government schedule listings and finding out there was a labor draft lottery the next day. They had maybe twenty-four hours.

They were caught between a rock and a hard place in a lot of ways. The Lunar economy was chronically short of low-end labor, and there were good odds that Ben and Garrison could find jobs working as tunnel-bore laborers or hydroponics maintenance workers immediately. But the labor draft could easily rule them to be *underemployed* in such a case. After all, they were highly trained scientists. What were they doing drilling tunnels? In such cases, the government could rule that their skills ought to be put to better use elsewhere. Therefore, scut jobs would be no protection against the draft and Garrison didn't even bother trying. They had to get real jobs that dealt with their profession—and *fast*. Since the government wasn't allowed to hire them, and since the government hired most of the scientists, there was a problem there.

Unfortunately, as Garrison rapidly discovered from the classified databases, the only other possible employers were the mining companies. Lucifer Technologies, for example, was not likely to hire them, whether or not LuTech had offered employment a few weeks ago.

But there were other mining outfits out there, and Garrison slogged through them all. For the whole morning, and half the afternoon he ground his way through the classifieds, making the calls, getting cut off, getting put on hold, being told "no." He called old friends and people who owed him favors—but it was all useless. Here and there were job slots that either Ben or Garrison might have filled—but the hiring process would take weeks, or even months, not hours.

There was nothing out there. That was becoming clear. In late afternoon, it became even more hopeless. The "sale" of their job rights began to hit the personnel computers at the businesses they called. Hiring them, once the employer was notified of selling the rights sale, was downright illegal. The government didn't like its draft labor pool diminished.

When six o'clock rolled around, there was really nothing

left to do but drag by the Riggs Bank office and cash the lousy nine-dollar checks. They slumped back to the Perimeter Hotel and said the hell with it for the day.

Ben lay awake that night, thinking hard. He turned and looked at his friend Garrison, trying once again to figure him out. Garrison had certainly demonstrated a skill for endless reckless, bullheaded stubborn determination back on Iceland. Once on the Moon, he had exhibited a cheerful zest for life that Ben had not expected. And yet, today, after the initial panic, Garrison had seemed to *accept* the whole situation with an odd sort of fatalism, something quite out of character for him. Maybe it was a sort of Lunar reflex the colonists developed. The Conners expected to be conned.

Deep down inside, Ben decided, Garrison had already reacquired the reflexes of a Conner, expressed so perfectly in that damned saying of theirs that explained *everything* that didn't make sense, every cockeyed screwup, every set of inexplicable rules no one could go against: "This is the Moon."

Ben whispered the phrase to himself in the gloomy darkness. He reached for his pants, hanging on a chair, and pulled out his wallet. Fumbling in the darkness, he extracted his citizenship rights cards. What kind of rights were these if the government could make them vanish at a whim, without appeal, without recourse? But there wasn't even any point in asking the question. "This is the Moon," Ben repeated. As if that explained it.

In his first full day here, Ben had certainly seen plenty of things no one should have to put up with, that no one *needed* to put up with. Things that easily *could* be changed—unless you had the mind-set that everything was inevitable.

He could understand, almost, that sacrifices might have to be made in a rough, pioneer society, in a fragile oasis threatened on all sides by the caprice of nature. Once, the Moon had been such a place. But Central Colony wasn't *like* that anymore. This was a comfortable, secure, even wealthy city. So why did the colonists put up with insults, privations, frauds that served no useful purpose? They could change things, if they really wanted to do so.

Maybe nothing changed because none of these fatalists made the effort to change them anymore. On the other hand, Ben wasn't much of a fatalist. How much harm could making the effort do?

"But this is the *Moon*," Ben protested to himself sarcastically. Garrison grunted in his sleep and pulled his pillow over his head.

Ben smiled to himself and went to sleep.

He hit Garrison with it the next morning over breakfast. "Listen," Ben told him. "You're the local expert, right? You know the Moon, how things work, what you can do, what you can't."

Garrison shrugged and poured himself some more tea. "So?"

"So we're screwed," Ben said baldly.

Garrison looked up sharply. "Hey, Ben, I'm sorry you're in the soup too—but it's not my fault. This is the—"

"Nine hundredth time I've heard that. I know, I know. I'm not blaming you, or saying we should have done different. All I'm suggesting is that you've done everything you could, and we're *still* screwed—how much worse can it get?"

"Not much. They can do whatever they want with us now. We don't have the money to leave again, and no place on Earth would have us anyway. Me, anyway. I renounced my old citizenship when I first came to the Moon. But you're still a U.S. citizen—they'd *have* to take you back. Is that your point? Look, if we pool our money, we might just have enough for *one* ticket back—"

"Forget it. LuTech could dust off those libel charges any time they want—and I think they might be able to buy a better lawyer than I could afford. Maybe they'd even make a down payment on a judge. Not for me. I'm not going back. My point is, the native-guide woodsy lore isn't getting us there—so we might as well go cause some trouble."

"What kind of trouble?" Garrison asked suspiciously.

"I say it's time we go fight City Hall. What have we got to lose?"

Garrison played with his teacup for a moment, wondering where the labor office would send the two of them. "Not much," he said. "Not much at all."

Hillary Wu pulled the door to the governor's office complex in Government House closed and locked it. Last out again tonight, just as she had been first in this morning. There were plenty of times she wondered who else gave a damn about the place. She tossed the keycard into her handbag and started to walk away, not paying much attention to the two men sitting in the lobby outside.

"Excuse me, Miss Wu?"

The quiet, perfectly civil voice startled her. She turned around slowly and carefully. Central Colony was full of weirdos. "Yes, what can I do for you?" she asked in what she hoped was a steady voice. There were two of them, grim-faced, rugged, heavy-bearded men. A big, tall, one, and a smaller redheaded one.

"You do work in the governor's office, don't you?" the redhead asked.

"Yes, yes I do," she said cautiously. These two looked familiar. "How did you know to ask for me?" she asked at random, stalling for time so she could think, remember who these two were.

"Ten bucks American to one of the lobby guards," the redhead answered carelessly. "We'd like to make an appointment with the governor," he went on.

In a sudden flash, she recognized them—and regained some of her panic. These were the two the governor had been so mad at. She recognized their faces from the files pictures. And now they were here to complain about having their lives ruined . . . "I'm afraid that's impossible," she blurted out, not knowing what to say. "The governor's schedule is quite full." She stopped suddenly. "It *is* you two, isn't it? Morrow and Musca—"

"Moscowitz," the redhead said. "So you know us. You were right, Garrison. It was the governor."

Hillary looked at the two of them, swallowed hard, and told herself there was not so much to fear. Not from people naive enough to think they'd get somewhere petitioning the governor. She tried to convince herself that they didn't look like psycho or claustra-freaked, and realized it was true. They appeared quite polite, perfectly sane. They just looked determined. Very determined.

She suddenly realized why she was still here listening instead of running, screaming for the guards. It wasn't because they looked nice. It was because she felt guilty about what she'd done to this pair. "*He* didn't do it," she said. "I did it." The two of them looked at each other, then at her, their faces startled and angry. *Oops*, Hillary thought. Wrong thing to say. "I *had* to do it," she went on quickly. "*He* wanted to sell off your right to due process and throw you in the Tycho Penal Farm. People don't usually survive to the end of their sentence in Tycho."

"So you dreamed up the right of free employment gag instead?" Moscowitz asked, now seeming a bit more looming and threatening. "Awfully kind of you."

Hillary looked from one to the other. "Listen, I can help you guys—but I can't talk here. Someone might see us. You go ahead and I'll meet you in the bar downstairs in five minutes."

"I'm afraid not," the big one, Morrow, said, speaking slowly and carefully. "We wait there five minutes, ten, twenty, then we come back up here to see what happened to you and you're gone—or there's a squad of security on the door and we get arrested for disturbing the peace and thrown in Tycho anyway. If you want to talk with us in the bar, we go together."

Damn it. Well, she couldn't blame them. *She* wouldn't trust anyone in their shoes. The hell with it. "Okay, we'll go down there right now," she said. She led the way downstairs.

Five minutes later they were seated in a rear booth of the bar, a tall pitcher of beer tea planted in the middle of the table. Hillary poured each of them a mugful.

There was something about the relaxed atmosphere of the bar and the ceremonies of hospitality that calmed her visitors a bit—as Hillary had known there would be.

"We pretty much have figured out what comes next," Garrison said, his voice a lot calmer than it had been.

"There was a labor lottery this morning. When the results are posted, our numbers will have come up, and that's it. We'll get stuck in whatever the nastiest gig the guv could think of is."

Hillary shook her head mournfully. "No, it's worse than that. The plan is a lot crueler: You didn't come up in the draft *this* time—you come up next month. In the meantime, you two can't get jobs, any jobs, and you're forced to spend all your money just to stay alive."

She hesitated and looked at each of them in turn, for a long moment. "Once you're tapped out, broke, depressed, all your options gone—then you get shipped out to Farside."

Chapter Thirteen

Garrison opened his mouth, shut it and opened it again. On the third try, he was able to get a word out. "*Farside?* That son of a bitch is shipping us out to *Farside?*"

"I didn't even know there was a permanent settlement there," Ben said.

"There barely is," Garrison told him sourly. "Last I heard, there was a small astronomy team there—visible, infrared, UV and radio. They're set down exactly smack in the middle of the Lunar Farside, as far as possible from Central Colony, so they've got the whole Moon to block out radio and light interference from Earth. By virtue of that fact, it's not exactly overcrowded there."

"There's also a small comm operation being set up there," Hillary mentioned. "Just getting underway, really."

"What the hell do you need a comm station for when there's no one there to talk to?" Garrison growled.

Hillary shook her head. "I really don't know all the details. Something about establishing an independent comm link between the Moon and the Settlements. Until we get that Farside link, we have to bounce Nearside's communications off Earth or Earth's comsats half the time, whenever a given planet or station is visible from Farside." She shrugged. "Politics."

"I don't get it," Garrison said. "Why do you route comm through Earth when the target is over *Farside?* And why not use comsats?"

"Because if *Farside* can see it, then it's eclipsed from *Nearside.* Think of Earth in the center of the Moon's orbit. Nearside is the inside always looking in toward Earth. Farside is outside, always looking away from Earth. We can't use communications satellites in Lunar orbit because there aren't any, for a number of reasons. Some of the possible orbits are too low to be over a given horizon for a usable length of time, or else they're already used by maneuvering spacecraft—and nobody wants a collision. Other orbits are too high to be stable. Earth's gravity cocks it up. Besides, the comsat wouldn't be stationary relative to the surface, and you'd need complicated tracking gear on the ground stations."

"What about the Libration points? Aren't they stable and stationary?" Garrison asked.

"Less stable and much fuller of rocks and debris than most people think. A comsat there would get swiss-cheesed in a month. Any of the problems could be solved if you wanted to spend a hell of a lot of money. Lunar comsats *could* be technically feasible—but they'd be a pain in the ass to operate and maintain. So we patch comm through the birds orbiting Earth. Sooner or later, the message gets where its going. But the Settlement worlds want something faster and more reliable for their relays, so they pressured the U.N. to build the Farside station, so as to make the Moon's communications independent of Earth."

"I'm surprised UNLAC let that one through," Garrison said. "They don't like the words 'Moon' and 'independent' to appear in the same sentence. Why should they deny themselves the chance to snoop on our phone calls, and the Settlers?"

Hillary smiled. "Probably they aren't much interested in what we say to the outer worlds. But my bet is that UNLAC got sold on the idea as an economy move. Save all that expensive relay work, avoid hanging expensive steerable comsats in messy unstable orbits around the Moon. A Farside station is cheaper."

Ben cleared his throat meaningfully. He was beginning

to notice how much Conners enjoyed talking politics and
hardware, any time, anywhere. "Look, just getting back to
the main point—are we definitely getting shipped out to
this Farside station place, or is that just a possibility?"

"Oh, it's definite. And it's a promotion, by the way,"
Hillary said sarcastically. "You," she said with a nod to
Garrison, "are to be the director, and you, Dr. Moscowitz,
the assistant director of the entire Farside Geologic Research Service. Also its first two—and only two—employees.
The salaries are pretty good—but what the hell will you
spend them on back there?"

"Why give us fancy job titles and good money if the idea
is to punish us for hurting the mining industry?" Ben
asked.

"Standard cover-your-ass stuff," Hillary said. "If two
highly skilled scientists were made janitors at minimum
wage, the labor draft board might notice it someday. They're
interested in getting the best possible use of the labor
pool. If you had ended up in the L-draft legitimately, you
can bet your boots you'd be assigned to work in your field.
And if you *were* made into janitors, you'd have proper
grounds for complaint to the board. As it is, on paper at
least, you won't have any grievance case at all. The record
will show you waived your employment rights—and there's
a forged record on file of your request for that rights sale.
It'll show you were unemployed—and that you were duly
assigned to jobs commensurate with your skills. What
right have you got to complain?"

"I suppose that we'll be required to pay our own way
there, too," Garrison said.

Hillary nodded. "Either cash up front, or by garnishee-
ing your pay for the full amount—plus interest—after the
fact."

"Wonderful," Garrison muttered. "And we can't afford a
rocket shuttle." He raised his beer glass to Ben in mock
salute. "See you on the SunWay, pal."

"What the hell's the SunWay?" Ben asked.

"A dirt trail to Farside. It's a long ride," Hillary said
absently.

"*That* is an understatement," Garrison corrected.

Ben shook his head. "Isn't there any way we could fight

this? Couldn't we hire a good sharp lawyer and sue somebody?"

Garrison shook his head "Not on the Moon. Lawyers are illegal."

Ben felt like his eyes were crossing and uncrossing. "How could *lawyers* be illegal?"

"Because they are," Garrison said wearily. Unspoken behind his words was the real explanation: *Because this is the Moon.* "Instead we have 'advocates,' and not many of them. They're licensed volunteers, and get paid a stipend—a small one—by the courts. Some *are* ex-lawyers from Earthside, but they aren't allowed to take a fee from a client. You *can't* hire your own counsel, that's the whole idea. When a case comes up, the court sees who's available from the pool of advocates and appoints one to the defense and another to the prosecution. The idea was to prevent the wealthy from buying justice, and to keep the legal system from getting overgrown. A nice little social experiment UNLAC could try out in its very own controlled laboratory here in Central Colony. But since the judge appoints *both* the advocates, and since all three judges on the Moon are appointed by the Governor . . ."

Ben drummed his fingers on the table and nodded. "Yeah, yeah, I get the picture." He took a careful sip of his beer and glanced at his watch. Thirty-seven hours. Thirty-seven hours he had been on the Moon, and here he was in a bar calmly talking about comsats and lawyers. He would much rather be screaming about being deported to some place worse than here. "Why are you telling us all this?" he asked Hillary abruptly. "Why cooperate in shafting us and then try and be helpful after the fact?"

"Because that's my job," Hillary said simply. "Or at least that's how I see my job." She looked at Garrison. "You've never seen the Governor, and *you* think he's a dangerous idiot. *I* see him every day. How do you think *I* feel? Every morning I go into that office and try to prevent as much damage as possible.

"The Governor was bound and determined to do *something* rotten to you. I did everything I could to make it not quite *so* rotten. Farside beats Tycho."

"Your tax dollars at work," Garrison said with a tired

smile. "Thank you, Miss Wu. C'mon, Ben, we'd better let her get on home." The two friends stood up and left, and Hillary Wu watched them as they left. Poor bastards. She took another swallow of beer and made a face. She suddenly had a very bad taste in her mouth, but the beer had nothing to do with it.

Garrison led the way back to the Perimeter Hotel in silence. Ben, still getting used to handling himself on the Moon, managed to keep up, if a bit awkwardly. Finally, he broke into his friend's thoughts. "So what are we going to do about this, Garrison?"

Garrison stopped and turned around. "Get ahead of the curve, I figure. We know where we're going to end up, right? Unless Wu was lying for some reason, of course, and I don't see the point of that. I believe her. So I say we head out to Farside *now*, while we can afford to eat and buy a ticket at the same time."

Ben nodded. "I was sort of thinking the same thing."

Garrison stopped and looked around him. They were on a lovely green pathway, halfway up the slope leading toward the hotel. The fragile buildings and pocket gardens of New Subbubble were laid out below them. Mist and cloud hid a part of the far wall and the blue-colored dome overhead was flecked with gold as the day simulator came around toward sunset. It was a beautiful place, whoever was in charge of it. Garrison stroked his beard thoughtfully. "There's not much holding us here," he said, "and I'd say the sooner we get out of here the better. I say we catch the next caravan heading out. Tomorrow at the latest."

"Hold it, just a second, though. I could do with a day or two here—"

"To rest up?"

Ben grinned. "No, to do some homework. Don't forget you're dealing with a nice Jewish boy here," he said sardonically. "You and I got kicked off Earth, now we're getting kicked off Nearside. Maybe this is all new to you, but I've got genetic experience in refugee work. There are ways to *handle* getting sent into exile. And I've got a few ideas."

"Like what?"

Ben grinned. "Like making a buck off it."

Garrison's mouth twitched into a reluctant smile—and suddenly he began laughing, right out loud, the laugh of someone who needed the emotional release. "Make a profit out of being deported *twice*? Kiddo, if you can pull *that* off, we'll make a Conner out of you yet."

Ben nodded enthusiastically. "So help me work it out. Start thinking." He gestured toward the city laid out below them. "Here we are in the New Subbubble of Central Colony, a shopper's paradise. So what are they likely to be short of on Farside?"

"Huh?" Garrison wrinkled his forehead. "What are you talking about?"

"Retail. I'm talking about selling retail on the frontier, like in the 1849 California gold rush where they paid five dollars for a fresh egg." Ben threw his arm around Garrison and they walked on. "Don't think of it as political persecution. Think of it as a classic market opportunity."

Garrison shrugged. "Okay, then the first thing to examine is shipping costs. Which means you'd better bone up on the SunWay."

"The SunWay?"

"The SunWay. Go look it up."

The Equatorial SunWay had an impressive name, and as written in the Armstrong library, it was a magnificent achievement. However, to a person actually *standing* on it, there wasn't that much—or even anything—to it. In places one might not notice it was there at all, if the surface in the area didn't take tread or wheel marks easily. Long-range plans called for a smooth, sleek-surfaced, four-lane highway to be built. That was all well and good, but at present the SunWay was not even paved. It was merely a trail, bulldozed smooth in a few places where rough terrain required it and high traffic volume justified it. Radio-locator transponders were set all along the roadway so that at least one would be in line of sight from the road at all times. Some were mounted on towers, others perched on crater walls. And that was about the limit of construction so far.

The SunWay threaded its way through the maria, through the highlands, through the crater fields, skirting round the higher-walled craters and other massive obstacles. One day tunnels would be bored clear through the craters' walls, considerably shortening the route—but for now, the money wasn't there to do the job—nor would the traffic density justify such a huge engineering project.

For that matter, the current traffic density didn't justify the *present* heroic engineering effort. Even the present SunWay, unpaved, bone-rattling, trail of tracks in the dust that it was, represented a visionary investment in the future. It was not the quality of the road that made the SunWay visionary, but the *scale* of the project.

For the SunWay girdled the globe, ran clear around the Moon from Central Colony to Farside Station and back, connecting with all the other permanent outposts as well, either by direct connection or by spur lines.

And no vehicle that drove on it need ever carry a power supply.

A solar roller could drive clear around the world without stopping to refuel or recharge—and that was what gave the SunWay its name. For it was intended for use by solar-powered vehicles. By maintaining an average speed of about twenty kilometers per hour, a vehicle could keep the Sun in view constantly as it traced its leisurely month-long journey across the Moon's sky. The trip from Central Colony to Farside Station took two long weeks—but it was cheap, reliable transport. You could carry bulk cargo and passengers clear around the world without expending a single molecule of expensive rocket propellant.

Unmanned solar-powered robotic vehicles, tracking off the radio transponders, could make the trip on their own, not once, not occasionally, but constantly, rolling on and on across the endless kilometers, circling the Moon every month, providing cheap but slow transport of mail, cargo—and passengers who couldn't afford anything better. It might be slow, and crude—but it linked a world together. By the very fact of its existence, it could make transport cheap enough to generate the traffic that would increase trade that would expand the whole economy to make the SunWay cost-effective. It was a dirt trail leading into the Moon's future.

And, at over fourteen thousand kilometers it was, needless to say, the longest single road—and the longest *one-way* road—in the Solar System.

Ben got very interested in the SunWay in the day after their talk with Hillary Wu, as part of his research into what would be their new home. He looked into the price of a roller ticket to Farside, and the price of accommodations at Farside, and the size of any trade goods they might want to carry—and came to some rather startling conclusions, conclusions he confirmed with a check in the public classified-ad database.

His next step was to dig his empty, crumpled-up duffel bag out of the top of the closet in their hotel room, open it, and turn it inside out. He grabbed onto the edge of the lining and pulled hard. It peeled away, and revealed something surprising. Between the lining and the canvas cover of the bag, dozens of small flat packets were neatly sewn into place. Ben got out his pocket knife and sat on the floor. Working carefully and methodically, Ben cut the packets out of the lining, one by one, stacking them on the floor as he went.

Garrison came in as Ben was working. "What're you doing?" he asked.

"Unpacking. And teaching you lesson one in how to be a refugee."

Garrison knelt down and picked up one of the packets. He opened a flap, looked inside, and let out a low whistle. In it were thirty U.S. one-thousand-dollar bills. "You've been holding out on me, son. Where did all this come from?"

"There was some family money, and I sold my house in Philadelphia while we were waiting to get berths to the Moon," he said with a studied lack of emotion. "What the hell, I'm not going back there again."

"Why the hell didn't you tell me you were carrying all this?" Garrison asked.

"I figured why have two of us nervous on the way through customs?"

"Why indeed. Though I could have told you there are no restrictions at all on importing currency up here. They love the stuff."

"Yeah, but there *are* a few rules about taking too much

out of the States. Besides, you've been doing a great job of keeping us alive on the cheap—you wouldn't have scrounged quite as hard if you'd known this was socked away."

Garrison laughed. "You're one sneaky dude, pal," he said, shaking his head. "So what are you going to do with it?"

"I'm going to spend part of it on a used solar roller."

"What?!" Garrison shouted. "What the hell do we want with a roller?"

"There's a cargo job in the ads today that I've got my eye on," Ben went on, paying no attention to Garrison. "It sounds like it could be just what we need."

"Just what we need for *what?*"

"First off, two round-trip tickets overland to Farside cost nearly a third of what a used roller costs. There's a glut on the market for some reason. Second, the prices for cargo shipment are even more ridiculous. Then I checked on the price of temporary accommodation out there at Farside. Insane. If we spent a month in a rented room out there then we'd have paid for the *other* two-thirds of the roller. But if we live in the roller until we find a permanent place to live, we'll save plenty."

"If the seals on the roller don't give out and vent our air," Garrison agreed. Something occurred to him. "Why did you check on the price of round-trip tickets, anyway? One-way is all we need."

"And round-trip is all they sell. The story is that it's a limited-resource area, whatever the hell that means, and they can't afford to clutter up the station's life-support system with poor slobs who spend their last buck getting out there and strand themselves. In real life, of course, they make more money selling return tickets. So I spend on a roller instead and they don't get any money at all."

Garrison held up the packet of money he had opened. "I take it some of this is going to go toward loading up that roller pretty good?"

"You've got it," Ben agreed. He pulled a notepad out of his pocket and flipped through his notes. "There's a population of about a thousand on Farside. There's lot of things they need—or want, but don't have. Brands of cigarettes they don't get. New varieties of flower and vegetable seeds for their gardens. Entertainment tapes. Spare parts kits for various machines they have out there. Datatapes and journals for the astronomers. Better test equipment for the comm workers. Toys for their kids. Books for everybody. Household gadgets."

"Hope there's room for us in that wagon with all that stuff," Garrison said. "But how did you get precise information about all this?"

"Mrs. Lumbroska at the front desk. She agreed to talk to some friends of hers who had been to Farside, buy the info from them wholesale and sell it to me retail."

"You're starting to get the hang of it," Garrison said approvingly.

"Thanks," Ben replied. "Does that mean I'm already a Conner, or do I still have a way to go yet?"

Garrison smiled. "You're getting there." He nudged the stack of money packets on the floor with one toe. "But I don't quite get it," he said. "You've probably got enough money here to keep yourself fat and happy for the next five years. And if Wu was telling the truth, we're going to be getting paid pretty well while we're out there, in the currency of our choice if they play by the rules. So why knock yourself out opening a general store?"

"I *could* live off this for a while—but what would I be doing in the meantime? And then, sooner or later, the money'd run out.

"Besides—*are* they going to play by the rules? So far they haven't. No one we've come across has. Not LuTech, not CRATER, not the Lunar government—hell's bells, even the Natural History Museum let us down. I figure I'd better take care of number one, because no one seems to be planning on doing the job."

Ben removed another packet of money from the duffel bag lining and went on. "And there's another reason, I guess. We're being sent where we can't do our right jobs. 'Assistant Chief of Geology for Farside,' my ass. According to Mrs. Lumbroska's people, there's not so much as a pick and shovel out there. No lab equipment, not even any available lab space. No computer support. I haven't been able to find *anything* worthwhile in Armstrong Library about Farside station's geology. As best I can tell, no one's ever even done a basic survey of the area. Which means we're going out there with no idea even of the questions to ask, let alone being able to get the answers. If you and I do want to do some research, we'll have to start from scratch. Completely.

"So if I can't be an effective geologist, I want to do *something* worthwhile. Do something so I don't go rock-happy staring out the window with nothing to do. I'm not just bringing in one cartload of goods and selling it off. I want to start a real business, with the capital and the equipment to sell to the people who want to buy. Make life a little more pleasant out there."

"Sounds like it makes sense," Garrison agreed. "If you need to hire a chief sales clerk, lemme know."

"I'll keep your resume on file," Ben said. "There's one thing that worries me—we're going to be nailed by the labor draft. What's to stop them from shutting me down? I mean, is there any law against setting up private enterprise?"

"There's all sorts of licensing stuff, so complicated no one can keep it straight. Don't worry about it. The big thing is to register with the sales tax crowd, and they're relatively honest. Then all you have to do is collect the sales tax properly, turn the money over to the government quickly, and you're all set. Whenever some government desk jockey comes after you for having violated some rule no one's ever heard of, just fill out all the forms he gives you, and make sure you overpay the fee by at least fifty percent. Do that, and everything will sail smoothly."

"But what about import laws and tariffs?" Ben asked. "Can I get in trouble for, I dunno, selling contraband?"

Garrison waved his hand deprecatingly. "No way. If the government banned smuggling and black marketeering, they'd lose half their tax base."

Ben nodded silently and went back to his work. He must be getting used to this place. Answers like that were beginning to make sense.

Chapter Fourteen

ABOARD THE *DAWN TREADER*

Shiro Ishida sat in the captain's cabin, a folder full of papers spread out before him. The *Dawn Treader* was at last under spin, and papers could safely be placed on a desk without fear of their floating away in the first breeze. Ishida disliked the inconvenience of zero-gee.

He examined the sheets of paper, each one a brief report on one of the people aboard the ship. Eighteen sheets of paper, eighteen people aboard, including the ship's crew. It was important to know, gauge, and appreciate the degree of each person's loyalty to him, as well as the causes, forms, and quality of that loyalty. All he had worked for would be lost it they failed to obey him. There was even a one-page report on Ishida himself. Like all the papers, he had prepared it himself. It served to remind him that he must also consider his own personality, his own strengths, weaknesses, dreams and fears as he plotted.

But that was mere formality, an effort at completeness. It was the others aboard he had to consider.

The *Dawn Treader's* crew he dismissed from his mind without a great deal of thought. They were simply employees, loyal not to him but to his pocketbook. Ishida had selected Captain Broadmoor because he was a nonentity. Likewise, the crew. He merely needed them, as he might need a hammer or a rice bowl. Like a hammer or a bowl, he would use them until they were no longer needed, and that would be an end to it. He would pay the crew, and there would be no further obligation between himself and them. Money would satisfy them, satisfy his commitment to them.

He should, he told himself, therefore have felt a complete indifference toward them—but their mercenary attitude distressed him. For this he chided himself. He had never wanted for anything in his life, had always had money and power in such abundance that they were unimportant to him, except as tools to greater ends. A thing was only valuable if it was rare—how would *he* feel about money if it was rare to *him*? After all, it was the chase after greater rewards that drove him on. Thus, in a broader scale, he was as mercenary as his crew. If he was equated with them, then surely they were worthy of his respect, balancing his displeasure at their love for mere money.

His feelings thus rebalanced into neutrality, he considered the other people aboard the ship. They could be divided into two further groups.

The first consisted of those bound to him by the laws they had all broken together—more accurately, the laws *they* had broken for *him*. They shared the camaraderie of fugitives. This he considered a far stronger link than money, but one that created a significant and potentially open-ended obligation for Ishida.

He had deceived them, in a real sense betrayed them, further complicating the bond, increasing the debt he owed them. Indeed, he had set out with the *intention* of manipulating them, betraying them—for the sole purpose of bonding them to each other and to himself. To do so had not been an honorable course of action. He consciously chose not to examine his emotions regarding those persons too deeply.

His feelings did not matter, he told himself, so long as he paid the debts he had incurred. Ishida paid all his debts. He would fulfill his obligations to these people, even if he did not allow himself to *acknowledge* the obligation.

But if they were outlaws because of him, they were also outlaws *with* him. That was the key point. That was the main purpose in involving them in crime. By setting the world against his followers, he had formed them into a cohesive group. He knew that if he treated them well, they would do anything for him.

Then there was one last group, the smallest. Only two people—but those two were here for no other reason than because they were well and truly *his*, Ishida's. Servants who were the children of his parents' servants, he had grown up with them. They had been his playfellows, his troops, his to care for and to be cared for by, all the days of his life. Trained by a lifetime of obedience, they would obey his every word with the selflessness that Westerners mistook for fanaticism.

But this group, too, he need not spend much thought on. They were utterly reliable, utterly known to him, their strengths and weaknesses as familiar to him as his own face in the mirror. *And yet, the mirror reverses all it sees,* he reminded himself. Human beings were capable of affording infinite surprise.

But nonetheless, it was the second group, those he had deliberately exposed to danger and legal jeopardy, that were the most unknowable to him, as well as the most important. The ones he betrayed were the ones whose situations demanded the best treatment from him. There was irony in that. He scowled, gathered up the papers, and closed the folder.

Shiro Ishida did not appreciate irony.

He pressed the intercom button on the desk. "Hoshiro, I would appreciate it if the ship's passengers and crew could be assembled in the common room. I have some words that might interest them." Having given the order, he sat and waited for a few minutes to allow the others to assemble, then stood up and made his way to the common room. He chose to arrive last.

They were all there, waiting for him, the lumpen Captain Broadmoor and two or three of his crew carrying notepads linked to the ship's instruments. They could monitor vital systems from here. Good. They would all be here to listen. His message would have been far less effective if some of them had received it second hand, or through the ship's intercom.

Ishida had given a great deal of thought to what he would say. He regretted that he was forced to speak in English. Although he was of course entirely fluent in English, he had always felt that the Western tongues did not have sufficient subtlety or poetry for a perfectly crafted speech. It was most important that he speak well, and precisely, for his words would mix truth and lies, he hoped in an artful and convincing fashion.

He walked to the front of the room. "Good afternoon to you all," he said. "I will now confirm something that many of you have suspected for some time—every person aboard this ship is here as part of a single team. We are here together to work against the dangers represented by Cornucopia. I have brought you all together for that purpose. I must also confirm that the work ahead will not be easily done, or completed quickly.

"Our efforts to engender bad publicity for Cornucopia were at least a partial success. Our revision of Dr. Morrow's report alarmed many people, and caused many others to feel for the first time an appropriate level of concern over this grave danger. We have thus educated millions of people. That is no small thing. I myself must take the blame for failures of judgment regarding the degree of adjustment made to the report, and the consequences to our party. Our benevolent fraud, intended only to alert the people of Earth, has been branded a criminal act. Fortunately, the laws of the state of New York and the United States cannot reach us here. We are safe.

"But we have set off on a journey into space for a far greater and better purpose than securing our own safety. Once again, many of you may have reached this conclusion as well, perhaps without surmising what that greater purpose was. For clear reasons of security, I have dared not reveal what our goal is. It is now my proud task to reveal to you the duty before us:

"We are bound not for Mars, but for deep space."

He paused, and looked about the room, his eyes gleaming. "We shall intercept the asteroid Cornucopia, board its control station—and divert it away from Earth, sending it back into the void from which it came!"

The room was deadly silent.

Cathy Cleveland swore silently to herself. A good idea, she told herself. A great idea. It could be done. Wonderful. *Then why don't I like it?* she demanded of herself.

But it was far too late to do anything but cooperate. She stared at Ishida, saw how his eyes gleamed, saw the enthusiastic expression on his normally inanimate face. She saw, in the set of his jaw, the flush of his cheeks, in a dozen microscopic hints, the passion of madness she had not been able to find when he ordered the video tampering.

So he was crazy, after all. It had just taken a while for the madness to reveal itself.

And this guy had decided to divert an asteroid.

Somehow, she was not surprised at Ishida's plan. And somehow, she knew he was lying.

CENTRAL COLONY, THE MOON

The hatch swung open and Ben hesitated on the threshold of the Central Colony thermal dome. He had never worn a pressure suit before, and it was a strange—and unnerving, experience.

He was standing in vacuum already. Intellectually he knew that, but there was no real hint from his senses that it was true. He was still inside, surrounded by walls and ceilings, protected. Stepping out into the vast unprotected expanse of the thermal dome was a big psychological step.

The dome was a pretty unnerving sight at that, Garrison had to admit. In point of fact it was nothing more than a medium-sized crater that had been domed over and left in vacuum—but its interior was vast. It probably represented the largest scale use to which nothing—that is, vacuum— had ever been put.

For many classes of machinery and material, vacuum is a superb storage medium. Machinery fares much better in airlessness than it does when exposed to the demons of air and water. Without exposure to the corrosive effects of oxygen, or the chemical reactions to other atmospheric gases, without air currents to carry invasive dust, without rust-promoting moisture attacking on every eddy of wind, machinery can last a very long time. Provided that such things as lubricated bearings are sealed, and that other elementary precautions are taken, spacecraft, rollers, tunnel borers and so on can be left for years, or even decades, in vacuum without the slightest deterioration.

But a wild, natural vacuum has its own demon that can wreck the works of humanity just as effectively as air and water: thermal shock. Temperatures on the lunar exterior ranged from a high of 100° centigrade down to minus 190°, and that range merely represented the surface temperature of the world itself. The bulk of the satellite itself served to moderate the extremes somewhat. Anything left on the surface could easily exceed either end of that range, as it both absorbed and radiated heat faster than the Moon itself could.

Heat makes things expand. Cold makes them contract. Different materials expand and contract at different rates. Without expensive engineering, even the simplest mechanism could be wrecked by the stresses induced by these differentials. Microelectronic circuitry could be wrecked by a contraction of even a few micromillimeters. Too-fast contraction and expansion could be most destructive. When, for example, a roller moved from light to darkness, a drop of two hundred degrees centigrade in a few seconds was not impossible.

Thermal locks were the solution. Every large settlement had one. All of them consisted of the same elements: a large covered area, left in vacuum and supplied with heatlights and a radiant cooling hookup designed to hold the temperature at a steady twenty centigrade. Special moderator chambers allowed for gentle gradual temperature-matching between the inside and outside.

Central Colony's thermal dome was just like every other thermal lock. Except that it was so damned big.

The New Subbubble was in fact somewhat larger than the thermal dome, but *its* vistas were of a painted blue sky, buildings, green living things that gave it scale. This place was dead, desolate, threatening, Ben thought, an airless artificial cave. The personnel entrance to the thermal dome was raised up on a platform a few meters off the floor of the dome, and Ben and Garrison were favored with a panoramic view of the chaos below. The interior of the old crater was littered with a weird assemblage of pressure igloos, storage dumps, and machinery, some of it abandoned and derelict, some of it very much in use, most of it quite unidentifiable to Ben's eye.

No effort had been made to pave over the floor of the crater or tidy up the surrounding cliff wall. The rough, boulder-strewn crater floor had been left alone. Smaller craters, from grapefruit-sized up to a hundred meters across, peppered the floor, but many of them were hidden from view by the bustling works of humanity.

Even though the dome was brightly lit, it was hard to see everything that was going on. The lighting was harsh and glaring, beating down from spotlights set into the dome above. All was glare and shadow, bright highlight and utter black gloom, with no place where the eye could find rest in gentler shades.

Rollers wheeled about in the distance along with anonymous men and women in pressure suits. Made tiny by distance, their movements made awkward by the bulky suits, they seemed like soulless automata, going about their business with an inhuman resolution of purpose. The whole interior flickered and glimmered as advertising signs flashed on and off, reflective surfaces moved and caught the overhead lights, welding torches blazed, and worklights moved about. Everything moved and flickered about in the disconcerting silence of vacuum, and the ceiling of the dome flickered and glowed as it reflected the light below. Even the raucous din this place would have had back on Earth would have been more welcoming, more reassuring and human than the unnatural silence. The place was a scuttling nightmare beehive of noiseless activity. It looked like some mechanical circle of hell that Dante had missed somehow, or the fields of Mordor made antiseptic.

Strange images for an oversized garage to inspire, Ben thought. He tried to calm himself. But the place was so damn *big*. Now, suddenly, he was ready to believe the strange idea that agoraphobia was just as prevalent as claustrophobia on the Moon. He had only spent a few days inside the safely enclosed spaces of Central Colony, and already here he was scared of open spaces. And this wasn't even the open surface of the Moon, just one mid-sized crater, roofed over to get out of the Sun. It didn't help matters to know there *was* vacuum out there, that one pinhole in his suit could kill him.

"Take it easy, Ben," Garrison told his friend over the intercom link. He could hear Ben's heavy breathing coming in over his own headphones.

"I'm okay," Ben said in a most unconvincing tone of voice. "I'm just not used to the idea of walking about in vacuum."

"These rental suits are safer than the Subbubble," Garrison reassured him in as soothing a voice as he could manage. "Everything in them is idiot-proofed, everything has a back-up system, they transmit complete telemetry back to the rental office constantly, they get a bonded inspection every time they come in, every time they go out. You're okay." Idiot-proof or not, the suits certainly *looked* idiotic. They were big, roly-poly things, all the edges rounded off, without any external attachments or controls at all. The air supply and other support equipment were hidden under a sort of hump across the shoulders of the suit. There was absolutely nothing the wearer could adjust or fiddle with. There were no hoses a panicky tourist could yank off in a fit of claustrophobia, and the helmets were nondetachable for the same reason. In fact the rental suits were deliberately designed so that it was impossible for a person to take one off without outside help. Garrison did not like the clumsy rental suits, but he trusted them. No one ever had injured anything but their pride by wearing one.

Garrison put his hand on Ben's shoulder and urged him to step out of the lock. Garrison was glad they had agreed to meet the roller salesman in the dome. It would give Ben a little time to get used to the suit. If they had met inside the city and gone out into the thermal dome together, the salesman would have seen Ben's initial nervousness. If this guy Yorg Reinhart was like most salesmen on the Moon, his carnivore's instinct would be intense enough *without* the chance of working on an intimidated customer. Ben wouldn't have a chance once Reinhart realized his customer was worried about whether he was going to keep breathing. Better to let Ben get used to the pressure suit in private and not expose the salesman to that sort of temptation.

The need for private lessons explained the intercom jack, too. The radio worked—but it was also publicly transmitted to the local horizon. A crafty salesman would be trying to listen in on their conversation as they walked to his office igloo—and all the salesmen on the Moon were crafty. Walking with the cable strung between them might be a trifle awkward—but it could save them a very pretty penny in the long run.

Reinhart might even try bribing the clerk at the Hertz office to get a repeater of the suit's telemetry. It could be very helpful to a used roller salesman if he could monitor his mark's heart rate and EEG . . .

Garrison wouldn't put that past the realm of possibility, but on the other hand there wasn't much they could do about it if the salesman *was* doing something like that. "C'mon," he said. "Let's not keep the man waiting."

Yorg Reinhart, along with many other roller brokers, had indeed given thought to buying customer telemetry from the suit rental people, but unfortunately the rental companies seemed to have hired only incorruptible people—quite an accomplishment in the vicinity of Central Colony. The incorruptible probably represented the smallest minority group on the satellite. Perhaps virgins were in shorter supply, though not by much.

No matter. But Reinhart's semi-legal video tap into the airlock cameras revealed another setback; these two were using a hard-wired intercom instead of radio. He couldn't listen in, but again no matter. He knew how to sell even without such help. He was in a selling mood today. Besides, the use of an intercom told Reinhart that Moscowitz's friend was no newie. That was a useful fact.

He stood up from his desk and reached on top of the filing cabinet for his helmet. Reinhart was in and out of pressure all day, and rarely bothered to remove his suit when he came inside. Too much bother to get back on. It saved time, but it cost him fortunes in dry cleaning. Nothing got gamier after a day or two than the inside of a pressure suit—and nothing cost more to clean, it seemed like. Still, it would never do to have customers passing out from odor every time he took his helmet off.

Reinhart fumbled his gloves on, stepped into the microlock and activated the air pump. Two minutes later he was out in the vacuum of the municipal thermal dome, watching his potential clients coming toward him from the direction of the main airlock, a kilometer away.

Nice location, he told himself, as he did every time he stepped outside. *Right smack in the middle of the dome.* He looked up at the flashing sign over his pressure igloo, just to make sure it was on.

REINHART ROLLERS
Best Prices Anywhere

Well, maybe not the *best* prices, he thought wolfishly, but certainly all the traffic will bear. And with that in mind, like any good wolf, he turned and watched his sheep, waiting for them to come to him.

Central Colony's thermal dome had long since evolved out of its original purpose as a storage area into a strange combination of an old-fashioned bazaar and a heavy industrial park. Pressure igloos dotted the landscape, repair yards worked on everything from surface scooters to spacecraft. All manner of hardware was being built, modified, repaired and sold. Ben and Garrison threaded their way through the haphazard collection of alleys and pathways, keeping their eye on Reinhart's huge sign as their only sure landmark. They passed a busy row of diners and more opulent restaurants, a massive tunnel-borer undergoing repair, and a line of wrecked machinery waiting to be scrapped and melted down.

They turned a corner and found themselves on Reinhart's back lot. Forty or fifty rollers, some nearly new, some of twenty-year-old design, were parked in neat rows.

"Hello!" A voice shouted in their ears as soon as they came around the corner. A portly figure in a rumpled pressure suit waved to them from the far end of the lot.

"Greetings, Dr. Moscowitz, Dr. Garrison! I am Reinhart!"
The salesman bounded up to them, covering the ground in
a series of rapid kangaroo hops.

"Ah, Garrison is my *first* name—" Garrison began, but
Reinhart was already into a rapid-fire sales pitch.

"Now, Dr. Moscowitz," he began while a meter off the
ground, "you said you had interest in cargo rollers. Now
let me tell you—" Reinhart paused half a moment to
concentrate on his landing. Ben had to backpedal a bit to
avoid being landed on. "Ummph! Pardon me. Let me tell
you you've come to the right place." Reinhart was close
enough to peer inside Ben's helmet, get a good look at his
face.

What he saw gladdened his heart. This was a newie
among newies, probably never been in vacuum before.

This one, Reinhart told himself, he could sell *anything*.

Chapter Fifteen

ABOARD THE *DAWN TREADER*

Cathy stared gloomily at the computer screen. The simulation was running again, in compressed time. The screen showed the arrangement of Cornucopia, the *Dawn Treader*, and the inner planets as they would be positioned over the next two years, until the *Treader*'s encounter with the asteroid a few million kilometers out from Earth. Already it all seemed dreary and dull, and they had barely been underway two weeks. And still two years to go. If the *Dawn Treader* had been a more modern constant-boost ship, they could have cut the travel time to a few weeks.

But a fast ship would not have worked into Ishida's plans. For one thing, a constant-boost ship was dead easy to track. Had they used one for a direct approach, the artificial intelligence system that ran the computerized space track network would have nailed them at once. The net would have spotted the fusion flame of a constant-boost ship, burning bright in the sky week after week. The AI system would have projected the orbit forward to its intercept with the asteroid, and immediately have alerted LuTech. No, only an old ballistic tub like the *Dawn Treader* could sneak up—and only by going slowly.

The whole point was to overtake Cornucopia fairly close into Earth, but before LuTech's crew was scheduled to go aboard. That required they arrive, preferably from an unexpected direction no one would be watching, and do so within a fairly thin slice of time. That moment was two years away.

All of which meant they had to stall for time, literally enough time to get lost. Out in the asteroids, no one tracked ships as relentlessly as the traffic controllers of the Inner system did.

Therefore: a slow ship. Ishida had worked it all out.

The *Dawn Treader*'s official flight plan called for her to boost for Ceres in the asteroid belt after departing Mars, and the real mission would resemble that flight closely enough. They actually would boost directly toward Mars, but then shift course to intercept Cornucopia. A two year journey.

If only they could have taken a faster ship . . . But even as it was, by the time they reached Cornucopia, they were going to be overdue at Mars by a few weeks. That would be long enough even for the Martians to notice, long enough to get people worried, get searches started. If they had taken a fast ship and been *years* overdue, that would be time enough for someone to find them.

Two years. There was no way out. She was stuck with the *Dawn Treader* for two years. She would take cold sleep for most of it, but even so.

Two years with the near-certifiable Shiro Ishida in command, two years with a fanatic running her life. *But it will be worth it*, she told herself again. *What's two years of my life compared to saving the Earth?* It bothered her that she was even asking that question.

Was she that shallow? Did she care so little about a whole world that such an exchange seemed unfair?

She had let the simulation run past the encounter maneuver again. She blinked and told herself to stop daydreaming. She hesitated with her fingers over the keyboard, then drew her hands away and sat, staring into space once again.

No, she told herself. *It wasn't the two years.* She reached out and started typing in commands.

It wasn't the two years. They didn't matter at all. It was the growing certainty, in the core of her soul, that Shiro Ishida wasn't the least bit interested in saving the Earth.

THE SUNWAY, OCEANUS PROCELLARUM SECTOR, THE MOON

The right front wheel found itself another craterlet and dove down into it with its usual enthusiasm. The weird, slow motion crash lifted Garrison and Ben inexorably up out of their seats. The Moon's weak gravity made even a violent impact into a drawn-out spectacle that moved at a leisurely dream-speed. The two of them hung in midair for a moment, held in place only by their seat belts. Then the overworked shock absorbers bottomed out and sprang back upward, slamming the two men back into their seats in a spine-rattling bounce that lifted the whole right side of the roller clear of the ground for a moment. The right front wheel spun free half a meter off the ground before it landed and got some traction again.

Ben grabbed the manual steering wheel in a cold sweat as the entire roller protested the violence done to it in a cacophony of squeals and clunks far above the usual background level of noise.

The rear of the roller, overpacked with cargo, rode even lower on its shocks than the front did, but the auto pilot was able to swerve the rear wheels out of the way of the crater. The hard swerve to the left set off its own series of clunks and bumps as the cargo rearranged itself against the restraint webbing.

Garrison, sleeping in his fully-reclined crash couch, opened a bleary eye, muttered to himself, and tried to roll over on his side—difficult to do while wearing both a seat and chest belt. Garrison was blessed with the gift of deep sleep, however. He didn't really wake up all the way and in a moment he was snoring again.

Ben peered at his friend through the double-thick gloom of the dimly lit cabin as seen through sunglasses. Lucky bastard. When it was *his* sleep shift, Ben woke at every twitch of the roller. Ben swore to himself and started resetting switches and knobs for the dozenth time that morning. That last little dance of the wheels had convinced Ben to set the steering to dodge smaller obstacles. Of course, that would put a lot more zigging and zagging into their travel, and Ben was susceptible to motion sickness. Too bad. He'd rather lose lunch than a drive wheel.

Even with the auto pilot reset, Ben continued to hover over the manual overrides. He was ready to shut down the self-steering gear altogether by this time. The "autonomous" guidance robot aboard the *Rock & Roll* required so much supervision, so many operator overrides and adjustments that he was almost as much in moment-to-moment control of the vehicle as if he was driving it manually. If the terrain got much worse—and it would—then they'd *have* to drive by hand.

And that possibility was starting to scare Ben. They *couldn't* drive this thing manually. Not nonstop, all the way around to the Farside of the Moon. It was tough enough just trading shifts back and forth to monitor the autopilot. Four hours on, four hours off—they *might* be able to keep that up for the full two weeks of the transit if the on-duty man was simply watching the dials—but not if they were actually *driving* this bolt bucket.

Their eyes would give out, for one thing. Even with glare filters on the ports and sunglasses on the driver it was tough. The harsh, unsoftened light of daytime on the Moon, the ink-black shadows alongside the dazzling brightness of the sunlit patches, gave Ben spots before his eyes that didn't quit for an hour after his shift ended. And that was while operating in the automatic mode, where he could dare to take his eyes from the road for a few moments. It strained his eyes to the limit when he tried to peer into the shadows.

Unfortunately, it was the shadows that he *needed* to look at. He was getting better at it, but he still couldn't read this kind of landscape well enough to tell a minor beshadowed dip in the road from a yawning pit ready to rip a wheel off. The *R&R* had two powerful steerable headlights right over the forward viewports, but by the time Ben could get the beams aimed at a black spot that got him nervous, the roller was already on top of the point in question.

Ben had thought at first that he could stay out of trouble

by following everyone else's tracks, but that was no good either. There were too many tracks, wandering all over the place. Too damn many cowboys had gone ripping over the course, and on vehicles that were obviously a lot sportier than this one—judging by the tread marks over boulders, through craters, and into the deepest crevices. Crazier drivers, too, by the number of abandoned wrecks he had seen. Ben had counted four so far since leaving Central Colony.

Ben glanced up at the Traffic Status Reporter, a fairly crude device in spite of its rather grand name. All it did was report the number and identity of vehicles between each pair of transponders on the road for fifty klicks ahead of and behind your position. That could be important information if your own roller went down—the ID numbers displayed on the reporter represented your only potential rescuers. Traffic was spread pretty thin, as best Ben could tell. Not more than ten or twelve vehicles reporting for the whole hundred-kilometer stretch. Given his current level of faith in the *Rock & Roll*, Ben would have liked more company.

The *Rock & Roll* ran into another patch of uneven ground and started swaying drunkenly back and forth. They had christened her that because she was a roller carrying geologists, but the name was taking on a second, more accurate, and less welcome meaning. Ben was getting all too good at imagining a roll-over.

The *R&R* was basically a big cylinder laid on its side and bolted to a drive chassis. A large array of steerable solar cells was attached to the roof of the cylinder. The array rack was far larger than the pressure cylinder, and hung over its sides and ends. That not only made it a more effective sunshield, it allowed for a larger array.

The trouble was that the array, and the complex of struts and supports that held it, were relatively fragile. If the *R&R* tipped over, the pressure cylinder would probably hold. But the array would be smashed to bits, and the drive chassis and the pressure cylinder would be exposed to the full glare of the Sun. They'd lose power to the charge/storage coils and the cooling system and cook within hours. . . .

Just as he was reaching that happy thought, Ben spotted another wreck by the side of the trail, an older-model roller that had smashed face-on into a craterwall. A rockslide had dropped on top of it. The wreck sat there, gleaming white in the perfect sunlight of a lunar vacuum, its paintwork pristine and perfect, though it might be twenty years since the crash. Up here, disaster didn't have the decency to rust away and disappear after a few years. Every wreck he had seen looked like that, as if it had happened ten minutes before.

Ben shivered involuntarily and checked the Traffic Status Reporter again.

The *R&R* hit one more chuckhole and then came around a curve into a wide, flat plain. Ben gave a sigh of relief and relaxed. Smooth sailing. For a while.

Garrison shifted in his sleep, grunted, woke, trying to sit up. The chest belt frustrated his efforts for a while, until he remembered where he was and what was going on. It took a few half-awake gymnastics, but he got the belt undone and found the release for the chair recliner. There was something not quite right in the chair's mechanism—a fact that Garrison once again remembered just barely too late. The chair snapped from reclined to full upright in a split second, throwing Garrison forward like a jack-in-the-box. "Yah!" he cried out, and managed to throw his arms up in time to keep from getting pasted into the right-side control panel.

Ben grinned without taking his eye off the road, his sunglasses giving him a rakish air of nonchalance. "Good morning," he said.

"Don't jump to conclusions," Garrison muttered as he untangled his lap belt and climbed out of his chair. Bracing himself with the handrails set into the walls and ceiling of the passenger compartment, he staggered back toward the head to get cleaned up. Five minutes later he came forward with two zero-gee drinking bulbs full of hideously expensive instant coffee. No one in a bouncing roller ever tried drinking something hot from an uncovered cup. At least, not more than once. Garrison handed one bulb to Ben and sat back down in the right-hand seat, careful to strap himself in before he got comfortable. "So how goes the trip, *mon* brave *capitan?*"

"Your brave *capitan* has got the royal screaming meemies. Driving along all by his lonesome with nothing to look at but rocks, craters, and the occasional abandoned wreck is tough on his nerves."

"We're hanging in there," Garrison said. "Still in one piece."

"So far," Ben admitted. "But I'm wondering if Reinhart gave us a good deal on this thing"—he patted the *R&R*'s bulkhead—"or just a good price. She's got lots of personality, to put it politely."

"You got a good deal. She's a nice old tub," Garrison said with a bit more confidence than he felt. He took a big swig of coffee and sat up in his chair. "Time to change shifts, friend. Switch the controls to this side." Ben flipped the switches. Garrison's side of the panel lit up and he looked over his board. He was checking over the last set of readouts when his eyes nearly bugged out of his head. "Jesus, Ben! Haven't you been watching the local suntime?"

"Huh?"

"Look at the indicator! We're underdriving like crazy! We fell a full hour behind the Sun on that last shift."

"My God," Ben said. The *Rock & Roll* was solar powered, and while her storage rings could hold enough power to keep her wheels turning for twelve hours of darkness, she had to keep the Sun in sight if she wanted to keep moving for long. Ben and Garrison had started their trek from Central Colony at local "noon," heading west with the Sun directly overhead. The idea was to pace the Sun exactly as it tracked across the Moon's sky from east to west over the course of the month-long lunar "day."

The technique was called the constant-drive strategy. You were supposed to drive just fast enough to keep the Sun in the same place in the sky all the time, bearing in mind that it was better to go too fast rather than too slow.

If they had gone too fast, overdriving the Sun, it would have sunk lower toward the eastern horizon behind them. In theory, a roller at top speed could overdrive its way clear out of the sunlight, past the terminator into the lunar night, creating a false sunset in the east behind them as they headed toward the west. That wouldn't be too serious—

all that was needed in such a case was to park and live off the batteries until the Sun caught up behind them.

But the *R&R* was *under*driving, not overdriving, letting the Sun get *ahead*. The sun was threatening to set for real, ahead of them in the west. And if it set there, it would be no minor inconvenience of a few hours. The Sun would be gone for two weeks—and by then, no one aboard the *R&R* would be alive to view the dawn.

So far, things were far from being that grim—but if they got that bad, there would be almost no chance of rescue. Not this far from a major settlement. The closer to the sunset line a roller got, the fewer vehicles there were on the road—for only desperate people would dare start a solar-powered journey across the Moon when the Sun about to set. There would be no place to run, either. Out here, settlements were hundreds or thousands of kilometers apart.

Garrison considered their situation. They had been falling behind the Sun since they had left Central, two days before. Solar roller drivers judged their position by the amount of Sun ahead of and behind their positions. The *R&R* had started out with seven days of light ahead and seven behind. Now they were at eight ahead and six behind. In other words, if the *Rock & Roll* stopped right where it was, in six days the sunset would catch them.

Clearly, they were in no immediate danger at the moment, but just as clearly they were headed for trouble. It had only taken them two days to fall a full day behind. If they continued at that rate, they'd run out of sunlight halfway to Farside.

The obvious thing to do was speed up—but it wasn't that simple. The *R&R* was a somewhat elderly machine, and one that had been sitting on a backlot for some time. Whatever the virtues of vacuum storage, she probably was not all that well-kept a machine. Both Ben and Garrison had been nervous about running her at high speeds. But now they had no choice.

There was another factor, once which Garrison didn't want to bring up. All the falling behind had happened on Ben's shift. He was being too slow, too cautious. And caution could kill them out here. It was up to Garrison to do something to increase the pace, if they were going to survive.

"We can't afford to get any further behind the Sun," Garrison said. "I say we've got to crank her up to forty kilometers an hour, minimum."

"No way the autopilot can handle that, even if the roller itself could," Ben protested. "Maybe the autopilot sensors are in bad shape or something, but the 'pilot can't even control us at *twenty* klicks an hour."

"Then we've got to shut it off and drive this thing ourselves," Garrison said grimly. "Otherwise they'll have to defrost us after they find us." Garrison looked at Ben's stunned expression and shrugged. "Listen, Ben, this has been the *easy* part of the trip, nothing but nice flat maria. Once we get past Earthrise Station it's craterfields all the way—we'll slow down to a crawl getting through that stuff. We have to sprint ahead *now*, while we have the chance."

"Garrison, we're only two days out, we're both punch-drunk already from too little sleep—and we haven't even been doing the driving!" Ben was not happy.

"Better punch-drunk than dead," Garrison said. "From here on in it's sprint-and-stop. We drive until we drop, stop and rest, and then drive hard again until we drop again. What else can we do?" Garrison waited a long moment for an answer, but Ben said nothing. At last Garrison pulled on his own sunglasses, cut out the autopilot, took the controls, and gunned the *R&R* up to forty.

Ben stared at Garrison in silence as he got the *R&R* up to speed. At last he unstrapped himself, stood up, took off his sunglasses and headed aft to freshen up and get some food.

Garrison sighed. The trouble was simple, really. Ben was still thinking like a city boy, and this was the frontier. Out here, you were on your own. Ben had yet to accept that fact emotionally. He was still thinking as if he was back home, assuming that everything was always safe, as if there were cops or rescue squads to call if you got in over your head, that safety engineers had smoothed out every divot in the pavement and made sure the road was safe. He was still assuming that you could call for help and actually get it.

On Earth, you could afford mistakes. The society, the culture, even the planet itself would take care of you, or at least let you live through a misstep. The cost of failure was low, and disaster was getting a stain on your suit.

Ben hadn't adjusted to local conditions, even after all the wrecks they had passed. Up here, the only question was how Nature would try to kill you if she got a chance.

On Earth, Ben's cautious driving would have been sensible. Better to drive too slowly on an unfamiliar road then risk wrapping a fender around a tree. Better still, don't take the chance of driving yourself. The car's autopilot would do a better job, handle the car more safely and smoothly than any human driver could. Better to trust that everything would work.

Except, up here, the autopilots were dumber, and the road wasn't even there. Either you took some chances, or you died playing it safe. Sometimes you died anyway.

Everything was riskier up here. Taking a walk outside. On Earth you didn't die if you tore your clothes. Ben would have to realize things like that, deep in his gut, if he was going to survive.

Garrison didn't say anything to Ben about *why* they had fallen behind, or whose fault it was—but even the change in plans was a form of rubbing Ben's nose in it. Garrison shrugged. So maybe Ben felt insulted. Maybe he had learned something too. That was how you got educated on the Moon. You made mistakes, and were lucky enough to survive them. And you had to be smart enough to know that sooner or later your luck was going to run out.

Garrison knew damn well he couldn't *teach* Ben any of these things. It was attitudes, assumptions, point of view, stuff down deep in the gut. The poor bastard would have to learn it all for himself. Or die.

A big crater swung upon them from around the bend. Garrison cut the wheel hard and dodged it.

Garrison was a little surprised by Ben's fouling up. After all, Ben had done all right on the north coast of Iceland, and *that* had been no day at the beach. The difference, Garrison decided, was that on Iceland your body got some signals. The place *felt* harsh and uninviting. The wind and the cold and the weather gave you some stimulation, some warning of danger.

But this was the Moon, an air-conditioned frontier. Out-of-shape pioneers with pot bellies living their perfectly climate-controlled, technologically sophisticated lives—with death by vacuum or heat or cold or power failure or food-chain collapse or asphyxiation always lurking invisibly beneath the surface. They padded about their cities in their slippers without fear of stubbing a toe—while the Sun roasted the surface above them to better than boiling point. No wonder the Conners were all a little crazy, with *that* dichotomy floating around in their heads and their lives. It was a wonder anyone survived.

Garrison wished Ben good luck and kept on driving.

Forty kilometers an hour sounds ridiculously slow. Less than twenty-five miles an hour. Horses could run faster than that. The speed limit in sleepy New England villages was higher.

But after two more days in a bouncing, careening, over-loaded, overage solar roller rushing across the raw rocks and soil of the lunar maria, with the Sun shaping every shadow into unreadable darkness, with every lit surface glaringly, blindingly bright—it was a breakneck pace, a wild ride that seemed likely to crack the roller like an eggshell, letting the killing vacuum in.

Garrison remembered a strange essay he had run across in English lit, a million years ago, back in college. "The English Mail Coach," by Thomas De Quincey. It was a vivid, even lurid description of the thrill of wild, uncontrollable speed, riding a mail coach across the wilderness of early 19th-century England, escaping a fatal accident at speed by the slightest of margins.

Garrison still got a secret thrill, remembering the vivid description of impossible swiftness, the rumble of the hooves and the clatter of the harness rocketing through the night. It had seemed to Garrison the most compelling description of reckless, headlong speed possible—except that De Quincey's heart-stopping adventure through the rural English night had proceeded at a sedate thirteen miles an hour.

As a student, Garrison had felt almost cheated by that fact. De Quincey trying to sell a slow jog as a death-defying thrill-ride! Of course, De Quincey admitted to taking a dose of opium during the ride, and Garrison had long assumed that accounted for it.

Not anymore. Not now. Garrison was prepared to believe that anything faster than standing still could be scary. Forty klicks an hour was a nightmare. There was simply no time to think, no time to judge the next obstacle, before it was time to act on it.

To human eyes evolved for Earth, Lunar distance, size, and perspective were hard to judge. Many of the visual cues were missing or distorted. There was no air to soften the details of far-off objects. It was often hard to tell if things were small and close or large and far off. The Moon's diameter was a quarter that of Earth's, and so the horizon was correspondingly closer—but the horizon *looked* the same general size and shape of Earth's. The eye tended to judge items on the horizon as farther off than they were—until you realized how close—and big—they were. Craters, hills, boulders and gullies seemed to leap toward Garrison as he drove along.

Nor could you judge sizes by knowing what you were seeing. On Earth, an observer would know at least roughly how big most objects were by knowing what *kind* of objects they were, which in turn made it easier to judge relative size and distance. If a man and a house were the same apparent height, it was easy and automatic to know the man was closer and smaller, the house larger and farther away. But on the Moon, rocks, craters, gullies and ridges came in all sizes—and at even a moderate distance, each size of rock and crater exactly resembled all the others. In was often impossible to tell a one-meter crater a hundred meters away from a ten-meter crater a full kilometer away.

Meanwhile, the "road," such as it was, was worsening with every kilometer. The futher east they went, the less traveled the road became, as each small settlement siphoned off some of the traffic.

Finally the road trickled down to a trail and then all but vanished. In the more populated parts of the Moon, enough drivers had done the run enough times that their tracks at least formed a consensus as to a good path between the transponders. Hundreds of wheel marks gave at least some clues to the "best" route, laid out by the trial and error of every driver and autopilot who had gone before.

That hadn't happened out here yet. As Garrison threaded the *R&R* between the craters, he crossed and recrossed dozens of wheel marks that seem to wander back and forth across a swath of landscape at least two kilometers wide. Judging by the track marks, no one seemed to have used the same route twice.

There was nothing to track by but the transponder beacons—and a few of the transponders were out of commission. When that happened, it was time to rely on the roller's inertial tracker to guide them toward where the map said the beacon had been. It was always a relief to pick up the next working beacon after a malfunctioning one and know they were still on course.

The only other excitement was the Wrong-Way Charlies. Although the SunWay was officially a one-way east-to-west-only road, there was a certain amount of travel east to west, running between pairs of settlements that were reasonably close to each other. Garrison couldn't really blame the Charlies—who'd want to drive clear 'round the Moon when you only wanted to go a hundred klicks in the other direction? Even so, the sight of a solar roller suddenly popping up from behind a crater, heading straight for you, rooster-tailing a fountain of moondust from every wheel, bounding and plunging across the landscape where it wasn't supposed to be at all—well, it was unnerving.

He glanced up at the local suntime indicator. At least there was some good news in that department. They were gaining, slowly but surely, on the Sun. Even with the brief rest periods they were taking, they had gained back almost all the suntime they had lost. It was just a trifle past local "noon" at the moment. He checked his wristaid. Almost time for Ben to take over again. Maybe, Garrison thought, he was getting used to the pace. Here it was the end of his shift and he was merely exhausted, not brain damaged.

Maybe they were going to make it.

Chapter Sixteen

ABOARD THE *DAWN TREADER*

Cathy sat alone in her cabin, curled up on her unmade bunk, desperately alone. She longed to step out into the passageway, venture into the common areas, find someone, *anyone*, to talk to. But she couldn't bear the thought of stepping out that door, only to find someone else as wretchedly miserable as she was. That would be worse, far worse, than merely being alone with her guilt.

She sighed and rubbed her forehead. She felt like a Judas. Thanks in large part to her, Garrison's life, his work, his career had been wrecked. Wrecked without seeming to accomplish a damn thing. Endlessly, day after day, she tortured herself with that knowledge. She didn't know how to stop, and she didn't want to subject the rest of the ship's complement to her moods. And so she stayed alone.

It occurred to Cathy that every person aboard was spending more and more time alone, but she did not have the training to know she should have been frightened by that.

Had the *Treader* been what she was pretending to be, a normal passenger liner on a typical long-duration run, there would have been someone aboard trained to spot the

warning signs. Even a slow old tramp of a ballistic ship—
especially a slow ship—was supposed to have at least one
crew member with some training in psychology. A slow
ship, her crew and passengers isolated from the outside
universe for months or years at a time, was precisely the
sort of craft that was most in need of psychological
monitoring.

A psych officer would have been seriously alarmed by
the state of the *Treader*'s passengers and crew. A psych
officer would have instantly spotted cases of delayed-stress
shock, depression, separation anxiety, gradually increasing
tendencies for claustrophobia, and half a dozen other serious problems as well. All Cathy knew was that no one she
saw was happy.

God only knew how Shiro Ishida was handling the situation. He almost never ventured out into the common areas
of the ship, but remained in his cabin, tended to by his
servants. Cathy couldn't even begin to imagine how isolation would affect *him*.

The deathly silence was broken by a courteous knocking
at the door to her cabin. Cathy cringed inwardly. There
were very few people she could bear seeing at the moment. "Who is it?"

"It's Bradford Choate, Dr. Cleveland," said a deep bass
voice, in smooth, cultured tones. "Might I come in for a
moment?"

Cathy breathed a sigh of relief. Bradford was probably
the only person aboard she could deal with at the moment. "Yes, just a moment." She got up, made a half-
hearted effort to smooth over the blankets on the bunk,
looked in the mirror to pat her hair into place and un-
latched the door. "Come in, Mr. Choate."

Choate stepped through the door and smiled down at
Cathy. She caught a whiff of bay rum and smiled back.
The smell would always remind her of the first time she
had seen him, as he came hurtling through the hatchway
into the *Dawn Treader* like an oversized beach ball.

There was no question that he was heavyset, but in
zero-gee he had seemed plumper than he really was, and
Cathy had not realized how tall Choate was until the ship

was spun up, and they faced each other with their feet on the ground. He was big. At least two meters tall.

His height suited him, made his portly girth seem impressive rather than comic. There was nothing flabby or soft about him, none of the sort of weak, exhausted breathlessness of a man tired out by hauling around his own body. Instead, there was a sense of strength, of solidity about him. He was wearing the same bright blue suit he had worn the day they had all come aboard. The color suited him, matched the piercing blue of his eyes.

His face was starting to get a bit jowly with age, but it still retained its character, rough hewn and earnest. His eyebrows were thick and bushy, making his gaze seem even more direct than it was. His, hair, once jet black, was shot with silver now, but if the color was beginning to change, there was as yet no sign of his hairline receding. He combed his hair straight back across his head, and kept it in place with the sort of pomade that had been fashionable twenty years before.

"Dr. Cleveland," he said. "There's a matter of some seriousness I'd like to discuss with you. I think you might be the sort of person I could confide in."

Cathy smiled uncertainly. "Of course," she said. "But I must admit I'm a bit surprised. You don't know me, and I don't know anything at all about you. Not where you're from, or how you came to be here."

Choate smiled. "I've made inquiries, and I've seen you aboard the ship, at meal times and so forth, chatted with you once or twice, talked to the people who knew you from the video lab in New York. I like to think I'm a very good judge of character. And from what I've seen of yours, I think you might be the person I need."

Cathy shook her head sadly. "Then you're a very poor judge of character, Mr. Choate. I'm not the sort of person anyone could trust."

Choate looked at her closely for a long moment. "I see," he said at last. "Might I sit down?"

"What? Of course." Cathy stepped back and resumed her seat on the bunk. Choate folded a seat down out of the wall opposite her and settled his considerable bulk down on it.

"You don't feel yourself a trustworthy person, then?" he asked. "Because of what Ishida maneuvered you into doing back on Earth? Spying on your friends, helping to wreck their work because he told you that would help *save* their work? Because you were manipulated and tricked and overawed into a foolish lie that wrecked their careers?"

Cathy grabbed at the fabric of her bulky sweater and knotted it up. "Yes. I guess that's close enough, anyway. I got Garrison into big trouble."

"You did no such thing, Dr. Cleveland," Choate said, with startlingly intensity. "It was all Ishida's doing. He used you. If he had decided that someone else would have been a more suitable tool, he would have used that other person. Blaming yourself is like blaming the bullet for being fired, or the gun for letting its trigger be pulled."

"Mr. Choate, I'm a human being, not a tool. I make my own choices. And—"

"It is most convenient to Ishida for you to believe those things. Yes, you make choices—but you can only do so based on the knowledge you have, the things you believe. And *those* are what Ishida manipulated. He set up a situation—a series of situations—where there was only one decision you could possibly make. For example, setting the fire—yes, I know about that. What did he tell you then? That he had proof Garrison was going to fake the results, make it seem like the asteroid had never existed?"

Cathy looked up at Choate, an angry light in her eye. "That's right. Later on, he told me that he was mistaken, and very much regretted my action—but that of course I should not discuss it with anyone, as they'd be sure to turn me in."

"He was lying from beginning to end—and counting on your basic faith in human nature. From then on you belonged to him. Partners in crime. He tricked you into doing his bidding. That is the one thing he is good at. In spite of all his intellect, all his cold charm and intimidating sophistication, all he knows how to do with all that talent and ability is to get people to do things for him. But he knows how to do that very, very well."

Choate hesitated for a moment and then went on. "And part of it is knowing what sort of people to use. And you are just that sort of person. That may sound like an insult, but it is not."

Cathy scrunched up her face. "It doesn't matter anyway. I feel like I deserve insults."

"Nonsense," Choate said flatly. "Ishida used you because you are kind, because you are trusting, because you care about things outside yourself, because you are ready to believe yourself wrong and someone else right. Those aren't the qualities of a worthless, untrustworthy person."

Cathy shrugged and looked down at her fidgeting hands. "I can't say that I agree with you. But it feels good to hear something nice about myself."

"Then, for the sake of argument, can we take it as read that you are a worthwhile person?" Choate asked, a hint of teasing in his voice.

Cathy looked up at him, and couldn't help but smiling at him. "I guess so."

"Then let me get back to the purpose of my visit," Choate said. "I think you and I have come to the same conclusions about our fearless leader—we don't trust him, or like him, but we need him and his resources, to keep Cornucopia safely away from the Earth."

"That's a pretty fair assessment," Cathy said, "but let's hope these rooms aren't bugged."

Choate looked startled and glanced around at the walls of the room, as if he thought he could spot the microphone. "That hadn't even occurred to me," he said, dropping his voice to a whisper. "But you're right, that would be his style."

"Unless he's so complacent about us he didn't even bother," Cathy said savagely. She thought for a second, noticing how *good* it felt to get angry at her situation. She stood up, pulled a player out of a drawer, stuck a record block in it, and switched it on. The finale of Beethoven's Fifth started to blast out of the player. She sat down again and leaned her head close to Choate's. "That music could be twice as loud, and I could still filter it back out in a second with the right equipment," she whispered. "In theory, he still might be able to hear us clear as a bell. But I don't think the equipment is aboard, and I don't think he or his flunkies would know how to use it. We should be safe. So what do you have to tell me?"

"It's complicated," Choate said. "I should start by saying I've been involved with CRATER for many years. I was part of it before it was radicalized, before Ishida had anything to do with it. The name used to stand for 'Citizens for *Restrictions* on Asteroids in Technological Enterprise Regions.' We were trying to get some sort of controls on how asteroids were handled near planets and habitats. We used to have a lot of support on the habitats. Then the radicals came in and took over the group, changed the name to 'Citizens for the *Removal* of Asteroids from Technological Enterprise Regions.' They demanded that *all* mining work on all asteroids everywhere stop. Not very practical, and not very popular—especially with the habbers, where we had actually been doing some good. The habitats are more dependent on asteroids than anyone, of course. What support we had dried up. Then Ishida came in and more or less took over a few years ago. For all intents and purposes, he has been the only source of funding for the organization. And since the radicals and Ishida came in, we've accomplished exactly nothing."

"I don't understand. If they've wrecked the organization, why have you stuck with it?" Cathy asked.

"Because," Bradford Choate said, "it's the only game in town. No one else is doing anything about the problem. Because I care very deeply about controlling the use of asteroids." He sat there, silent, for a long moment before speaking again. "I'm from England, originally," he said, his voice deep and sonorous. There was a hint, not so much of sadness, but of remembrance in his tone. "Some years ago, however, when I was still a young man, I emigrated to High Manchester."

Cathy breathed in sharply. High Manchester. Suddenly she understood everything, understood Choate very well indeed. The very name of the lost habitat was synonymous with disaster, with catastrophe in space.

Choate, lost in his own memories, didn't seem to notice her response. "High Man was one of the earliest Unassociated Habitats, you know." He smiled for a moment. "We all went blue in the face explaining to visitors that the term 'Unassociated' had nothing to do with politics. Everyone always assumed it meant we weren't allied with either Earth or the Settlers. All it *really* meant was that the habitat wasn't *physically* associated with a planet. That is, the hab was neither in orbit or in a libration point—what they call a planetary habitat. UnHabs are in free solar orbit, never coming near a planet.

"To a habber, whether or not your habitat is planetary or unassociated makes a big difference. How long are your supply lines? How long will it take for emergency cargo to arrive? Do you have to contend with planetary magnetic field and Van Allen belts, or straight, raw solar radiation, or both? Will there be interruptions in sunlight caused by eclipses by the planet? How far from the potential markets for your products will you be?

"Sit two old habitat engineers down and they'll bore you to tears talking about that sort of thing. There are some very significant design differences between a planetary hab and an UnHab.

"But High Man. . ." he said in a voice that was more than half a whisper. Bradford Choate leaned back in his chair and stared intently up at the ceiling, his piercing blue eyes seeing things long distant and long lost. "High Manchester was built in Earth orbit and towed to its intended orbit, well off the ecliptic and about midway between Earth and Mars. And when I say it was an UnHab, I'm not exactly speaking the truth. We *were* associated with a planet—but only a very small one. We went out to that godforsaken orbit because there was an asteroid, a rock there. No name to it of course, not before we got there. And we just called it the Mine."

Bradford Choate's face hardened for a moment, as if he were trying to avoid thinking about something. "The orbital dynamics of two such relatively small masses are tricky sometimes. In theory, we were in orbit of the Mine, and in theory there wasn't any reason not to be in a *very* close orbit. And it made sense to be as close as possible—why make the transit time between the two any longer than it had to be? Besides, a distant orbit would be much more unstable.

"High Man was a cylinder about two kilometers long,

and the Mine was a misshapen lump of rock about the same size, but much denser of course—the hab was hollow, and the Mine was solid rock. We put High Man ten kilometers away from the Mine.

"Everything was fine for a long time. Everyone took the rock in the sky for granted. It was normal, nothing to worry about. There were about eight hundred people in High Manchester, the population headed up, income improving nicely—when they hit the gas pocket."

The music had ended without either of them noticing it. Cathy knew she should reach over and start it up again, drown out their conversation again, but she could not bring herself to move, to interrupt what Choate had to say.

"The Mine was a burnt-out comet," he went on, "like a lot of asteroid-sized bodies. Comets are dirty snowballs, as the old saw has it, and the Mine was basically the dirt that was left over after all the hydrogen and other light elements had boiled away in the Sun's heat. But the boil-off hadn't been complete, for some reason. One pleasant surprise was the relatively high concentrations of hydrogen in the rock we were mining. Hydrogen is damned useful stuff, and we were glad to have it.

"Except the Mine had one more surprise for us. Deep in, near its core, was a large pocket of hydrogen that had been trapped in its frozen state billions of years ago, when the Mine congealed out of the evaporating comet. The trapped hydrogen had partially melted down, of course, but a few kilometers of rock are good insulation, and a good pressure seal. There had been some leaching—which accounted for the high hydrogen content throughout the asteroid. But there was still a large pocket of slurried hydrogen under pressure trapped beneath the surface.

"And they were using oxygen torches to cut through the rock. The first small blast cracked opened the oxy storage tanks.

"The Mine was structurally pretty weak, and the main explosion shattered it all together. Fragments blasted in all directions, at high speed."

Choate was silent for a long time. "And High Man was only ten klicks away. High Manchester was prepared for a few meteor strikes, of course. We might even have been able to handle ten or twelve large impacts smashing through the hull at once. But we weren't prepared for thousands. Some of the fragments were the size of a house, or larger. Big enough to do major structural damage, snap bearing beams. The hab was under rotation, and without proper support, the structure of the hab started to give way, tear itself to pieces.

"We were on the other side of the Sun from Earth, nearly as distant from Mars. No help could reach us in less than a few weeks. Most of the population was killed outright—my wife and my children died. By chance, I was aboard a ferry craft when the Mine blew. Our craft took a few hits, but we escaped major damage. We managed to link up with three other ships, and together we just barely survived until the rescue teams from Mars arrived. There were twenty-nine of us. We were the only survivors."

Choate shifted in his seat and folded his hands in his lap. "So as you can see, I have my reasons for fearing asteroids too close to a habitat—let alone a world. But I know enough, understand enough to realize you can't ban all bridges because one bridge collapsed. What you do instead is build safer bridges. But now CRATER wants to do the impossible and ban asteroid mining altogether. *That* would kill a lot more people than the Mine explosion ever did.

"There are a great number of people who rely directly on asteroid products for their day-to-day survival. They eat food grown from soil and nutrients manufactured from asteroidal material, just for example. And no matter how close they come to closing the ecologies of the habitats, increasing populations are going to require that more raw asteroidal nitrogen, carbon, oxygen and hydrogen be brought in every year. And needless to say, all their exports and trade goods are made out of asteroidal matter."

Cathy waved her hand and smiled weakly. "Spare me the details. I understand all that."

Choate looked surprised and smiled himself. "Forgive me. I'm too used to explaining things to people who *don't* understand."

Cathy thought for a moment and chose her next words

carefully. "But if you don't agree with what CRATER wants to do, and if what CRATER wants to do anyway is impossible—why you are here?"

"To help Ishida do what he says he's going to do—and prevent him from doing what he *really* wants to do." Choate hesitated, and leaned in close to Cathy. He whispered earnestly into Cathy's ear. "I don't think he just wants to keep Cornucopia out of Earth orbit. I think he wants to steal the asteroid for himself."

Choate stood up abruptly, as if alarmed by his own statement, and stepped through the door without another word.

Chapter Seventeen

SUNWAY, EASTERN LIMB SECTOR, THE MOON

Flat-out exhausted, feeling like his entire blood supply had been replaced with caffeine, Ben barely noticed when the rough track turned into a legitimate, worn down path as two or three side trails merged into the main road. It had been too long and wearying a trip for a minor thing like that to register. Lack of sleep had burned out most of his higher functions; about the only parts of his brain still working were the ones that were steering the damn roller, automatic responses and reflex, nothing else.

But even in his condition, the first road sign in a thousand kilometers couldn't help but catch his eye. It was, after all, hard to miss, even it was half a kilometer to his left and still far off ahead. After thousands of kilometers of rock, rock and rock in all its myriad forms, the eye was naturally drawn to a gleaming white perfect rectangle, a pleasant, reassuringly human-built thing in the endless wilderness, a sign of human occupation and civilization.

Of course, it didn't hurt that the thing was fifty meters tall and a hundred across either. Ben pulled out the binoculars and gave it a look through tired eyes.

EARTHRISE STATION
FIFTY KLICKS
EATS BEDS SHOWERS REPAIRS

it announced. Vastly encouraged, Ben hit the accelerator and hurried on toward the promised oasis.

He was perhaps five kilometers further along when he noticed something strange at the edge of his vision. There was a long, straight line, running parallel to his course, half a kilometer to the south. He dismissed it at first as a long ridge to be avoided—but then it suddenly struck Ben that it lined up exactly with the big billboard. He gave the "ridge" a peek with the binoculars and whooped with joy. It was a *road*. An actual, honest-to-God, certifiable, ruler-straight paved *road*. Vacuum-concerete by the look of it, shining white in the sunlight.

He swung the steering wheel hard around and headed for it. Five minutes later he eased the *R&R* up onto smooth pavement.

The sensation was incredible. The banging, rattling clatter, the bone-jarring, nerve-wracking bouncing vanished as if they had never been. All the dreadful cacophony faded away, replaced by faint, reassuring mechanical noises Ben had never even known were there. The smooth, purring vibration of the drive-motors transmitted itself through the chassis to fill the pressure cylinder with a gentle hum, the ventilator hissed quietly. For the first time since they had left the thermal dome at Central Colony, the *R&R* was a calm, peaceful place.

The absence of noise actually awakened Garrison, a true indication of how drastic the change was. Garrison sat up, fumbling as usual with his chest belt. "What is it?" he asked. "Have we stopped?"

"Stopped, hell! We're doing fifty kilometers an hour!" Ben laughed. "Take a look out the window."

Garrison did. "Hot damn!" he exclaimed. "A *road!* Where did that come from?"

"I think the owners and operators of Earthrise Station decided it would be good for business."

"If they think that way, they think right. How far *are* we from Earthrise?"

"Just under forty klicks."

Garrison grinned. Earthrise was almost exactly half way between Central Colony and Farside Station, and it had taken them only six days to get here. Six of the longest, most unpleasant, grueling days of his life, granted. But they were here, ahead of schedule. "Ben, I think we've earned a stop at Earthrise. Take us on in."

Ben nodded enthusiastically. "You read my mind, kiddo." He hit the accelerator. There had to be another little bit of speed he could squeeze out of the *Rock & Roll*.

Forty-five minutes later, Ben followed the road up over one last crater wall ridge and paused at the summit. There, laid out below them in the center of the crater, was Earthrise Station. It was perhaps an unfairly romantic and evocative name for such a scrappy, tumbledown outpost on the edge of nowhere. But not to Ben. He took a long look at the few half-buried huts, the rough landing field, and the ramshackle shipping depot that made up the station. He had never seen a better looking sight in his life.

Ben dropped the roller into low gear and began to make his way cautiously down the steep slope. It was a modest-sized crater, as such things went on the Moon, only ten or twelve kilometers across. The paved road led right through it, running straight through the station proper. Ben drove up into the center of town, such as it was, and pulled off the pavement alongside one of the larger pressure huts.

Working as slowly and carefully as they could in their eagerness to get out of the *Rock & Roll*, they powered down the roller, then got into their pressure suits, each checking all the seals on the other's suits. These were not idiot-proof rental models, but used suits bought on a wing and a prayer. Ben and Garrison had tried them on and tested them as best they could in Central Colony's thermal dome—but it still required a leap of faith to trust in a used suit. Garrison was determined to trust to fate as little as possible.

"Okay, listen," he said to Ben once they were suited up. "We're going outside, and we're to do it as carefully as we can. I want to let the reserve electric storage rings charge up as much as they can while we're at Earthside. We'll need to power down the *Rock & Roll* to get maximum charge." The storage rings were high-density, high-temperature superconductors that could store a tremendous amount of power. It was a basic tenet of lunar lore to keep them charged to the hilt at all times. Solar arrays were known to fail, and then a traveler might need every erg of stored power. "That means depressurizing the roller so we're not wasting power on life support. But I want to stay inside, under pressure, ready to come get you in case you get into trouble. That means you go through the lock first. The second you've cycled through to the outside, I'll hit the crash-repressurize button and get into the lock myself. I'll be right behind you, ready to yank you in if anything goes wrong. Even if you're suit fails altogether, I'll have you back inside before you can get into trouble, okay? Once I'm satisfied that you're okay, I'll start powering down and depressuring the roller. When I'm done, I'll meet you outside."

Ben nodded, a bit nervously. Garrison's voice sounded small and tinny through the pressure suit's elderly radio speaker. "Now we've got bargain-basement suits here, so we've gotta be careful with them," Garrison continued. "Take your time cycling down to vacuum, and then I want you to stand in the lock and watch your suit air pressure for a solid five minutes before you open the outer hatch. Make sure you flex all the joints while you're waiting— better they should crack in the lock than on the surface. If you get *any* pressure loss at all, any at all, dump the air back into the lock and get back in here. Come back on in if you even *think* you see the pressure drop. Don't tell yourself it's nothing, or just a piddling little pinhole that you can ignore since we're not going far. Leaks get bigger, not smaller. Sometimes they get bigger real fast. I'll be listening on the radio link."

Ben wanted to complain about being nurse-maided, but he thought better of it and kept his mouth shut. He realized that he *agreed* with the precautions. Everything Garrison had said was right, sensible, prudent. He remembered something Garrison had said once. "Not all Conners are paranoid—only the live ones are." Ben stepped into the lock and shut the inner hatch. If he was starting to think that way, maybe he was getting to be a Conner at last.

Ben stepped into the tiny airlock—designed to fit one suited person normally or two if an emergency meant they wouldn't mind crowding—and pulled the inner hatch shut. He double-checked the seal on the inner hatch, twisted the lock control knob to *slow depressurization* and waited for the air pumps to do their work.

He felt the suit stiffen slightly as the air left the lock. The control valves in the suit's back pack kicked in with a quiet *clunk* and a slight hissing. Ben was alarmed for a minute until he remembered what it meant. As the air from the lock was removed, the suit naturally had to expand slightly. Reduced external pressure let the suit swell out a bit. With the same amount of air contained in a suit whose internal volume had grown larger, obviously, the suit pressure dropped slightly. The suit's automatic controls were pumping in a bit more air to compensate. It was a normal phenomenon.

The lock's pressure indicator dropped to 0000.01 millibars and stayed there. One hundred-thousandth of an atmosphere was the best vacuum the scavenger pumps could provide, but it certainly ought to be good enough. Ben checked the watch sewn onto the suit's sleeve. Five minutes. He began waving his arms back and forth, bending his knees, twisting back and forth as best he could in the confines of the small lock.

It wasn't easy to wiggle around like that and watch the old-fashioned pressure meter on his chest-display at the same time, but Ben did his best—and was alarmed all over again by the results. The meter needle was jittering back and forth wildly. The suit was going nuts! Better get back inside right away—Ben's hand was on the pump controls before he stopped and thought for a second.

Of *course* the meter needle was jittering! Every time he moved a muscle he was bending and twisting the suit, changing the suit's volume. Besides which, his physical exertion was heating up the suit—and heat sure as hell affected air pressure. What else could the air pressure do but change? He stood still and watched the pressure needle again. Rock solid. He flexed the suit vigorously, stopped and watched the pressure indicator, and repeated the sequence two more times.

No change in pressure, but Ben found he had broken into a sweat with even that mild exertion. It was easy to get out of shape on the Moon. He checked his watch and found that the five minutes were up. He clenched and unclenched his fist nervously, then reached over and opened the outer lock door.

Moving with exaggerated care, he made his way down to the last rung of the ladder, a meter above the surface. Gingerly, gently, he swung his feet clear and used his arms to lower himself to the ground below.

For the first time in his life, Ben stood on the unshielded surface of the Moon, with no outside barriers between his suit and that barren, wild world. This was no sealed lock that could be crash-pressurized if something went wrong. There was no sunshield overhead, no thermal lock to keep the temperature steady, no paved-over surface beneath his feet. This was real. This was the Moon.

He should have been frightened. All there was between himself and death were a few layers of fabric, a fragile bubble of transparent plastic for a helmet, a collection of tiny pumps and thin tubing that let him breathe. He held up his gauntleted hand to his helmet. It was most strange to realize that there was nothing, literally nothing at all, between the helmet and the glove. He carried a tiny and imperfect simulacra of Mother Earth's sheltering habitat on his back—but between his face and his hand was another world, the Moon's native environment. He could never truly be part of that world, never truly experience it, unless he did so in the act of dying. He raised his hand to his face and tapped a finger against the plastic. He heard the quiet *plunk, plunk* inside the helmet, knowing there was no sound at all in the world that surrounded him. This was an alien place, he felt—and then reminded himself that *he* was the alien here. *All* life was alien here.

He turned and looked back through the tiny port in the *R&R*'s airlock. He could see Garrison standing inside the lock, watching Ben's every move. Ben's radio was on, but he didn't feel like talking. He waved to Garrison, and Garrison waved back.

Ben walked a few steps, looking around at the bleak landscape, his back toward the huts and buildings of the station. He lowered the helmet's sunvisor into place to cut down the glare.

The naked Sun shown down from directly overhead, safely out of the limited field of view afforded by his helmet visor. Still it cast a painfully bright light on the crater floor. There were almost no shadows with the Sun at its highest point in the sky and the whole crater floor seemed perfectly flat and featureless, roasting in the intense, undiminished sunlight. The crater wall rose up, surrounding the empty plain, a high ring of cliffs that seemed somehow to hold in the emptiness as they held out the velvet darkness of the sky.

There was a sad beauty here, a silent and abiding loveliness of loss, of an unfinished, impoverished world, patiently enduring the failure of its destiny. This tiny world, Ben thought, so perfectly placed at just the right distance from the Sun, could have *lived*. Had it just been a bit larger, had the proto-moon gathered in just a bit more mass, a bit more water, had it retained and evolved its primordial atmosphere instead of losing it to uncaring space—then this world *would* have lived.

There *should* have been life here—water, air, clouds, wind in the sky. The craters should have been washed away by the gentling rain, the soil should have bloomed forth with plants and trees and flowers. The familiarity of the home world belonged here. And yet life here would have to be wildly different from Earth's. The reduced gravity, the month-long days—what wondrous creatures might have come to be here?

Lifeless and grey, that moonscape spoke to Ben somehow, in a language he could not explain, although he understood it perfectly. This lonely, empty, barren world was an invalid, badly wounded by numberless accidents and disasters in the four billion years of her existence. Only now, in these latter days, was she finally the abode of life. On the home world, humanity had been the wrecker, the destroyer of life. Even today, many on Earth did not accept that humankind must be the steward, not the master, of all it surveyed.

There, on the home world, humanity had an endless debt to pay, a duty of penance to perform until the end of time. The damage done could never be completely repaired, but the husbanding, the caring, the nurturing, the research, had to go on.

Here, on the Moon, there was no debt—but there was a duty. As the steward of life, humanity owed both the lifeless world and life itself the chance to grow here. For the first time, Ben could understand the colonists' passion for their gardens, for their flowers, for their pets. This empty world *needed* life, hungered for it, after four billion years of loneliness.

Ben walked a bit further on, turned toward the east and looked along the crater wall. He froze in astonishment and wonder.

Five minutes later, Garrison found him there, standing stock still, staring at the eastern sky. Garrison was alarmed at first, and hurried toward his friend—until he happened to look in the direction Ben was facing. He caught his breath and stared himself, transfixed by the sight.

Earth does not, as commonly thought, stand still in the Moon's sky. It would do so if the Moon revolved in a perfect circle about the exact center of the Earth, and if the Earth thus stayed precisely still in relation to her satellite, but that is not the way orbital mechanics works.

The Moon travels an elliptical orbit about the Earth. When it is closest to Earth, it moves faster, and when it is farther away it moves more slowly. The Moon also rotates about its own axis, a lunar "day" being exactly as long as one orbit about the Earth. Since the velocity of the orbital motion varies, while the speed of rotation is constant, the two movements do not exactly match, moment by moment, though they average out to match exactly over time.

The Earth's orbital motion falls behind the speed of rotation at apogee, then catches up and gets ahead just a bit at perigee, before slowing down again as the Moon heads back toward apogee and slowing again, over and over again in an endless cycle.

As seen from the Moon, this combined motion is seen as a slight "wobble" of the Earth in the sky.

From most points on the Nearside of the Moon, this motion is so slight as to be undetectable. The Earth hangs too high in the sky for anyone to notice the tiny movement.

This is not so at the line dividing Nearside from Farside. At Earthrise Station, directly on that line, Garrison and Ben looked on the Earth, blue, lovely, fragile and perfect, hanging just over the eastern horizon, framed by the crater wall. Over the course of the Moon's month-long orbit, the Earth would slowly rise, peek over the edge of the crater, spinning each day on its own axis as it hung in the sky, and then slowly slide back down below the edge of the world, to be lost to view for another two weeks.

The Earth was in half-phase, balanced on the crater wall, the sunlit half highest in the sky, riding above the darkened nightside on the knife-edge of the horizon. The nightside was not wholly black, but was visible in the lights of cities, and in the reflection of moonlight and starlight gleaming off the cloud tops. Four times the size of a full Moon, and far brighter, the shining world sat poised on the edge of the sky. The liveliness of Earth, the brightness, the swirling clouds and changing weather, all served to make the dead moonscape below seem all the more lifeless. The contrast could not help but remind them how great a prize the Earth was.

Ben and Garrison stood, staring at the achingly lovely sight, for a moment that might have taken a minute—or an hour. How long they were there didn't matter, for the image would remain with them always, as timeless, as enduring, as fragile, as the blue-and-white vision before them.

There she was, Garrison thought. The world that he had sworn to defend against Cornucopia. Staring at the Earth as she floated serene in the sky, he knew he wasn't crazy. It didn't matter if the danger she faced was centuries away, if no one else could see it, if no one else believed in it, or cared about it. All that was unimportant.

He would defend her.

Chapter Eighteen

At last Ben and Garrison reluctantly turned their backs on the view. They headed back past the roller toward the Station settlement.

It seemed almost a sin to turn away from the splendid sight of Earth on the horizon. Leaving that loveliness behind to look on a place like Earthrise Station seemed downright blasphemous. If the view *from* the Station was sublime, the sight of the Station itself was ridiculous.

The outer perimeter of the Station looked more like a junk yard than a settlement. Half-disassembled rollers of various vintages littered the landscape, many of them modified almost out of recognition. Some had portable thermal shields rigged over them, but it was impossible to tell which of the rollers were being fixed, which were being stripped for parts, and which had simply been abandoned. Ben and Garrison wandered through the repair field, looking at the strange debris. Smaller machines of uncertain purpose and unidentifiable bits and pieces of gadgetry were strewn about on the dusty surface. Here and there someone seemed to have made half-hearted attempts to sort out the junk and organize the salvage into various heaps of similar parts. The effort obviously hadn't gotten very far.

"Ben!" Garrison called out. "Come take a look at this!" Ben had to look about for a moment before he could locate Garrison—the suit radio could give no idea as to which direction a voice was coming from, or even from how far away. Finally he turned completely around, and saw Garrison in the middle distance, looking up at a big cargo roller, three times the size of the *R&R*.

Moving carefully in the awkward suit, Ben went over to his friend. "What is it?"

Garrison pointed up at the big vehicle. "Look what they're hauling."

Ben looked up at the cargo roller. Unlike the *R&R*, its pressure cylinder took up only the front of the drive chassis. The rear three-fourths of the chassis was a flatbed, open to vacuum, with its cargo carefully strapped down on the bed.

Ben looked over the equipment on the roller, and suddenly recognized it. The details of the design were a bit different, but the family resemblance was there. It was deep-drilling gear, very similar to the system they had used on Hrisey, on Iceland, a few weeks and a million years ago. "What the hell would they be drilling for *here*?" Ben asked.

"Practically everything. You're forgetting, the deep-drill stuff we used was based on lunar equipment," Garrison said. "A lot of valuable elements and materials are scarce or totally absent from the Moon's outer crust. They're present in the Moon, but only much deeper down. You get at them by deep-drilling, going much farther down than we went on Hrisey. You drill down, then blast-inflate a subbubble with heat-intensified nuclear bombs. That wrecks your drill hole, of course, so you redrill down and send robot mining machines down the new drill shaft, and the robots start excavating the subbubble.

"Sometimes you can use mass meters and gravity sensors to locate an old asteroid or carbon-rich comet that buried itself on impact. Those are the major pay dirt: you might come up with metals, carbon or even hydrogen bound up in various compounds. But that's not the real point. Take a look at that shipping label."

Ben grinned. "How about that. 'Ship to: Farside Station Cargo Facility.' Maybe they'll have some work for the Farside Geology Section after all."

Garrison slapped Ben on the back, a bit awkwardly through his clumsy gauntlet and Ben's heavy suit. "C'mon, let's get inside and see if we can't get some scuttlebutt on this."

They turned toward the center of the Station and headed for the largest of the half-buried huts. There was an airlock at one end of the long narrow hut. A sign outside read:

WELCOME TO EARTHRISE STATION BAR & GRILL
WE BREW OWN BEER
ALL ALCOHOL DISTILLED ON PREMISE
SERVING THE FINAST FOOD FROM AROUND THE GLOBE (LUNA)
FAMILY HOTELL-NICE RATES
LUXURY GRAND-SWEET ROOMS INCLUDE MATTRESS SHEET PILLOW

Luxury, Ben decided, was relative—and so were grammar and spelling, it seemed. The idea of a mattress being a special feature for a hotel room struck him as a real sign of the frontier. Of course, a soft mattress and pillow on the Moon weren't strictly *necessary*. Logically, even a rock-hard surface should be comfortable enough when the sleeper only had one-sixth of earthside weight pressing him or her down. In practice, of course, people liked their familiar comforts.

Ben followed Garrison into the airlock and they cycled through together. Their suits collapsed slightly as air was pumped into the lock. Garrison opened the inner lock door and they stepped through the hatch into a long, low-ceilinged room.

A very strange room. Reading from front to back, it seemed to combine the functions of a tavern, a repair shop, and a hotel lobby. A long waist-high counter lined the right side of the room. The low wall behind it revealed what went on behind each section of the counter. The first part was lined with bottles, the second covered with tools and parts bins, and the last held a set of mostly empty pigeonhole mailboxes.

The left side of the one big room was taken up with tables, a rickety line of pressure-suit racks, and at the far end what seemed to be a large open hatchway set into the floor. The top of a ladder stuck up from the hatch, and Ben correctly assumed it led to tunnels connecting up with the rest of the buildings and the underground portion of the station. The inevitable masses of plant life—spider plants, mostly—hung from pots bolted to the wall. Oversized decorative palms loomed up from huge urns, crammed onto the floor wherever they would fit. Wallplant ivy was growing almost out of control, clamoring up whatever bare wall it could find. Considering the dim lighting and the smoky air, the greenery seemed remarkably healthy.

Shuttling back and forth between the bar and repair sections of the counter, a swarthy, heavyset woman seemed to be doing several things at once; serving up drinks to a noisy knot of customers at the tavern end, arguing with an unseen someone over a headset clamped over the thick braids of hair coiled atop her head, and working on the parts of some sort of broken gadget spread out over the middle section of the long countertop.

There seemed to be two or three heated arguments going on at the bar, the barkeep was doing her best to keep up her end of her telephonic debate, and a speaker was blaring out some unidentifiable form of music. At the far end of the room, behind the hotel part of the counter, a thin, sallow-faced young man sat straight up in his chair, fast asleep.

Given pride of place at the far end of the room from the airlock was a huge portrait of a stern-looking elderly man in a musical-comedy military uniform. A candle sitting on a table in front of the painting flickered in the smoky air.

Ben looked at Garrison, and Garrison looked at Ben. Aside from that, no one in the place took the slightest notice of the newcomers.

Ben opened his suit helmet and instantly wrinkled up his nose in distaste. The place smelled, smelled of more things than he could identify. Stale tobacco smoke, good strong stew on the boil, a little whiff of marijuana, spilled beer and booze, human bodies, burned-out electric motors, fresh coffee, boiled cabbage, a cat box that needed changing, the loamy, pungent flavor of soil and fresh-cut ivy. Other odors, too subtle to identify when overwhelmed by all that competition, hovered in the background. Ben coughed, sneezed, inadvertently breathed in again—and found to his surprise that the stench wasn't quite as bad as he had supposed. He took another cautious sniff and found the smell fading away even as he tried to sample it.

He shouldn't have been surprised. After spending the last week in the overfiltered air of the *Rock & Roll*, and the week before that in the carefully hygienicized confines of Central Colony, *any* sort of smell was more than his nose was used to. It simply took a minute or two to acclimate. He took another deep breath through his nose and decided the place had character. What he was breathing here made the air he had been using for the last two weeks seem bland by comparison.

Behind him, Garrison was already half out of his suit. Ben got his helmet off and set it on the top shelf of an empty suit rack by the door. After a few minutes of wrestling and wriggling, Ben got out of the body of his suit and hung it carefully in the rack.

Garrison put his own suit away, grinned, scratched his beard, and nodded toward the bar. "Let's go see what that locally distilled alcohol is like." They walked across to the bar, found an empty pair of stools and sat down.

The heavyset barkeep—one look at her and you *knew* she was the owner, not just a barmaid—instantly appeared in front of them.

"Hold off, Fred, must serve two high-class customers just come in," she announced into the headphone's mike. "Welcome to Earthrise, friend. Saw your roller come a while back on the outside watch camera."

She stuck out a meaty hand that had a thin film of machine oil on it. "I'm Nadezhda Konstantinovna Pevtrovka. I own joint." She was a big, strong, heavyset woman. She had a solid, determined face that fell easily into a smile, revealing two steel teeth among the ivory ones. Her bright blue eyes sparkled, handsomely set off by rosy cheeks. She was of indeterminate age, perhaps thirty, perhaps fifty. She was dressed in a bright blue jump suit that seemed to be mostly zippers, pockets, and patches. Tools and gadgets sprouted from every pocket, and a tool belt clattered at her ample hips. Judging from the way she used it to keep her hair in place, the headset seemed to be a permanent part of her outfit.

Garrison took her hand first and almost got his hand crushed. "Good to meet you, Nadezhda Konstantinovna," he said, pronouncing the Russian name perfectly, and obviously pleasing their hostess. "I'm Garrison Morrow, and this is my friend Ben Moscowitz. We're on our way to Farside Station."

"Hello," Ben said as his own hand crumpled under her strong grip. "Nice to meet you."

"Moscowitz," she repeated. "You Jew? Russian Jew?" she asked hopefully.

"Yes, Russian Jew, about eight generations back," Ben replied cautiously. "I'm American."

"Pah!" she said in annoyance. "*Never* do they come through here. Russians on the Moon must all be hiding, or always stay in one place. Never travel. Never do I get to speak my own language. Always English, English, English. You find where Russians hide, you tell 'em come here for a visit. Well, never mind, we know how to welcome Yankee Dooleys too!"

"Start us off by selling us some of your beer, then," Garrison said. "And what meal are you serving at the moment? Breakfast, lunch, or dinner?"

"Open twenty-four hours, always serve all meals. But," she said in a confidential whisper that could be heard at the far end of the room, "stay away from porridge just now. I leave it on the stove another hour and then use to patch pressure leaks." As she spoke, she made two big steins of beer appear on the counter, each accompanied by a chaser of what seemed to be vodka. Interesting local drinking custom, Ben thought.

"How about two bowls of that stew behind you, then?" Garrison suggested.

Nadezhda Konstantinovna beamed happily. "*Knew* you were high class—Yes Fred what the hell is it now?" She interrupted herself halfway through her own sentence to bark into the headset mike again. She listened to the earphone for a moment, and covered the mike with her hand. "Moment, friends, please. Idiot partner could not repair paperweight without advice. Is outside now working on failed charging link." She served up two big bowls of stew and big hunks of black bread to them as she shouted into the mike. "No, no, NO! Storage coil must be *shielded* before opening access panel. Shield from Sun. Above fifty centigrade and is scrap! What? Say again?" She bustled down to the middle of the counter, squatted down and pulled a fat dogeared manual out from a low shelf. She flopped it down on the counter and riffled the pages. "Calibration values are one hundred ten volts, thirty amps. Da." She put the manual away, hustled along the line at the bar, and refilled everyone's glass without invitation, effortlessly remembering what everyone was drinking.

Ben was expecting her to come back and chat with them, but, the barflies being sated for the moment, she was already back working on whatever broken gizmo was lying on the workbench. She screwed a jeweler's loupe into her eye and examined a small part critically. Obviously, her attention was going to be elsewhere for the moment.

"C'mon, let's take this to a table," Ben said to Garrison. The bar was just a bit too crowded, and the customers just a bit too unsteady, for a guy to eat in comfort.

It took two trips to get the bowls, bread, spoons, beers and chasers to one of the less-dirty tables. Conversation was a bit lacking for a while as they both set to work on the rich stew. It was amazing to Ben that anything could taste that good. A steady diet of concentrates and lukewarm handmeals eaten in a bouncing roller tended to reduce your gastronomic expectations. For that matter, even before Iceland Ben hadn't exactly been a gourmet. He was, like many bachelors, more of the food-as-fuel persuasion. You needed the stuff to stay alive, but somehow cooking for one didn't make it. It was easier, and somehow less depressing, to zap a food tray and snarf it down, rather than go through the ritual of cooking and then eating a decent meal alone.

Ben made a resolution to start making *real* meals when

they got to Farside. Even this plain old stew was terrific. Ben couldn't quite identify the meat in it—rabbit, probably, as they were the easiest to raise on the Moon. But that didn't even matter. It was fresh, it was hot, it had character. The black bread was strong-flavored, and took a bit of chewing—but that was the way it was *supposed* to be, not the result of some compromise to make packaging easier. The beer was perhaps just a trifle thin for Ben's taste, and there was something about the taste of the vodka that made him think it was only a few hours old. So what? The food and drink were *real*, they were made by people, they were made as an aid to enjoyment, to living *well*, and not just to allow for survival.

It was a lot to conclude from merely eating one meal. Maybe the poetry of Earth in the sky was still with him. Whatever it was, Ben made a promise to start *living* instead of just marking time. In a way, he had already started doing that. A year ago, he had been back in his dull little lab in Philadelphia, day after day, running the same damn tests on an endless stream of rock samples, never really knowing or caring where the samples came from, or what the results meant. He never would have dreamed then that he would be here now, eating rabbit stew on the borderlands of Lunar Nearside.

Strange thoughts at mealtime. Maybe it was just that he was tired, more tired than he had ever been. But his mind couldn't stop. And there was a lot to think about.

His past back on Earth was lost to him, his future was unknown and unknowable. There was danger ahead, from the Moon's harsh environment, from the whims of politicians and the rules of a frontier culture he didn't understand. No smotheringly paternalistic arm of society was going to take care of him. No weekly pay deposit, no insurance policy, no cops to call, no social justice officer. None of the people running the Moon could or would take care of him if he got in trouble. Except for Garrison, there was no one but himself he could rely on. He was surprised how good that felt. It was beginning to sink in. For the first time in his life, he was on his own. Twice over an exile, he was *free*.

"This is great," Ben announced.

"What, the stew?" Garrison asked absently.

Ben shrugged. It was too hard to explain. But it felt *right*. He was here through his own efforts, depending on himself more than he ever had before. It meant something. "The stew, the bread, getting here—everything. I just feel good."

"You and me both," Garrison said happily. "A hundred meters *thataway*—and we're on the edge of the Farside, halfway there. I didn't think we could do it at first, driving ourselves clear round a whole planet—but it was your plan and we did it. In your bargain basement used roller."

"That reminds me of something I've been meaning to ask," Ben said, a little embarrassed and eager to change the subject. "Why *are* rollers so cheap? You've kept telling me that machines are expensive on the Moon. We bought a used one, but even the new rollers I priced were *cheap*. I'm not arguing with the price—but there's a contradiction there."

Garrison thought for a moment. "Okay, lemme see if I can explain it. Suppose you wanted to sell eggs on the Moon. What would you import, eggs or chickens?"

"Chickens, of course," Ben said. "Or probably fertilized eggs, let 'em hatch here."

"Minor detail. A fertilized egg is just a chicken in compact packaging. But the point is the same. Since eggs are something everyone can use, it's worth shipping in a whole egg factory—that is, the chicken—rather than importing the finished product, the egg. You sell a million eggs cheap and make your money on volume. Now, suppose you wanted to important caviar. What do you ship in—the fish eggs or the sturgeon?"

"The caviar, obviously."

"Right. Not only is the fish harder to take care of than a chicken, but a lot fewer people are going to want the product. So if you're going to make a living selling caviar on the Moon, you're not going to have much volume. You send the price through the roof to compensate."

Garrison took a sip of his beer and went on. "What's expensive on the Moon are the caviar machines, things you only need a few of if you need them at all. Specialized high-tech stuff. Like the automated ID booth you were expecting. Or maintenance robots. Or luxury items, like those automatic hairdressers that were such a big fad when we were in New York. They'd cost too much, so the Conners get along without them and tell themselves they're better off without them. If we ever get back to Central, ask Mrs. Lombroska her opinion of automated hotel systems. That's the caviar stuff.

"What *we've* been riding in is a chicken's egg. There are *thousands* of rollers around, because some UNLAC lab on Earth designed a whole roller factory. They built it, shipped it here, switched it on, and stepped back. It's been cranking out rollers ever since. They've tweaked up the design a few times, and they put out a few different models for different jobs. Cargo versions, oversize jobs like that big guy out front. Besides dialing in what model to make, they just leave the factory alone. Which makes rollers cheap. Basic supply and demand.

"The kicker is that the factory is *totally* automated, right down to raw materials. I got a tour of it once. They have robot bulldozers that feed dirt into the hopper of a soil-cracker, and dedicated long-distance robot haulers that supply ore for lunar-rare elements like nitrogen from nearby mines. They fabricate the parts right from raw materials. Robot labor assembles it. They call it a half-von Neumann machine."

"Meaning what?"

"A von Neumann is any machine capable of replicating itself. Then the replicas replicate themselves, and soon you're up to your keister in von Neumanns. There have been some gimmicky lab gadgets that could copy themselves but no one has ever built a worthwhile true von Neumann. A half-von Neumann can endlessly duplicate a machine simpler than itself."

"They can't do that with an entire roller," Ben protested. "It's too complex."

"You open up that control panel when we're back aboard and see how many parts there are in it. They've got the things boiled down to absolute simplicity."

Ben frowned for a second. "Wait a minute. Solar powered factory, right?"

"Right."

"So they've got free power. And they're getting the raw materials essentially for free, digging the dirt out of the ground and refining it. Robots mine the raw materials and build the rollers, so you don't have any labor costs. Power, material and labor free. Aside from the cost of building the factory, it doesn't cost them *anything* to make the rollers! So what do they base the cost on?"

"'The value of a thing is that which it will bring,'" Garrison quoted. "They sell for whatever the market will bear. At the moment, the market is flooded, so rollers are cheap. Another good run of immigration, and the supply will dry up. Or else they can just turn off the factory for a while until it's needed again, and drive the price up a bit. But you've spotted a real problem there. How do you run an economy when things of value cost nothing to produce? The roller plant is an example, not an exception. Lots of common items on the Moon are produced that way."

"So how *do* they run the lunar economy?"

Garrison shrugged. "UNLAC? I think they just ignore it and hope it will go away. I mean, Christ, you've got a whole planet here that doesn't even have its own *currency*. Instead we use everyone else's money—and half of that is in confetti-denominations. From an economic standpoint, the whole Moon is sheer chaos, but it works somehow. I think the policy people are afraid that if they try to fix it, people will notice it can't possibly work, even though it's been working for years. Confidence would collapse, and the whole place would go to hell in a hand basket."

"Food good?" a booming voice asked from behind them, making them both jump. Nadezhda Konstantinovna sat down between Garrison and Ben.

"Yes," Ben said. "Everything's delicious."

"Good," she said. "You go to Farside, then? For short visit?"

"To live," Garrison said. "We got caught by the labor draft." That was enough explanation for now. No point going into the whole story.

"Bad luck for you," she said seriously. "But you have your own roller, I see," she said more cheerfully. "Much more pleasant than riding in nasty public roller. Same size as yours, twenty people in it for two weeks! Huff! Terrible.

But if you go to Farside Station, you should convoy with Mohammed. He travels there as well." She turned and shouted toward the bar. "Mohammed! Come here a moment. There are people you should meet."

A tall, lanky young man detached himself from the mob at the bar and came over to the table, carrying his drink with him. He sat down at the fourth chair, opposite their hostess and between Ben and Garrison. He was a strikingly handsome young man, lean-faced, dark-skinned with jet black hair and perfect white teeth that fell naturally into a disarming grin. "What's up, Nadia?"

She shook a finger at him. "A good Muslim like you, drinking alcohol. Satan is working on you," she warned in mock anger.

"He's working on *you*, if you tell lies like that," Mohammed replied evenly. "This," he said, raising his glass, and addressing Ben and Garrison, "is some vile fruit juice concoction Nadia tries to poison me with every time I come through. Fortunately, I've built up an immunity." He turned back to Nadia. "I must write and warn the Patriarch about your sliding back into the sin of lying," he said sternly.

"Back in Moscow, you think he has time to read love notes with the whole country going to hell? The czar ought to retire, abdicate and let his daughter take over," she said, nodding to the huge portrait at the far end of the room. "Listen, Mohammed, say hello to Ben and Garrison. They're headed to Farside Station. I tell them convoy with you."

Mohammed nodded. "Sure. Always glad to have some company out there. Rolling on your own, then?"

"They are, in a ten-year-old roller that's overpacked by the look of the suspension," Nadia answered for them. "Springs half smashed flat. What you *got* in that thing?"

Before Ben could reply, Mohammed cut in. "Ten-year-old roller? What's your call number?"

"CC-260-3S-5," Garrison replied. "Named the *Rock & Roll.*"

"Yeah, I passed you guys four days ago. I remember wondering what a roller with an old local government registration was doing way the hell out here. You were barely crawling, so slow I figured you *had* to be making a local trip. How'd you get here so fast?"

"We shut off the auto pilot and drove nonstop at forty kilometers an hour," Ben said simply.

"Forty KPH?" he asked, incredulously. "In *that* thing? No offense, but you're lucky to be here. Or even alive. Why so slow and then so fast? And why the hell did you turn off the auto?" Mohammed asked.

"Because the auto was what was slowing us down. It couldn't handle the terrain at even twenty KPH, and we were losing the Sun. We *had* to sprint to make up for it," Garrison explained.

Nadia frowned. "Bad planning," she said sternly. "You *must* be first timers on this run. Who you buy roller from?"

"Reinhart Rollers in Central," Ben answered.

"*That* gouger!" Mohammed growled. "He had no business selling you that thing for long-distance haulage. That roller is configured for light-duty transit in the populated areas."

Ben and Garrison exchanged an uncomfortable look. It wasn't any fun being a greenhorn.

Nadia switched on her headset again. "Fred! Next job on schedule. Roller CC-260-3S-5, parked on east side of station. Install real auto pilot, beef up suspension." She shut off the set without waiting for a reply.

Ben shifted in his chair uneasily. "Ah, but I'm not sure we can pay for—"

"Want your future business, and is no repeat trade from dead customers," Nadia said bluntly. "We work out fair deal later, but you need job done if you want to survive drive through Farside craterfields. Fred will do job."

All of a sudden, Ben didn't feel quite so self-reliant and independent. But he was starting to realize you didn't stay alive out here if you turned down help. These people knew the score. "Thanks," he said.

"Forget it," Nadia said. "Excuse now, must go back to fill hollow legs of drunks at bar."

"Is that your big cargo rig out there with the deep-drill gear on it?" Garrison asked Mohammed.

"Yeah, sure is. And it's the last shipment, too. It's

been a nice contract while it's lasted. Drive the stuff from Central to Farside, then deadhead back around the other side back to Central. Pretty relentless schedule, but at least there was money in it for me to get off the road for a while now."

"Why do they need deep-drill gear for way the hell out there?" Garrison asked.

"Laser array."

"Huh?"

"The comm laser array they're building out there."

"Right, we'd heard about that," Garrison replied. "But what do comm lasers have to do with deep-drill mining?"

"They're shipping a whole laser *factory* out there, and they need a bunch of materials that aren't available on the surface. It's the old factory that built the Nearside array."

"A whole factory just to build a few comm lasers?" Ben objected.

Garrison shrugged. "You have to put the factory somewhere. Cheaper to ship it than haul the final products halfway around the Moon, even if you only need a few lasers."

"They need more than a few," Mohammed said. "With the space traffic density they're projecting, they'll need to track maybe two, three dozen comm-targets at once—most of the interplanetary shipping, plus the Settlements on Mars, the Belt, and the inner and outer planets. *Plus* you need back-ups for all of those, and you have to have lasers at several frequencies for various dull reasons. Right off the bat, they'll need about a hundred frequency-tunable comm laser units. More with eventual expansion, and for replacement of broken units. Makes sense to build them on the spot. Besides which, the laser units aren't small. Each comm laser unit will be self-contained. Each one with its own solar cells and storage coils and pointing mechanism and so on.

"If they had built 'em at Central Colony, and shipped 'em from there, *maybe* I'd have been able to fix two of them on my roller at a time. Shipping two per trip, and one trip a month, it would take over four years to get 'em all out there. That would cost UNLAC plenty, more so if they hired several oversize rollers to get it done faster.

There aren't that many outsizers around, and they cost plenty to hire. It's cheaper, faster, and easier to ship a robot factory out there. In fact, most of the factory is already out at Farside Station. The deep-drill mining gear is the last component to go in."

Garrison opened his mouth to ask a question—but something suddenly struck him. There, suddenly, in his mind, was a bright, clear perfect idea. An idea that felt *right*, simple, obvious. The bits and pieces of it fell into place in his mind so naturally and perfectly it frightened him. A complex, full-blown plan appeared in his mind, flawless and complete.

He, Garrison was in exactly the right time, the right place, and the right situation to make it work. It was so *simple*—but it would require a great subtlety to pull it off. And great audacity. He would have to be careful. And maybe a little bit crazy.

Chapter Nineteen

EARTHRISE STATION

The as-yet unseen Fred was already at work on their autopilot by the time Garrison and Ben were finished eating. Ben's thoughts immediately turned to the luxury beds with real sheets, pillows and mattresses. Ben and Garrison wanted to check in to their room, but the young man behind the hotel desk section of the long counter was still fast asleep.

Nadia took time out from her various duties behind the bar to stalk down to his end of the counter and shout in his ear. "Josef! Wake up, lazy brain! Guests to check in!"

The young man's eyes bounced open and he almost knocked over his stool as he jumped in surprise. "All right, Ma, take it easy. Jeez." He blinked once or twice to get the sleep out of his eyes and looked around dazedly, trying to get his bearings. He didn't zero in on his customers immediately as he peered about, but finally he spotted them on the other side of the counter. "Ah, there you are. Welcome to Earthrise Station."

"Check in these two men, good room with no airleaks," she ordered, and then glanced at the newcomers in embarrassment, thinking she might have unnerved them. "Is joke."

"We know," Garrison said gently. "So this is your son?"

"Da." Nadia beamed proudly at her son, reached over and rumpled his hair. "He good boy, hard worker. Just come off night watch is all. Not get enough sleep. But smart boy."

"Knock it off, Ma," Josef muttered in a tone of voice that proved he had no hopes that she would. He ran a hand through his hair to smooth it down. "I'll take care of them, you get back to your customers." He waited until his mother was safely out of range and offered his hand to Garrison. "Hi. I'm Joe Pevtrovka."

"Garrison Morrow, and this is my friend Ben Moscowitz."

"Good to meet you. C'mon, I'll show you to your room." Apparently, a handshake was it in the way of check-in procedure. Joe hopped over the counter, moving with the easy grace of someone used to low gravity. He headed over to the hatch set in the floor, more bouncing than walking, and simply dropped down the hatch, rather than using the ladder. Garrison was about to follow his host's lead, but then stopped and shouted down the hatch. "Hold on just a second!" He hurried back to the racks by the airlock, and grabbed his suit and Ben's. "Lot of good these would do us by the door if there was an accident." He handed Ben his suit and hopped down the hatch after Joe.

Ben looked through the hatch and found the floor of the tunnel below seemed just a bit too far down for his liking. He chose a more conservative approach, climbing down the ladder one-handed as he lugged his suit and helmet in the other.

The tunnel was covered with dark green wallplant. The walls and ceiling were completely hidden from view, and even the floor was thickly carpeted in it. The flat-leaf ivy gave the air a pungent, musty flavor. The tunnels were brightly lit, apparently to suit the vegetation, and the air was warm and humid. Ben had seen wallplant before, but never so much of it. Usually it was raised to supplement the air system and provide a food source for domestic animals. Here it didn't seem so much to be cultivated as taking over the place. Ben was careful at first to tread gently on the vines underfoot, until he noticed Garrison and Joe were taking no such precautions.

Joe led them through a tangled maze of tunnels that seemed to lead in all directions at once. Ben was startled when a pair of brown furry streaks shot past them headed the other way, chasing each other down the corridor. He shouldn't have been. Cats were popular on the Moon. Joe paid the kittens no mind, but led on.

They dropped down another hatch to a lower level, and at last Joe stopped in front of an airtight door. Someone had painted a sloppy 27 on it a while back. Drips of dried paint trailed down from the bottom of the 7. Joe brushed the wallplant back from the latches, undogged the door and stepped through into a surprisingly pleasant room. Nothing fancy, but it did have two genuine beds in it. "Bathroom's down the hall," Joe announced. "One dollar U.S. a minute or equivalent for the shower, no charge for toilet or hand basin. There's a map of the place on the bureau, all four levels—but don't trust it toward the south end, we're doing some fresh tunnelling back that way." He glanced around the room to make sure all was in order, and nodded in satisfaction. "That should do it," he concluded. He hadn't given them a key, and Ben noticed the door didn't have a lock anyway. Joe stepped out into the hallway, then remembered something and turned back. "Oh, and you might want to keep the door shut between 2000 hours and 0100," he said. "That's when we let the bunnies out for their run. They can get into mischief in the rooms sometimes."

"Bunnies?" Ben asked.

"Bunnies. Rabbits. How else do you think we keep the wallplants under control? Or make the stew you were eating?"

Ben was asleep almost before he hit the bed, but, genuine mattress (albeit a foam rubber one) or not, for once it was Garrison who couldn't doze off. Ben was the one who usually did the worrying, but this time Garrison had legitimate cause for staring at the ceiling. The brilliant idea that had seemed simple over a bowl of stew, requiring mere audacity and a small dose of fibbing to accomplish the impossible, now seemed hopelessly complex, riddled with unknowns, dangerous and murky.

Such as the fact that Garrison was not a good liar, not a good schemer, not a good conspirator. Look at the mess he had made of Iceland! But this time would have to be different. He *had* to pull it off. The whole damn fool idea was a ridiculous long shot, but never again could he hope to have odds even this good. He rolled over and forced himself to get some sleep. Considering what Nadia was likely to demand in barter for the use of this bed, it seemed a crime to waste it. Besides, tomorrow they'd be back on the damn roller.

It would be nice to move in convoy, Ben thought. A dose of human contact at Earthrise Station had made the barren lunar landscape seem all the more lonely. It would be good to see someone else rolling right alongside. He pulled his seat belt on and glanced up through the forward viewport just as Mohammed's oversize roller, the *Ali Akbar,* began to move. "Happiness is the planet Earth in your rearview monitor," Mohammed announced over the radio.

Ben switched on his own radio transmitter. "What the hell is *that* supposed to mean?" he asked as he powered up the *Rock & Roll.* Solar cells, storage ring power, cooling, cabin pressure, transponder link. Everything go. He punched up the autopilot and the *Rock & Roll* moved forward.

"I'm not sure, exactly," Mohammed's voice replied through his headphones. "They say it a lot out at Farside Station. I think it's a paraphrase from some old 20th century American song about a guy being glad to leave his home town. Most of the people at Farside are exiles of one sort or another. Maybe it makes them feel better to think they're getting rid of Earth instead of the other way around."

Ben looked at his own rearview monitor. He felt a lot of things as he watched Earth slide lower and lower in the sky, but happiness was not one of them. It might be months, or years, before he saw Earth again. In fact, there were no guarantees he would ever see it again. This was the wilderness, the frontier. People died out here from more things than old age.

And never mind wondering if he would *see* Earth again.

Would he ever *walk* upon her again? An exile twice over, would he, could he, ever return home?

Maybe the Farsiders had a point, he thought, pretending that they like leaving. With infinite sadness, Ben watched Earth drop back behind the eastern horizon.

ABOARD THE DAWN TREADER

The days were long aboard the *Dawn Treader*. There was little work to do, and much time for thinking, and for conversation. Even with the precautions needed to guard against snooping, in the small bits and pieces of time they could snatch without raising suspicion, Bertram Choate and Cathy Cleveland found the time to talk. In quiet, careful conversations, in bits and pieces over many days, Cathy told the whole story to Choate—everything that she had done, everything that had happened to her since Hrisey. He said very little himself, and chose not to say anymore at all concerning his suspicions of Ishida. It was as if he were hesitant to say more, commit himself further to Cathy's trust, until he knew her better.

It was in a talk in her cabin, some days after Cathy had told him the last of her story, that Cathy finally got Choate to speak his piece. Even then, Cathy had to press him a bit before he would talk. "Come on, now, Bertram," she said at last. "I've practically told you my life story. Either you trust me by now or you don't. I haven't been able to spot any listening devices, and I've rigged up the best bug-jammers I can, just to be on the safe side. No one else can hear us. If it's ever going to be safe to talk, it's here and now. So what is it that Ishida's got in mind?"

Choate hesitated, but then leaned close to Cathy and spoke in low tones. "Very well. You're right. But please don't be offended at my caution. It wasn't just that I needed to know I could trust you, though that was part of it. I needed to hear your story, see if the facts you could report fit into my theories. I'm afraid your adventures fit in alarmingly well." Choate stood up and began pacing back and forth across Cathy's tiny cabin. "I'm only guessing at what Ishida has planned—but I think I've gotten close to the truth. My theory starts with the assumption that Ishida has so far done exactly what he set out to do. His *apparent* failures were all really well-disguised successes."

Cathy knitted her brow in bafflement. "What are you talking about?"

"He apologized for wrecking Morrow's video show, right?" Choate asked. "Convinced everyone that it was an accident, a miscalculation. *I* think that in reality, he knew perfectly well what was going to happen. He had it all figured out. He *wanted* that disaster to happen—not just to make us all into fugitives, and force us to stick with him—but also to wreck Morrow's work. Ishida *needed* Morrow to fail. Right from the beginning, he only pretended to support Morrow. And his pretension can be most convincing."

Cathy knotted her fingers together. "That, I know, Jesus, Ishida talked me into committing *arson* against Garrison. Ishida had me believing that burning down Garrison's supply shed was going to expose Garrison as a fraud or *help* Garrison by forcing LuTech's hand."

"Proof that he's good at mixing the truth in with his lies," Choate said with a humorless smile. "He *did* want to make things sticky for LuTech, there's no doubt about that. That *was* one thing he intended, I'm sure. It was important for him. And, in a way, he was telling you the truth. After all, the arson plan worked. I'll bet it was the arson that got Morrow's people suspicious about the source of the funding.

"But Ishida had a much more important reason for weaning Morrow away from LuTech's covert support. *Ishida* needed to discredit Morrow, and do it his own way, so as to make LuTech look bad at the same time. My guess is he needed LuTech looking weak and discredited for some move of his down the road. But he also needed *Morrow* to fail.

"If Garrison had been effective and *believable* on that video show, maybe he'd have scared enough people and kept them scared long enough for effective action to be taken. Cornucopia could have been diverted away from an Earth-encounter orbit by now. There are some big fusion engines strapped onto that rock, along with some rather hefty fuel tanks. I'll bet there's enough rocket power aboard

Cornucopia to do the job right now. Query the computers and see what you get. Five to one you could divert that rock into an orbit that'd miss Earth by twenty million klicks any time in the next six months. Try it."

Cathy frowned. She had never looked at the problem from that direction. She had only considered the procedures for diverting the asteroid once it was already close to Earth. Now, for the first time, it occurred to her that waiting until that terminal phase made no sense at all.

She had been studying trajectory and maneuver techniques for weeks now, training herself as a navigator. As a simulations specialist, she found the skills of space navigation closely resembled her own work. She was learning fast.

One thing she had picked up early on: as a rule of thumb, the closer you got to your target in space, the more energy a course correction would require. Indeed, that was more than a rule of thumb—that was close to a primary axiom in orbital navigation. Because a course major change done late and close in might leave no time or power available to correct an error, pilots considered it bad form to make their maneuvers late. It allowed them no time afterwards to second-guess themselves.

Cathy had learned other bits of pilot folklore: all other things being equal, it was more difficult to control high-power maneuvers precisely, as opposed to low-power ones; and it was tougher to handle course changes near a strong or complex gravitational field rather than in deep space.

If they tried to knock Cornucopia off course once it was close to Earth, they would have to do all those things. It would require less power, less precision, and far simpler calculation to do the job early, while Cornucopia was still in deep space.

Given a choice between administering a gentle, almost casual tap of thrust to the asteroid in the roomy depths of the void, and hitting it with a sledgehammer blow of rocket thrust—one that had to be struck with micrometer precision —in the crowded, fragile china shop of near-Earth space, Ishida had set up a situation where only the latter technique was possible. The *Dawn Treader* was a slow, low-powered ship. She could not possibly get to

Cornucopia until the asteroid had almost reached Earth space. Cathy ran the program on her own, private, portable computer, since she was sure it was quite unlinked to any datanode aboard the ship. It took a bit longer to run the program, and the 3D graphics weren't as smooth as they would have been on the main ship's system—but privacy was worth a few sacrifces.

Besides, the answer came, just the same. It would take the merest of love-taps to knock Cornucopia irrevocably out of its Earth trajectory, not only keeping it from arriving now, but keeping anyone from ever dreaming of recapturing it again with any sort of economy. A quite modest burn *now,* in *this* particular direction, would send the asteroid toward Jupiter. Then the giant planet could be used in either of two ways to get rid of the rock. Either a gravity-assist maneuver could send it whipping out into the outer System on a wild, unrecoverable orbit, or the asteroid could be dropped *into* Jupiter. The latter was a daring idea, but Cathy couldn't see any reason against it. After all, there wasn't any solid surface on Jupiter for Cornucopia to damage. The best it would be able to do would be to raise a splash.

But none of that was possible now. They had no way of sending remote command codes to the asteroid, and the *Dawn Treader* couldn't get there in time to board the rock and lay in the commands manually.

Cathy grunted and wordlessly shoved the computer over so Choate could look over the screen. "Okay, you're right," she said, once Choate had examined the display. "But maybe all that means is that Ishida couldn't afford a faster, more modern ship." Even as she said it, she knew it sounded unconvincing.

Choate snorted derisively. "Poppycock. His uncle runs one spaceline, and his brother is a big stockholder in Boeing, to mention only two obvious, *overt* connections. I've studied our boy Shiro Ishida for quite a while. He could have afforded a fast constant-boost ship."

Choate paused in thought for a moment. "Let's go back to my theory that whatever Ishida ends up doing, he *meant* to do all along. If we postulate that, and assume that he deliberately colors his successes to look like failures, what does that mean? If he always gets the results he wants, what things can those results tell us about? Pretend you're back in your college analysis class."

Cathy thought, treating the question as a pure reasoning exercise, ingoring the obvious absurdities. "Given your postulates, current results tell us what his original intentions were. Things as they are suit him just fine, because things are as he planned. So, in order to find out what he wanted, we just have to look at what he's gotten." She stopped and looked up at Choate. "But things are in a mess. He's on the run from the law, he's in public disgrace, and he failed to stop Cornucopia."

"Thing are in a mess for him only if stopping the asteroid was his *real* intention," Choate said eagerly. "But if we take a look at a few features of property law and rules of jurisdiction—"

"*Property* law? What the hell are you talking about?" Cathy demanded.

"Well, space property law, I suppose, if you want to get specific," Choate said. "And the issues drift over into admiralty law as well. I think that what Ishida is trying has a lot to do with the state of rules and regulations regarding ownership and territoriality in space. The questions can get sticky. For example: Who owns Mars?" Choate demanded abruptly.

Cathy look at Choate strangely. "The Martians, of course." She hesitated a moment. At least, that is, the Martian government, I suppose."

"Then who owns Earth?" Choate asked in the same rapid-fire tones, obviously trying to force a quick answer.

Cathy opened her mouth, shut it, and then thought for a minute. "I was going to say the Earth government, but there isn't one, not really. And certainly none of the sovereign nations have ceded their rights to the U.N. But if I answer that the governments of Earth's nations own the planet, parcel by parcel, that would be wrong, too, wouldn't it?"

Choate smiled mischievously. "You escaped the second part of my trap. Yes, that would be wrong as well. And of course, I'm deliberately mixing up the concepts of ownership and territoriality. For example, the United Kingdom includes the territory of, say, London, or Wales, or Dublin, for example—but it's the shopkeepers and landlords and homeowners that actually *own* the property the cities are built on—except of course the various city councils hold various forms of authority as well. The nation, or city, or the council, or whatever local authority you wish, can at times compel the property owners to do various things— such as pay taxes, or surrender their land under the right of eminent domain. If the owners connot control their property, or prevent others from taking it, how can *they* be said to own it? And you're not quite right in saying the nations have not ceded rights to the U.N. Under rather special circumstances, the U.N. can wade in and claim eminent domain, on the legal theory that it is acting on behalf of all humankind.

"So you tell me: Who *really* owns the Rising Sun pub around the corner from St. Paul's Cathedral in the City of London? The proprietor? The City of London? The London Corporation Council? The United Kingdom? The U.N.? They all exercise some form of control over it and can claim things from it, if they choose to.

"And that's a simple example. What happens in a war, when the government that established and guaranteed the laws surrounding a property deed and title is overthrown? Or when a colonial power pulls out and takes its legal system with it? Or when the U.N. declares a trust territory, and a member nation registers a counterclaim, the way the Argentineans did with Antarctica? What about the oceans, or the sea floor, or the atmosphere, or the Earth's core? Various groups have laid claim to part or all of those places with varying degrees of sanity and success. There are tangled precedents and conflicting laws and theories of law regarding all these questions.

"The real, honest, answer to the question 'Who owns Earth?' would have to be: nobody knows. There were kingdoms and countries and alliances for centuries before the question ever meant anything. With hundreds of years of law and precedence and tradition for parceling out the landscape—none of it contemplating the thought that Earth might have to speak with one voice, or be considered as a single legal entity—well, in short, it was easier to ignore the question, sweep the loose ends under the rug, rather than turn every property law upside down. The realization that Earth had to be treated as a single place for many purposes came too late to organize things neatly." Choate paused for a moment. "The *practical* answer for everyday use is of course to ignore the question. There are various legal fictions that have been cooked up, but mostly people have found ways of not dealing with the issue. The U.N. does its best, but even it is constantly caught up in lawsuits over sovereignty infringements."

"To come around a little closer to the matter at hand, when the lawyers and the law makers and the diplomats came face to face with the fact that people were going to be colonizing—excuse me, *settling* various worlds in space, and in some case building their own artificial worlds, outside the jurisdiction of any then existing court or law, they had both a legal crisis and an opportunity on their hands. They had the potential for a real mess—and a chance to make things tidy.

"They came up with a few basic precepts. *No sovereign nation could own or claim territorial rights over a planet or natural astronomical body, or any portion thereof.* There was already a U.N. treaty that said as much, before the Americans reached the Moon for the first time in 1969. Once the migration into space really got under way, that concept was expanded and firmly established in other treaties of one sort or another. The one exception, of course, was that the U.N. managed to establish its own claim to the Moon.

"Tradition and the precedents of international law extended the no-claims rule to any government, *anywhere*, coming into existence after the treaties were signed. In theory, that rule might have been ignored—except it takes government-sized assistance to start a settlement on a new world. And there was another rule established quite clearly. *No nation could plant a colony on another world, or by other means attempt to extend its sovereignty outside of Earth space.*

"So instead of establishing a colony, an Earthside government would assist in the creation of a new nation-state, settled primarily by people from the Earthside country, and allied—at least as first—with the home country. The old nation would not allow the new nation to be established until it had signed all of the space territory treaties.

"Following all this, so far?" Choate asked.

"Yes, more or less," Cathy said cautiously. "Tell me the truth, though—you used to be a school teacher, right?"

Choate smiled bemusedly. "In my former life. I was a lecturer at High Man's one and only school. All grades, all ages under one roof. The old habits die hard."

"I thought so. For what it's worth, you were obviously a good one. But if what you are saying is right, then the off-planet governments—and nations—don't actually have any territory."

"True. No nation is allowed to possess a planetary body."

"But—if, say the Commonwealth of Ceres,—doesn't possess the territory of Ceres—what does it have sovereignty over?"

"Everything human-made in, on, about or attached to or made from Ceres. Everything occupied or used by humans. Everything about Ceres that the government—or its citizens—control. Which, for all practical purposes, means Ceres. Any bit of the planetoid that isn't controlled in some way by humans comes under the jurisdiction of Ceres government the moment someone uses it. The idea that the people and government of Ceres don't 'own' their planet comes down to being yet another legal fiction—but an important fiction.

"For that matter, if John Smith, private citizen, sets foot on an unoccupied, unused lump of asteroidal rock somewhere out in space—he *is* the government of that asteroid until he leaves it or ceases to make use of it, even if he wasn't the first one there. Within broad limits to allow for temporary absences, prior claims are invalid. If John Smith leaves and doesn't come back, and then John Doe comes along and spends five minutes on that rock—it's his. But, if Doe leaves it and does not return for a period of two years, *he* loses all claim to the rock.

"The idea of the no-territory laws is to prevent the sort of foolishness that made a mess of the map of North America when it was colonized. Virginia's original border didn't *have* any western limit, for example. In theory,

Virginia owned a swath of California coast. Private citizens were deeded tracts of land the size of the mother nation, including wilderness no European would see for a century. What sense does that make? And if I have this straight, there was some great foolishness about the Pope deeding Japan to the Portuguese at one point—though the Japanese emperor was unaware of it at the time. And of course the European colonization of Africa is *still* causing nightmares. No one will ever get those borders settled to everyone's satisfaction.

"The law seeks to keep someone from sticking a flag onto a planet and claiming it when they can't control it, possess it, or use it in any way. Or what's to stop someone from rigging a way to drop a flag onto Jupiter and claiming it in perpetuity?"

An odd look came over Cathy's face. "I think I see where you're going with this," she said quietly.

"Then let me add one more piece to the puzzle. LuTech is in trouble, serious financial trouble. They were having problems long before Garrison Morrow started drilling holes in Iceland. Their main asset has always been the mining asteroid Lucifer, of course. But they made some bad mistakes and had some bad luck with leasing arrangements on parts of Lucifer.

"Lucifer was the first asteroid in Earth orbit, and it was placed in a distant, conservative orbit. That makes shipping costs for Lucifer quite high, compared to the later rocks. Lucifer's extraction and processing gear is far less efficient than what the competition is using. The long and the short of it is that the other mining companies have been able to undercut LuTech's prices, even in the protected Earth market. LuTech's utterly hopeless trying to sell to the Settlement markets, of course. Which brings up one last problem—the supply of asteroid products in the Earth/Moon system is far larger than the demand."

"Then why bring in Cornucopia?" Cathy asked.

"It's a high-grade rock," Choate said. "It has some extremely large concentrations of high-profit compounds. And most of the potential markets for those materials will be in a low-earth orbit—in energy terms, close to where Cornucopia is supposed to go. Factor in the lower shipping costs, better-grade raw materials, and the efficiencies of a new-style processing plant, and you've got a real formula for profit. LuTech is gambling that it will work. And they're betting heavily. They've spent practically every dime they have on the Cornucopia project. If Cornucopia doesn't come through—well, it'll take some creative efforts to keep them out of bankruptcy, at best."

"So," Cathy said, "by keeping Cornucopia out of Earth orbit, Ishida can bankrupt LuTech, its owners. And by setting foot on the rock two years after Lutech personnel have last been aboard, he can legally register his own claim," Cathy said. "LuTech has to bear all the expense of moving an asteroid, and Ishida gets to take it away from them. But what good does that do him if Cornucopia is in an unusable orbit?"

"You should know better than that. Run the projections, Cathy. Track the asteroid's orbit after we've performed the planned course-change on it."

Cathy's eyes widened in shocked understanding. How had she missed that? It was so obvious. Cornucopia would remain on a closed solar orbit after the *Dawn Treader* team had knocked it out of its Earth-orbit insertion path. And what goes around, comes around. She grabbed her computer again and ran the problem. "Jesus H. Christ," Cathy said. "Three years. Cornucopia's new orbit is eighteen months long. Every three years, every other orbit, Cornucopia has a close encounter with Earth. For every three orbits Earth does, Cornucopia does two—and they meet up again. Its path and Earth's keep crossing and recrossing. Some of the encounters are very near misses."

Choate nodded grimly. "But Ishida won't leave it that way. He just has to have his people occupy the rock long enough to protect his own claim, wait until it comes back around and he can knock it into close Earth orbit himself, three years, two Cornucopia orbits from now. Without LuTech's debts or problems, he can step right into the orbital mining business. He can, quite legally, steal an asteroid. And in the process of capturing it three years from now, he'll expose Earth to all the dangers he's protesting against now."

There was dead silence in the tiny compartment.

Cathy shivered. "Unless, of course, something goes wrong with his plan after we've shifted the orbit," she said. "Say *he* goes bankrupt, or dies, or winds up in jail. Then Cornucopia will stay in that orbit, using Earth for target practice every three years for the rest of time. Until someone else steals it, and brings it into a dangerous low orbit. Or until it impacts on its own."

Choate sat back down and looked intently at Cathy. "So. How do we stop him?"

SUNWAY, HERTZSPRUNG SECTOR, LUNAR FARSIDE

It was incredible how much of a change a new suspension and the proper autopilot made. The *Rock & Roll* moved smartly along between the rail transponders, keeping an orderly one-kilometer separation from Mohammed's *Ali Akbar*. The two rollers kept up a thirty-kilometer-per-hour pace, even through the roughest crater fields. They *needed* to keep up the pace, too—threading their way through the craters added perhaps fifty percent to the length of their route. On average, it took them fifteen kilometers of zigzag driving to move a straight-line distance of ten klicks. They were just barely keeping pace with the Sun as it tracked slowly across the lunar sky.

But the best news was that the *R&R* could now handle itself on autopilot. Mohammed's pilot was unquestionably a better rig than even their new one, as it allowed him to herd the *AA* single-handedly, but whatever hardware Fred had put into the *R&R* did the trick far better than what he had taken out.

Ben and Garrison were able to let the roller handle itself with only occasional operator intervention. Fred had even rigged an alarm that sounded whenever the pilot thought it *might* need help. All the on-duty driver had to do was sit back, relax, and enjoy the show. The situation was improved even more when the two vehicles were within line-of-sight with each other. Then the two autopilots could use comm lasers to trade data back and forth, affording two views of each obstacle.

In a suddenly much-enhanced vehicle, after a good rest,

with a week's experience of endurance roller-driving under their belts, the Farside leg of the trip was easier to handle then either of them had dreamed. But even so, the endless wilderness of craters, crevices, and boulder fields would have been tough to traverse alone, no matter how much better the *Rock & Roll* or her drivers had gotten. Mohammed and the *AA*'s autopilot knew the route, and Mohammed was a past master of tracking exactly with the Sun as they moved. He kept them precisely at local noon as they moved. He wasn't about to let them run out of daylight.

Riding through the endless vacuum-baked noon as they chased the Sun around the Moon, Ben and Garrison each spent a good deal of time essentially alone, on watch while the other man slept. There were long hours alone, and not much to do but think.

A hundred times in those silent hours by himself, Garrison wanted to wake Ben, talk with him about his plans. Garrison wanted, needed, to bounce all the wild ideas off someone, anyone, but especially off his best friend. But his ideas were just *too* wild for that, and the first steps Garrison would have to take alone, anyway. What if Garrison failed before he ever began? No, it would be better to wait, share his plans only when there was some hope of their succeeding.

On the third day out, his resolve collapsed. There was too much quiet surrounding them, too many doubts in his mind, too much fear of attempting even the first step of such a daunting plan completely alone. Ben was just waking up, getting ready to go on shift, and Garrison had spent the long hours of eternal light worrying. The endless *brightness* was starting to get to him. Garrison missed the comforting darkness of their Earthrise Station hotel room. The searing glare of the lunar noon seemed more relentless than ever now. Garrison wished passionately for *night*.

Probably the glare was serving to make him worry more—but he barely needed the excuse anymore. "Ben," Garrison said as his friend returned from the head and settled back into his couch, "there's something I want to talk to you about."

Ben looked over at Garrison and nodded calmly. "I

thought there might be. You've been a little strange ever since Earthrise. What is it?"

"An idea. An idea that sounds nuts."

"Okay, shoot."

"They're going to assemble that automated factory at Farside, right? To build the laser units. Run off about a hundred of them and then shut the thing down."

"Yeah, so?"

"So what if they forget to shut it off?"

Ben sat up a little straighter in his chair. "It'd keep cranking out laser units."

"And since this factory is on Farside, where no one is watching, really, no one would be likely to notice if the thing was still running." Garrison spoke without looking at Ben, staring straight ahead at the landscape, watching it with far more care than he needed to take. "Yeah, if they went looking, sure they'd find us—but why would they look? No one would notice, probably, right?"

"Right. Go on." In a burst of inspiration, Ben suddenly realized what Garrison was leading up to. His stomach snapped into a tangled knot and his mouth went dry.

Garrison swallowed hard and clamped his hands tightly around the steering wheel. "So," he asked in a voice that was nearly a whisper, "how many of those lasers slaved together would it take to blast Cornucopia right out of the sky?"

Chapter Twenty

SUNWAY, HERTZSPRUNG SECTOR,
LUNAR FARSIDE

It took a half day of driving for Ben to decide Garrison wasn't insane. The whole idea of message lasers blasting an asteroid out of the sky seemed incredible, impossible.

At first just to humor his friend and prove him wrong, and then to confirm the astonishing truth that he was right, Ben ran through a long series of calculations again and again. There was a lot of guessing involved, but the range of possible answers was impressive to say the least. Garrison stayed behind the wheel while Ben worked out the questions.

There were a lot of unknowns, facts and figures Ben just couldn't get at while rolling along the lunar maria. Range, power dispersion, power ratings and efficiencies, size of target, accuracy of the laser pointing system. It was frustrating to realize that a good number of the answers were probably buried in the journal and datablocks he had packed away in the back of the *Rock & Roll*. Unfortunately, there was no way to get to those references until they stopped and unpacked. Ben wished more than once that Cathy Cleveland had been there to help them. Maybe she had betrayed Garrison—but Ben himself wasn't innocent on that score, and Garrison had always felt that Cathy's crimes were committed with the greatest reluctance. Garrison still thought of her kindly, at the very least. That much Ben knew, if it meant anything when Garrison talked in his sleep.

But wandering into those sorts of side issues wasn't getting the problem solved. Ben plunged into the figures on his own, determined to do his best. Even in the absence of hard numbers, he could make a reasonable ballpark guess at most of the variables. In some ways the problems were pretty straightforward. Mostly it was a question of figuring how much energy the attack on the rock would take.

Cornucopia was shrouded in a highly reflective white bagnet that would make the job tougher. The white reflective coating would throw back most of the visible laser light—but if Ben remembered what he had read about the asteroid, and if the pictures he had seen of it were right, the stress cables overlaying the bagnet were dark in color, and should absorb heat nicely. Those cables had to be under a fair degree of stress. If they could get enough of them hot enough, they ought to weaken and ultimately snap. With enough cables lost, the whole support structure for the asteroid ought to come apart. If they could develop a few holes and tears in the net, they'd expose the dark asteroid surface underneath—and that *ought* to heat up very nicely.

And it would not be necessary to melt out the whole rock. Snapping the support cables and wrecking the bagnet would be half the battle. The asteroid's internal structure hadn't been very strong to start with, and it had been weakened considerably by the stresses of capture and launches. The cables and bagnet were, after all, there to hold the rock together. Without the cables and net to offer structural support, the spinning asteroid would break up on its own without much encouragement. Then it would merely be a question of targeting the larger fragments, heating each of *them* until they melted down to vapor and gravel.

It wouldn't take all that much power to accomplish the

job. Well, yes, actually, it would, Ben admitted to himself. By any normal standard, it would take *incredible* amounts of energy to smash Cornucopia down into harmless rubble. Ben looked out at the blazing sunlight blasting down on the lunar surface. What was gradually dawning on Ben was that they *had* incredible amounts of power out here. Unlimited solar power, free for the taking. By the standards of what the Moon got from the Sun, the power needed to wreck an asteroid was chump change.

If they could get their hands on enough lasers that fired light of the right frequencies, the idea was workable. All they had to do was gain control of the "off" switch for the laser factory. If they could get in charge of the laser construction project they'd have it made.

But that was a big if. A huge if. It occurred to Ben that most of the *engineering* problems the plan presented had in large part been met by the UNLAC engineers who designed the robot laser factory in the first place. All that was left was an enormous political challenge. Garrison and Ben had to get control of the laser operation.

That was going to be tougher than pumping a few terawatts of power into a rock from a few million kilometers away. So how did two exiled geologists go about gaining control of a major engineering project? Ben leaned back in his chair and started to contemplate the question.

He didn't realize at first that he was already thinking about how to zap Cornucopia, and not wondering if they *could* blast the rock.

At last Ben shut off his computer monitor and turned toward his friend. "Garrison. I think the damn thing might be doable. *If* we can get our hands on that laser system."

Garrison hadn't looked away from the forward viewport once since he had asked about the lasers, but now he turned and grinned at Ben. "That's what I figured, too. *That's* the tack we've got to take at Farside. Convince them we ought to be in charge of things before they even think to ask. Find out who's in charge of the laser construction system and convince him that since the factory involves mines, and mines come under geology, that *we're* in charge. Just barge in there and take over. And take it from there."

"So who's in charge of construction?"

"Hell if I know—but Mohammed would," Garrison said.

Ben reached for the radio switch. "So let's ask him."

Garrison almost reached over to stop him, and held himself back just in time. "Just don't be obvious," he said.

"This from the master of subtlety?" Ben replied with a grin, punching up the radio. "Mohammed, this is Ben. How are you doing in there?"

"Just sitting here dreaming of the bath I'm going to take at Farside," Mohammed's voice replied. "What's up over with you?"

"Oh, not all that much," Ben said. "Just sort of wondering what happens when we get there. You going to take off again right away, or do you have to lay over and get your cargo handed over to the boss there?"

"Believe me, I've earned a layover," Mohammed said. "But I don't *have* to stay around. All I have to do is wheel up to the cargo hatch, drop off the gear, and get a receipt. There's barely any boss at all, fortunately. If there were, I bet I'd have to fill out a lot more forms or wade through some damn inspection drill or something."

"There must be someone in charge," Ben objected.

"Well, there's a bureaucrat back at Central Colony who's the official UNLAC engineer in charge—but would *you* roll all the way to Farside if you could avoid it? He handles everything over the phone. The only people on the scene are four locals they hired as construction technicians. The Farside Administrator General is a nice old coot, Dr. Hari Prathnabar. He's supposed to watch over the project, but he's barely able to keep up with the regular colony work. If he could dump the job on someone else, he would. In fact, if you guys aren't careful, he'll stick you with the job. After all, it involves mining."

Ben switched off the radio for a second and said, "And the mining part is the thin edge of the wedge." He switched back on and kept the conversation going, so Mohammed wouldn't get suspicious. "So what are your plans after you finish the layover?" he asked.

"I'll drive around in circles for someone else, of course. What else am I equipped for?"

"Not much, Mohammed, not much," Ben replied with a laugh. "See you when we get there. Moscowitz out."

Garrison turned to his friend. "My God," he said. "I think we might actually get away with it. All we have to do is convince this Prathnabar guy that we're doing him a favor by muscling in."

The *Rock & Roll* and the *Ali Akbar* moved on through or around the massive landmark craters. It took them over a day to cross Korolev Crater alone. The brooding emptiness of the sunbaked moonscape, the endless harshness of the noontime light became more and more oppressive. These were not happy or friendly lands.

They never stopped once in the whole week's journey. No one admitted it, but they were all reluctant to halt in a place where the very land seemed to tell them they were not wanted. More and more of the transponders were out of commission as they pressed on. They were forced to trust the *AA*'s auto pilot to remember where the missing beacons *had* been. Mohammed very carefully logged all the outages so as to report them to a SunWay maintenance team—for what good it would do. Many of them he had reported more than once before.

But then, a day past Korolev, the beacons stopped failing. They were close enough to a station for someone to bother taking care of the transponders. It was a tiny thing, the mere absence of failure, but it was a sign they were getting close, and it was heartening.

Then, at last, they rolled over the brow of a crater wall, and paused on the lip of Daedalus Crater, home of Farside Station. The two rollers paused at the summit ridge to look down at their destination. In spite of their altitude above the crater floor, Daedalus was big enough and the horizon close enough that they could not see the opposite wall of the crater—or even its center. There was no sign of life, nothing before them but an empty walled plain, dotted with small interior craters. It looked exactly like all the other big holes in the ground they had passed through to get this far.

"Mohammed, I thought we were there already," Ben said into the radio mike.

"We are."

"So where the hell is the Station?"

"Almost at the horizon. See the two largest interior craters? Use your binoculars on the northern one. You should just be able to look down into it from here."

Ben signed and fished out the field glasses and trained them on the crater-in-a-crater. Another letdown. He was getting used to anticlimactic arrivals on the Moon, but even so he was a bit disappointed by his first view of the Station. There was little to be seen at this distance except a few huts on the surface. It seemed not much larger than Earthrise Station. There didn't even seem to be any astronomical instruments around—and Ben wasn't ready to believe *they* were underground.

"Some booming metropolis, Mohammed," Ben said.

"If you've got five minutes I'll show you all the swinging night spots," Mohammed said cheerfully. "C'mon, let's get down there." The *AA* took off down the slope, roostertailing a stream of dust behind.

Ben punched a few buttons and the *Rock & Roll* took off after her.

Dr. Hari Prathnabar settled his old-fashioned spectacles more firmly on his nose and smiled faintly to himself as he watched the pick-up off the exterior view camera. New people arriving! Mohammed and his roller full of mining gear, that was expected, and much looked forward to; but the second roller, that was a surprise. A bonus.

The Station was a small, isolated town, the kind of place where everyone got to know everyone else far too quickly and far too well. The inhabitants of Farside Station were always hungry for new faces, new visitors. But Dr. Prathnabar enjoyed meeting newcomers even more than most. *Naturally gregarious*, he told himself, *that's what you are, old boy*.

Dr. Prathnabar was a quiet, unassuming man, perhaps a bit more advanced in years than a man in his position ought to be. It didn't really mean much, but, officially speaking, he was the Administrator General for the entire Farside of the Moon. Seventy-eight years old and in charge of half a world! He still marveled at that.

Ten years ago he had been exiled to Farside Moon by his own government, for the crime of publicly suggesting that India should perhaps grant certain expanded civil and religious rights to the citizens of Occupied Pakistan. No one wanted to hear that, not even from a respected old astronomy professor. And poof! Out he went. Exiled.

It wasn't an *official* exile, of course. The Indian government didn't do anything as unsubtle as that anymore. But they saw to getting rid of him just the same, eliminating all other possible postings or jobs to him, until the choice came down to accepting a position at Farside Observatory or starving.

At length he had settled in. It helped that nearly everyone else at Farside was in much the same predicament. Disoriented, exiled, cut off from their old world. Some of the scientific staff were transients, here voluntarily for a brief time to run their experiments and leave, but all the permanent residents were Moon-marooned exiles of one sort or another.

Scientists, engineers, writers, pilots, politicians, parolees from Tycho Penal. All of them people someone had declared undesirable somehow, all of them shoved off Earth or the Settlement Worlds or the habitats, foisted off on the Moon because the Moon's government had never been granted the power to control its own immigration.

But the powers-that-be on the Moon didn't want the worst of the troublemakers hanging around the larger settlements. UNLAC found ways to push them and prod them all towards Farside—or worse, to Tycho.

Such was Prathnabar's own fate, exiled to this empty and lonely place. And yet he commanded half a world! Well, yes, it *sounded* quite grand, if you forgot that the AdminGen had very limited authority. And of course there were only a few thousand people in this one lonely settlement, plus a few mining camps, on the whole of Farside. And the main reason he had been offered the job was that no one else wanted it.

But Dr. Prathnabar was an essentially cheerful man, and he shook off his gloomy thoughts. There were new people to meet. He put his work to one side and made his way to the main airlock section.

                            *   *   *

Down they came from the crater's rim into the central plain of Daedalus. Dead ahead, with a well-marked trail leading straight to it, was a smaller interior crater, Farside Crater, named for its position and for the Station. It drew closer and closer, and at last they climbed one last slope and rolled down into Farside Crater.

From the rim of its crater, Farside Station looked a little more impressive, Ben conceded. Even after two weeks of practice, it was hard to read the scale of things on the lunar surface. But as best he could judge, the scattered surface huts were larger than Ben had thought from the rim of Daedalus, and there were more buildings visible from this angle.

"Time to ring the doorbell," Garrison announced cheerfully. "Farside Control, this is Roller CC-260-3S-5 *Rock & Roll*, traveling in convoy with Roller UN-HT-127 *Ali Akbar*. Do you read me, over," he said.

"Welcome to Farside, *Rock & Roll*. This is port control. We are activating the follow-me strobe on thermal lock entry three. You should be able to see a repeated triple-flashing light. Follow that into your berth. Disregard double-flashing light, that is for *Ali Akbar*."

"We copy, port control. On our way." Garrison drove down the steep slope and followed the strobe to the massive thermal lock doors.

The outer doors swung open and the *Rock & Roll* eased its way into the moderator chamber of the thermal lock. At the moment, the moderator chamber's temperature was matched to the harsh lunar noontime temperatures, 100° Centigrade—the boiling point of water.

The moderator chamber was designed for gradual heating or cooling. Depending on the need, radiators and heaters were gently used to bring the temperature of anything in the lock to 20° over the course of a few hours, at which time it was moved through the inner doors and down into the underground thermal-control storage area.

But Ben and Garrison weren't expected to wait in the lock all that time. A robot access tunnel snaked out from the side of the thermal lock and docked itself to the *R&R*'s hatch. That was a pleasant surprise for Ben. No pressure suits required. Ben opened the inner lock door, stepped into the lock and checked the exterior pressure gauge. There was air out there, sure enough. He opened the spill valves, letting pressure match between the roller's interior and the access tunnel. Ben felt his ears pop at the slight pressure drop. He swallowed to make them pop again and clear, and then opened the outer door.

It swung open—and Ben breathed a sigh of relief. These were the last steps of the journey. They had arrived. Nothing more could go wrong. Six thousand-plus kilometers of Moon had failed to kill them. Ben felt a release of anxiety he did not even know he had been feeling. Now that there was nothing to be afraid of, he could at last afford to acknowledge his fear.

A comfortable, welcome sense of his own tiredness swept over him as well. No nervous half-sleep in a crash couch tonight, pitching and heaving along with the roller across the wild landscape, his subconsciousness half-expecting to be rudely awakened at any moment. Tonight he could *really* sleep. *That* thought settled his mind. Sleep, real sleep, real comfort and rest.

He slung an overnight bag over his shoulder and stepped into the access tunnel, the introspection of a moment before forgotten, nothing on his mind but the nearest shower. Never mind the price, he was going to have a good hot thirty-minute hose-down. He had never needed —or deserved—one more.

Ben walked through the tunnel and out into what seemed to be the main lock area for the station. There was a small knot of people there who seemed to be waiting for some excitement that was about to happen. Ben glanced around himself nervously and caught Garrison's eye as he came out of the access tunnel behind Ben.

Suddenly it dawned on Ben that Garrison and he were the excitement. After all, they didn't get many visitors around here. Great. They wanted to give the two of them a formal welcome—and Ben knew he and Garrison had to smell like a pair of dead moose.

An elderly Indian gentleman stepped forward from the little crowd. "Greetings to you," he said almost shyly, a small smile on his lips. "I am Dr. Hari Prathnabar, Ad-

ministrator General here. Welcome to Farside Station."
The little speech prompted a brief flurry of applause from
the small crowd that had gathered. Ben glanced around
nervously at the little knot of people.

"As you can see, we are always eager to welcome visitors," Prathnabar said. He spoke in a high, pleasant, gently
lilting voice that had almost a singsong quality to it. "We
look forward to meeting you and hearing something of the
outside world."

Ben stepped forward, feeling a bit self-conscious in front
of all these strangers' faces. "Hello," he said awkwardly.
"I'm Ben Moscowitz and this is my friend Garrison Morrow."

"Welcome to you both," Dr. Prathnabar said, taking
Ben's hand in a firm handshake. Ben found himself staring
in fascination at the kindly old man's face. He blinked and
glanced away, trying not to seem rude. That only brought
his eye around to stare at other faces. He felt his eye
drawn irresistibly to each face in turn, every one seeming
a miracle of a life's history drawn on flesh and bone.

Ben blinked in bafflement and looked again. These were
just ordinary people, ten or twelve men and woman with
nothing so remarkable about their looks. Their faces were
just faces—old, young, all ages and conditions, but nothing that should make him stare in slack-jawed fascination.
He realized what the matter was—he was not used to
seeing people anymore. Humans are social animals, and
Ben had been starved for company. After spending most of
the last two weeks with no one but Garrison to look at, he
had forgotten the infinite variety of human appearance.

Garrison, unaware of Ben's confusion, stepped forward
and shook the AdminGen's hand as well. "Dr. Prathnabar,"
he said. "It's good to meet you."

"Thank you very much, young man. I am likewise pleased
to make your acquaintance. Will you be visiting with us
for long?" Prathnabar asked politely.

Garrison cleared his throat uncomfortably and shifted
his feet. "I'm afraid we're here for the duration, doctor.
Permanent residents."

Prathnabar's face fell. "Oh dear, there has clearly been
some mistake. I have not received any notice about new
residents. I am much afraid we have no accommodation

available, beyond the transient barracks, which are not suitable for a permanent home whatsoever. If we had received some word . . ."

"That's our fault, I'm afraid, Dr. Prathnabar," Ben said, coming back to himself a bit. "Two weeks ago, we received advance word that we were going to be transferred here two weeks from *now*, and we just decided to get here early," Ben explained. It was the best kind of lie—so close to the truth it nearly *was* the truth. "We're supposed to start up a geology section out here. I'm surprised that you haven't received some sort of word about us by now."

"Geology?" Prathnabar asked. He knit his brow for a moment, as if trying to remember something. "Oh yes, of course," he said. "I received a message concerning you just yesterday, though I was given no names. I was notified that two geologists were to arrive in the *next* light period, three or four weeks from now—you're a month early or so, that is all. We have no place ready for you as yet. But I am sure we can make arrangements. Please, do let me escort you."

Ben and Garrison followed Prathnabar out of the airlock section, and the small crowd broke up, no doubt to tell their friends and co-workers about the new neighbors. The last of them were leaving just as Mohammed came through another access tunnel. "Ah, Mr. Ul-Haq," Prathnabar said happily. "It is good to see you again. I'm afraid that you have been upstaged by your traveling companions." Prathnabar smiled at Ben and Garrison. "Usually, it is Mr. Mohammed Ul-Haq they all come out to see. He has many friends here."

"That's okay, doctor," Mohammed said. "I was looking forward to the chance to slip away quietly for once so I could get cleaned up."

"Oh, yes, of course." Dr. Prathnabar frowned and looked over at Ben and Garrison, obviously noticing for the first time just how grubby and rumpled they looked. His nose twitched involuntarily, and Ben immediately felt more self-conscious than ever about his own aroma. Prathnabar seemed to be gauging not only how dirty his guests were, but the degree of delicacy required in mentioning it. "Forgive me, I was not thinking of your comfort," he said.

"No doubt you two as well would welcome the chance to refresh yourself. But perhaps you would be my guests at dinner in two hours time?"

"We'd be delighted, Doctor," Garrison said. "But if you could show us to that transient barracks, or wherever we might find a shower . . ."

Mohammed grinned and pointed down the corridor. "Just follow me that away. And if you lose sight of me, just follow the smell of old sweat shirts and sneakers."

The transients' barracks seemed like a pretty small place to have such a big name, but it did have bunks and a shower and a place to shave. Ben didn't get his half-hour soak-down, not with Mohammed and Garrison both eager for their turns, but the five-minute shower got him clean, and that was the main thing.

They got through dinner with Prathnabar somehow, then collapsed into bed.

Even Ben slept soundly. Being in a bed that wasn't moving felt too good for insomnia to have a chance.

Chapter Twenty-One

PORT VIKING, MARS

Angela Hardin wanted to go home. Go home to Ceres and leave these fools to do their worst without the chance to trouble her about it. There was nothing else left for her to do here on Mars. Nothing to do but wait for the next disaster—which should not be long in coming. McGillicutty and his people had forced through their tax refusal bill. Henceforth, no resident of any Settlement world would be required—or even permitted—to pay any taxes to the U.N. or any nation on Earth.

Since the U.N. still required tax payments of any terrestrial citizen who wished to go home without being thrown in prison, it wasn't hard to see that McGillicutty's bill meant nothing but trouble. Earth would be forced to respond, sooner or later.

But Angela knew she couldn't go home. Duty would not permit it. She had no choice but to stay here and limit the damage.

It was not a job that seemed likely to be very rewarding.

FARSIDE STATION

Farside Station was a big, rambling sort of place, burrowing out in all directions from the central station for kilometers. It was one of the very few joint efforts of the Settlement Worlds and Earth. Who had jurisdiction over which function became so blurred with the passage of years—and Farside proved to be so spectacularly unimportant —that no one really knew or cared who ran the place.

The Station certainly *looked* as if no one knew who was in charge. Outbuildings seemed to have been planted at random over the landscape of Daedelus Crater as this project or that program of those workers needed some sort of isolation—electromagnetic, vibrational, or personal—from some other operation. The largest part of Farside Station was the Farside Research Center, which functioned as a sort of scientific Siberia for both Earth and the Settlement worlds. The FRC was the ultimate dumping ground for scientific malcontents, eccentrics, and political unreliables from all the populated worlds. Department heads the length and breadth of the Solar System, seeking ways to get rid of their eccentrics, incompetents, irascible geniuses and resident curmudgeons all found ways to get their problems transferred to FRC. Trouble-making scientists from Titan, Mars, the asteroid belt, the habitats and Earth all tended to end up there, shipped away temporarily—or permanently —to a place where they couldn't give the front office any more headaches.

Unlike the original Siberia—or Tycho Penal—there was no forced labor, no actual incarceration, and very few of the Farside inhabitants were actually *deported* per se. Just as happened to Garrison and Ben, most of the permanent scientific staff were pressured into a path of least resistance toward the one place that would have them. As in Siberia, and other such places in history, the Farsiders discovered that exile is not all bad: being out of circulation also means being out from under. Farside was too remote for the powers that be to bother with surveillance. There was little or no supervision, were no political reliability tests, no annoying bureaucrats to joggle one's elbow. In short, it was a freewheeling, easygoing place, where some of the best thinking and research in the Solar System was underway.

Indeed, some Voluntary residents—most of them temporary postings, to be sure, but a even few permanent—had started moving to Farside. For obvious reasons, the Exiles and Voluntaries didn't understand each other very well.

By far the largest part of the FRC was the Observatory, the original reason for having a Farside Station in the first place. With the glaring Sun below the horizon for two solid weeks at a time, with the scarcely less blinding Earth forever hidden from view, with the whole endless electromagnetic din of terrestrial civilization permanently eclipsed by the bulk of the Moon, Farside was an ideal spot for an astronomical station, and boasted superb instruments for examination of optical, radio, X ray, and gamma ray emissions. Like everything else at Farside, half the astronomical hardware was paid for by the Settlers, and half paid for by Earth. It was not always clear which half was which.

With such divided authority and responsibility, it was not surprising that Farside wasn't run very well. Even so the astronomers were happy. They, after all, knew what they were doing. Clearly no one else in the place did.

Garrison wished *he* knew what he was doing. As the days went by, he was finding himself rediscovering the fact that conspiracy was not easy. That much he should have remembered from his previous foray into the profession, back in Iceland—if it was possible to dignify the way Ben, Cathy and he had tripped over themselves plotting against each other with the term "conspiracy."

But it was obvious that Ben and he couldn't pull this job off alone. They were going to need help. How and where they were going to get that help was much less obvious. They didn't know anyone here, or really understand how the place was organized, or what the political leanings of the populace were. Presumably UNLAC was not much favored by a group of people who had been deported by UNLAC, but it was a long stretch from there to joining some damn fool cabal that wanted to use asteroids for skeet-shooting practice.

There were other difficulties. Being discreet and unnoticed were two obvious prerequisites for getting into the conspiracy business. Unfortunately, in the days that followed, it also became clear that the good people of Farside Station weren't going to give two prominent newcomers the chance to be discreet or unnoticed. The two of them were a real draw around the commissary table, and Ben found himself the happy focus of a good deal of female attention.

But it wasn't just that they were newcomers. Further complicating matters, Ben and Garrison had a certain notoriety at Farside long before they had arrived. Hardly anyone at Central Colony or Earthrise Station had known or cared about the Mjollnir incident and the forged video— but they sure knew about them at Farside.

Maybe it was because the big observatory at Farside raised the general interest level in things astronautical. Maybe it was just that the lonely, isolated Farsiders were always hungry for *any* sort of news from the wide universe beyond their tiny outpost. Certainly the Farsiders were news junkies, true infomaniacs eager to know about everything. Newsheets were very much in demand, and the ink was half worn off the plastic before they could be recycled. Trivia games were taken very seriously at Farside.

Whatever the reason for strong local interest, Ben and Garrison found themselves telling their story over and over again. Ben had brought along record blocks of the video in both the authentic and forged versions, and cheerfully permitted anyone who was interested to make as many copies as they liked. As they settled in, it gradually occurred to Ben and Garrison that their notoriety, and people's reactions to their adventures and the video simulation, could serve as an excellent gauge of potential reaction to Garrison's plan.

In the meantime, there was a lot more that needed doing. The transients' barracks were all right for a night or so, and Mohammed was good company, but the three of them might just as well have been sharing a broom closet. As per his original plan, Ben set about turning the *Rock & Roll* into temporary quarters until such time as a vacancy came free—or, more likely, until the maintenance people could find the time to drill some more tunnels and compartments. Prathnabar arranged for a convenient parking space in the thermal lock, and provided a permanent access tunnel between the roller and the pressurized section of the station. With the access tunnel in place, they could go back and forth to the R&R without resort to airlocks and pressure suits. That made life more convenient. Once the R&R's interior could be rearranged, they could have a pleasant little temporary address.

The trouble was that Ben's merchandise was blocking most of the roller's deck space. Much of it could survive vacuum, and Ben promptly stacked that part of his stock outside the roller, right outside the front windows where he could keep an eye on it. He was pleasantly surprised by how rapidly the rest of his trade goods melted away. Apparently, he had chosen his stock well, back at Central Colony, and the Farsiders were more than willing to pay a fair price for types of merchandise they hadn't seen in a long time. He didn't come close to making a profit on the run, once the cost of buying the R&R was figured in, but the numbers showed promise for the future.

In the meantime, they pressed forward on their real plans. What they had expected to be the toughest part, getting control of the laser manufacturing process, was all but effortless. Prathnabar was delighted to find someone volunteering to take on the management of the operation, and didn't even ask Garrison why he was interested in the project.

Garrison was actually able to make a real contribution to the manufacturing operation. A rather unnerving German by the name of Alois Hofmeister was in nominal charge of laser construction, but his team had not exactly been setting productivity records. Hofmeister didn't seem much interested in getting down to work under Prathnabar's haphazard supervision. But Hofmeister took an immediate and inexplicable liking to Garrison, and that made all the difference. The project had been badly behind schedule, but Garrison quickly got it moving again. The minehead got drilled, blown, and redrilled according to plan and the mining robots went down the drill hole and got to work. The factory got assembled and tested. The first laser units were expected to come off the line a month after Garrison and Ben had arrived.

The question rapidly became who they were going to get to operate the lasers. They needed bodies.

Slowly and carefully, Garrison and Ben built up a list of people who seemed to understand the danger Cornucopia represented, and who had some sort of skill the plan would require. The two of them agreed early on that no one would be signed on merely because they seemed to fear the asteroid. They had to be useful to the cause, not just friendly to it. Conversely, they agreed that no one would be signed up merely for the sake of professional competence. The risks of betrayal were too great.

At least that was their original theory. They quickly came up against the problem of Hofmeister. He was the laser expert. There were several candidates for most of the other positions they might need filled—tracking, guidance, computer operations—but there was no one else at Farside who knew more about building and operating high-power lasers. His skill and knowledge were irreplaceable.

"So what do you think?" Garrison asked Ben. At the end of a long day, they were back in the *R&R*, getting ready to bed down for the night. "Can we trust the guy, or what?"

"The real question is: what choice do we have but to trust him?" Ben replied. "We can make all the rules we want about only recruiting true believers, but we need this guy."

"What do you know about him?" Garrison asked.

"Not much. You've seen his personnel records. Birth, arrival on Moon, citizenship status, that's about it. It looked to me as if someone had done a very thorough job of removing anything unpleasant from his computer file, and there wasn't much left afterwards. I've gotten a lot more from the rumor mill. Supposedly, he did some time at Tycho Penal, for what, nobody seems to know. He definitely runs one of the best stills at Farside. It's supposed to give a whole new meaning to the term moonshine."

Garrison smiled. "I'll have to get a sample of that stuff."

"He seems to dabble in the black market a lot, but if

that were true, you wouldn't think he'd be so friendly to my coming in with a wagonload of goodies to sell. He's been one of my best customers. He smiles a lot. He doesn't strike me as being very respectful of authority, and probably wouldn't have many qualms about breaking a few rules. If there was something in it for him, I think he'd go along with just about anything, though I don't know what we'd have to offer him. That's all I can tell you about him. Except that, without his help, we might as well pack up and go home."

Garrison flopped down on his cot and sighed. "That's about what I expected to hear, even if I was hoping for better. I guess we've got to take the chance. How's our list of other potential recruits?"

"Good. I think we can put together the rest of the team from people we can trust."

"Then I guess it's time to start spreading the word. Tomorrow, we start having some quiet little chats. A week from now I want to have a meeting."

Jody Holmes was an odd case. She was *glad* to be at Farside. Even stranger, she had come to Farside of her own free will, and counted herself lucky to get there.

Her first choice and original plan was to spend two years at Charon Station, compared to which Farside was a dazzling cosmopolitan metropolis. Charon Station, orbiting Pluto's large single moon, was in a prime location for the study of Oort Cloud proto-comets, and Jody had been greatly looking forward to the posting, not really minding the long months of cold-sleep storage she would have had to spend in transit back and forth. But the posting had fallen through, and that was the end of that. With the tensions building between Earth and the Settlers, maybe it was no bad thing to stay on Earth's side of the line. There were some reports of terrestrial citizens getting a fairly tough time of it out there at the hands of the Settlers.

And as second choices went, Farside was first rate. True, the Oort was distinctly further away from here compared to the Pluto/Charon system, and it was tougher to do low-temperature observation—but for two weeks of every month, the full bulk of the Moon shielded her instruments not only from the radio noise of Earth, but also from the heat and glare of the Sun. With that huge and annoying presence below the horizon for such long periods of time, she had gotten some really first-rate super-long exposures of several proto-comet objects. Once, she had managed a full two-week exposure. With the enhancement devices available at Farside, the resulting data was a real triumph. It was going to make a great paper someday.

Jody was a rather unlikely-looking astronomer. On the other hand, she would have made a rather unlikely-looking *anything*. Short, a bit pudgy, shy and withdrawn, awkward in social situations, with a squeaky little voice, she was almost twenty-five, and no one could ever believe she was over seventeen.

She was a native of Jamaica, and was proud of her lilting island accent, even if she was determined to use nothing but absolutely standard English usage—and that determination probably did nothing for her slight stutter. She sported a short, puffy, rumpled, rather old-fashioned afro cut. Typically, she wore her hair that way more because it was easy to care for than because she cared for how it looked. She was even secretly glad that cosmetics were hard to come by at Farside, particularly in shades suitable to a dark-skinned black woman. Otherwise, she would have been obliged to try and use them, and she was hopelessly bad with such things.

In fact, she thought of herself as hopelessly bad at *most* things—practically everything, in fact, besides using the tools of her trade. But even she was willing to concede that she was an incredibly gifted astronomer, not only good at the art and science of observation, but a brilliant theorist. The People's Republic of Jamaica knew it too. They were the ones funding her sojourn here. The PRJ's pockets were not noted for being deep, but Jody's work in the Chilean observatories had been impressive enough to convince them she was a world-class talent—and the PRJ had never been shy about showing off its successes. Somehow or another Jody had been declared a national treasure.

But national treasure or not, she wasn't comfortable

around other people. It made her nervous to talk to strangers. And when that new fellow, the redheaded American who had just come in on the roller started talking to her, it made her very nervous indeed. Unfortunately, when he sat down next to her in the commissary and started to talk with her, there wasn't much she could do about it.

"You're Jody Holmes, right? The comet expert."

"Pro—proto comets," she corrected, stuttering just a bit. "Yes. I work on proto-comets, that's right," she answered, privately kicking herself for speaking so badly.

"Glad to meet you. I'm Ben Moscowitz. I just got signed onto the geology section here."

"Yes. I—I heard about you. They had that simulation video of yours running in the astronomy building the other day. I saw it. Par—part of it." Why couldn't she say a whole sentence at once, the way other people could? Why did it all have to come dribbling out in bits and pieces like that?

"What did you think of it?" Ben asked her.

"Well—it was awfully dramatic," she said doubtfully.

"You mean the altered version?"

"No, even the or-original. It *could* have happened that way, I suppose. But no one could ever know for certain if it happened the way you showed it."

"We think we proved pretty conclusively that the asteroid hit."

"No, there is no doubt that the asteroid hit—but there is no way you can show what sort of trajectory the object had, or what time of day it struck." She noticed that, as usual, she had started talking in complete, confident sentences the moment the topic shifted to astronomy. Why couldn't she always talk this easily?

"Wait a second," Ben said in bafflement. "You're objecting to our showing the impact happening in *daylight?*"

"It's an unwarranted assumption. How could you tell what time of day it came down?"

"But what difference could it possibly make?"

"But if you take that attitude to the limit, what difference does *anything* make?" Jody asked severely. "We always need the best information, the most accurate information, possible. What good does it do to make things up that cloud the issue?"

"But there are other kinds of truth than science," Ben said. "Truths that are more important. It would be irresponsible to subordinate them to some slavish determination to avoid mistakes."

Like many shy people, Jody had a temper that flared up unexpectedly on occasion. Facts, truth, certainty, were the core tenets of her world view. "*What* other truths?" she snapped. "What could be more important to you, a scientist, than knowing and telling precisely what happened? What truth could be more important than that?"

"This one: 'Life is good,' " Ben said gently. "I don't know how you could prove that scientifically, but it's true, and what we were trying to do was in the defense of life."

Jody looked as if she were going to say something, but she kept quiet.

Ben thought for a moment and then went on. "We *did* make up some of the details for that simulation, and yes, doing so was not rigorously scientific. Actually, some of the imaginary details were much more significant than what you're objecting to—we showed a calved fragment striking in Greenland, and that's pure guesswork. We showed an ice age happening as a result, and we just don't know if that's true. We projected a semi-permanent giant hurricane over the impact site, and that was only a mathematical construct. None of that was more than possibility, imagination. And who knows what effects the impact had that we never thought of?

"We *could* have made a simulation that didn't make guesses, and avoided the chance of missing effects we hadn't thought of by saying straight off we were going strictly by the facts, and were only concerned with documented reality. Most likely, that would have ended up being not much more than a black-and-white outline globe of the Earth being struck by a featureless blob, and maybe a very orderly cross-section view of the Earth's interior, showing how Iceland developed. It wouldn't have any guesses in it.

"But we couldn't have shown the people what they *needed* to see. There wouldn't have been any *juice* in a simulation like that, nothing that could scare people, make them worry that it could happen again. Make them scared of dropping a planet-wrecker of our own onto Earth. Yes, we made things up, but only to show a higher truth—an asteroid can kill a living world.

"*Something* like what we showed happened, we know that. If it hadn't, we'd still be up to our asses in dinosaurs. We'd never have evolved. The details of what happened that day aren't important in and of themselves so long as they are guessed at responsibly, with reasonable accuracy, and support the central facts we do have proof of. What Cathy Cleveland and the CRATER people did was wrong because it deliberately controverted the known facts in support of a central lie." Ben not only liked the way the conversation was going, but was pleased with his own eloquence. "Maybe it's the difference between art and artifice. At least that sounds good, even if it doesn't mean much."

Jody blushed, feeling mightily embarrassed for no reason she could explain clearly. But there was more to it than that. She was enjoying this argument—well, this discussion, and sensed that Ben was too. This was good old-fashioned intellectual philosophizing. "I s—s—see your point, Dr. Moscowitz. But I'd be more con-convinced if it had *worked*. But no one on Earth cares about Cornucopia. You colored the truth in support of some higher goal. You—you're saying the ends justify the me—me—means. But you didn't a—achieve the ends. I'm sure the people who doctored your video could defend themselves just the way you have. By saying that saving Earth is worth any price, even fal—fal—falsehood." It was clear that from Jody's point of view there was no conceivable crime more serious than falsehood.

"The difference is that Garrison and I didn't run away from the consequences—and we didn't betray anyone's trust. Garrison was arrested and thrown in *jail*, for God's sake. We gave up and left Earth for the Moon because we were forced to. No one back on Earth would let us work again. We didn't jump, we were pushed. Not like the CRATER crowd. They vanished into thin air before anyone had a chance to see the video. To this day, no one knows where they are. They knew what trouble they would cause, and they ran away from it—leaving Garrison holding the bag. That doesn't tell me they have the courage of their convictions. We took our lumps."

"For the sake of your goal, you were willing to harm yourself," Jody said, not even noticing her stutter had vanished for a moment. "They were willing to harm others. That *is* a big difference." She frowned and looked at Ben. "But that doesn't change the situation. The asteroid is still heading for Earth."

Ben smiled. "No, nothing's changed. Not yet. Let me ask you something. Do *you* care—do you understand the danger from Cornucopia? Enough to take risks to stop it?"

"Yes. Of course. But th—there's nothing I can d—do."

"Maybe not. But Garrison and I have a little idea . . ."

In the finest tradition of conspirators everywhere, Ben leaned his head closer to Jody and spoke to her in low tones. Jody leaned closer herself to hear what he was saying, and her eyes grew wider and wider. Still listening intently, she pulled out a notepack and started to run some calculations. She couldn't believe what she was hearing. But numbers don't lie . . .

If Ben's chat with Jody went satisfactorily, Garrison was far less satisfied with the results of his talk with Hofmeister. It *went* well enough, but Garrison had the distinct and uncomfortable feeling that he and Herr Hofmeister were talking past each other.

Getting a chance to talk privately with Hofmeister wasn't the problem. Garrison had a work meeting with him daily in Garrison's private office. (It was one hell of a comment on something or other that while there was no place in Farside for Ben and Garrison to *live*, office space was going begging. The planning section hadn't been doing its work.) But knowing how to start with the man was difficult.

The two of them got through the last of the routine work-progress items, and Hofmeister was standing up, getting ready to leave, when Garrison decided to take the plunge. "Herr Hofmeister," he said. "Sit down for a moment. There's something else I'd like to talk with you about."

"Yeah, sure, Herr Doctor." Alois Hofmeister grinned meaninglessly through crooked, discolored teeth and sat back down.

Garrison looked at him thoughtfully for a moment. Hofmeister wore his sparse and balding hair in a rough close-trimmed crewcut, and usually seemed to be sporting about a two-day's growth of beard, giving him a rather stubbly appearance overall. His face was lean and angular, his grey-pallored skin drawn tight across the bone and muscle underneath. As usual, he was wearing a pair of musty grey overalls.

He looked like a man half-starved to death, or like a prison inmate who hadn't seen the sun in years. In times past at Tycho Penal, no doubt he had been both of those things. Garrison still didn't know what had gotten Hofmeister dumped at Tycho. Murder? Forging a check? Staging a protest or annoying some government somewhere? Jaywalking? Any offense great or small, or any official ruling, thoughtful or capricious, could get a man landed in Tycho. The real question was how Hofmeister had gotten back out.

But all that had been years ago, and Hofmeister looked as if he was still doing time. It was as if his past still rode on his shoulders, making him grey and emaciated. Garrison had seen him under the sunlamps, and at meals. The man took care of himself, the man ate. So why did he look like a living skeleton? Garrison sighed and forgot about it. None of that mattered. What mattered was that Hofmeister was as strange inside as out, an off-putting combination of brashness and guile, boldness and servility.

Garrison didn't trust him. But he didn't have any choice. "Herr Hofmeister. We should be getting our first lasers off the production line in a week or two. At the planned production run of two a day, we should be ready with our one-hundred-laser system in about two months. Can we speed that production rate up? And could we run the line longer, produce more lasers if we needed to?"

Garrison knew the answer to both questions was "yes,"

but he wanted to hear it from Hofmeister, hear how the man reacted.

If Garrison had been expecting caution or uncertainty, he was disappointed. Hofmeister nodded enthusiastically and smiled in a way that seriously frightened Garrison. "Yeah sure, you bet. We can run system at least twice that fast. Schedule plan made up by super-careful Earth fatheads. We can get out full run in a month."

"What about extending the run?"

"Run that damn system forever!" Hofmeister said excitedly. "Very well built, good back-ups, self-repairing. You bet we extend run."

Garrison swallowed nervously. It was as if Hofmeister had been expecting these questions, *hoping* they'd be asked. Just what Garrison was in the mood for. More mysteries. "If there was a good reason for doing it, would you be willing to run off more lasers?"

"Naturally. You tell me good reason, glad to help." Hofmeister said. "What is reason for lasers?"

Garrison hesitated one last time and took the plunge. "We want to shoot down an asteroid," he said.

Hofmeister looked at him strangely for a moment, and then burst out laughing. It was not a happy sound, but rather sent a chill down Garrison's spine. There was something very cruel about that laugh. "Asteroid! That's good! That's very good. Sure, sure we build lasers all you want to shoot asteroid. I do some figures, see what we need to do." And with that, Hofmeister stood up and walked out of the room, still chuckling.

Garrison stared at the door and cursed under his breath. He was supposed be running this conspiracy, keeping the secrets, building the cabal. So why was *he* the one wondering what the hell was going on?

Both Garrison and Ben were pleasantly surprised at how easy it was to recruit for the conspiracy. People here seemed to understand the danger. Perhaps that shouldn't have been so surprising. Farside was mainly a scientific installation, after all, here for the express purpose of running an observatory. Living in a crater field helped bring home a clear idea of what an asteroid impact could do. And out here, very few people seemed to give a damn what the authorities thought. In any event, Garrison and Ben were able to get together a core group of people.

All that remained was to lead them. And keep from getting caught. Which led to the meeting in Garrison's office a week later. It was crowded, with eight or ten people wedged into the small office, and there was some trouble scaring up enough chairs, but it wasn't exactly the sort of meeting you could sign up one of the public rooms for. Ben had come up with punch and cookies from somewhere and laid them out on Garrison's desk. There was something more than faintly ridiculous about serving chocolate chip cookies for a meeting about building the greatest weapon of all time, but Ben knew what he was doing. For one thing, he couldn't offer anything stronger without running the risk of offending Mohammed—or some other member of the team who happened to be Muslim. Serving refreshments made the meeting seem a bit less audacious, and provided a social lubricant. People had to hand the cookies around and pour the punch. It got them talking to each other, made them more relaxed.

At last it was time to get started. Garrison stood uncomfortably at the head of the room. "If everyone could take a seat, please." He gave them a moment to settle down and went on. "There aren't many of us, and at a guess there are some people in this room that don't like each other very much," Garrison said. *Hello, Hofmeister*, Ben thought.

"But I'm going to have to ask you to trust each other, in spite of that," Garrison said. "Please do *not* speak to *anyone* else about what we're going to talk about here. Or we'll all end up in Tycho. Ben?"

Ben stood up and looked around the small group. "In ones and twos, here and there, all of you have been told roughly what we have in mind. Briefly put, we want to beef up the comm laser array and use it to knock out Cornucopia before it can get into an orbit that threatens Earth." There was a small buzz of muttering and foot-shuffling from the group. All of them knew what the plan was by then, but it was unnerving to hear it stated so baldly.

Hell, it got *Ben* nervous. He waited for the group to quiet down and continued. "What we need now is to plan how we are going to do the job. As you know, Garrison and I have been working with Herr Hofmeister on the mining and laser manufacturing operation. It should be fairly obvious why that is important to our plans. We hope to use the factory to crank out the planned number of comm lasers, and then leave it running for our own purposes. Simply put, we're not going to turn off the factory when the normal production run is complete. Herr Hofmeister is of course the factory manager for the laser plant, and he will be in charge of producing the laser units—and in charge of augmenting the lasers to make them more effective for our purposes.

"So we should have a tool, a weapon, for the job. But we need some way to point it at our target.

"Jody Holmes of the observatory staff will provide the tracking and control data we need—secretly, of course.

"As to other requirements, the first things Garrison and I discovered when we sat down to decide this plan was that we needed a lot of things we can't get here. We need a way to get them. Bluntly put, we need to put together a smuggling operation. Mohammed Ul-Haq and I are setting up Sunchaser Shipping. Mohammed?"

Mohammed stood up and looked around the little group, wondering what in Allah's name he was doing here. "Ah— hello. There's not too much to say about Sunchaser yet. It's going to be a legitimate shipping operation, working the SunWay routes, using surplus rollers that we'll buy up where we can. It should make a profit, and so provide the money we need to finance the operation. Of course, it will also provide a cover for smuggling what we need and can't get otherwise. I suppose one key point is that it's going to be a pretty limited operation. We should be able to get you any small vital parts you need—but not a spare spacecraft." That drew a small laugh, and Mohammed sat down gratefully.

Jody Holmes self-consciously raised her hand, feeling as if she were back at grad school, not quite understanding what the professor had said. "B—Be—Ben, one thing just

doesn't make sense to me. You're talking about mes—
message lasers here. How could they possibly be powerful
enough to melt an asteroid? Th—they only put out a few
hundred w—watts, right?"

Garrison cleared his throat and turned toward the laser
chief. "Herr Hofmeister, perhaps you could explain."

Hofmeister leaned over the back of his chair and smiled
unpleasantly at Jody. "These lasers very much over-
designed. They want to build them and forget about them,
never bother go fix them. They are intended to have
hundred-year operational life—but they lose about one
percent of initial efficiency per year. By the end of hundred years, they losing half of power potential each year,
various lasing elements deteriorate. Mostly tuneable fluid
crystals begin to break down.

"So we build lasers with about one hundred times capacity of their maximum power requirement. Also, that
maximum power requirement is much higher than you are
thinking. Much more than few hundred watts. Yes, receiver only needs maybe a few milliwatts of power to pick
up signal. But on most ships receiver eye is only about
size of your hand. Basic rule in electromagnetic radiation
message systems—smaller surface of receiver lens, mirror
or antenna, less sensitive it is, and stronger signal must be
to compensate. Pocket phones on Earth can have tiny
antenna because orbital antenna size of soccer field.

"Also, message beam must be deliberately defocused to
provide large reception area at plane of intersection for
ship. To provide that few milliwatts at receiving eye, must
spread signal over large area. Maybe cross-section ten
thousand square kilometers.

"Other problems also means we need much power. To
hit dome colony, say on Mars, you have to punch through
atmosphere and dust. Extra power needed to cut through
that. Maybe one hundred-thousandth or -millionth of original signal power will be received at other end if you are
lucky. Maybe much less.

"So in normal operation we have laser working at small
fraction of power spreading its beam out wide. If we focus
beam tight and at same time use laser at maximum power

instead of one-percent rating, we will get at least about ten-to-sixth increase in effective power. That's one million times augmentation. Build enough lasers, we melt all the asteroids you want." Something about what Hofmeister said seemed to amuse the man greatly, and he seemed to struggle a bit to keep from laughing.

Garrison cleared his throat and continued the meeting. He had thought that the UNLAC cops might be the biggest danger to this operation. Now, looking at Hofmeister, he was starting to think otherwise.

Chapter Twenty-Two

CANNON FIELD, LUNAR FARSIDE

No one really knew who had started to call it Farside Cannon. The name seemed to spring up, unbidden. But no doubt it was appropriate. So far the Cannon was little more than a few doodles on a few hopefully-secure computer screens, but even the mere idea of it was unnerving to consider.

So too was the amount of work to be done. Virtually all of the manual physical labor was going to be handled by robotics, and they were going to have a certain amount of artificial intelligence help in design and management, but even the amount of work left after that was daunting—and there were only eight people on the initial team, all of them with official jobs they still had to do.

But they had time. That was important. They had over a year to think, to plan, to build and design. Jody was out here now in order to do a little of that planning. If she was going to be in charge of targeting the laser, she felt she had to see what it was she was going to be targeting.

Hofmeister had brought her out here to get a look at one of the early production models of the standard laser unit. Hofmeister was planning to program some augmentations to the basic design, but this was pretty much what the final units would look like. It sat there on the bare lunar surface where the crawler had dropped it off, a brooding shape that seemed insectoid somehow, like a strange half-living, half-mechanical monster.

It was big. That was the first thing that surprised Jody. She had seen pictures, drawings, diagrams, but none of them had offered a clear idea of scale. The base of the laser was easily three meters on a side and two meters high, a boxy no-nonsense shape designed to hold the electronics and the superconducting storage coils, without any concessions to appearance or aesthetics. Atop the base sat a massive turntable. A heavy-duty Y-shaped yoke sprouted from the center of the turntable, and the barrel of the laser tube itself hung between the two arms of the yoke. The laser tube was nearly half a meter in diameter and perhaps three meters long. Jody saw that the design allowed the laser tube to swivel vertically from horizon to horizon on its yoke, and that the turntable could spin the whole yoke/laser assembly through a full circle. It was a very simple, straightforward mounting that could direct the laser tube to any point in the sky. The whole arrangement resembled certain kinds of optical telescope mounts.

A few meters away, connected by a thick cable, sat a second, identical boxy base unit, sporting its own turntable. But this mounting held not a laser tube, but a large high-intensity solar array. The yoke and turntable arrangement allowed the solar array to track the Sun and charge the superconducting storage coils. Jody was impressed. "Bu—but what about the receiver?" she asked. "I've never seen any mention of the signal re—re—ceiver."

"It looks like solar collector," Hofmeister said. "In fact *is* solar collector, with slight modifications. This unit here could use its own collector to receive laser signal. Lose charging time pointed away from Sun like that, though, so they make third version of base unit with optical receiver dish, like collector but optimized for comm laser frequencies. But standard collector like this makes good back-up just in case. Good design. Now let's see what *laser* end of system does." There was a portable control panel velcroed to his backpack, and he reached around to pull it off. He clipped the panel's lanyard to his belt, then went over to the laser unit, knelt, and opened an access panel. He plugged a cord from the control panel into a socket inside the panel.

Hofmeister stood again and backed up a few meters before punching a series of commands into the control panel.

The massive turntable rotated smartly onto its new heading, almost due south. The fat cylinder of the laser tube itself swiveled up in its yoke until it was aimed at a bright star high in the southern sky. Jody was surprised at how quickly the pointing system could redirect the laser to a new target.

Hofmeister worked the controls again and then let the portable panel drop from his hand to hang at his belt. "There," he said. "Now we are sending message beam to Sirius. We can come back in eighteen years to see if we get answer."

Jody looked at the laser in surprise. She *knew*, intellectually, that in vacuum she would not be able to see the laser beam itself, but even so it was disconcerting to look and see nothing. If the beam had been firing through air instead of vacuum, it would have been not only visible, but glaringly bright, because the air molecules themselves would be knocking photons out of their proper path, diverting them toward the viewer's eye and keeping them from reaching the target. By variously absorbing, reflecting and diffusing a laser beam's photons, air robbed a laser of its power even as it made that power visible. Vacuum left the laser alone. The fact that it was unseen made the power of this device no less real.

But somehow none of that was convincing. Jody still expected to be able to *see* something. "Are you sure it's working?" she asked doubtfully. "Isn't there some sort of light meter or something—"

Hofmeister laughed and stooped to pick up a rock. "You watch," he said. "You see there's something there." He held up the stone in his hand. "This rock is asteroid, and this laser is like all lasers we going to build." He hefted the rock for a moment and then threw it to cross a few meters in front of the laser tube.

There was a flash of blinding sun-bright red, and a

soundless explosion that was almost too fast to see. A halo of sparks, microscopic fragments of what had been rock a moment before, leapt out from the path of the beam, glowing with intense heat. They flashed out in all directions, still in the process of vaporizing as they travelled. A few of the sparks struck Jody's helmet. They were too tiny to hurt the tough suit, but it was unnerving even so. It certainly proved there was something there. "Why did you have to do th—th—that?" Jody asked querulously. "One of those sparks could have burned through my suit."

"No, no, too small. Besides, you wanted to see if laser could blast rock. Our lasers, they damn sure be able to blast asteroid." Hofmeister's voice sounded like churning gravel in Jody's earphones, and his low, throaty chuckle sounded even worse. "We be able to blast *anything*."

The lasers streamed out of the factory, most of the first ones carried to the comm laser array site south of Farside Station. The robot haulers shuttled back and forth between the factory and the array site. No one noticed that the haulers were also heading *north* toward the Cannon Field, depositing the first of the Cannon's lasers there.

The plan seemed to be going well, at least in its early phases. Garrison and Ben were less novel, but no less popular with the small populace of Farside. Ben's fledgling shipping business had a lot to do with that, but so did the nature of their expulsion from Earth and Central Colony. Everyone at Farside had been kicked out of somewhere, but few had done it with as high a profile, or as dramatically, as Ben and Garrison.

Rumors began to spread: that it was no whim of the Central Colony bureaucrats that had brought them to Farside, but their own careful plan, that they were out here as part of some undefined elaborate scheme against UNLAC. It wasn't true, of course, but it was close enough to make Garrison uncomfortable.

The rumors had their own strength. The two of them rapidly grew to folk-hero status, leading citizens of Farside Station.

And that did not sit well with some people.

*   *   *

Dr. Hari Prathnabar hesitated a long time before inviting Dr. Garrison Morrow to visit the AdminGen's office. Even two months after he had concluded that the evidence was overwhelming, Dr. Prathnabar told himself repeatedly that he could be wrong, that he might be forming a hypothesis based on inadequate information, that to do so would be most unscientific. But he was deceiving himself, and knew he was doing it.

Dr. Prathnabar was a proud man, careful of his own dignity. He knew that he was careful of it, perhaps overcareful, and deep in his heart he knew that his pride was the difficulty, not any doubts about what he had learned. Dr. Prathnabar knew that his was a very limited authority, that he did not have much power. That merely made it harder for his pride when someone flouted that limited authority.

As Dr. Morrow was doing now.

There came a buzz from the door control, and Dr. Prathnabar pushed the *open* button on his desk without even asking who it might be. The door came open, and Morrow stepped in, looking more the guilty schoolboy than the dangerous plotter.

"Do have a seat, Dr. Morrow," Prathnabar said, gesturing his visitor toward a chair without rising himself. Keeping his own seat was a minor thing, but it served to remind who had the higher status here.

"Thank you, sir." Morrow sat down, his movements betraying at least a slight degree of nervousness.

"I shall not beat around the bushes, Dr. Morrow. I know what is going on. Your secret is quite exposed."

Garrison did not trust himself to speak, but merely nodded.

Dr. Prathnabar tented his fingers and stared intently at Dr. Garrison Morrow. "I am a scientist, you know, and the administrator of a colony, and I am not bereft of intellect or imagination. You come here, perhaps by the caprice of Central Colony, perhaps by your own design. You are on the Moon because you opposed the Cornucopia project. You are obviously a young man of great energy and determination. You arrive and immediately take over a project that has only the most peripheral connection with your area of expertise. I found all this curious. It would have been hard *not* to find all this curious. It didn't take much thought to connect the two sides of the story. You are planning to use the lasers against the asteroid."

Garrison Morrow looked Prathnabar straight in the eye for the first time. "Yes. Yes we are." Prathnabar looked at Morrow. There was an unspoken second statement in Garrison's expression, the set of his shoulders, the calm quiet of his voice. All of them said the same thing: *We are doing it, and there is nothing you can do to stop us.*

That, too, was something Prathnabar had figured out for himself. Prathnabar was grateful that Morrow had not spoken the words out loud. Pride and self-respect would have demanded a response—and disaster. As it was, Prathnabar could and did choose to ignore Morrow's wordless defiance.

Instead he nodded quietly. "Thank you for not dissembling further. That would have been an insult to both our intellects. But you never seriously expected to keep your secret, did you? Not here, not in this tiny outpost full of busybodies. By my count, there are eight people in your operation. That is seven—or perhaps eight—more than the optimum number for keeping a secret."

The ghost of a smile showed at the corners of Morrow's lips. "You are well-informed. In answer to your question, I never seriously expected the project could be kept quiet forever. Sooner or later, the whole station was going to know that *something* was up. I suppose the most I ever hoped for was that it would be a respected open secret around the station, not discussed in front of strangers. But I suppose that's a forlorn hope now."

"Not necessarily," Prathnabar said. "I know what you're thinking at this moment. Your plans are already too far advanced for me to be able to stop them. Perhaps you already have a hundred laser units at the ready. By the time I could get word to Central Colony, get through to someone who would believe me, get them to take me seriously, and have them do something about it, by the time they could assemble a team to come out and stop you by force, you might have another fifty or a hundred lasers built. More than enough to defend yourself with.

And you might even have time to relocate the manufacturing operation, hide where you couldn't be found. And each day of delay in finding you and trying to stop you is another day when more lasers come on line, another day when you become stronger. Perhaps you would be able to hold out long enough to stop the asteroid. Perhaps not.

"The trouble is, you are playing a very dangerous game—and playing it against a background of forces you don't understand. Even without Cornucopia, these would be hazardous times. Earth and the Settlers have not finished their business with each other."

Prathnabar hesitated before speaking again. "I really ought to stop you. I really ought to notify the authorities. UNLAC doesn't have an army on the Moon, but they could put together some sort of force of ill-equipped policemen in vacuum riot gear. Maybe you'd win, maybe they'd win. I ought to do that, because I do not approve of what you are doing. You are claiming for yourself a power so great that not even a government should possess it, let alone an individual.

"But the difficulty is—I am an astronomer, and every day I look out onto a crater field. I know what Cornucopia will do, and I too know it must be stopped. So I will not block you, but I will not join you. Given the chance to look the other way, I will do so. Force me to take notice, force me to take action, and I will."

Prathnabar stood up and looked hard at Garrison. He looked old, tired, frail: yet a threatening light seemed to gleam in his eyes. "You are young, healthy, strong. You are popular, personable, likeable. You gather power to yourself, more kinds of power than one. And the times are changing. The day will come when this office will be surrendered to a leader selected by the people, and not imposed by fiat. The times will demand it. It will be well, at that time, if the office is held by a man willing to step down peacefully. The politics, the theater of the moment, will require a cooperative villain for the piece. I will play my part, and you will play yours.

"I believe that you will take my place then. But I do not believe you will hold it long."

PART THREE

ENCOUNTER

Time is an illusion.

It is life that creates the illusion of time. At the very least, it is life and the busy activity of a changing, evolving world that brings meaning to time. On the planets of the Solar System that are still unsettled, barren, and lifeless, time changes nothing. Night has no mystery, and morning means nothing more than a slight warming of a lump of rock. Nothing is made new.

Even without life, a world might in a sense be lively and changeable, but it is not so on any of the planets of our Solar System, save Earth alone. On the other inner planets, there is no rain, no surging of the ocean, there are no tides. Even the very crusts of the other terrestrial worlds are rigid and unchanging, compared to the restless Earth. In the gas giants, vast energies churn in the atmosphere, but the weather patterns are stuck in a rut, centuries, perhaps millennia, old. Nothing changes.

On these dead and deadened worlds, change comes with glacial slowness—and time can only be measured by the changes it makes. Entropy, the collapse down toward disorganization, is the only true measure of change where life does not exist. Humanity is bringing life and change, death and the birth of new life to these worlds, bringing

293

time on the scale of living things, but the effort will take many lifetimes.

But the lifeless worlds are changeable indeed compared to the immutable eternity of deep space. In space, there is not even slow collapse for use as a time scale.

In space, the cycles of predictable change that make humans believe in such nonobjective things as days, or seasons, or years simply do not occur. In deep space the universe is always shrouded in dark, the stars forever shine, the Sun blazes in heat and glory without end. All is always as it was.

There are patterns to the movements of the planets across the sky, of course, but in the dark between the worlds they are insignificant, tiny pinpricks crawling across the endless dark, too small, too slow and unnoticeable to make time important.

But here, too, humanity has planted change. They have wrapped a burnt-out comet, a once-nameless asteroid, in white. They have named it Cornucopia, and sent it out on a new path through the sky. Now it rises out past the orbit of Mars and begins the long falls back in toward the Sun, back toward the orbit of Earth. Telemetry devices measure the changelessness aboard the asteroid, the quietude of the instruments and devices, and radio them back to bored technicians orbiting Earth.

Far away from the asteroid, and drawing slowly closer, is a tiny ship. Aboard her there is scarcely more activity than on the asteroid. One by one, virtually all those aboard the Dawn Treader have chosen cold sleep over the interminable waiting. Only two crewmen and Shiro Ishida have remained awake, the crewmen because they must, and Ishida for reasons he could not explain even to himself. All the rest sleep through the endless sun-drenched night of space.

But on the Moon, on the Farside, there is activity. Great activity. There, they work against illusory time, racing against a deadline that may be too close already.

For Cornucopia and the Dawn Treader are coming.

Chapter Twenty-Three

ONE YEAR LATER

UNITED NATIONS HEADQUARTERS, NEW YORK

Hiroshi Suzuki walked out of the conference room, feeling genuine pain and hurt. There was nothing metaphorical about the anguish wracking his body. This pain was real, as real as if his fellow delegates had stabbed knives deep into his gut. Perhaps this latest disaster had at last given him the ulcer the doctors had promised was impossible.

But, no, this pain was not caused by any physical injury. This was the torture of heartbreak, of betrayal. It was as if his own children had turned against him, eagerly agreed to ignore all his counsel. Away they ran, willfully chasing after a momentary passion, knowing full well that it could only end in their own destruction.

Embargo. The damnable fools were actually going to declare a full and complete embargo against the Settlement worlds. Total cessation of trade, complete stoppage of travel between Earth and the Settlement worlds. Where could that lead, where could that *possibly* lead, but to disaster?

It was all doubly frightening because of the enthusiasm and unanimity with which they rushed toward disaster. Suzuki had counted on at least the Americans to show some shred of common sense. How often had protectionism failed for them? But no, *they* had led the way, forced the early vote that insured victory.

Only the powerless Inner Planets Administration Council had voted against. IPAC, nominally a United Nations entity, at heart pro-Settlement—their vote was no surprise. But even UNLAC had voted for embargo, and that was a chilling sign of how far the madness had spread. More than half the Moon's economy was tied up in trade with the Settlers.

Suzuki made his way to the elevator and rode up to his office, half wondering why he bothered. In all likelihood, he would be out of office before the week was out—perhaps before the elevator reached his floor, considering how capricious the council had become.

But that would be the least of the damage they could do. This embargo was an engraved invitation to McGillicutty and his bunch of rowdies to force Angela Hardin out of office and take over the Settlement Council. And what good would *his* bully boys seek to do for Earth?

The radicals were winning, on both sides.

LASER CANNON FIELD, FARSIDE STATION

The ground rattled beneath their feet, and they could feel a symphony of vibrations through the boots of their pressure suits. There should have been noise, deafening noise, to go along with the scene they were watching—but this was the Moon, and all was deadly silent.

It was night on Farside, ten days into the two-week darkness that robbed the Moon's surface of every erg of heat and light. Massive floodlights blasted down on the factory, illuminating the scene for the benefit of human eyes.

The huge, tank-treaded hauler rolled out of the shadowed maze of the factory, a dazzling confusion of darkness and bright reflections. A massive piece of machinery was strapped down on its roller bed. The solar array was folded, and the main laser barrel was strapped down for transportation, but even so it was recognizable as it rolled out of the range of the floodlights and into the preternatural darkness that surrounded them.

A laser station, number 4362. Behind it, in the robot factory, number 4363 was already on its way—and 4364, and 4365. . . .

Ben shook his head and turned to Garrison. "Just how long can you keep this up, do you think? Sooner or later someone from the outside is going to notice."

"They won't notice," Garrison said with a hard edge to his voice. "Besides, who is there *to* notice? There hasn't been anyone from UNLAC Central through Farside since we arrived. The one real danger of exposure we faced was from Prathnabar. He could have made things nasty for us—but he's protected us pretty well by not doing anything.

"Most of the rest of the colony has taken their lead from him and not asked any questions. Even the comm people are happy. They got the last of their lasers twenty months ago and set up shop. Once they were in business sending and receiving messages, they didn't care what we were doing. Some of the Farsiders *have* to know we're up to something hush-hush, but they don't want to rock the boat. As far as they're concerned, this factory shut down a year ago. They don't want to know anything different. It's officially on standby since then, for manufacture of spares should they be needed."

"There are over a hundred people in and around Farside who know what we're doing here, to one degree or another," Ben protested.

"And how many have called up UNLAC Central to warn them about us in the last twenty months?" Garrison said calmly. "Zero. Why should they start now? They don't owe the authorities anything. We were all put out here on the theory we couldn't do any harm, and there was no need to keep an eye on us. You're looking at the inmates to warn the jailers, Ben, and the jailers are halfway around the globe. Probably there's some UNLAC intelligence officer who's got a file on us. Maybe a rumor or two drifts in once in a while. By the time he gets around to doing anything about it, it will be too late. It's too late already, for that."

Ben had heard it all before, but he still didn't quite believe Garrison's scheme was working—in spite of more than a year and a half's evidence to the contrary. "How many lasers?" Ben demanded. "How many is going to be enough?" he asked.

"As many as we can get," Garrison said. "The best we can do is build as many units as we can before Cornucopia gets in range. And at the current rate of construction, that will be about five thousand."

"Roughly fifty times the intended capacity of the comm station—and the intended station including a full set of spare units," Ben said quietly. "If that's not enough, I don't know what would be."

"Except we've had to set up some of those lasers to defend the Cannon Field," Garrison said regretfully. "I don't like giving those up."

"You'll still have over four thousand units," Ben objected. "That ought to be enough."

"Maybe. But we need enough firepower to destroy the asteroid on the first try—because we won't *get* a second try. Right now I don't know if we're going to have that by the time Cornucopia approaches Earth. And there's the targeting problem."

Each laser unit was self-contained and self-steering—but each unit had to be told where to point. The comm lab's computers were designed to handle an absolute maximum of one hundred lasers, each pointed independently.

Garrison was proposing to wire up nearly five thousand lasers without benefit of the pointing computer, instead using a far simpler surplus computer Ben had smuggled in from Central. The only thing that made the idea even remotely possible was that all of those five thousand cannon units were to be pointed at the same object. Just getting together enough fiber-optic cable to link the laser units to each other and the control system had been a struggle. Ben had smuggled in a pocket cable plant and solved that problem—but there weren't any targeting computer plants to smuggle in, let alone robot software engineers. Who the hell was going to program the damn thing? Jesus Moroz was one of their original cabal group, and he was working on the problem, but Ben worried about how fast his progress was. According to Jesus, it should be possible to get each unit directed properly using Ben's computer for data and using the laser's own on-board pointing gear from there. But despite what programming tricks they used, there was no question that controlling the lasers was going to be tough.

On the other hand, it would be even tougher to install the surplus laser units into the comm section's computer without arousing suspicion. After all, using comm section undetectably was impossible. Any alternative had to be easier.

And of course they were counting on Jody being able to give them good tracking data on the asteroid, which she would have to do by stealing observation time.

No one said this would be easy.

"Come on, Garrison," Ben said. "Let's head back to the ranch. We've got a meeting to get to." Ben hit a button on his radio link and shut down the floodlights. The factory worked on through the darkness. The two of them turned on their helmet lights and walked back to the *Rock & Roll.* Sunchaser Shipping had purchased quite a fleet of rollers over the past two years, but Ben still drove the *R&R* for reasons of sentiment. He and Garrison had lived in the damn thing for three months until a couple of apartments in Farside Station had opened up.

The *R&R*'s inner and outer airlock doors were wide open, the cabin exposed to vacuum. They climbed up into the cabin, left the airlock open and stayed in their suits for the short run back to the station. Ben took the controls and cranked the roller up to fifty kilometers an hour. He had gotten to be a much better driver in the past year or so, and this was a route he knew well.

Ben rushed on through the darkness, a lumbering crawler looming up as he sped past, leaving the mammoth carrier behind as it scrabbled toward the Cannon Field.

"You want to hit Cornucopia on the first shot?" Ben asked. They were bogged down in another of the endless planning meetings for the attack. "No way. We aren't that good. Not yet. We've got a complicated device here, and we need to test it before we use it for real."

"But once the outside worlds know about the Cannon

they'll go berserk," Garrison objected. "What's to stop them from dropping a nuclear bomb on us?"

"There's nothing to stop them trying, but you not been doing homework," Hofmeister said nastily. Most of the resident exiles of Farside Cannon were decent people unfairly thrown out of their homes, their nations, and their lives, but Alois Hofmeister was one of the exceptions that made Garrison think that maybe a case could be made for exiling certain people, just on general principles.

Hofmeister himself certainly didn't have any principles, general or otherwise. Perhaps that wasn't fair—he really seemed to care about stopping Cornucopia. It was just that he wasn't all that choosy about what methods they used. At heart, Garrison had decided, Hofmeister was nothing more than an old-fashioned crook. Or perhaps nothing less than an old-fashioned psychotic.

"Bombs is not much use in a vacuum," Hofmeister went on. "They give no blast effect or shock wave without air to carry their force. That leaves only other bomb effects. First, shrapnel and fragments, second, heat plus other electromagnetic radiation, and third, heavy atomic particles. We get all three of those every day of week anyway, in form of micrometeoroids and what Sun dumps on us. So we're hardened against all that stuff. Besides of which, lasers are pretty well dispersed. Bomb close enough to take out a few laser stations on the east side wouldn't be able to touch the ones on west side of the crater floor. We could ride out bomb attack pretty easy," Hofmeister concluded happily.

"But the bomb wouldn't ever have to reach us," Ben put in. "What's to stop us from using the Cannon to zap their bombs—or anything else they can think of to throw at us? If Jesus can get the programming together—and we can get some decent tracking gear—we'll be able to *defend* ourselves with the Cannon."

Jesus Moroz grimaced and hunkered down in his seat, making his incongruous leather jacket rumble and pop as the worn fabric bunched up and creased itself. "That is easy to say, Benjamin, but hard to do." He looked at Ben earnestly, his jet-black eyes compelling behind his hooded eyelids. He frowned, and the dark, pockmarked skin of his face looked as rumpled as his bomber jacket. "I can *write* a program to control the Cannon lasers, yes—but how do I test the program? *I* need the test shot, beyond all question. As to the defense system tracking problem—we are starving outside of a gourmet restaurant. The Farside Observatory's radio telescope would make an ideal radar antenna, and their optical instruments would serve the purpose superbly. But we can't use them, no?"

Ben shook his head vehemently. "No, we can't. We can't even think about it at this point. Most of the Observatory staff are from Earth, and we're not going to figure prominently in their native sympathies. If there is still a risk of our hand being shown, it's through the Observatory crowd. Especially with the political situation in the shape it's in. There's already been a few nasty arguments in the commissary between some of the Observatory people and a few of the feistier exiles. There was even a fist fight last night. No offense, and present company excepted, Jody, but we can't risk it."

Jody smiled shyly at Ben. "It's—it's okay, Ben. I agree with you. They're pretty sus-suspicious of you over there already."

"Question, please," Hofmeister cut in. "Why not use same tracking system we use to spot Cornucopia to run defense program?"

"It is a totally different problem," Jesus said unhappily. "Believe me, if we could go that way, we would. But you see, we know Cornucopia's orbit, down to two or three decimal places. In theory, we don't even *need* tracking data for it. If we just plugged in the numbers that say where it ought to be, we would be able to hit it. That is a nice theory, but in practice some small deviation may have occurred. But only a small deviation. So all Jody has to do in order to spot Cornucopia is search a very small piece of sky centered on where the asteroid *should* be. The defense system would have to watch the entire *sky*, from horizon to horizon. An attack could come in very quickly, from any direction. That will require many more sensors, of far greater ability. So how do I watch the entire sky?" Moroz asked plaintively.

Garrison picked a marker up off his desk and doodled on his desk blotter. "You plan on the assumption we commit further crime and treason," he said. "We have the defense lasers in place, right? Cable them through the hardware we've got as if you *could* use the Observatory equipment. Jody should be able to get you the specifications. If push comes to shove and we *need* defensive tracking, presumably it'll be because the bad guys are on the way. Therefore it will be too late by then to wonder if the astronomers are going to warn someone. Furthermore, if they were led to understand someone wanted to drop nuclear warheads on them, they might be open to reason on the subject of cooperation. If not, and we've got the choice between being radioactive or impolite, I'll take impolite."

There was a flurry of nervous laughter at that, but there was a sense in the room that they had all just crossed a line. They were acknowledging that they were willing to take the astronomers' equipment by force if need be. Jody and Ben exchanged an unhappy glance even as the last of the laughter was fading. They were willing to hurt others, not just themselves. It was a small thing, arguably— borrowing a few telescopes during an emergency—but it was also the thin edge of the wedge. How far would it go? How many people were they prepared to hurt?

"So let's operate under the assumption that we'll be able to hold off an attack," Garrison went on, either unaware of the uneasiness in the room or willfully ignoring it. "We *should* have the firepower for the job, to keep the baddies at bay for as long as we want. But I can't get rid of the idea that that's not good enough." He leaned back in his chair and sighed. "Something in my gut tells me that there's no way this will stay under control. Once the outside knows what we've got here, *everyone* will go crazy. Earth, the Settlements, everybody."

"So let them go crazy," Hofmeister said belligerently. "None of that is our concern. It is mere politics. *I* sure as hell am not caring about Earth pols or the Settlers. I just want to keep that rock from getting close to Earth and hitting my family maybe." There was something overly virtuous about his tone of voice. Hofmeister paused to

light up one of his noxious cigars and gestured eagerly.
"Use Observatory sensors hooked up to lasers, and we be
sitting behind invulnerable shield. Let them try and come
get us." He plugged his mouth up with the cigar, puffed at
it, and waggled his eyebrows maliciously.

Ben spoke quickly, jumping in before anyone would
have a chance to start another argument with Hofmeister.
"You might be right, Herr Hofmeister, but I don't know if
we can take the chance. I think we need to go ahead with
Sidebet."

"I agree," Moroz said. "In theory we ought to have an
invulnerable system here—but we won't know for certain
whether it is or not until we abruptly find out the hard
way that it isn't. We need a backup. A hole card."

Garrison looked unhappily from Jesus to Ben. "Anyone
else got any thoughts on the subject?" No one spoke. "I
hate to admit it," Garrison said at last, "but I'm getting to
the point where I'm inclined to agree with you."

"It will require diverting much of our resources away
from the Cannon," Hofmeister said warily.

"How many lasers will we lose?" Garrison asked.

Hofmeister shrugged. "Five hundred, perhaps."

"Not that many," Wiggins objected. Bill Wiggins was
Hofmeister's assistant—and largely responsible for doubling the robot laser factory's output. "Ben and I were
going over it, and we can do the whole breakdown and
transfer of the factory during one light period. Two weeks,
maybe only ten days. Another five days to reassemble.
We'd lose twenty days' production, maximum. Three hundred lasers, absolute tops."

"But what about raw materials?" Hofmeister objected.

"Two phones to the chief of mine operations at Mare
Orientale and we'll have all the raw materials we possibly
need stockpiled by the time we need 'em," Ben said. "I've
seen to it that they ran up quite a debt with Sunchaser.
I've let them have luxury goods on credit. They'll supply
us in exchange for clearing the slate."

Garrison grinned at Ben. "Planning ahead, I see. And I
wondered if you'd ever be a Conner. But can they handle
our needs?"

"Are you kidding? They're the second largest mining

operation on the Moon. This job will be chump change for them."

"But how will we ship the raw materials?" Hofmeister protested. "All our cargo rollers will be tied up at the same time, shipping equipment from here."

It was Ben's turn to grin. "Oh, they'll be able to manage. It'll be a bit hairy, but they can express ship whatever we need."

Garrison turned to Mohammed. "You're the shipping guru. What's your guess? How fast can we set up Sidebet?"

"We can do it—or rather we can watch the robots do it—in two weeks, certainly."

Garrison stared down at his desk and thought. "I hate to lose even that many lasers—but we need the insurance. Ben—you ready to go for it?"

"Damn straight. We'll have sunrise here in another four days. Bill and I can put the final plans together tonight and get started on the move by local dawn." Ben was pleased that he had won an important round, but there was another big problem. "Getting back to the main issue," Ben continued, "we need at *least* one test shot to calibrate. Not only to calibrate, but to make sure the lasers can work at maximum power, and what their effect on a target will be. Without a test, we won't have any idea what we're doing when we fire."

Garrison leaned back in his chair and shrugged, feeling to be in an agreeable mood. "Okay, I don't like it, but I can't really see any way around it. Jody, can you find us a target?"

Jody looked around nervously. Everyone was looking at her. "I'll do my b—b—best," she managed to squeak.

Jody's best was pretty good, of course. She got to work on the problem during her next shift.

There had once been a time when it was difficult to find asteroids and comets. At times, Jody wished she had lived back then, before astronomers had gotten out of Earth's atmosphere and hooked modern sensing devices up to their mirrors and lenses and antennae. Nowadays, the sky seemed to be fairly crawling with sub-planetary objects. It required massive amounts of computer space to keep track of them all, and doing so was a bother, no matter how essential. Without a good catalog of what might cross an observational area in a given time, any number of delicate observations might be ruined. Of course, object tracking was not just for astronomical purposes. It had its uses in navigation, as well, but that was secondary. At least to Jody. Most pilots and navigators would disagree with that assessment, but what did they matter?

There were currently a hundred thousand sub-planetary objects to be kept track of, with new adds sprouting up all the time. There was simply too much clutter in the sky.

On the plus side, when Garrison had said he needed an object to simulate Cornucopia for a tracking exercise, it was five minutes' work with the Farside Observatory's tracking computer to come up with a suitable lump of skyrock. It was going to come in from a different direction and at a different velocity than Cornucopia, but that shouldn't matter. Jody punched up a request for a complete report on the object. The printout surprised her. Not only was the object unnamed (which wasn't at all unusual), it was officially undiscovered. It had been spotted by one of the automated skytrack systems, but never brought to the attention of a human being.

Jody had "discovered" the comet inside the computer memory. And discovery confers certain rights on the discoverer. Jody smiled and typed in a few commands to the computer, and an anonymous number, and a lump of rock and dust in the darkness, never seen by human eyes, magically became Comet Holmes.

GOVERNOR'S OFFICE, CENTRAL COLONY, THE MOON

Things were not going well.

Needless to say, that was a gross understatement. Governor Jose Neruda was trying, with only moderate success, to remain calm.

The embargo was threatening to cause riots at Central. Already there had been demonstrations, loud, noisy gatherings that seemed to be less *for* anything than *against* everything. The split personality of Central Colony was becoming exposed. The lunar colonists had a natural sympathy for the Settlers—but just as strong a link with Earth.

But Earth was rapidly losing points on the Moon. It was the U.N. that had declared the embargo. Without their markets in the Settlement worlds, a lot of colonists were going to find themselves out of a job. And if the Conners were angry now, just wait until times got a little rougher. Neruda reached a hand up to his lapel and fingered his boutonniere nervously. He should never have agreed to vote for embargo. Damn UNLAC! It was their pressure that had forced him to instruct the delegates to vote yes.

It never occurred to Neruda that he didn't have to listen to UNLAC's pressure if he didn't want to. That was not the way he viewed the governor's job. But what he should or shouldn't have done was all spilt milk by now—he had a situation to deal with. The latest news had sent the colonists into an uproar. The Settlement Council had met and booted Angela Hardin out of office. McGillicutty had taken over the chair and promptly packed the Council Secretariat with his own Martian cronies.

McGillicutty had announced that the Settlers would regard any effort to enforce the embargo as an unfriendly act. The U.N. Customs Authority had immediately announced that, should a ship refuse a board-and-search order from a customs cutter, UNCA was prepared to use "surgical" laser shots to burn off antennae or disable engines. McGillicutty responded by announcing that any Settlement spacecraft harassed while entering or leaving Earth space would be authorized to defend itself.

What *that* meant, when no one owned any spacecraft more heavily armed than the customs cutters, was anyone's guess. The cutters carried fairly heavy-duty laser systems, but beyond that no one had ever bothered to equip a ship with so much as a sidearm. In a peaceful Solar System no one saw much point in carting the dead weight of useless weaponry around. No proper naval craft or armed merchantmen existed except on the drawing board—for the moment. No doubt old ship plans were already being dusted off.

But for now, there were no warships in space besides

the cutters. There was only one way a fusion-powered craft could defend itself—by turning its fusion engines on an opposing ship. In short, any merchantman who tried to break the embargo and got caught had the choice between surrender and vaporizing a customs cutter. Most of the Settler trade ships would no doubt respect the embargo out of plain fear, but it was almost inevitable that sooner or later someone would smell enough money to make the risk worthwhile. An incident was almost inevitable. When it happened, almost certainly it would be serious.

And news of that incident—or of the latest resolution from UN Headquarters that could be interpreted as anti-spacer, or of the next outrage from the Settlement Council—indeed, *any* news at this point could set off serious trouble at Central Colony. Riots, mobs, chaos.

Neruda remembered what he had seen as a boy in Santiago. Like so many who had seen anarchy take hold of their world, he had a paranoid fear of dissent—and a knee-jerk faith in the rights of the authorities. He did not intend to let Central Colony get as far out of hand as Chile had, so long ago. But how could he prevent it, when he was powerless to control events?

It suddenly dawned on Neruda that it was not events on distant worlds that infuriated the populace. It was the *news* of those events that brought on reaction.

All he had to do was shut off the supply of news. *That* would keep the mobs quiet. It had worked in Santiago, at least for a while. He pressed the intercom button on his desk. "Miss Wu, step in here, please."

Hillary Wu slipped in through the door to the outer office and took her usual seat, notepack at the ready.

The governor stared thoughtfully at his desktop and spoke without looking up at his assistant. "I am ordering a complete news blackout," he announced.

Hillary looked up in surprise. "No more news out of the governor's office?" she asked.

"No. No more news on the Moon. Period. Until further notice, all newspapers, news programs, fact sheets and all other such instruments of reportage are to cease publication, transmission, broadcast or dissemination of any kind."

"Sir?" Hillary stared at her boss in astonishment. Now what sort of boneheaded idea did he have?

"Am I failing to make myself clear?" Neruda asked in a threatening tone of voice.

"Ah, no sir. But, sir—there are the free press rights—"

"Rescinded. You will order the Bureau of Rights to refund the purchase price of all freedom-of-press rights certificates that have been issued. Have communications section disconnect any and all comm net lines that will be rendered unneedful by the change. Lines from news offices into the video net for example, and lines from incoming news sources as well."

Hillary stared in shock. "Sir. You can't do that. The press rights—"

"Are rescinded," Neruda repeated. "At least temporarily. I am granted broad powers in an emergency, and I judge the Colony to be in one now."

"Sir, people will get the news anyway. Outsiders will beam radio and message lasers at us to get their point of view across. People will pass rumors. Every computer that's hooked into a network is a potential news node. You can't stop—"

"I think I can," Neruda said flatly. "It is the news from the outside that is stirring people up. If we can squelch it, we can regain control of the situation. I expected that you wouldn't understand, Wu. But I also expect that you will do as you are told. I want an action document outlining the means for achieving this plan on my desk ready for signature by close of business today. I want the plan put into effect within seventy-two hours."

Hillary just sat there staring at her boss for a long moment before she could even react. He returned her gaze with a withering glare. After a moment she snapped out of it and stood. There wasn't any point in discussing the matter, and she couldn't think of any way of discouraging this latest brainstorm. But if Neruda thought Central Colony was restive *now*, he was in for a surprise in three days.

ABOARD THE *DAWN TREADER*

Shiro Ishida was always careful to do his homework, and

one apparent threat to his plans still remained—LuTech's own recovery ship, the *Jumpstart*.

The *Jumpstart* was a specially-built craft, designed, built, and equipped solely for the job of boarding Cornucopia and bringing the asteroid into Earth orbit. She had launched from Earth orbit a week ago, and was due to dock with the asteroid a week from now, well ahead of the *Dawn Treader*.

The *Jumpstart* was built at a shipyard owned by one of Ishida's cousins, and that had been a great help to Ishida. He had been able to derive much useful intelligence on the ship and its mission from that fact. Much of what he knew about the Cornucopia project came from the shipyard.

But one thing had gone from Ishida to the *Jumpstart*, unbeknownst even to the cousin who had provided such great assistance. It was a device controlled by radio. Ishida had kept the operating transmitter hidden in his own cabin for the entire journey, but now was the time to bring it out.

He removed the device from its hiding place and considered it for a long moment in the seclusion of his cabin. A small green light shone from the control panel. While it glowed, *Jumpstart* would live.

Ishida paused to consider. This would be murder, killing merely for the sake of money, victory, power. How had he dared frown on the *Dawn Treader*'s crew merely for being mercenary, if he was prepared to go even this far?

And yet he *was* prepared. He had come too far, worked too hard, waited too long, to stop for anything. Now, before the *Jumpstart* came close enough for anyone to notice the explosion. He could act in perfect safety, leaving no clue behind. His own people had been promised that the *Jumpstart* would be delayed. They would need to know nothing else. He flicked off the safety, turned the activator key, and plunged home the button.

A fusion engine easily becomes a fusion bomb. A heat flux, a burble in the magnetic field, that was all it took.

Far off from the *Dawn Treader*, unnoticed and unobserved, a new star flared briefly in the firmament.

Shiro Ishida watched the green light on the detonator wink out, and knew that five men and women were dead.

He put the thing away and stared resolutely at the wall, marvelling that he was mad, knowing that he was mad, and not caring that he was mad.

He thought again of the dead, and apologized to their spirits. He promised them, and himself, to aid their widowed spouses and children. Secretly, quietly, untraceably, but it would be done.

Honor required it.

Cornucopia was drawing near. After her long two-years' stern chase, the *Dawn Treader* was finally closing in on her prey. It was almost time to go to work. The *Treader* would dock with Cornucopia in three weeks.

Ishida ordered the entire ship's complement brought out of cold sleep in preparation for the job ahead. Cathy was one of the first roused from her slumbers, and woke feeling as if she had the worst hangover of all time. Stiff in all her joints, dehydrated, a persistent taste in her mouth like a small rodent had crawled in there to die, she was brought back to the world of the living feeling more than half dead. She could look forward to a week or so of insomnia before her body restored its scrambled diurnal cycle. Cold sleep had its disadvantages.

As did zero-gee, but that couldn't be helped. A spinning ship would make the already complex maneuvers hair-raising in the extreme. Captain Broadmoor ordered spin-down, much to the annoyance of the queasy-stomached unfortunates coming out of cold sleep.

Cathy had planned the *Treader*'s course so that the asteroid stayed between Earth and the ship, effectively hiding them from any prying eyes back on Earth. That was merely a precaution. In all probability, it wouldn't occur to anyone to look for a ship in the vicinity of the asteroid in the first place, and the *Dawn Treader* was too small a craft to be found at this range, so long as she kept radio silence and did not fire her engines.

Even with every radio blaring and the engines roaring at full power, the odds would have favored the *Dawn Treader* keeping her privacy—at least for the moment. Once they boarded the asteroid, of course, all hell was going to break loose. But that was trouble that hadn't happened yet, Cathy reminded herself. There was enough trouble around at the present time without borrowing against future supplies.

She wanted Choate's help. Seemingly following the old law of nature that the perversity of the universe tends toward a maximum, Choate was awakened last of all the ship's complement. Cathy was left to worry and fidget for three whole days as the medical robots brought the crew and passengers out, one by one.

Unfortunately, the cold-sleep process hit some people harder than others. Choate was never in any danger, but he was stuck in sick bay for another three days. There were three other crew members who had suffered reactions to the process in bed in the same room, making private conversation impossible. And Choate wasn't really in any state to talk anyway.

Cathy, almost in spite of herself, kept very busy while she waited for her co-conspirator. There was a great deal to do in preparation for landing on the asteroid.

Slowly the gleaming white shape grew in the ports and the viewscreen. At first it was a mere pinprick of light that seemed to shimmer in the sky, its brightness flickering in a regular pattern as the asteroid rotated on its axis. Then surface detail could be picked out with modest magnification, and then with the naked eye. Most of the crew took to wearing sunglasses when they looked out the port. The perfect white of the luminous surface seemed to glow against the jet black of space.

The looming presence of the flying mountain lumbered closer and closer until it took up half the sky. The *Dawn Treader* fired her engines, stopping the ship relative to the asteroid. The *Treader* could have gone into orbit around the asteroid, but they still wanted to hide behind the rock as long as possible, avoiding any chance observation from Earth. The captain set up a station-keeping program that would fire maneuvering thrusters once an hour to hold the *Dawn Treader* in position. The two traveled on in orbit, keeping perfect formation.

A lot of careful and precise work needed to be done before the *Dawn Treader* could dock at the north pole of this worldlet. First and foremost was a gravity survey of the rock. Presumably LuTech had done their own gravi-

timetry, and knew precisely how much mass Cornucopia
had, and where it was distributed—but they hadn't made
it public. The CRATER team aboard the *Treader* needed
to make their own measurements if they were going to
maneuver the asteroid precisely.

Making the measurements was fairly straightforward.
Crudely put, all they had to do was stop the ship alongside
the asteroid and see how fast they fell toward it, and in
what direction. First they would do a baseline over the
equator of the worldlet, and then move to the south end
and slowly move north, making repeated measurement
drops.

But there were other jobs at hand. They needed to
listen to the asteroid, or more accurately, to the telemetry
signals it was sending back to Earth, in the opposite direction from the *Treader*. The information was being sent
over a tightly beamed radio signal, with very little leakage
in any other direction. The radio engineers aboard the
Treader, with no specialized equipment on hand, weren't
able to pick up any of the rock's telemetry until they were
right on top of it. Ten kilometers from the transmitter,
there was enough signal leakage for them to read. The
data was not encrypted, and the CRATER team rapidly
learned a great deal of detailed information on the asteroid's control system.

Besides filching the telemetry, monitoring the signals
confirmed the CRATER team had not yet been detected.

Right now they were burglars looking in the window
from the darkness, unseen, not taking any action. They
wanted to get as much data with passive snooping as
possible. Once they landed, they were breaking the window and climbing in, and presumably the alarm bells
would ring and they would be detected—and they would
have no time to waste before they alerted the cops. So
they wanted to know as much as possible before landing.

Cathy spent long hours examining the asteroid, both
through the viewports and monitors and through her
computers and simulator programs. She didn't have to
worry about people being suspicious of her motives—half
the rest of the crew was there by the port all the time
anyway.

It was a sight worth seeing. The massive white-shrouded asteroid hung impossibly in space, spinning ponderously about its long axis, illuminated in about half phase by the distant Sun. Cornucopia was traveling with its axis almost perpendicular to its orbit. The asteroid's north pole, where the *Dawn Treader* would land, was pointed at the North Star, Polaris.

The featureless white of the huge bagnet was broken up by the dark grid of reinforcing cables strapped around the bagnet's exterior. One set of cables ran from pole to pole, and another wrapped around the circumference of the asteroid at regular intervals. It looked as if someone had drawn out lines of longitude and latitude on the asteroid.

The bagnet was cinched up tight around the body of the asteroid underneath, revealing every lump and bump of its topography, and the regular grid followed the rumpled bagnet faithfully. The *Dawn Treader* was holding station directly over the "equator" of the rock, precisely over the terminator. Half the tiny world was in light, and half in darkness. As the skyrock rotated, sidelit by the Sun, the shrouded landscape of the world wheeled up from behind the sunward horizon and vanished into darkness directly below the *Dawn Treader*.

The gridmarks imposed over the irregular landscape, the jarring distortions written on the landscape by the constantly shifting shadows, the weird admixture of wilderness in space with a massive engineering effort all fascinated Cathy—and the rest of the crew. Including Ishida, if the reports of the first officer were to be believed. According to the second in command, Shiro Ishida spent endless hours staring at Cornucopia out the port in his cabin.

And Ishida was the key to the whole problem. She had had her doubts at first, but by now Cathy was completely convinced that Ishida planned to hijack the asteroid and later claim it for himself. It was the only explanation that fit all the facts.

She had ideas about stopping Ishida, but they were all rough sketches, not anywhere near final plans. By the time Choate had recovered she had learned enough that she was forced to reject two plans—and vastly improve three others.

But the most important thing that she learned was that it *could* be done. Cornucopia could still be kept out of close Earth orbit—and not just for the moment, but for good. It was still possible to keep Ishida from stealing Cornucopia and dropping it into Earth orbit three years from now.

But Cornucopia hid half the sky from their view, and from that half of the sky, no news could come. They could know nothing of what happened on the Earth and the Moon.

Or on Comet Holmes.

Chapter Twenty-Four

CONTROL CENTER, FARSIDE CANNON

In a silent, robotic mass ballet, four thousand laser barrels turned as one and locked onto a tiny spot in the sky. Garrison watched from the pressurized observation bubble hanging halfway up the side of the crater wall, two kilometers from the edge of the Cannon Field and half a kilometer over the crater floor. He glanced down at the remote box in his hand. A thick cable led from it into a socket set into the airlock panel behind him. The remote was hooked into the master controls for the laser cannon. Master Control was dug into the safety of the crater wall behind him. The rest of the team were watching their computer monitors. No doubt the computers would provide better information, but Garrison wanted to *see*.

There was a sealed airlock between Master Control and Garrison's observation bubble, just in case something went wrong. Garrison knew he should have been in a pressure suit, but for some irrational reason he felt the need to be as unconfined as possible at this moment.

And it felt good to be out from under Farside Station. The place had gotten more and more tense every day since Neruda's press ban. The fiberlink cables to Nearside could carry an almost unlimited amount of programming and information—and now they were all but silent. Garrison had never realized how dependent on the cable Farside was. Without any comsats, the cables were the only links to the outside world—and the other end of the cable was shut down by the press ban.

All the video news programs and newstext services had been pulled, as were any entertainment programs that made the slightest reference to politics or current events. Telephone service had been severely restricted, and even personal text messages were carefully controlled. A rather paranoid artificial intelligence program ruthlessly expurgated anything that it thought might be even a coded or slanged-up reference to current events. The astronomers especially were going berserk as the robot censor slashed their scholarly papers to ribbons.

Garrison hadn't realized, either, just how important the fiberlink cable was to Farsider morale. The Farsiders could handle the physical isolation all right—but the news ban made for a much more crippling psychological isolation.

Well, they wouldn't be cut off much longer. The world would soon pay a great deal of attention.

He looked out at Farside Cannon, and was astonished by what he had built. He picked up a pair of binoculars and looked down on the ranked lines of laser units. The perfect, widely spaced rows marched off toward the horizon, the laser barrels and solar collectors gleaming in the brilliant sunlight, all the lasers pointed in precisely the same direction. Well, not *precisely* the same direction—the Cannon Field was so large, and the comet so close, in astronomical terms, that each laser on the Cannon Field had to be pointed in a slightly different direction to zero in on the comet. Fortunately, each laser had its own pointing control. All Moroz had to do was relay to each laser the same three-dimensional spatial coordinates, and each laser automatically pointed itself independently. The difference in angle between lasers was invisible to the naked eye—but it meant the difference between hitting or missing the comet. Garrison swept the field glasses over the broad expanses of the Cannon Field, half hypnotized by the perfect repetitions of detail repeated over and over again in each unit, every detail of the closest laser unit repeated clear out to the far-distant crater wall opposite.

"We've got 98 percent lock-on, Garrison," Jody's voice announced in his ear. He smiled, knowing she was wrapped up in her work—he could tell because the stutter was gone. "No, just a second—a few late arrivals at lock-on. Make that 99 percent."

"Wish Ben could be here," Garrison said.

"They've got our private fiberlink cable hooked up at that end and we're feeding them all our camera views," Jody said. No one in officialdom knew about the cable Ben's team had laid as it traveled, and even if the brass had known, they couldn't do anything about it. It represented the only uncensored, unmonitored link between Farside and the rest of the universe. "Don't you worry, Garrison. They're watching."

Garrison nodded. "Yeah, I know." He didn't even try to explain to Jody that wasn't the point. Ben could see the show just fine from the Sidebet site, but that was no comfort. Garrison needed Ben *here*. It was a month now since Ben had left with the Operation Sidebet team, and Garrison had been constantly surprised by how much he missed Ben, missed his friendly presence and sensible advice.

"Three minutes," Hofmeister announced gruffly. "Showing power control positive. Herr Doctor Morrow, if you must watch from out there, please to put on your flash-goggles. If a laser tube blows or does a skewing defocus, it could blind you—or kill you. Better you should come inside."

"Thanks, Herr Hofmeister," Garrison said gently. He set down the field glasses and strapped on the goggles. "I have them on now."

"Tube pre-excitation commencing. Showing high response rate, 98 percent-plus," Jody announced.

"Nice programming, Jesus," Garrison said.

"Two minutes. Observation scopes locked on Comet Holmes. Data blocks recording." Jody's voice betrayed an undeniable hint of pride whenever she spoke the comet's name.

Garrison peered intently through the dark goggles, eager for the test to start. There would be nothing to see, of course. Laser beams were invisible in vacuum. It wouldn't really be much of a show—unless a defective laser blew. *That* could get exciting.

"Stand by to fire," Jody whispered. "One minute."

Garrison felt a wild impulse to rush back, pull open the airlock, order them to stop, shut it down, forget it before it was too late.

But it had been too late for a long time. The tool, the weapon, the Farside Cannon had been built. Sooner or later it would be used. And if Earth were going to be protected from Cornucopia, it had to be used now.

But many other forces besides laser light would be unleashed when Farside Cannon fired. When the combined might of four thousand laser beams struck the comet, the light show would be visible throughout the entire Solar System. Observers on every world would see something was happening, and rush to find out what it was—and all of them would want to do something about it. Garrison could order the lasers shut off, but he could never put out the political firestorm he was about to start.

"Thirty seconds."

By a deliberate act of will, Garrison forced himself to act. This thing must be done. They needed this test before they could stop Cornucopia. And Cornucopia must be stopped. The damn thing would be here in a month. But *he* had to do this. It had to be his act that set these things in motion. No robot or computer could be allowed to do it, and he did not have the right to leave the ultimate act to subordinates. "Switch control to my panel."

"Switched over, Garrison. You have control. Ten seconds to firing command."

Garrison watched the countdown in his remote panel, and felt his throat go dry as the numbers reached toward zero. He reached toward the fire button with a finger he tried to keep as steady as possible. He looked up toward the Cannon Field, determined to look what he was doing straight in the eye.

"Fire," he said, his voice solemn and sad. He slammed the button home, knowing that nothing would ever be the same again.

He watched expectantly, knowing he would see nothing. *Laser beams were invisible in vacuum, remember?* he told himself. But it still seemed to him that he ought to be able to see *something*.

There was an air of anticlimax about the unchanged scene laid out below him. Enough energy to vaporize anything material was surging into the sky—and it seemed that nothing was happening. He glanced down at the read-outs on his remote panel. According to the instruments, the Cannon was working exactly as intended. But there should have been something more than numbers on a display panel to signify an act affecting the fate of worlds.

Garrison looked up into the sky, in the direction the laser tubes were pointing. There, in that direction, out where the dark, burned-out comet moved through the blackness, there would be something to see, and soon.

A laser beam is invisible in vacuum—except from one vantage point: the direction it is pointed in. The reasons for this are simple: Laser light consists of monochromatic coherent light. This simply means the light is one color and that all the light is traveling *in the same direction*. To state the same thing another way, the photons that make up the light beam must all be of the same energy level and moving parallel to each other, all the light moving in exactly the same direction. Coherent light is also referred to as "collimated" because it moves in a straight line or column, rather than spreading out.

Since light travels in a straight line, anything or anyone not on the straight line between a laser in vacuum and its target will be unable to observe the beam, just as the light currently on its way from the Sun to Mars is invisible from Earth. However, when that light strikes Mars and is reflected back into space, some of it shines on Earth—and Mars becomes visible.

The light from the lasers of Farside Cannon was just as invisible to the outside universe—except from the surface of Comet Holmes. There it was more than visible. It was blinding bright.

From the comet, the image of the Moon was blotted out, lost in a blaze of blood-red energy that blasted down onto the surface.

Comets in the solid state are creatures of the cold, composed in large part of compounds—such as water and methane—that turn to liquids or gases at quite modest temperatures.

When they venture too close to the Sun, young comets boil off these volatile elements into space, where they form the glowing comet heads and tails, glories of reflected sunlight, which most people associate with comets. For the most part, all these gases are lost to the comet, escaping into the vacuum of space. When the comet retreats back into the dark and cold of deep space, whatever is left of it refreezes. Each time a comet's course brings it close to the Sun, more volatiles are boiled off, and the comet loses more and more of its substance. Finally, the comet has boiled off all of its surface volatiles, and can barely manage to form even a faint glowing cloud of gas and dust when heated by the Sun.

But other volatiles remain, locked under the surface of the comet and bound up more firmly in the dusty surface of the comet itself. Such was the state of Comet Holmes when the laser light of Farside Cannon struck at it.

Tumbling slowly through space, Holmes seemed at first unaffected by the torrent of light. It heated slowly at first, quiet under the sudden blaze of light energy. But its dark, dusty surface was an ideal collector for visible light energy, and tended to hold what energy it took in, rather than reflecting or reradiating it. Even with the whole surface available to absorb the energy, Comet Holmes soon began to overheat. The comet's fragile surface, a loosely bonded aggregate of dust particles and ices, began to expand as it heated, cracking and shattering, exposing still-cold subsurface material.

Frozen gases, trapped for millions of years in rock crevices, began to jet out, further weakening the surface. Water ice, carbon dioxide and methane, heated past their sublimation points, suddenly flashed directly into gas and rushed out into the surrounding vacuum. A faint gas cloud began to form about the comet, began to glow weakly as it absorbed and reflected the relentless beam of heat and light storming out from the Cannon.

Larger and larger chunks of the surface broke up under the stress of heating. Larger pockets of frozen gas exploded out, smashing through to the surface, flinging rubble clear of the dead comet.

The combined beam of the laser was not perfectly focused on the comet. Over the millions of kilometers that separated the comet from the Moon, an error of even a microscopic fraction of a degree could add up. The beam was over five kilometers wide at the distance of the comet—larger than the comet itself. As the comet broke up, its fragments floating out away from it, they remained in the beam, and did not escape its relentless heating, but continued to melt and vaporize.

Now the whole comet was crumbling under the brutal pounding of the Farside Cannon. Its core was exposed to space, molecular bonds formed four billion years ago broken for the first time since the creation of the Solar System.

The Sun was too weak to force Comet Holmes to form a head or tail, but the Cannon had the power to melt out the gases, and set them glowing and shining in the blaze of laser light and sunlight. Hours after the first laser light struck it, Holmes was a naked-eye object from Earth, a flame-bright point in the sky.

The point of light swelled and expanded, growing into weird, contorted shapes. It was impossible to miss.

At the Operation Sidebet site, Ben had long ago left the command station to stand out on the surface and look out at the comet with his own two eyes. He stood there, alone on the blasted plains of the lunar surface, watching in wonder and delight as Comet Holmes blossomed into the sky. It was about time the Solar System received its introduction to the Farside Cannon.

He felt as if they had won a great battle—even as he knew the fight had not yet begun. But Farside Cannon was a secret no longer.

He wondered how Earth and the Settlers would take the news.

EARTH

It was noon in New York when Comet Holmes, high in the northern sky, first became noticeable. It had been visible hours before in the late-night skies of Asia and Europe, but few other than astronomers paid it much mind. In the busy skies of the twenty-second century, with massive satellites, stations, spacecraft and habitats in any number of orbits, few people paid much mind to odd lights in the sky anymore.

But even to the jaded citizens of Earth, a blood-red apparition, a glowing blob of angry scarlet in the noonday sky was alarming—doubly so when it rapidly became clear that no one knew what it was. Whatever harried astronomers the press could find were hounded to death, and what they had to say didn't make any sense at all, nothing but double-talk about coherent light and purity of color not found in nature, and the object having an impossibly high temperature.

The long and short of it was that the astronomers knew just as little as anyone else.

In the absence of hard information, rumors started.

It was the long-awaited aliens finally making their arrival, and the scarlet wound of light was their star-drive red-shifting out of faster-than-light speeds. That was nonsensical techno-gibberish, of course, but it sounded good enough to convince some people.

Or else it was a massive, experimental fusion engine going haywire. That idea started a radiation scare, and sent a large fraction of the population scurrying inside, searching for whatever cover they could find. No radiation meter could detect anything, but that convinced very few people. Obviously technology was not to be trusted if it couldn't explain what that blood-red eye was.

It was the long-awaited, much-delayed Second Coming, or Judgment Day, or Gotterdammerung, or some other of a seemingly infinite number of long-predicted religious apocalypses. It was, in short, the end of the world. True believers eagerly filled the streets and the places of worship, about equally divided between frantic penitence and frantic bacchanalia. By the time the Sun again stood at noon over New York, riots had lit the night in every major city in the world.

By then, the astronomers were beginning to understand the incredible truth. Any number of brilliant theories had blossomed for brief moments only to die just as rapidly. One hapless Harvard grad student, holding to the idea that coherent light was not found in nature, suggested that the phenomenon might be artificial, but that mad idea was as completely ignored as it deserved to be. But under closer scrutiny, every other explanation fell by the wayside, leaving the artificial-event theory in sole contention of the field, more or less by default. Even for the researchers who were prepared to entertain the idea, it was a vast leap of faith in measurement to accept that anything human-made could have the power to melt a comet. But it fit all the facts—and when the same grad student suggested a refraction-angle measurement that might pinpoint the source of the light, his colleagues were prepared to listen immediately.

The resulting answer was communicated immediately to the New York offices of the United Nations Lunar Administration Council. The news was not welcome. In point of fact, it was instantly declared top secret, and a passel of FBI agents materialized at Harvard's astronomy department.

Everyone was panicky.

In the offices of Lucifer Technologies, Leonard Brattleby looked up at the sky just like everyone else, and knew instinctively that this was no natural phenomenon. Humans were doing this, somehow. Without his understanding what he saw, or having the faintest idea what it was, he knew it meant danger. If this could be done to a dead comet, it might threaten Cornucopia. Either intuition, or justifiable paranoia, told him that it *was* a threat to Cornucopia.

Others concluded it was artificial, but Brattleby had a slightly different perspective than most. The rest of the world had forgotten the dust-up two years ago over Cornucopia, but not Brattleby. And he was very much aware that Cornucopia was now less than a month from Earth encounter, and that the *Jumpstart* had disappeared. His business, his fortune, his life's work were gambled on that asteroid. If it was not safely in orbit and producing ore within a few months, Lucifer Technologies was doomed.

And still, somewhere, there were people who wanted to stop Cornucopia. That Morrow fellow, and those CRATER wildmen. He had defeated them all, two years before. He tried to tell himself they had all vanished, or been exiled— and weren't anything to worry about—but he knew, deep in his heart, that Morrow was not the sort of person to give up.

MARS

John McGillicutty, newly elected chairman of the Settlement Council, tried once again to gavel the meeting into some semblance of order, but none of his fellow Council Members paid him the slightest attention. He had packed the Council with his own rowdy allies so as to impose control over it—but right now, the operative word was "rowdy." No one could control this mob.

The Martian technicians were a bit quicker off the mark than Earth's. The Martians had concluded that the object was a dead comet being irradiated by laser light—and even identified the source as the Lunar Farside—within hours of Comet Holmes becoming visible. Twenty-four hours later, it seemed that Earth still did not know for certain what it was that had appeared in the sky.

At least the *people* of Earth did not know what they saw. McGillicutty had no doubt that the U.N. and the major powers knew exactly what it was. After all, they had built it.

Suddenly, irrationally, he wished Angela Hardin were present. He had whipped up hysteria, using fear and anger toward Earth as a weapon to gain the chairmanship. But hysteria was an easy weapon to lose control of. Hardin was the one who knew how to coax, compromise, lead through calm example. And calm was going to be desperately needed in the days ahead.

McGillicutty pounded the gavel again, beating the table so hard he thought he was going to break something.

"Order!" he barked. "Order! We are not going to solve this problem by shouting at each other. Not this time. The intelligence officer will give his report—without interruption. Mauser?"

The spindly, bloodless little man stood up nervously, clutching at a single page of notes as if they were some sort of talisman that might protect him. McGillicutty looked at his intelligence chief and swore. In peacetime, the Settlers, safe behind the broad distances of space, could afford to appoint someone's ineffectual brother-in-law to run the joint intelligence service. Not now. "Come on, Mauser. Get on with it."

"Yes. Yes sir," Mauser said, clearing his throat warily. "I could go into our complete threat estimate, but I think it might be best to summarize. Obviously, the Earth powers have constructed an offensive weapon, a massive battery of lasers."

"We know that, man. How the hell did they build it without our detecting it?" one of the council members demanded.

"We don't know. The very odd thing is that we *should* have known. Our field people are very good," Mauser went on, unconsciously inviting unpleasant comparisons with the headquarters staff. "There are a lot of Settlement sympathizers in the various U.N. offices and commands, especially the space-based ones. We have infiltrated virtually every major command, and have eyes and ears—both human and electronic—almost everywhere. They should have seen reports on this weapon. I am completely convinced that none of the offices that *should* have known about it were kept informed. I can't imagine this big a project being that tightly held.

"But, obviously, it *was* kept quiet. We suspect that it was built under cover of building a laser communications array—a joint Earth/Settlement venture. We do not know Earth's intentions. We do not know what they plan to do with the laser battery. We do not know why they chose this moment to fire it, or why they fired on the comet. Presumably to make a most impressive demonstration of the laser battery's power."

"And now that they've got us so scared we're wetting

our pants, it's just a matter of time before the ultimatum," said a sour voice from the far end of the table.

McGillicutty ignored the interjection. "But what could they do with the laser?" McGillicutty demanded, still holding out some hope that it wasn't as potent a device as it seemed. "What are its capabilities? How powerful is it?"

Mauser's face was shiny with sweat. "There are already a lot of numbers, a lot of information about power potential and so forth. We can tell roughly how much power is being pumped into the comet by measuring the light and heat it is giving off. The figures are rough, of course, but—"

McGillicutty clenched his fist on the table and growled at Mauser, trying to keep from shouting himself. "Dammit, man, but *what*?"

Mauser cringed visibly and swallowed. "It could wreck any ship in space. If the power of that laser battery were directed at this city, it would overheat the environmental control system, probably wreck the bubbledome, and render Port Viking uninhabitable within a few hours. It could do the same to any other sealed settlement."

The meeting degenerated into a madhouse, and Mauser shrank back, looking as if he was about to take cover under the table. McGillicutty did not even attempt to gavel the meeting back into order. He tasted fear, and paid no mind to the pandemonium that surrounded him. They had pushed the terrestrials to the edge with their bluff and bluster, and now came time to reap the whirlwind. Earth was prepared to fight.

The Settlers could not tolerate the existence of that weapon. It had to be destroyed, somehow, anyhow. No matter that the Settlers had no military—now they would have to create one.

Finally the shouting began to die away, and McGillicutty gaveled the room back into order.

He spoke, trying to keep the tremor of panic from his voice. "We will need no discussion to agree the Settlement Council cannot accept the existence of this weapon. We cannot survive as independent governments so long as it is pointed at us. How, then, ladies and gentlemen, shall we neutralize it?"

Nobody spoke. The implications of his words were clear, frighteningly so. McGillicutty leaned back in his chair, closed his eyes and listened to the stunned silence in the room. McGillicutty felt ill, physically ill. He had only sought to shake off the last vestiges of colonialism, make Earth accept the other worlds as equals rather than vassals.

Instead, he found himself wondering if he was making the opening moves toward the first interplanetary war.

FARSIDE STATION

The pressurized section of the main cargo bay, the largest open space in the Station, had been pressed into service as a meeting room, but even it was not going to be large enough to take in the press of people. Everyone who could not shove in found a video hookup somewhere to watch.

The wraps had come off very rapidly, once the Cannon fired. Those who had kept the secret for so long could at long last talk—and those who had suspected the truth, or something close to it, likewise wasted no time demonstrating their sagacity. What had long been merely one of many rumors was now official: Garrison Morrow was going to go asteroid hunting.

And there were very few people among the population at Farside stupid enough to miss the implications of *that*.

Dr. Prathnabar wasn't missing anything. He stood on a large packing crate that served as a speaker's platform, and leaned gingerly against the stack of smaller boxes that made up the improvised podium. He looked out upon his audience. An angry, excited buzz of conversation emanated from the mass of people pressed up against the stage. Neruda, UNLAC's puppet governor, had only himself to thank for what was going to happen here tonight. He had long symbolized the system that exiled these people, but no one had ever taken him seriously enough to hate him. The press ban had changed all that overnight, made Neruda and his government the focus of anger for these people.

Prathnabar, however well liked he was personally, was the local representative of that authority. And Garrison

Morrow was making a massive, public gesture of defying that authority, all authority.

So. The evil day had arrived at last. Perhaps he could retain his title of Administrator General, hold onto the modest trappings of his office, but today was the day he lost whatever real power he had held at Farside. It was ironic that a man clearly not interested in that power would now take it up. And Prathnabar must play his part, ceding graciously that which would be taken by force in any event.

He switched on his microphone, raised his arm for quiet, and began the meeting. "My friends, my friends, please. Let us have quiet. Please. Quiet down now."

The murmuring buzz faded slowly away. "Thank you, thank you. Now then. We know why we are here, and I will not waste your time explaining what you all already know. So I invite Dr. Garrison Morrow to speak with you all."

A great shout rose from the crowd, and, to Prathnabar's surprise, a loud chorus of booing as well. Perhaps Morrow would not have things all his own way. He looked down at the foot of the stage to Garrison and gestured for him to come up.

Garrison gracefully vaulted up to the top of the two-meter box, taking full advantage of the low gravity. Prathnabar made way for him. Garrison stepped to the podium, took the hand mike from Prathnabar, and looked out at the people, wondering what he could possibly say to them all.

This was his moment, he knew. All that he had done up to this time was as nothing if the Farsiders would not go with him. Building the Cannon was little more than telling the robots and the auto factories what to do, programming the autopilots of the crawlers to tell them where to place the laser units. The actual human labor involved was minor.

But stopping the asteroid, while defending Farside against a presumably hostile outside universe—that would require more. Much more. He needed help.

And *"Stop Cornucopia"* would be no rallying cry here. These people were seething with anger, all the long-tolerated frustrations of their exile finally made intolerable by Neruda's ham-handed tactics.

That was the place to start, Garrison realized. First tell them what they needed to hear, and then they would be willing to hear what he needed to say.

He raised the mike to his lips and spoke. "I need you all," he said quietly, wondering even as he spoke if his words were cynical manipulation, or a new leader bowing to the will of the people. It didn't matter. In the end, they would have to fight for each other's causes. "I need you all to join me in the struggle for your own freedom."

This time the cheers were deafening, and the booing could scarcely be heard.

Chapter Twenty-Five

OPERATION SIDEBET HEADQUARTERS,
THE MOON

"I wish I'd had the time to look at it more," Ben said
sadly. "It was a hell of a sight while it lasted, though." The
Cannon had shut down, and, bereft of its source of illumination, Comet Holmes had all but vanished from view.
There was only a faint halo of Sun-reflecting dust left to
show where the gaudy thing had shone. "How's things
back at Farside?"

"We've got a pretty solid front here," Garrison's voice
announced happily. He sounded tired to Ben, but his
image on the video screen looked relaxed, at ease. "UNLAC
and Neruda did us some favors. Once I played to that, we
were in business. The only serious holdouts are in the
Observatory staff. They're already pretty burned because
our test shot on Comet Holmes wrecked some set of
observations, and they don't want to cooperate in using
their gear for the defense ring."

"That's not good." Without the Observatory gear, the
lasers set up to shoot down any incoming warheads would
have no way to track their targets. "Listen, without a
defensive system, you guys are in big trouble. If someone
decides to attack the Station instead of the Cannon Field—"

"One nuke could spoil our whole day," Garrison agreed. "I know. I've already started on dispersing people. Maybe dispersal would save some lives, but tactically it won't do much good. Anyone who wanted to take a crack at us would have a lot more bombs than targets. I ordered it as much to throw a scare into the Observatory people as anything else, to make the threat seem real. So far they aren't very scared."

"Listen, you're talking survival here," Ben said. "Can't you just wade in and take over the instruments you need?"

"Who's going to operate them?" Garrison objected. "Jody can't be everywhere at once, and she's the only astronomical technician we've got. We need the astronomers' active *cooperation* if this is going to work. Besides, it wouldn't make anyone else here too happy if we started playing bully-boy. We'd lose a lot of local political points."

Ben thought for a moment. He was about to speak, when a slight tremor rattled the ground underneath him. The tremor seemed to give him an idea, and he smiled mischievously. "Are the astronomers refusing to help for political reasons, or because they don't believe in the danger?"

"Mostly the second, a little of the first—and maybe a touch of Ivory Tower complex—they can't really get interested in anything but their own work. They're so wrapped up in their studies they *can't* get involved in outside issues."

"So if you could shake them up a little, get their attention—"

"Then it might be different." Garrison studied Ben's image in his own monitor. "You look like a man with an idea."

"That I am. Let me work on it, and I'll let you know how it works out."

"Okay. Just do it fast if you can. Lemme see. What else is on the docket here?" Garrison checked his notes. "Did you manage to get the press release out?"

"Yeah, but it took some doing."

"Good. I hope it buys us some time. Speaking of which, I've got some damn meeting in five minutes."

"What's this one?"

"Attack planning. We need to get some more details down about how we're going to hit Cornucopia. We don't really have a good simulations specialist here. I wish to hell Cathy were around. We could use her."

Ben looked up sharply at his friend. Garrison didn't mention Cathy very often anymore. Usually, when he did, it wasn't a good sign. It meant that Garrison was worrying, or scared, wishing he were back when life had been simpler and he had been in love, back before his love had betrayed him.

Well, right at the moment, Ben couldn't blame Garrison if he wished for simpler times. He decided to let it pass. "Yeah," he said at last. "I know what you mean. Have a good meeting, and we'll talk later."

"So long, Ben." Garrison cut the connection, leaving Ben alone with enough worries of his own. For starters, wondering if the press release deception was going to be worth the effort taken to get it out.

The release itself hadn't been tough to work up. It was just a simple text message, no graphics, no visuals—but getting it sent had been tricky nonetheless. The hookup had not been easy. Sidebet had the cable they had run from Farside, and had laid a fiberlink cable from Sidebet to Earthrise Station. Earthrise was plugged into the Nearside cable net, and in theory that should have let them patch into Central Colony—but Central was still refusing all outside contact. The lid was down tight there.

Still, Ben was getting to be a pretty resourceful Conner—and at the moment, he had a number of resources to work with. Garrison's words, relayed over the fiberlink from Farside to Sidebet by fiber-optic cable, were lasered out to Earth, High New York, High Singapore, and the rest from there.

And as lies went, Garrison's wasn't bad at all.

Right now they *needed* a good lie. It would be another twelve days before Cornucopia rose over Farside's local horizon and the Cannon could open up on it. That still might be time, somehow, for LuTech to figure out what Garrison had planned and maneuver the asteroid, keep it out of line-of-sight with Farside. If Garrison could keep the issue sufficiently confused long enough, maybe no one would figure out what was going on.

Jody promised that it was impossible to shift Cornucopia's course enough to keep Farside from seeing it, but issuing a phony press release wasn't much effort to take to insure against the impossible.

Ben glanced over his own hard copy once again. It certainly seemed to be boring enough to be real. Maybe enough people would buy it for long enough.

RESEARCHERS SURPRISED BY COMET BRIGHTNESS

Scientists at the Farside Research Station have completed a fluorescing experiment, conducted with the use of the Farside Communications Relay, and in doing so were reminded just how unpredictable comet chemistry can be. Nearly all one hundred lasers of the Relay were focused on Comet Holmes, a small, dark body currently on a close approach to Earth.

The researchers were surprised by the resulting brightness of the comet, which was far in excess of the expected levels, and far above the energy output of the laser array itself.

The researchers believe that Comet Holmes must contain an exotic chemical structure, and that the laser light experiment must have unexpectedly initiated some sort of photochemical reaction. Apparently, the laser illumination raised the energy level above a certain threshold, at which the unexplained chemical reaction was possible. Much as a match can set fire to a log, releasing much more energy than the match itself contained, the Farside Laser Array apparently touched off a complex and powerful chemical reaction inside the comet.

Farside scientists have already put forward a number of possible chemical reaction sequences that could account for Comet Holmes' unusual brightness. The unusually strong carbon lines in spectra of the illuminated comet suggest that a carbon/oxygen reaction played a large part in the event. . . .

Ben shoved the release to one side. No one would ever read past that point. The question was, would anyone believe a single word up *to* that point? Would they have that kind of luck?

After all, a lot of breaks had gone their way already. Without Neruda's press ban, getting the Farsiders to cooperate with the laser attack would have been a lot tougher.

Poor Neruda. Poor Prathnabar. From their points of view, it was all entirely rotten luck. Without the Cannon to rally the people, they could have held on to Farside. They had literally been ruined by a bolt from the blue— well, a bolt from the black, anyway. Their positions were wrecked by something they never could have expected.

Ben frowned, and a knot formed at the base of his gut. Nothing had ever gone this well for Garrison before. Something was bound to go wrong. What surprises were waiting out there, waiting to wreck *their* plans?

Another slight tremor shook the compartment and Ben smiled, remembering he had a surprise of his own to arrange for Farside's astronomers. Whatever wild cards the universe had for *him* would just have to wait.

ABOARD THE *DAWN TREADER*

The *Dawn Treader* gently fired its maneuvering jets and floated out over Cornucopia's north pole. A brilliant double star slid over the asteroid's horizon as they rose above the asteroid's bulk. The Earth and Moon, hanging perfect in the darkness, gleamed like blue and white jewels against the black velvet of space.

Already they were close enough for Earth to show a discernible shape, a tiny blue-white crescent. The Moon, smaller and dimmer, still showed only as a point of light. The *Dawn Treader* was a long way from home, but the double planet was a welcome sight, nonetheless.

Cathy, alone in her cabin, had the view on her screen,

but she didn't notice much about it, or take time to admire the scenery. She had an asteroid to steal, and plenty to worry about.

She was glad that the landing was about to happen. Clearly, nothing could be done until the *Treader* was safely down on Cornucopia. Just setting down onto the asteroid would simplify matters greatly. Cathy chewed her lip nervously and waited for Captain Broadmoor to complete the docking. Or was it a landing when you set down on an asteroid—or should it be called a docking anyway, because Cornucopia was fitted with engines and controls and was therefore technically a spacecraft? Whatever. When Cathy was in this kind of a mood, she knew she'd worry about *anything*, just to provide an outlet for her anxiety. She felt like she was back in grade school the night before a big test, worrying about whether her pencils would break.

Once they were down on Cornucopia, things would get busy, and Cathy knew she would feel better. The key to the plan was getting Ishida out of the picture, and *that* was already taken care of, assuming Cathy's computer finagling with the environmental system had worked. Ishida was quite thoroughly imprisoned, whether he knew it or not.

A thump and a bump bounced the *Treader* back and forth as Captain Broadmoor corrected his approach. The docking maneuver was the key to getting Ishida locked up. Once Captain Broadmoor ordered everyone to acceleration stations, Cathy knew exactly where everyone on the ship was—and Ishida's acceleration station was in his cabin. Cathy had used the computers to reset the air pressure controls. The air pumps should be working already, putting the corridor sections surrounding Ishida's cabin into vacuum. Once the pressure dropped far enough, Ishida would be trapped behind the cabin's airtight doors. Even if Ishida and his servants kept pressure suits in the cabin, it wouldn't do them any good. The air pressure differential was enough to seal the doors shut most effectively. At sea level air pressure inside the cabin and vacuum in the corridor, the door was jammed shut by the equivalent of a 17,000-kilogram boulder.

The ship's environment system would keep them alive,

but Ishida and his servants weren't going anywhere. And since Cathy shut down the intercom as well, they weren't going to talk with anyone, either.

Except everyone would *think* they were talking to Ishida. Cathy dimpled at that thought. She had stolen a page from Ishida's own bag of tricks. Waiting in the computer system to intercept any intercom calls to Ishida was a small voice-simulator hooked into an artificial-intelligence program. Anyone calling Ishida would get the computer simulating Ishida's voice, saying the things Cathy and Choate wanted him to say.

Of course it couldn't fool everyone forever. Ishida rarely left his cabin, but sooner or later someone would wonder why he never came out at all. Or Ishida would figure a way out of the trap. But by then it would be too late. She hoped. Cathy started worrying again.

She glanced at her wristaid, wondering why the docking was taking so long. She could not afford to waste time. Once aboard the asteroid, they would not have much time to shift its orbit.

Cornucopia was approaching the Earth/Moon system from the west. LuTech had planned to use a gravity-assist maneuver around the Moon to slow Cornucopia, then allow it to drop in toward Earth orbit and firing the braking bomb at perigee, slamming the asteroid into its intending close orbit.

Ishida's announced plan was to wreck the nuclear braking bomb, so that Cornucopia would simply sail past Earth. Presumably, his unannounced addition to that plan was to wait until the asteroid came back around to Earth. Then, Ishida would grab the asteroid for himself.

Cathy's plan was a bit more elaborate. She wanted to fire the asteroid's fusion engines *now*, before they reached the Moon, changing their approach path to the Moon so that the gravity assist maneuver would *accelerate* Cornucopia, rather than slow it down. The maneuver Cathy had planned would throw the asteroid out of the plane of Earth's orbit altogether. It would be terrifically expensive to recover the asteroid from there but the new orbit would still intercept Earth's orbit occasionally. Thousands of years from now, it might intercept the Earth itself. A second fusion-engine burn after the gravity-assist would shift the asteroid's perihelion inward toward the Sun, eliminating that possibility.

Once safely out in deep space, Cathy proposed to unship the braking bomb, bore a hole into the equator of the asteroid, and stuff the bomb into the hole. If positioned properly, the bomb should shatter the asteroid down to a cloud of vapor, pebbles, rubble and dust, harmless small debris drifting in an orbit that would never again approach the Earth.

It *ought* to work. It ought to save Earth from the danger of serving as target practice, and possibly prevent another mass extinction. But as the *Dawn Treader* set down at the north pole docking complex of Cornucopia, all she could think of was how pleased and surprised Garrison would be.

She wondered where he was. Back on Earth, probably, working in his lab somewhere. She knew, deep in her heart, that saving the Earth was not the reason she was doing what she was doing. It was for Garrison. She owed him—and smashing Cornucopia ought to make good the debt.

She smiled, a thing she had done only rarely for a long time. She would be the first woman in history literally to move worlds just to please her man.

The clang of hatches sounded throughout the ship. "We are docked," a voice announced over the intercom. "You may secure from acceleration stations." Cathy hurried toward her cabin door. Now the trick would be in getting the fusion engines started before Ishida could think of a way out of his cabin.

FARSIDE STATION

The first impact came an hour after Ben's call.

It caused the merest teacup-rattler of a tremor, but even that was enough to send people sprawling in the Moon's gentle gravity. Garrison had been sitting with his feet up on his desk, and promptly found himself flat on his back.

He climbed back to his feet and started reaching for a phone to ask what the hell had happened. Before he had the chance, the answer appeared on the external-view monitor that now hung a bit cockeyed on the far wall. Garrison crossed to the flatscreen, staring at the image as he straightened the screen on its wall hook.

Whoever was running that camera was good, no doubt about it. It was already panning over to the geyser of dust and rock that was still climbing into the sky, spreading out in a fountain-spray of parabolic trajectories. A good-sized crater that hadn't been there a minute before sat precisely between the administration building and engineering.

Something had just crashed into the ground right smack in the middle of Farside Station. A natural meteor strike? The odds were very high against that, but—

Two more dust geysers suddenly blossomed, the first crater perfectly centered between them. The debris ring from the first strike started to come down out of the sky, and there was a rattling clatter on the outer hull of the station, like hail on the roof back on Earth.

Garrison, knocked off his feet once again, didn't bother to get up this time. Or rather, he couldn't get up. He was laughing too hard. Ben. It *had* to be Ben. And if *this* didn't throw a sufficient scare into the astronomers, nothing would.

OPERATIONS SIDEBET HEADQUARTERS

Ben thanked the Mare Orientale engineer and punched the hang-up button. Quick service—but then from Mare Orientale Mining's point of view, it wasn't much of a problem.

Most of Orientale's customers were in orbit, and that was where Orientale delivered most of what it mined. They used a powerful, highly sophisticated linear accelerator to send the ore where it was going. The LineAc was basically a three-kilometer-long magnetized rail. Specially-built carrier pods rode the alternating magnetic fields of the rail. By sending a pulse of magnetism through the rail, the carrier pods could be accelerated at hundreds of gravities. A load of ore would be loaded into a pod. The LineAc would fire, and the carrier pod would flash down the rail, releasing the ore at its midpoint. The ore would fly clear, moving fast enough to escape the Moon's gravity altogether, and the carrier pod would be braked to a halt as it rode down the second half of the LineAc.

What worked for getting ore to orbit could work just as handily for getting ore to another point on the Moon, if you didn't mind it landing a little hard at the other end. It just meant punching a different set of coordinates into the LineAc's targeting computer. Orientale had been launching Sidebet's ore that way all along, and all Ben's crew had to do was dig their raw materials out of the target crater.

And what worked for delivering ore to a point on the Moon could be used for scaring astronomers back at Farside. It wasn't even dangerous for them: Orientale's targeting computer was precise enough to land the loads within two or three meters of the target point. Ben had asked Orientale to keep up the "deliveries" to Farside until further notice, but he made a bet with himself that the astronomers would be willing to cooperate in a few hours.

Even then, he'd keep up the deliveries. No doubt Moroz's defense programs could use the target practice.

GOVERNOR'S RESIDENCE, CENTRAL COLONY, THE MOON

Governor Neruda straightened his tie and looked admiringly at his reflection in the mirror. No panic here! It was only a bit more than twenty-four hours since the fuss over that comet had started, and here it was, over already.

Apparently, these Farside yokels or whoever it was had shut off their overpowered message laser a few hours ago. It was reported that the dramatic sky display had stopped as abruptly as if a light switch had been thrown, leaving but a faint cloud of dust for the Sun to illuminate dimly.

It was over as suddenly as it had begun. A stunt, that was all. The scientists playing with a new toy. Neruda shook his head in condescending wonder. All that fuss over a message laser! Wu had written a report of some sort on the event, but Neruda hadn't bothered to do more than skim it, once it mentioned the Farside press release that explained what had happened. After all, it was not wise to pay too much attention to these teapot-tempests.

That could be most distracting. Indeed, he had made a point of not so much as looking at the comet.

Others might choose to panic over the news of Comet Holmes, but that was not Jose Neruda's way. Instead, Neruda simply chose not to know about the crisis in the first place, actively avoiding detailed knowledge of the situation. And thus, he had kept calm. No doubt *some* persons in authority had lost their nerve, but not Neruda!

He had spent a great deal of time over the last month or so demonstrating his nerve, his ability to deal with difficult situations. And he had proved victorious—he had held control and kept the lid on his own domestic crisis.

Very few outsiders knew about the press-ban riots at Central Colony, and even fewer were aware of how fierce the riots had been. But the small, beleaguered contingent of UNLAC security forces had held firm in spite of all— just barely. Even Neruda conceded that it had been a close thing. Stopping the nascent revolt had required a certain degree of ruthless resolve—and the depressurization of a corridor full of rioters—before the colonists were able to understand the weakness of their own situation.

Now the security forces could get back to their proper work of jamming signals and tracking down illicit transmitters and receivers. And they were good at their work.

Even if the press ban had caused some part of the trouble, it had also been a major part of the solution. Neruda had also seized control of the news reporting coming *out* of Central Colony. Not one word about the uprising had reached the outside press.

Silence had also been helpful on the domestic front. Only rumor and back-street gossip had carried words of the trouble to the colony. The gossip was unfortunate, but even if the rumors were damaging, they were nowhere near as bad as the truth would have been.

And, most important, the colonists had not been stirred up into a frenzy by irresponsible reporting. Hard times had hit Central, very suddenly, with the embargo against the Settlers—but no one outside the governor's office staff knew just *how* bad.

Yes, news control was a wonderful thing. UNLAC may have voted for the embargo, but by a miracle, Neruda had succeeded in planting the rumor that UNLAC had voted *against*, and that the common reports to the contrary were lies. Without any independent source of information, people were prepared to believe it. Perhaps life had been made easier for Neruda's rumor because the colonists couldn't believe that their own government would betray its citizens that thoroughly.

If the Conners had known for sure that UNLAC had been in part to blame for the crash of the lunar economy, indeed that UNLAC and the big Earth nations had brought about the crash as an act of deliberate policy—then the governor's residence would have been a smoldering ruin by now.

As it was, the residence was the sight of a splendid dinner party tonight. Neruda straightened his tie, added a last splash of cologne, and left his bedroom, heading for the drawing room to await his guests.

Neruda loved parties.

GOVERNMENT HOUSE, CENTRAL COLONY, THE MOON

Unread. The governor's computer listed the damned report on Comet Holmes filed as *Unread*. Hillary was working late again, taking her turn as night duty officer. She didn't like sitting at the DuOff desk. She could access her own computer files from here, but she was forever shuttling back and forth to her own desk for this or that piece of paperwork. She kept her personal notepack on a strap slung over her shoulder to keep the shuttling to a minimum, but it seemed a law of nature that half of what she needed would not be loaded into it.

At least drawing night duty gave her a chance to catch up on her housekeeping chores. Among these was wading through the governor's electronic in-box, seeing what was pending and what he had already dealt with.

And even she couldn't believe this one. *Highlights Examined*, the status screen said hopefully, but Hillary Wu knew how much that meant with the governor. Very likely he had let the computer select the highlights and then let them scroll past on the screen without actually "examining" them at all. He hadn't even taken a hard copy.

The man was becoming more and more detached from
reality with every passing day. Hillary looked over the
document summary screen one more time and swore out
loud this time. The computer cheerfully reported that he
had read the press release from Farside in full.

Hillary knew the governor well enough to spot another
outburst of wishful thinking. Probably alone of all the
people in the Solar System, he chose to believe that
pathetic attempt at a lie. No one knew the real reason the
laser had been fired, but no one else was buying the
experiment story.

That settled it. Hillary shut down the summary program
and set to work in earnest preparing a video presentation
on the comet for the governor. He could be allowed his
illusions about many things, but not about this. He *had* to
be made to see the importance of the laser array. Preparing the presentation was a fairly straightforward job, merely
a question of calling up images and figures from various
sources and storing them in her file section of the main
computer. It took her about an hour to get a rough draft of
what she wanted, and Hillary decided to take a quick tea
break before cleaning it up. She got up and went to the
kitchenette at the rear of the main office. Damn Neruda!
How the hell could she convince him—

A high-pitched beeping started up, and the red phone
on the DuOff's desk started to blink. A priority message
coming through. *Wonderful*, she thought. *More bad news*.
Hillary ran back to the desk and snatched up the phone.
"Night Duty Officer. Governor's Office," she said.

"This is Captain Dubois at UNLAC Message Center.
We've just got an emergency lasergram from Lucifer Technologies to all heads of government. They've got an asteroid called Cornucopia headed inbound to Earth orbit. And
the damned thing just started maneuvering without command. Somebody's hijacking the asteroid."

"Oh my God."

"That's all the information we've got so far. I'll pipe all
data into your computers as we receive it."

"*That's* all you've got?"

"That and a bunch of trajectory numbers no one's ana-

lyzed yet. Our orbital traffic control center is just getting
the details now."

Hillary felt a wave of cold fear wash over her. "Right.
I've got to go alert the governor. I'll switch to my beltphone.
Keep me posted."

Hillary hung up the receiver and switched on her
beltphone. Her immediate impulse was to race off and
alert Neruda, but two minutes of thought first would certainly pay off.

Cornucopia. She didn't need to check with her notepack
to remember *that* story. The big scare in the Earth media
two years ago. The governor had bit her head off for letting
the two men responsible arrive on the Moon. She had
even met them before they got deported to Farside—

Her blood turned to ice as she made the connection.
Now she *did* grab at the strap around her shoulder and
unsling her notepack. She instructed it to run a search in
the main computer. *Query, geologists deported to Farside,
last three years.*

The answer snapped up on the tiny screen. *Morrow,
Garrison and Moscowitz, Benjamin.*

Report current employment status, Hillary typed.

*Chief and assistant chief, Farside Geology Section, with
special responsibility for laser array maintenance—*

But Hillary had already reslung the notepack and was
moving at a dead run, notepack and beltphone banging at
her hips, before she could finish reading.

She had to stop running to answer the beltphone again.
It was Dubois again, this time relaying the Settler's
ultimatum.

MARS

The conference room smelled of too many bodies in too
small a space for too long a time. The whole room, and all
the people in it, seemed to have gone grey, turned ashen.

All the passion was shouted out of them. Their work was
done, but none of them seemed to have the energy to move.

McGillicutty looked unhappily at the document they
had just ordered broadcast out across the Solar System. It
was full of legalese, and the delegates all seemed to be
suffering from delusions of history. Practically every one of

them had inserted his or her own Whereas clause into the ultimatum, citing this or that grievance against Earth in what amounted to a declaration of war. No doubt they were all thinking about the Magna Carta, or the American independence declaration, bravely imagining their own words in the history books. McGillicutty, reflecting on it all with an uncharacteristic, contemplative fatalism, saw two major flaws standing in the way of those ambitions.

First, Jefferson was a better writer than any of them.

Second and more important, history was written by the winners.

McGillicutty did not see any way the Settlers could win against Earth and that damned laser. They would try, of course. Shipyards in the asteroid belt had already received orders to begin the construction of warships—but what use were ships against a weapon that could melt ships down to slag from millions of kilometers away?

But none of that mattered.

McGillicutty read the words over again, skipping the Whereas thises and the Whereas thats, going straight to the meat of the document.

. . . .It is the solemn declaration of this Council that, unless the aforementioned Laser Array is immediately deactivated and disassembled, with such disassembly proven to the satisfaction of this Council, then a state of war shall be considered to exist between the Settlement Worlds and Earth as of midnight, Universal Time, seven standard days after the issuance of this declaration.

That was all, but that was enough. They could not tolerate the existence of this weapon. McGillicutty could see no other possible course for his people.

Nor could he see any chance of success.

Chapter Twenty-Six

GOVERNOR'S QUARTERS, CENTRAL COLONY, THE MOON

Governor Neruda was just about to take his first bite of the fish course when the butler stepped back into the room, walked noiselessly to the head of the table and whispered into Neruda's ear.

Neruda listened, growing more and more annoyed the more he heard. "Must she see me right now?" he asked the butler querulously.

"She was quite insistent, your excellency. It appears to be a matter of some urgency."

"Oh, very well." Neruda rose from his chair and lay his napkin down beside his plate. He smiled apologetically at his guests. "Ladies and gentlemen, please do excuse me. There seems to be a matter my assistant feels requires my attention. Please do carry on. I'll be back as soon as possible."

He turned and followed the butler out of the room, his smile vanishing the moment he turned his back on his guests. It was an act of supreme self control to wait until the door was closed on the dinner party before he snapped at the butler. "I don't pay you to interrupt my dinners,

Hennessy," he said in his most intimidating voice. "This had better be good."

"I am sorry, sir," Hennessy said, quite unperturbed, "but as I said, Miss Wu was *most* determined to see you."

"Where is she?"

"I've put her in the drawing room, sir."

"All right. You go to the kitchen and tell them to hold the next course a few minutes. This shouldn't take long." Neruda strode purposefully down the hallway, stepped through the open door of the drawing room and shut the door behind him. There was Wu, a strange, wild look in her eyes.

"I'm sorry to disturb you sir, but several important things have come up all at once," she said.

"Well, then, you'd best get on with it." Neruda strode across the room and seated himself in an armchair.

Hillary hesitated, not quite sure where to begin. "Sir, the Settlement worlds have issued an ultimatum. They say they will go to war with Earth unless the large laser complex on Farside is removed."

Neruda crossed his legs impatiently. "In the first place, we don't *own* the laser complex. In the second place, it is far too small to pose a threat to anyone. You should know that, Wu. You flagged that press release from Farside for my attention. It's no affair of mine if the Settlers panic over some foolish light show. The Farside laser complex cannot harm them. I'm sure that if we all remain calm, we can demonstrate the truth of that to the Settlers." Neruda made a move as if to rise. "Now, if you will excuse me, my guests are—"

Hillary wanted to scream at the top of her lungs, grab this idiot by the throat and throttle him. She forced herself to keep calm and spoke in the steadiest voice she could manage. "Governor, before you hurry back to your guests, allow me to suggest that you haven't quite absorbed the significance—and the urgency—of what's happened concerning the laser system on Farside, and the serious danger it puts us all in. You *must* hear this."

Neruda glared at his subordinate and snorted loudly—an impressive performance, thanks to his patrician face and aquiline nose. "Well, make it quick, for heaven's sake.

This nonsense has taken up enough of my time already. I have a reputation as a host to maintain."

Hillary stared at the governor in wonderment, as if he was a strange sort of bug she had found under a rock. How could his priorities be that far out of whack? "You didn't read my report on the laser, did you?" she asked reprovingly.

Fury swept over Neruda for a moment. Her insolence was insufferable. But her eye caught his, and there was something there that frightened Neruda, frightened him badly, the look of a cornered beast that knew it was doomed and no longer cared. He shook his head dumbly.

"No?" Hillary asked. "Pity. I had it in your terminal two hours after the comet peaked. You ought to read more, sir. It's really most broadening." Hillary smiled, a wild, alarming leer that flashed on and off in a moment, an eye-blink view of the madness of panic. "Let me take a moment or two more of your time."

There was a small comm console in the corner of the room, with a wall screen behind it. Hillary hurried around behind the console and set her hands on the controls of the display, instructing the console to link up her data files in the governor's offices' main computers. All she had was the rough draft of her presentation, but it would have to do. The keyboard chuckled as she rattled in a series of commands. "I know you chose not to look at the comet when it was illuminated, but I must insist that you look at a recording of it now." Neruda stared at Wu in alarm. No one had ever dared talk to him this way before, but Wu didn't even seem to be aware of what she had done.

"It is flat-out impossible that their press release was telling the truth," she went on. "There is no conceivable way the comet could have contained that much energy. Once you see what that laser actually *did* to the comet during that 'experiment,' maybe you'll understand that."

A blank graph sprang up on the wall screen. "This is the light curve off Comet Holmes," Hillary said. "The brightness of the object charted over time." The governor, Hillary thought, had just about the technical proficiency to operate his wristaid, but perhaps even *he* could understand this.

A line started to draw itself across the bottom of the

grid, moving in a flat line left to right, then suddenly turning almost ninety degrees, shooting nearly straight up. "The first part of the graph is only an estimate, because the comet was so dim no one could see it without training a powerful telescope on it—and no one bothered to do that with such an ordinary comet. Where the graph starts to head up is where the 'fluorescing experiment' began," Hillary explained. "Bear in mind that this is a logarithmic scale—each horizontal line represents a power-of-ten increase in luminosity. As you can see, Comet Holmes went from a 10th-magnitude object, far too dim to be seen with the naked eye, right up to negative 20th magnitude, about as bright as a full Moon seen from Earth—over a period of *hours*—and kept going.

"And this is what it looked like, what you refused to see." Hillary shifted the controls again, and the image of the comet itself burst onto the screen, a phantasmagoric sprawl of light, a twisting, whirling starburst of reds and oranges, three separate tails writhing, undulating, out from the core, catching reflections and refractions from the laser light.

The governor stared at the image in shock, understanding for the first time the fear this thing had inspired. As he watched, a bright flash of light swelled up from the center of the comet head and then vanished. "Outgassing," Hillary said. "Violent outgassing. To put it another way, you're seeing the comet boil. An ice ball ten kilometers across, and they set it to *boiling*."

A note of hysteria started to creep into her voice. "This was after about eight hours of laser fire, and they fired at it for just over twenty-four hours. If they had kept it up, the comet would have been vaporized altogether in less than thirty-six hours. As it is, Comet Holmes is now only half of its original size. The rest of the comet is now a diffuse cloud of gas and dust. And they did this at a range of about five million kilometers from the Moon." She pulled out her handkerchief and wiped a thin film of nervous sweat from her brow. Hillary turned toward the governor and pointed over her shoulder at the screen.

"*That* is not the light of an unexplained photochemical

reaction. That is the unmistakable reflection of coherent laser light. You must understand that."

Hillary took a deep breath and went on. "The one true statement in that damned press release was that the comet was irradiated by the Farside Laser Relay. We triangulated back from the angle of light reflectance and confirmed that. It was a fairly straightforward matter to calculate the amount of energy Comet Holmes had absorbed, and from there to back into an estimate of the Relay's *actual* power. The UNLAC Technical Center estimated that, instead of one hundred laser units slaved together, the Array fired four to eight thousand laser units, each powered by its own solar collector, each refocused and amplified to run at perhaps a million times standard power."

Hillary stood up and walked in front of the screen, a short, spindly figure silhouetted by the glorious, glowing riot of color on the screen behind her.

"There isn't a single orbital habitat it couldn't destroy. There isn't a domed Settlement on any planet whose environmental system it couldn't wreck within hours, simply by heating the whole dome past safety limits. There isn't a ship in space that it couldn't incapacitate in ten seconds, or wreck altogether in under a minute.

"We don't know anything precise about the design of the laser array, but I did some rough figuring. If the laser units were spread out over a large enough area, no bomb or other weapon could knock out enough of them to affect it—and if they had any sense, the Farsiders would have used some of the lasers to set up a defensive screen that ought to be able to shoot down any missile that could be launched against them.

"But the power output and capabilities of this laser aren't the most frightening thing about it. I've just discovered who, exactly, is in *control* of this little toy. It's almost a truism that every malcontent intellectual and crackpot scientist in the whole Solar System ends up at Farside Station sooner or later. One of these malcontents is a gentleman by the name of Dr. Garrison Morrow—who, as you may recall, can thank this office, and you, *personally*, sir, for being stuck there.

"I am virtually certain that it was Morrow who built the

laser—and I think I know why. As you might recall, he ended up at Farside because he was trying to stop Cornucopia—and now this laser fires just as Cornucopia is approaching Earth. It was a test shot, before he tries destroying the asteroid.

"We must therefore assume that a man with a personal grudge against this office, a man who sees himself with a mission, is now in charge of an impregnable weapon of immense power, whose elements are either well dispersed or well dug into the lunar surface, a weapon capable of tracking and destroying any ship, bomb, or missile that could be launched against it.

"At any rate, I respectfully ask the governor to consider the political ramifications of such a dangerous weapon being on Farside of the Moon—a point from which it can strike—and destroy—any point in the inhabited Solar System. Every point except one: Earth.

"None of the other inhabited worlds can possibly tolerate its existence. They'll fight to destroy it, if need be. They may be out gunned by Earth, but they can't possibly let that weapon exist. We received the Settlers' ultimatum half an hour ago. They have quite understandably assumed that it is our weapon under our control. They demand that we shut it down and destroy it. They will consider themselves at war with Earth within seven days if we do not comply.

"Except, of course, there is no way *for* us to destroy the Farside laser complex, or even get near it. Obviously we ourselves do not control it, but I doubt the Settlement worlds will believe *that*, since it is on our territory—and the man who presumably built the laser is on the government's payroll.

"I might add another point that would represent an emergency even if none of this was happening. The asteroid Cornucopia has suddenly started to fire its engines without being commanded. It is shifting its orbit. I would expect that a crew under Morrow's control has boarded it and is adjusting its orbit to give him a better shot at it. As it was originally targeted to within a thousand kilometers of Earth, that is obviously a delicate maneuver. If they get it wrong and it impacts, it could snuff out half the life on

Earth. Garrison Morrow *has* to be insane. It would require delusions of godhood to take chances like that."

By now there was no chance of mistaking the hysteria in Wu's face, the rigidly-controlled terror in her voice. She stepped closer to Neruda, leaned over his chair, and smiled madly at him. She gripped his shoulder and her fingers clamped down on his flesh like the jaws of death.

"We face the likelihood of war on one side, and the possibility of mass extinction on the other, and we must assume the man at the center of it all is a monomaniacal madman. And you, *personally*, put this madman where he could do this much damage. All in all, it represents an interesting set of problems, perhaps interesting enough even to be worthy of your attention. Wouldn't you agree, sir? Wouldn't you?"

Neruda shrunk back from his aide, her eyes gleaming, her breath coming in short, panicky wheezes.

She licked her bone-dry lips and leaned even closer to him. "The United Nations Security Council will be convening in about fifteen minutes, and have asked you to join them by telelink. Perhaps the governor would reconsider, and let his dinner guests fend for themselves just this once?"

Chapter Twenty-Seven

Nuclear warheads were easy to come by in space. Every fusion rocket engine was a potential bomb if something went wrong accidentally. All that was required to make a bomb was to induce the same sort of malfunction deliberately—and teams of technicians were working feverishly to do that very thing on a dozen surplus fusion engines. The order had come through from U.N. H.Q. an hour before.

Other workers rushed to prepare the carrier rockets for the missiles, assembling them in jury-rig fashion out of whatever parts came to hand. No one had tried to fight a war in space before. Aside from the usual brushfire wars that seemed to be a permanent heritage of Earth's poorer nations, *no* one had fought any sort of war in a long time.

Even if the military planners had come up with recent experience somehow, it wouldn't have done them much good. No one, anywhere, had dreamed of trying to manage this kind of attack. Farside was going to be a tough target to hit.

But Earth's leaders knew they had better try and do the job—unless they wanted the Settlers to do it for them.

352

The bombs would be ready in another few hours, available for launch toward the Moon.

GOVERNMENT HOUSE, CENTRAL COLONY, THE MOON

"But what are they *doing*, Dubois? What in the holy name of God are they *doing*?" Neruda leaned in toward the viewscreen, a strange pleading note in his voice.

Hillary sat watching the performance nervously—and by the looks of Captain Dubois on the screen, he wasn't too at ease with Neruda's behavior either. The governor was falling to pieces, stunned by the Security Council's reasoning. The Moon was three hundred thousand kilometers closer to the asteroid than Earth; any likely course for the asteroid would bring it extremely close to the Moon; the Farside laser array was on the Moon. In short, the Moon was in the front lines as far as the two entangled crises were concerned, and Neruda was in charge of the Moon. The United Nations Security Council concluded that a lunar problem required a lunar solution.

In short, they had put Neruda in charge.

That sounded reasonable on paper, but would surely seem like madness to anyone who knew Neruda. Unfortunately, none of the Council members had ever met him. Besides, no course of action seemed likely to solve this mess—and no one back on Earth wanted to take responsibility for those decisions.

The Council had agreed on one thing—that it was only prudent to assume the worst case scenario—and so it must be assumed that the asteroid hijackers were working in concert with the Farside laser people, and that they were planning to crash the asteroid into Earth.

To Hillary, those assumptions didn't quite hang together. After all, Morrow's *de facto* deportation had been for the crime of trying to keep the asteroid away from Earth. After her own panic had subsided, she had started to think about Morrow. She had met him only once, but she remembered him clearly—and he had not seemed a madman. Far from it—he seemed a very sane and sober man. It worried her now that she had planted the idea of Morrow's madness with Neruda. Once he got hold of an idea he didn't let it go—and by now Neruda was steadfastly convinced that Morrow wanted to crash the asteroid into Earth.

Hillary could only think of one argument that suggested they were maneuvering the asteroid toward an impact on Earth. If they were hijacking it to get Earth out of harm's way, why did they leave it until the last minute? They could have intercepted Cornucopia any time in the past two years.

Hillary leaned her head against the back of her chair, shut her eyes, and listened to Neruda and Dubois that way for a while. Her screaming fit in front of Neruda had left her feeling drained, at low ebb—but also far calmer, as if she had exorcised her demons of fear and frustration. God knows her job was enough to drive anyone crazy. But after freaking out like that in front of the boss, she felt far calmer, far *saner* than she had in months. And it seemed to her that the Security Council's sensible-sounding words hid as great a panic as she had felt. They were *scared*. Hell, they had every right to be scared. But it was keeping them from thinking clearly.

"Sir, we don't know what they have in mind," Dubois said to Neruda as calmly as he could. "The hijackers are performing a very gradual throttle-up of the asteroid's fusion engines. That's pretty much all anyone would be able to tell you. We have no direct means of measuring their thrust vectors or levels properly, so we can't even calculate what their new course will be. The best we can do is to perform constant radar tracking of their course moment by moment in real time and project from that."

Neruda blinked rapidly and loosened his tie. "Wait. Wait just a moment," he said, rubbing his forehead in agitation. "You just said you can't tell how they are shifting the asteroid's path, and then you said we can track their course constantly. Which is it?"

Dubois hesitated. "It's complicated, sir. Both statements are true. They are firing the engines, but we can only get a rough idea of how hard and in what direction—we can estimate within a few percentage points, but their orbit is so complex, that's not good enough. Potentially, a few meters a second in velocity could be the difference between heading off into deep space and impacting on the Earth or Moon. Furthermore, we don't know how they might repoint the engines or throttle them up or down five minutes from now.

"What we *are* doing is tracking them on radar moment by moment. It's very accurate, but unfortunately it just gives us what their straight ballistic course *would* be if they stopped maneuvering at the moment the radar beam illuminated them."

"What use is that if they keep firing the engines?"

"It gives us a database to estimate from. We can track what their projected unmodified course was *supposed* to be against what their actual course *is*, moment by moment. That gives us a good indirect reading on their acceleration and thrust vector. Given enough time, we should be able to use *that* information to estimate what their ultimate course will be."

"So you should be able to tell if they get onto a collision course with the Earth or the Moon?"

Dubois hesitated. "Yes sir, we'll be able to spot that. But we won't have any way of knowing if they will maintain any given course."

"Very well. If your projected track for the asteroid brings it toward an intercept with Earth or Moon, let me know at once."

"Yes, sir."

"On a different subject, Dubois. As I understand it, this Farside Laser Array was supposed to be patterned on the Nearside Laser Array that your office operates, except that they added many more laser units to the Farside system, and then modified each of the lasers?"

"They didn't exactly modify them, sir. It's more a question of jacking up the power setting and narrowing the focus."

"That's what I thought. How rapidly could you make similar adjustments to the Nearside Array?"

"Just a question of issuing the commands through the control computer. Maybe twenty minutes. But sir, even adjusted for maximum power and focus, we won't have anything like the power of the Farside—"

"I realize that, captain, but we may need some firepower, and it's good to know we have it. One last thing—has news of Cornucopia got out yet?"

"Definitely not on the Moon, sir. The security teams are clamping down harder on leaks. Everyone on Earth knows about the Farside laser system, of course, and the Settlers made their ultimatum very public. There are reports of riots and demonstrations in front of government and U.N. offices. No one on Earth has made any announcement about the Cornucopia hijacking yet—but anyone with a telescope who happened to look in the right direction would spot some strange fusion lights and wonder what was going on. Everyone's underground here, we don't have that problem. The people on Earth will find out soon enough. And the rumors will be flying on the orbital habs. It's going to leak, and soon."

"Yes, of course. Thank you, captain."

Hillary opened her eyes and looked at her boss. Neruda stood up and started pacing back and forth. "I don't want this," he announced pettishly. "I do not want this responsibility." He took a deep breath and blurted out the next words, as if they were some shameful confession. "I am not qualified to make these decisions." Hillary almost smiled at that. As if anyone could be qualified to stop an asteroid and save the world. "But I am here, in charge of this foolish little world, which might be all that stands between Earth and doomsday. *I* have to decide what to do."

Hillary didn't say anything. The terrible thing was that this nincompoop *wasn't* having delusions of grandeur. He had just summed up the situation with perfect accuracy.

PERIMETER HOTEL, MAIN SUBBUBBLE, CENTRAL COLONY, THE MOON

Genia Lumbroska's bracelets and bangles clattered noisily as she lifted the binoculars to her eyes and peered out across the subbubble. Good. No sign of the UNLACs from here, and the code signs from the other high point in the subbubble—a potted palm in a window, a certain set of window shades half-drawn, the unlit "V" in the "No Vacancy" sign at the Lunar View Hotel—all reported that there was no UNLAC activity. It was probably safe to transmit. The only real danger was from collaborators—and there weren't many of those. Collaborators seemed to have trouble remembering to wear pressure suits when they went through airlocks.

The various wholesale rumor and information merchants had moved in on the market when Neruda had issued his press ban—and operating trading data, right under the eyes of the UNLAC thugs required a certain degree of cooperation.

It was tricky. They had to keep their real info-trade completely invisible while at the same time letting the UNLACs find an occasional transmitter or a stack of leaflets. The idea was to keep the thugs busy enough to believe they were keeping a lid on the information trade—without getting anyone caught and thrown into Tycho Penal.

But business was too good, and information prices had gone too high, for Genia to be scared off by the risks. Of course, the *real* money was going to her sources. She paid top dollar, and they got their data for free.

There might be a press ban on the Moon, but there certainly wasn't one elsewhere. The do-gooders on Earth and the large habitats were beaming news programming at the Moon, *giving* it away, and all that was required to get the stuff was a concealed antenna somewhere on the surface. Of course, the folks in that end of the business took greater risks than Genia—but all that money selling what you got for free!

Genia set down the binoculars and checked her watch. Almost time. She locked the door to the office, opened the closet, and unlocked a small hidden compartment at the rear of the closet, revealing a battered suitcase. She pulled the case out and opened it. There were stacks and stacks of money in it, large-billed denominations from every large Earth nation. The information business was good.

Genia's hope was that if the UNLACs found the cache, they would get no further than the money. All that dough ought to seem a sufficient reason for the secret compartment. Maybe they would not look further once they found it—or maybe they would just skim a share of the money—or even all of it—and leave her alone.

Better they take all her money than her means of making more. She closed up the case and put it to one side. She reached deeper into the hidden compartment of the closet. She pulled out the message maser and the tripod Benny had sold her. The maser was an ugly thing, about the size and shape of a shoe box, with lots of rough edges to it and the controls labeled in grease pencil. But none of that mattered. It worked.

Lasers were not much good for covert communications in atmosphere—the beam, refracted by air molecules, was plainly visible for all to see, pointing straight from sender to receiver. Masers, on the other hand, microwave lasers, were first rate. Especially the ones Benny built. Highly directional. Invisible beam. High enough frequency to send thousands of words of coded text in a few seconds.

Genia set up the maser on its tripod and sighted it carefully at the dimmed-out "V" in Vacancy at the Lunar View Hotel. The wall behind the "V" was transparent to microwaves, and Naomi's receiver and recorder would pick up everything.

Genia slipped a data block into the maser and pushed the *transmit* button. Not much for Naomi this morning, just more rumors from outside workers about that weird blob of red light in the sky two days before. Genia had tried to track down the story, but there hadn't been much to go on in the street gossip. Few people were allowed outside access these days. The UNLACs didn't want people wandering around outside listening to the off-planet news services.

That suited Genia—it drove up the demand for her own news and gossip—but it made it damn hard to get any word on this red light.

Ten minutes later the maser was carefully packed away in the closet, and Genia was eagerly pulling her datablock out of her own concealed receiver. Naomi sold news from the High New York downlink, and their news service was always good—even if it reached Genia 48 hours late. Maybe today there would be some explanation of the light in the sky. Genia sat down and began to read.

Within half an hour she knew nearly as much about Cornucopia and Comet Holmes as the governor did.

Normally, Genia could only sell a retail news story five

or six times, because only that many people would be interested enough in the information to pay her rates and make it worth her while. But Genia knew a gold mine when she saw one. She sold the story fifty times that morning, retaining a twenty percent kickback fee for any resale. In another six hours, half of Central Colony knew about the twin crises.

ABOARD THE *DAWN TREADER*

Shiro Ishida slammed his battered shoulder against the airtight door again, and once again bounced off it like a rubber ball against a concrete wall. It was hopeless. He gave up, knowing full well that he would be back at it in a few hours, when the frustration overwhelmed him again. It was vital to save face in front of his servants, demonstrate his calm, not give way to the torrents of anger surging inside him. To have come this far, to actually have the ship docked on the asteroid, and then to be trapped like a rat in a cage. Even having weight again was a defeat. He had heard the countdown, felt the surge of power as the asteroid's engines relit, felt the weight of his own body being gently tugged down onto the deck. Against his wishes, against his plans, against his authority, the asteroid was maneuvering.

And he had heard the false orders that made it happen— had heard them in his own voice!

His betrayers were wrecking his plan by simulating Ishida's voice—and there seemed no way for him to speak himself, no way to get through to the captain. He glared over at the ruins of the intercom panel, smashed in a fit of rage hours ago. That outburst had been unwise. Perhaps, if the device had been left intact, he and his servants could have found a way around the clever programming that cut it out of the ship's communications loop. But now the intercom would never work again.

But worse, a thousand times worse than not being able to speak, was being able to hear. The public announcement speaker in the overhead bulkhead was still functional, and over that came conversations between Captain Broadmoor and the computer simulation of Ishida's voice.

Oh, there was irony in that. To be defeated at the end

by his own weapon, a computer simulation of a human being.

Ishida was not a man who appreciated irony.

Ishida forced himself to calmness, to sober thought.

There had to be a way out. There had to be.

FARSIDE STATION

Garrison shut off the comm unit and slumped back in his chair. Ben had relayed the word from the High New York news feed. He couldn't believe it. The Settlers were going to declare *war* over the Cannon? Riots back on Earth? He had expected people to get upset, yes, but he'd never dreamed it would all go so far. There was a gnawing pain at the base of his stomach, and Garrison wondered just what sort of disaster he had unleashed.

Ben, still at Operation Sidebet headquarters, was able to get line-of-sight on Earth and some of the habitats, and so relay Earth's side of the story from there. But from the Settlers came nothing but silence. Garrison certainly had the communications hardware to talk to the Settlement worlds easily enough—but *they* wouldn't talk to *him*.

The Farside Station comm section was transmitting a message of his peaceful intent over and over again, beaming the signal to every Settlement that was visible in Farside's sky. None of them were responding.

No doubt they assumed Garrison was lying when he told them of Farside's peaceful intent and its *de facto* independence from Earth. And he *had* lied when he had claimed that Comet Holmes had gotten so bright because of a chemical reaction. It seemed that made him the boy who cried wolf; it wasn't going to help his credibility much. Maybe they regarded his protestations as strategic deception. Maybe they were concerned that any response beamed back at him would provide the Cannon with updated targeting data. Maybe they refused to speak with a man they assumed to be a mere military commander, and chose instead to confront his supposed masters back on Earth. In any event, the Settlers remained silent.

The obvious thing to do was take the wraps off the real purpose of the Cannon, announce publicly Farside's intent to destroy Cornucopia. No doubt plenty of people had figured it out by now.

But announce now, confirm it—and suppose they *hadn't* figured it out? LuTech still might have time to maneuver the asteroid, find some tricky orbit that would keep it out of range of the Cannon—or else, more likely, LuTech and UNLAC might find a way to destroy the Cannon.

Garrison shook his head, trying to clear it. This mess was too complicated, with too many people coming at it from too many directions. He needed to think, to figure out—

The comm unit beeped again. Garrison hit the *answer* button.

Ben's face came on the screen, his expression blank with shock. "Garrison, Cornucopia has started to maneuver. It started about twelve hours ago, but they've only just now released the news to the general public. We can't see it from here yet, but she'll be rising over your horizon much sooner than expected. Nobody knows who's doing it, or why, or where they're going to take her. But they're blaming us."

ABOARD THE *DAWN TREADER*, DOCKED TO CORNUCOPIA

"I am pleased to see the course adjustment is going well," Ishida's voice said over the intercom.

"Yes, sir, it is," Captain Broadmoor said absently. "I will report to you again in an hour. Bridge out."

Cathy, sitting at the navigator's station on the bridge, looked anxiously at Broadmoor, but he seemed not at all suspicious. He had no inkling that he had been talking to a computer simulation of Ishida's voice. If only the damned computer would come up with different phrasing! It was using almost precisely the same words every hour on the hour when Broadmoor reported. On the other hand, so was Captain Broadmoor. The man had no imagination, certainly—but that was an advantage to Cathy and Choate right now.

As were Ishida's solitary habits. He had not been seen outside his cabin for over twenty-four hours—but by now, everyone was used to his reclusive and unpredictable behavior. Broadmoor had not even acted surprised when Ishida had ordered the new and drastically different maneuvering plan.

"All right, boys and girls," Broadmoor said. "Let's take the rest of our status check. Asteroid systems?"

"Asteroid engines showing nominal. All the slaved-through controls are working fine."

"Navigation?"

"Still on course, right on the money," Cathy said.

"Life support?"

"All systems nominal, captain."

Cathy breathed a sign of relief. Her diddling with the cabin pressure outside Ishida's cabin was still undetected. Luckily, the cabin was normally off limits anyway.

"Communications?"

"Not much to report, captain. All the suit radio systems are fine. Still receiving multiple calls on all standard hailing frequencies, and we are still ignoring them."

"Quite right. They may wish to speak with us, but why should we speak with them?" That sounded very bold and buccaneering, but Cathy knew the real reason for radio silence. The crew of the *Dawn Treader* hoped to get away from this little operation without either their ship or themselves being identified. The ship's standard issue comm system automatically transmitted an ID code on a side band whenever it sent any sort of signal. That was required by traffic control rules, to allow for automatic ship tracking in busy orbits. The system was sealed and tamperproof.

They could have rigged a home-built radio system that sent no ID codes, but any radio or laser transmission might reveal some juicy clues—a voiceprint, a slip of the tongue, an identifiable background noise of some sort that might lead to the ship being identified. And besides, why *would* they want to talk to anyone?

The communications operator went on with his report. "We still have one work crew out there, checking on the nuclear device systems—and they report a healthy bomb. But I've heard some strange news broadcasts. We're still way out of range or beam angle for most of the news signals, but I'm getting bits and pieces of something from signal fringes. We're the lead item, of course, but there's something else," the comm officer said. "Some kind of nutcase fired a big laser at a comet a day or two ago. No one knows why. It must have happened while we were hidden behind Cornucopia. Supposedly it was quite a light show."

"Well, it doesn't sound like anything to do with us. Engineering?"

Cathy didn't hear the rest of the status check. She *did* have an imagination. And she had a nasty feeling it was about to run away with her.

U.N. OPS CENTER, HIGH NEW YORK

The attack force, such as it was, was ready for launch. Twelve jury-built fusion bombs, hurriedly mated to their boosters, hung in the void a few hundred meters from the habitat. The computers aboard the habitat transmitted the appropriate signals, and, one by one, the missiles fired their engines and set out on the fifteen-hour flight to the Moon. If all went well, they would all home in on Farside Station at the same moment, aiming not for the unknown location of the Cannon, but for the Station itself, in the hope that the control station was there.

In all likelihood it wouldn't work. Farside would be able to shoot down all the missiles. But maybe, just maybe, even a failed attack would help convince the Settlers that Earth did not control Farside Cannon.

If it was still possible to convince the Settlers of anything.

GOVERNMENT HOUSE, CENTRAL COLONY

It was quiet in the governor's office. Perhaps it was the only place in Central Colony that *was* quiet. The news of Cornucopia and the Farside laser had leaked out somehow, and the panicky mobs had sprung up again, roaming the streets and tunnels, unruled, unguided, uncontrolled. So far the riots hadn't started, but it wouldn't take much.

But all was quiet in the governor's office, as they waited for news. There was nothing Neruda or Hillary could *do*, but it seemed almost inevitable that something more would happen. This was the place to be.

Neruda had grown thoughtful as the evening had drawn

on, more so than Hillary had ever seen him. The crisis was demanding the best of this man and, incredibly, was calling it forth. For the first time ever, Hillary realized, the governor was thinking of the people he led, of the world outside himself, and not of his own image and prestige.

He sat behind his desk, at long last reading over all the material available—on Morrow, on the laser array, on Comet Holmes and the asteroid. Hillary stayed with him, sensing his need for company.

At last the governor shut off his reading screen and turned toward his assistant. "I have a theory, Wu. In fact a pair of them."

Hillary nodded encouragingly. "Yes, sir?"

"The first is fairly straightforward. The Settlers hijacked the asteroid as a response to Morrow's laser. Somehow they rushed a crew aboard it, or found a way to take it over by remote control. They plan to smash it into Farside and destroy the laser that way.

"The second theory is a synthesis of two contradictory things that have been suggested. One, that Morrow's people hijacked Cornucopia and are shifting its orbit to give his laser a better shot, and two, that he's built the Cannon as a super weapon to dominate the Solar System. Those two don't quite make sense side by side. It requires one sort of mad man to make an insane and needless effort to save the world from crashing asteroids—and quite another sort to try and dominate the Solar System with a mega-laser.

"But suppose the hijacking *is* his doing—but *not* because he's trying to line up the asteroid for a better shot? There's a much better reason for grabbing Cornucopia. If he *were* out to conquer the Solar System with the use of that laser, what's the one place he couldn't threaten with it? What is the one place in the Solar System it could never hit?"

Hillary's face drained of color. "Earth. Oh my God, Earth. It can never be seen from Farside. The Farside laser can't hit Earth."

"Exactly. Even if he made himself some sort of mad emperor of space, Earth could still threaten him.

"Therefore, before he can rule the rest of us, *he first must get rid of Earth.* I've sat here and thought it all out a dozen times, and I'm convinced that it's one of those two. Either the Settlers plan to hit *us* with the asteroid, or else Morrow's people plan to crash Cornucopia into Earth.

"And it's up to us to stop them, quickly, quietly, secretly. If we announce our intent, we'll be bound to touch off more panic. The moment Dubois gives me an orbit projection that intercepts Earth or the Moon, I will order him to open fire on the asteroid's engines with the Nearside Array before they achieve the intercept course. We will cripple their engines and keep them away from our worlds."

Chapter Twenty-Eight

ABOARD THE *DAWN TREADER,*

Bertram Choate, huge in his pressure suit, walked down the corridor and hesitated at the entrance to Ishida's cabin. He had gotten into the depressurized corridor section by using a pair of airtight doors in the adjoining corridor section as an improvised airlock, sealing the section off and depressurizing it before opening the door to this section.

The bridge indicator had shown a drop in pressure in Ishida's cabin, and Choate, for reasons he did not clearly understand, had volunteered to investigate. At least Cathy had managed to get Ishida's simulated voice shut down when the indicator had gone off. If indeed the cabin had gone into vacuum, it was going to be very awkward explaining how Ishida had kept talking afterwards.

And, Choate realized, *that* was the reason he had volunteered. Whatever the cause of the vacuum alarm, resolving the problem seemed likely to require tidying up a few unpleasant details. Either it was a trick on Ishida's part, and they were all inside the room, ready to jump Choate—or else there was a real malfunction, in which case Ishida and his servants weren't going to be ready for much of anything.

Choate checked the status board for the corridor first.

The corridor was still in vacuum, of course, but Choate wanted to check the valve controls. Cathy had set them so that the valves opened out onto empty space. Yes, they had held that way. Until those valves were closed, any air that reached this corridor would simply whistle away into space.

Choate turned back toward the cabin door. He was reaching for the handle when he spotted it. A neat hole, a perfect circle perhaps five centimeters in diameter, punched through the door by a high-power laser cutter.

Choate cringed inside. Deep inside, he had known all along this would be what he would find. Ishida had taken a chance, a gamble, and drilled through the door. If Cathy had merely pumped the corridor into vacuum and kept the spill valves shut, it would have worked. The air in the cabin would have roared out through the hole, decompressing violently—while the escaping air repressurized the corridor. Once the pressure had balanced, Ishida could have stepped through the cabin door, and sealed the hole in it somehow.

There would still be a pressure differential holding the door to the next corridor section sealed, but if they burned another hole through the airtight door in the corridor, air from the ship would have spilled in, again equalizing pressure. They would have escaped with no injuries worse than popped eardrums and nosebleeds.

But Cathy had set the spill valves open, and all the air rushing from the cabin to the corridor had kept right on going, right out into space. Choate shut the spill valves now. It wouldn't do for anyone else to note they had been left open. The trick now would be to keep people—especially Captain Broadmoor—from asking the wrong questions.

Still, that was a minor point right now. Choate forced himself to consider the thing he was unwilling to face—that they were all dead in there. Choate closed his eyes, and the carnage of High Manchester flitted through his mind. The exploded bodies, the wheeling bits of debris, the black-red smear of vacuum-dried blood.

He did not want to see it all again, but there was no choice. He turned the door handle and stepped through.

With vacuum both inside and out, the door swung open easily. Ishida was there, sprawled out on the floor, staring through sightless, glazed-over eyes at the ceiling, the laser cutter still in his hand. The two servants lay face down on either side of him.

Choate looked mournfully down at the dead men, then knelt gently and pulled the cutter from Ishida's hand. This had to be made to look like something other than an escape attempt, or even as stolid and stupid a captain as Broadmoor was bound to start asking questions. Choate fired once at the wrecked intercom, to account for the damage to it, then two or three times at the interior walls and furnishings, and then once more, straight through the outer hull. He knelt again by one of the two dead servants. Hoshiro, was that the man's name? Strange to have spent two years on a ship with a man and not know his name. But Ishida's servants had scarcely ever ventured outside this cabin. And that fact would help Choate's story. He put the cutter in Hashiro's hand.

Choate stepped apologetically over the bodies, went back into the corridor and out through his jury-rigged airlock. He had committed grave crimes, but there was no choice, and now no turning back.

Five minutes later he was back on the bridge, his suit helmet cradled under one arm. "They're dead. It looks as if one of the servants went berserk. Isolation madness, violent claustrophobia, something like that. He got a cutting laser from the emergency kit. He shot up the cabin, wrecked the intercom, cut a hole through the door—and then burned a hole clear through the outer hull."

"Dear God," Broadmoor said.

Choate looked straight at Cathy. "It was not a pretty sight. I'm glad you did not have to see it. But we have to decide what to do now."

Cathy looked wide-eyed at Choate, at the captain, through the viewscreen to the beshrouded shape of Cornucopia outside. "We go on," she said in a strange tone of voice that only Bertram Choate could know the reasons for. "We go on with what Shiro Ishida wanted done when he died. We get this damned asteroid away from Mother Earth once and for all."

Cathy turned and stared out at Cornucopia. Was what she had done murder? "Captain, you will continue the rocket burn as planned."

FARSIDE STATION

"We have no information, Garrison. N—n—none," Jody said unhappily. "We don't have any numbers or tracking at al—*all*. Ben has picked up a bu—bunch of news reports that say the asteroid has lit its engines, but no one knows where th—they are going. The news broadcasts don't give any tracking data, of course, and we can't exactly call over to Cen—Central Colony and ask UNLAC for the data."

She sat, small and sad, in the visitor's chair of Garrison's office, fidgeting with her notepack. "All I can tell you about is classes of orbits. All the possible paths for Cornucopia are pretty sim—similar. They are too close, too deep into the Earth-Moon gravity well for them to change things drastically." As usual, Jody had lost most of her stutter while talking shop. "But even a small change could cause a very big shift in outcome.

"No matter what they do," she went on, "the asteroid will make a close approach to the Moon and have its course swung around almost ninety degrees to drop straight in toward Earth. Then it will do one of three things: pass Earth on the west, strike the planet, or pass it on the east. An east-side pass would make it much harder to recover the asteroid later, so that would be the superior choice for someone trying to keep it away from the orbital miners.

"The problem is that the difference between an eastward pass and a westward pass is just a few tens of meters a second—with all the Earth-impact trajectories in between. So they *could* be trying for an eastward miss and still show an Earth-impact trajectory for a while. We don't know. We can't know until it's too late."

"Okay, I understand," Garrison said. "We'll have to wait until they come over our local horizon and track them ourselves. Or actually, once they rise over Sidebet." Ben's Operations Sidebet team was ready to go, just a few kilometers away from Earthrise Station, well to the west of Farside. "They've got tracking gear, of course."

Jody stared down at her lap and nodded silently.

"You're worried about Ben being out there, aren't you?" Garrison asked gently.

Jody looked up and blushed. "Ye—yes."

"Don't be. Believe me, he ought to be more worried about your being *here*. Which reminds me. What's the story on evacuation?" The odds were going up all the time on Farside being a target for somebody, and Garrison didn't want anyone there who didn't have to be.

"It's looking g—g—good. All the children are cleared out, and most of the dependents. Earthrise Station took in a lot of them, and Mare Orien—ta—tale. We have an emergency shelter put together at Mare Moscoviense to the n—n—north. No one in it but a skeleton crew, but it's there if we need it."

"Good. Let's hope we don't—and hope we get some numbers on Cornucopia, while we're at it. See you later."

Jody got up and left. Garrison punched in the call-code for Ben at Sidebet, stood up, and started pacing back and forth across the room.

Ben's face popped on the screen. "Garrison. You there? I can't see you on screen."

"Sorry." Garrison went back to the desk and twisted the camera to show the part of the office he was pacing in. "There, now you can see how calm and relaxed I am. Who is it, Ben? And what are they doing?"

"We just spotted the asteroid coming over our horizon, and bounced all the standard hailing codes off them immediately. We don't know. As to what they're doing, well, there are only two possible answers. Either they're knocking the damn asteroid away from Earth—or they're about to drop it *on* Earth. We can't read the orbit yet. Even if they're trying to throw the asteroid clear, somewhere during the burn the projected orbit could intersect the planet. The original orbit had the rock getting so close to Earth, that's almost inevitable. That's what made it so dangerous in the first place. By the time Cornucopia rises over your horizon, we'll know for certain."

"But who the hell *are* they?"

Ben looked through the viewscreen at his friend, pacing back and forth across his office like a caged animal. He had a guess, a wild guess. He and Garrison had vanished into the woodwork for two years, until the world forgot them—and until they had their chance to stop the asteroid. Why should they be the only ones to do that?

It had to be CRATER. It *had* to be Ishida and his crew. Cathy had to be there, aboard the asteroid. He had no proof, no evidence, no logic, but it had to be right. He *knew* it, deep in his bones. But Garrison had enough on his mind without that to distract him.

"I don't know who they are, Garrison," Ben said. "I can't even guess."

GOVERNMENT HOUSE, CENTRAL COLONY

The telephone bleeped and Neruda hit the answer button so fast Hillary barely had time to hear the sound. "Neruda here."

Captain Dubois appeared on the screen. "Governor, you asked to be notified of any possible Earth-crossing orbit."

"Yes, yes. Go on."

"Sir, there can't be any doubt. If they continue this burn for another hour, the asteroid will strike the Earth."

Neruda shut his eyes and slumped down in his seat. The perfectly dressed dandy of a few hours ago was gone, a rumpled and tired old man left in his place. "Very well. I formally order you to direct the Nearside Array at the asteroid and fire until her engines are incapacitated."

"Sir. There is another possibility. If, once they achieve an Earth-impact orbit, they continue to fire for another five minutes, they will then be back to a near-miss trajectory."

"That would be a very long five minutes for planet Earth, Dubois. Would you want to take the chance that the engines would not malfunction during that time even if they had the best of intentions?"

"No, sir."

"If we fire now and wreck the engines, would the asteroid strike Earth?"

"No, sir.

"Then you have your orders, Captain. Please keep me apprised."

Dubois had been expecting the command, and had made the needful preparations hours before. His small force of lasers was ready for action.

The Nearside Array opened up on Cornucopia two minutes later.

HIGH NEW YORK, ORBITAL TRAFFIC CONTROL CENTER

"Holy Jesus Christ!" Sid Pearson reached out hurriedly to turn down the gain on his optical tracking screen. Cornucopia had just turned bright red. He punched a button on his console and talked into his headset to his supervisor. "LuAnn, those sons of bitches at Farside just illuminated the god-damned asteroid."

"Get real, Sid," the calm voice in his headset replied. "Look at your line-of-sight display. Farside can't even *see* Cornucopia yet."

"Yeah, *you* look at the line-of-sight. That damned piece of rock turned red. *Somebody's* zapping it."

LuAnn Barrowman was famous for appearing with magical speed when there was trouble, and now she lived up to her reputation, getting in behind her tech almost before he had finished speaking. "Damn, Sid, you're right. But it *can't* be Farside. Get a fix on where the beam's coming from."

Sid checked the backscatter pattern. "From the reflectance angle, it's gotta be on the Moon. Zeroing in here— let's see, hold on, I think I can get some coordinates here. Sunnovabitch. Those bastards! Those lousy, traitor *bastards*! That's the Nearside Array shooting!"

"What the hell are they doing?" LuAnn demanded.

"Isn't it obvious?" Sid demanded. "It's the Settlers who grabbed the asteroid, everyone knows that. They want to drop it on the Farside Cannon and knock it out. The damn Nearsiders just want to piss off the Settlers, make it tougher for Earth while they do a favor for their crummy Farside chums, cook the asteroid's engines so they can't direct it to an impact with the Moon. *Bastards!*"

LuAnn Barrowman looked down at Pearson. Orbital

Traffic Control was a high-stress job, and it looked like maybe Sid was due for a little vacation. But the contact was for real, whatever the reasons. She'd let 'em know in Operations. Who knows, maybe they were crazy enough to come up with the same explanation as Pearson. She plugged her headset into an empty panel and keyed in the number. "Yeah, give me Carson. We've got a little development with Cornucopia."

CORNUCOPIA

The universe turned red. "Attack!" The comm officer screamed. "We're under attack!"

Captain Broadmoor leapt to his feet. "What the devil are you talking about?"

"Laser fire, sir, extremely intense laser fire directed at the midsection of the asteroid. Right where the fusion engines are."

"Nothing to do with us, captain," Cathy said savagely. "Just some nutcase shooting at an asteroid."

"Skin temperature of fusion engines rising," the engineering officer warned. "That's what he's after. He wants to overload the cooling system for the engines and knock them out."

"Can we shut down the engines?" the captain demanded. "Will that cool them enough to do any good and keep them from overheating?"

"No sir, not enough to be worthwhile," the engineer answered in tones that tried to sound calm and professional, tried to hide the fear in his eyes. "It might buy us a few seconds, but they can keep firing as long as they like. And the closer we get in toward the Moon, the more rocket power it will take to change course. We're right on the edge of fuel reserves now. If we shut down, we won't have sufficient power later to get into the course we need."

"How long until the engines overload from the heat?" Broadmoor asked.

"Not long, not long at all. I'm checking temperature readings for the whole asteroid. Temps much lower at the two ends of the asteroid, much higher amidships, where the main engines are. They've targeted precisely enough to concentrate their power right where it can hurt us the most."

"But how long do we have?"

"Sir, I don't know these engines. Maybe five minutes, maybe an hour. One thing that's saving us a bit is the asteroid's spin. They can only hit three out of four engines at any given moment, and the fourth is shielded by the bulk of the asteroid for a few seconds, giving it a little time to cool. But that won't be enough. Something will give out. A fuel line or a tank will overheat—or the engine bells themselves will rupture."

CISLUNAR SPACE

The tiny fleet of missiles launched by High New York was now only a few thousand kilometers from the Moon, moving at tremendous velocity and accelerating. Each missile was far distant from its companions as each took a separate course toward Farside, so as to hit it from all directions at once.

But a new command came in on the control frequency, and four of the missiles shifted course toward a new target. There was panic abroad, and fearful people were forced to decide too many things far too quickly.

Four nuclear warheads were diverted toward the Nearside Array. It was a much shorter and more direct course than the other. They would take only a few minutes to arrive.

CORNUCOPIA

"Engine two hydrogen tank reaching critical!" the engineering officer announced. "It'll blow any—"

There was a sudden, bone-rattling lurch that threw the crew against their crash couch restraints and sent loose objects flying about the bridge.

"Number two tank has blown, taking the engine with it. Other engines pivoting to compensate for off-axis thrust and engine loss and throttling up to maintain constant thrust. That will make them overheat all the sooner."

"Cut all engines!" Cathy shouted. "Cut them now!"

Broadmoor glared at her angrily. "I'll give the orders around here. You heard the man. We must use the engines to complete this burn now. We use them or lose them *now*. If we shut them down, the laser fire will destroy the engines, and we won't have them later to perform the maneuver."

"I said *shut them down!*" Cathy shouted. "Three days from now we reach Earth and fly past it. With another two minutes of thrust, our course will have changed enough to intercept the Earth instead of being a near-miss. Five more minutes of full power after that, seven minutes total, and we'd be okay, we'd have shifted course enough to come *out* of the intercept on the other side.

"Except we don't have full power anymore—and we just lost one quarter of our fuel supply! We don't have the fuel to make the full burn—and if the engines blow while we're in an intercept trajectory we'll have no way to get out of it."

Broadmoor frowned and tried to work his way through the problem. But he didn't have much time for quiet reflection. Two more violent lurches rocked the *Dawn Treader*'s bridge. "Engines and tanks one and three gone," the engineer announced. "Engine four throttling up to compensate."

"One engine left," Cathy hissed. "Three-quarters of our fuel gone. And the last engine is not going to hold together long enough to move us through the intercept zone. If the last engine blows while we're in intercept, there will be nothing we can do.

"But if we shut down *now*, we'll stay out of the sensible atmosphere, cross within a hundred fifty kilometers of the planet instead of striking it." A number changed on Cathy's display panel. "Make that a hundred forty. *That's* why they're firing on us—they think we *want* to drop this rock on Earth. And we're letting it happen."

Broadmoor opened his mouth vacantly and stared at the engine status board.

"Our miss distance to Earth is now one hundred thirty kilometers," Cathy said, as coolly as she could.

"Shut down!" the captain ordered. "Shut down remaining engine."

The engineering officer slammed down the control buttons.

But nothing happened.

Cathy felt a horrible sick feeling in her stomach. She brought up a repeater of the engine status board on her console.

Engine four was still firing. In fact it was still throttling up, gaining in power.

"We have lost control of engine four," the engineer announced. "The other engine explosions must have wrecked its onboard controller."

"What the hell does that mean?" the captain asked.

The engineering officer swallowed hard and looked at Broadmoor ashen-faced. "Engine four will continue firing as per its last instructions before its controller was wrecked. It will try to throttle up and re-vector to compensate for the lost engines. I am trying to call up the backup control circuit."

All eyes turned toward Cathy, and she checked her panel.

"Miss distance with Earth now ninety kilometers and dropping," she said.

Broadmoor turned toward the engineer. "Damn it, man, *get that engine shut down!*"

"Eighty kilometers," Cathy said. "That's put us well inside the sensible atmosphere. The asteroid will bore a hole right through the air at orbital velocity." *The sonic boom alone will kill and deafen billions*, Cathy thought.

"Sir, I have no control of that engine yet," the engineer said, pasty-faced with fear. "Both the engine and its control systems are badly damaged and not responding to command. The engine is firing at over 120 percent of rated thrust capacity and I can't throttle it back."

"Don't give me technicalities!" Broadmoor screamed. "Shut it down!"

"I'm trying, for God's sake! Backup systems are balky as well. I don't know them well enough to do this job."

Broadmoor turned to Choate, who was sitting at an observer's station on the bridge. "What will happen if he can't shut it down?"

Choate looked through the captain, seeing again the horror of High Man before his eyes and the coming catastrophe that would make in three days the loss of

High Manchester seem as nothing. "It will keep burning, trying to complete the burn on its own, until it ruptures altogether or until it runs out of fuel. And it will run out of fuel before it can get us into an orbit that misses the Earth."

"Sixty kilometers." Cathy said the words without feeling. It was over. Nothing could stop this. Another three minutes of thrust, and not even the braking bomb could kick them clear of Earth impact. Three days from now, this rock would smash the home planet. How many billions would die?

"Engine four overheating!" the engineer cried, a mad hint of hope in his voice. "Approaching rupture temperature. The laser's finally cooking it. Come on, you damn monster, blow." Panic was in his voice as he chanted the word. "Blow up, damn you, blow up—"

NEARSIDE ARRAY

No one had thought about defense when the Nearside Array was laid out. None of the precautions taken at Farside had been made here. The array was built conveniently close to Central Colony, its laser units were clustered close together, and there was no tracking system to spot incoming missiles—or lasers designated to fire at them. The four shrapnel-enhanced bombs from High New York detonated within five seconds of each other, the first a bare kilometer over the Array—throwing the follow-on bombs off course to land wherever they might. One detonated harmlessly in an unpopulated area, another hit the spaceport, and the last exploded a few hundred yards from the New Subbubble. The solid rock walls protected the Colony from catastrophe, but could not prevent quakes, landslides, and blowouts of isolated corridors.

At the Array itself, not a single laser unit survived.

CORNUCOPIA

"Laser fire has ceased," the comm officer said in horror. "They've stopped shooting."

"And the damn engine temp is dropping! Engine restabilizing. I still have no control. Diagnostic computer trying to run a work-around on the backup systems."

"Miss distance fifty kilometers." The *Dawn Treader*'s bridge was deadly silent, listening as Cathy counted down toward the moment that would seal a planet's doom. "Forty. Thirty."

"Oh my God, I'm sorry," Broadmoor moaned. "I'm sorry. I did not mean to do this thing."

"Twenty. Ten."

"Zero." Cathy closed her eyes and began to weep. "The asteroid will strike Earth seventy hours from now," she said.

No one spoke, and the silence of death pervaded the bridge.

Nobody noticed or cared, two minutes later, when the backup circuits finally came on line and shut the last engine down.

Chapter Twenty-Nine

FARSIDE STATION

The defense lasers snapped around on their turrets and fired before Jesus Moroz could even look up to react. The black sky was suddenly bracketed with starburst-bright explosions of color. Within ten seconds, eight missiles were detected, tracked, fired upon, and destroyed. It happened so quickly that Jesus wasn't even sure what had happened until he ran back the data at low speed. Jesus was delighted by what he saw, the clean, precise pattern of the defense moves. Nice to know his programming all worked.

Of course, if it *hadn't* worked, he'd never have known, but Jesus didn't stop to think about that.

Garrison was not as pleased by the news. What would happen the next time? Moroz's hardware would have to take its chances, but the people of Farside could not rely on it working perfectly all the time.

It was high time and past to evacuate the Station. Most of the children and dependents had been moved already, but it was time for the core staff to go too. Preparations for the move had been made long before, and the destruction at point-blank range of eight nuclear warheads was argument enough to silence anyone who might have complained about the disruption. Rollers, every roller Sunchaser owned, every roller at Farside, started loading up for the run to Mare Moscoviense. The advance team there made the final preparations to the snap shelter (which was little more than a large bubble dome). The remote command center for the Cannon at Moscoviense was powered up and tested. Garrison was relieved to find that the fiberlink between Mosoviense and Farside Station worked flawlessly.

It would take two days to get everyone to the snap shelter. Garrison would be in the last group to go, traveling via the *Bouncer*, the one and only rocket vehicle at Farside. A small sub-orbital pogo flier, the *Bouncer* could make the run to Moscoviense in twenty minutes. Everything was running very smoothly.

Until Ben called in. Garrison, overseeing the evac operation from his office, took Ben's call there—and knew the news was not good.

"It's going to hit," Ben said, and Garrison didn't need to ask more. "Our best tracking guess shows they were trying to move the asteroid into a better miss-Earth trajectory."

"Then some yabbo at Nearside panicked and took a potshot at them, knocked out their engines at exactly the wrong moment—and you know the god-damned rest. They're moving faster than we had hoped, too. You'll have a much shorter firing time than we had planned."

"Will it be enough time?" Garrison asked. *Hit the Earth? They had come this far to stop it merely threatening the Earth and it was going to hit?*

Ben looked at Garrison and spoke the hardest word he had ever said.

"No."

GOVERNMENT HOUSE, CENTRAL COLONY

The riots had started in earnest this time. There couldn't be an UNLAC security man alive by now. DuBois, in fact the whole communications section, were all dead, killed at the Array. The spaceport was half-wrecked. A half-dozen tunnels had vented.

The mob was screaming for blood. Neruda's blood.

Hillary was with the governor as he stood by the wall screen and flicked back and forth through the news channels. The news people had all put themselves back on the air, in simultaneous defiance of his orders. The riots, the looting, the burning, the crowds surrounding Government House played across the screen.

Hillary had always thought she would rejoice when Neruda finally resigned, but she found herself with tears in her eyes. The right decision, the one *right* decision he had ever made—that was the one that went wrong. Another minute and they would have stopped the asteroid. But then Earth had attacked the Moon. By now, everyone knew what had happened. And Central Colony would never trust Earth again, even if Earth survived. They had lost all their tracking data with the Array, and had no way of knowing whether the asteroid had been stopped.

Poor Neruda. After all the idiotic decrees, the pointless and petty harassments of the Conners, it was the decision to protect the Earth—and Earth's own panic—that started the revolt. Perhaps Earth's own panic had doomed Earth.

Neruda shut off the screen at last. "It's over," he said. "Earth can never rule the Moon again." He sighed and sat down wearily behind his desk. "I suggest," he said, "that if you wish for both of us to survive, that you declare my arrest and the establishment of a provisional government. Tell them I am out of power, or else we will both be hacked to bits when that mob breaks in here. You play your part and I will play mine."

Hillary nodded mechanically. She had reached the same conclusion. "I'll call the news people," she said. "Sir, I am sorry. You did the right thing, with the asteroid."

"Doing the right thing," Neruda said thoughtfully. "I don't think you've accused me of *that* very often." For just a moment, the old haughtiness showed through. "Doing the right thing, Wu—doing the right thing has rarely been the criteria for success."

FARSIDE STATION

Garrison felt his jaw tense up, his heart turn cold with

fear. But there wasn't time for that. "Even if we're going to fail, we've got to try. How long until Cornucopia is visible over our horizon at Farside?"

Ben checked his read-outs. "Four hours, twenty minutes. You'll have about twelve hours of firing time before you lose them."

But Garrison wasn't listening. "Ben—they don't know we're here." Something like hope sounded in his voice.

"What? Who doesn't know?"

"The people who grabbed Cornucopia. If they had, they would have contacted us, arranged to cooperate on knocking out the asteroid. They kept themselves secret, and so did we."

"If they were hiding out, say behind the asteroid itself, and maintaining radio silence, they could have missed Comet Holmes altogether."

"So what? Garrison, we have some major problems here! We can't worry about that right now."

"Ben, *we can't stop that asteroid by ourselves* any more. They tried, and they couldn't stop it by themselves. Maybe we can pull it off if we cooperate. At the very least we can warn them to get off the asteroid. You're in line-of-sight. Use your comm lasers and patch me through on a voice channel to them."

"Garrison, let Sidebet take a crack at them—"

"Dammit, Ben, Earth just dropped *nukes* on us! Maybe they bombed Nearside too, and that's why Nearside quit shooting. You don't have adequate defenses, you don't have the firepower to do any good—and we might need you later. Put me through to Cornucopia."

"Just let us—"

"Do it!" Garrison thundered. "It's a long shot, but if we don't do *something* Earth is doomed."

Ben set the switches and ordered a laser unit to swing around to Cornucopia. He knew, he *knew*, who would be on the other end. "Channel open, Garrison. Go ahead and talk."

"This is Farside Station calling via secure comm link to those aboard Cornucopia. We must speak with you. If we work together, perhaps we can stop the asteroid. Come in please—"

CORNUCOPIA

"—Come in please."

The comm officer listened to the call. He had his orders. Ignore all incoming contacts. But this voice said it could stop the asteroid, and in a choice between Earth and Broadmoor's orders—

"I have a new incoming contact," he announced. "I'm putting it on the main speaker." He threw the appropriate switch.

"—arside Station calling Cornucopia. Come in please. Do you read me? If so, respond on any standard laser or radio frequency."

Cathy stood bolt upright in shock. That was Garrison's voice! Garrison Morrow at Farside Station? "Give me a secure channel back," she ordered.

The comm officer looked over at the captain, but the poor sodding bastard wasn't even aware of what was going on. He shrugged and set his panel. "Speak into the intercom on your crash couch arm," he said.

Cathy switched on the intercom. "Garrison, this is Cathy Cleveland aboard Cornucopia. Is that really you?"

For a long moment, there was dead silence on the other end of the line. "Cathy? What the hell are you doing there?"

"It's a long story, Garrison. We were trying to knock Cornucopia away from Earth and it all went wrong. My God, I can't believe it's you." Too many emotions flashed through her heart at once for her to even know what she was feeling. Shock, delight, surprise, deep sorrow that they should meet again now, at the end of all things. The others on the *Dawn Treader*'s bridge looked at each other in mystification.

"I sure as hell didn't expect *you*. My God," Garrison's voice replied. They heard him clearing his throat, trying to pull himself together to sound businesslike. "We're here to try the same thing ourselves. We have a large laser array we plan to fire at the asteroid, but your maneuvers have cut down on the length of time the laser will have line-of-sight. We're going to try it anyway, and we at least wanted to warn you we were about to fire."

"You shot at us before," Choate objected.

"That wasn't us," Garrison said urgently. "Check your own charts if you don't believe me. That came from Nearside, probably the Nearside Array. Whoever it was, they were scared, and I can't blame them. God knows what's happening on Earth and at Central.

"We're on the opposite side of the Moon, in Daedalus Crater. Right now we're talking through a relay link near Earthrise Station. Our lasers can't even *see* you yet."

Cathy leaned in toward the intercom mike. "How long until you can commence fire, and how much power do you have?"

"We can start shooting the moment you come over our horizon in four hours—and I'd estimate that we have at least forty times the power of the Nearside Array that shot at you before."

"*Forty times?*" Choate asked incredulously. "How can that be?"

"We've been planning this for a long time," Garrison said wearily. "It isn't going to be enough as things stand. But if you can strip the bagnet off the asteroid . . . It's white and the asteroid underneath is dark—"

Cathy was trying to think fast. "Garrison, I see what you mean, but there isn't time to talk, and I don't know yet if we can do it. There *might* be a chance to make this work, but I need to check it out with some good numbers. Can you transmit some real detailed data to me, your engineering records, everything?"

"Ben, give me a data side band," Garrison ordered.

Ben cut into the conversation for the first time. How could Garrison be *listening* to her? She had just helped pilot Cornucopia into a collision course with Earth! "Garrison, you can't be serious. We can't trust these crazies!"

Cathy drew in her breath in surprise. But it made sense. Ben and Garrison would have stayed together.

Garrison shouted down the fiberlink to his friend. "Ben, god damn it, give me the data side band! We *have* to trust them, it's the only chance the planet has. *Earth is about to die.* If they're lying, how can they hurt us anymore than *that?*"

"They've hurt us plenty already, Garrison. Don't give

them another chance. We might be able to wreck the asteroid alone."

"And if we fail? If we failed because of some petty, personal sorrow and billions died?"

Cathy heard the hostility, the *hatred* in Ben's voice, and knew it was directed at her. The planet might die, and Ben was resisting the one chance to save it because she had betrayed Ben's friend, in work and in love. Well, she asked herself, why *should* he trust her? But there was no time to convince him. "Ben, please," she said in low, pleading tones.

Again there was silence on the line for a long moment. "Data side band open," Ben said at last.

"Cathy, I hope you have some smart computers. Here comes a lot of information."

"Keep the line open, Garrison. I'll call back soon."

Cathy set her computer terminal to index the masses of data that was about to arrive. This is what she was good at, what her job was. Loading data in one end and finding a solution out the other end.

The comm officer looked at Cathy in bewilderment. "Uh, Dr. Cleveland? Who *was* that?"

Cathy didn't even look up. She shook her head as she stared at the screen. "No time."

Bertram Choate went over to the comm officer. "I've heard a lot about this Garrison Morrow from Dr. Cleveland," he said. "He sounds like a remarkable man."

"Well, who *is* he? What kind of guy is he?"

Cathy looked up for half a moment before diving back into her data. She had to explain Garrison to these people. They *had* to know what she knew. But there was no time, and she searched for the briefest of descriptions. "I'll tell you what kind of man he is," she said.

"Garrison Morrow is what you make heroes out of."

Chapter Thirty

EARTH

Chicago, Paris, Dar es Salaam, Tunis, Rio de Janeiro, Moscow, Perth. The panic was everywhere. The disorders Comet Holmes had kicked up were as nothing. Now there was official, confirmed news of the ultimate doom, with no escape. There was no crime, no sin, no blasphemy left uncommitted. No place of worship that was not packed with bodies, no crackpot solution that did not have impassioned adherents. There were riots at every spaceport as hysterical people battled to the death for a spot on a flight, any flight, off-planet.

Rumors as to where the asteroid would strike were everywhere, and there were panicky mass exoduses from half a dozen cities where the hammer was supposed to fall.

The governments of the world searched frantically for a solution. But there was no hardware that could fix this problem, and no time to build anything. Many hopeful engineers remembered the small fusion-braking bomb Cornucopia still carried, (if it had survived the laser attack from Nearside) and went hopefully to work with their figures, searching for the place and time to fire the bomb and kick the asteroid clear.

386

But the braking bomb was too small for the job. It had been designed to give the final burst of braking power after the fusion engines had done most of the work. It did not have the power to kick the asteroid clear away from Earth.

Nothing did.

CORNUCOPIA

After Captain Broadmoor broke down completely in a sudden outburst, Choate had been forced to sedate him. It was unfortunate to see the poor man go to pieces, but at least there was no longer anyone on the bridge who might conceivably challenge Cathy's authority. She had no legal right whatsoever to command, but by now her orders were obeyed without question.

At least Cathy had a plan, even if she was were making it up even as the crew were executing it. One step at a time, that was the way to do it.

Cathy punched up an outside camera to see how the spiders were managing. The spider-robots had worked to capture this worldlet and tame it, two long years before. Now, they once again scuttled across the surface of the asteroid, their ferocious mechanical jaws snapping down on the thick support cables that strapped the bagnet to the asteroid. Other spiders clawed through the net fabric, tore it off in huge swatches of fabric that sailed off Cornucopia's surface, thrown clear by the asteroid's rotation. A third team of robots chopped through the underlying network of cable. Lengths of cable fell away from the surface and joined the shredded pieces of bagnet that now hung in a cloud of debris about the spinning asteroid.

The robots worked with a demented, metallic speed, almost too fast for the human eye to follow. But Cathy could see the results in the stress gauges and structure integrity indexes. Garrison's idea had been right on the money. Without the cables and netting to hold it together, the asteroid was a far weaker piece of skyrock—and even more importantly, a darker one. The dark greys and browns and blacks of the asteroid's surface would absorb and retain heat far better than the bright-white bagnet would have.

Cathy glanced up at the countdown clock. Two hours to go. Two hours until Farside Cannon would open up on the asteroid. No one on either side had spoken, but everyone knew that the Cannon would fire whether or not the *Dawn Treader* was clear or not. They would have no choice.

The comm link blinked on again. "Cathy, these are the coordinates I want you to use," Garrison said. "You should be able to hit them. Ready to transcribe?"

"Ready, Garrison."

"One hundred seventy-nine degrees five minutes west, four degrees five minutes south."

Cathy punched in the figures, told the computer to locate them for her, and swore. "Garrison, that's where—"

"I know. I know. And I think it has to be that way. Even if you just get close, I think it ought to be good enough. Don't worry about us here, we'll be well away. Just do what you have to do."

Cathy bit her lip. Would they be away in time? Never mind. If Garrison was lying about this, she had no right to question him. He knew what the stakes were. "All right, Garrison. We can use those numbers with no problem. You just try to hit our end of Cornucopia."

"We'll zero in right where you're sitting," he said mischievously. "So be careful. And hurry."

"Don't you worry about that. We'll commence our roll program in five minutes. *Dawn Treader* out."

There was only one large maneuvering engine left, and very little fuel for it, but Cornucopia still had its small attitude control rockets, and Cathy wanted to use them before the spiders got around to chopping through the cables that held them.

The aft rockets fired, and slowly, ponderously, the huge asteroid came about to its new heading, shedding a new cloud of debris as more bits and pieces of cable and bagnet and equipment wrecked in the laser attack broke loose. Cathy, still in the navigation couch, guided the monster craft so its nose would point straight at the Moon at perilune, the asteroid's point of closest approach with the Moon's surface. Cathy glanced up at an outside monitor to see the lunar Farside already rushing far too close. The endless wilderness of craters and mountains loomed closer, a deadly, lonely landscape, harsh and shadowless in the searing heat of full sunlight.

Well, it was going to get a hell of a lot closer.

Something creaked and moaned, and there was a clattering on the hull as some bit of debris bounced off.

FARSIDE STATION, CANNON CONTROL

Garrison watched on the monitor as the last of the rollers took off on the lonely two-day ride to Mare Moscoviense. If all went well, he would beat them there. The *Bouncer* was standing by, already preprogrammed for the quick rocket hop to the Sea of Moscow. If all did not go well—he'd never get there at all.

He turned and looked at Alois Hofmeister, his sole remaining companion at the station. He had finally figured out something about the strange laser expert.

Ben had reported something from Earth that gave him the clue. Ben had told him about the theories wherein Garrison was planning to declare himself emperor of space—with the power of the Farside Cannon to back him up.

It was *Hofmeister* who had planned to do exactly that, build an oversized laser and use it for his own purposes, long before Garrison and Ben had ever arrived at Farside. Garrison knew it had to be true the moment the thought occurred to him. Maybe Hofmeister planned to demand tribute, maybe he planned to set himself as some sort of king at Farside—or maybe he was crazy enough to try and use the laser to conquer the Solar System.

It seemed nuts even to Garrison, but it was the only explanation that made sense, that explained Hofmeister's strange behavior, that explained why he never quite seemed to believe that the real purpose of the Cannon was shooting down asteroids.

Presumably, Hofmeister had thought—and perhaps still thought—that Garrison was after more than that. Had Hofmeister simply gone along with the plan all this time, waiting until all was ready and he could take over the laser? What did he plan for Garrison, then, when this was over? A knife in the ribs, perhaps?

Garrison shivered. It all seemed mad—but then, they

had all always known Hofmeister was crazy. And it made Garrison feel all the more certain about what he had decided to do.

In the meantime, he would keep his back to the wall at all times.

"How much time do we have, Hofmeister?"

"One hour until Cornucopia rises over horizon. We're ready."

CORNUCOPIA

The *Dawn Treader* shoved off from the half-wrecked asteroid, all as much in readiness as it could be. The spider-robots could still be seen at work, chopping and shredding away the skin and sinews of the asteroid.

The comm officer ran nervous fingers over his console. They were running the asteroid by remote control now, and it all went through his panels. If something went wrong with his systems—but that didn't bear thinking about.

Besides, hadn't a great deal gone wrong already? Surely they had used up their share of bad luck by now.

Of course, the comm officer thought sadly, things didn't really work that way.

OPERATION SIDEBET HQ

Just at the moment, there was a part of Ben that wished Sidebet had been set up on the opposite side of the Moon, at Mare Smythii, instead of here next door to Earthrise Station. They had built Sidebet here, at the line between Nearside and Farside, not only as a backup to Farside, but as a look out post that could keep an eye on Earth. That had been smart. Sidebet had been vital for spotting and communications up to now, and so that was all to the good. But now things were going to get hairy.

Ben looked out over at the Sidebet Laser Array. There were only three hundred lasers in it, and if that were not enough, that was too bad. It was all the lasers they had been able to make once they moved the factory here. They dared not fire them yet, just in case Earth still had a few fusion bombs tucked away, say at one of the LaGrange points. But later, the Sidebet array might well be worth something.

If Garrison and Cathy's little plan worked right, most of the debris would be heading in Sidebet's direction. Being at Smythii on the opposite side of the Moon from *that* seemed only sensible. But Ben had picked the Sidebet side himself, and could only blame himself if things broke the wrong way.

Of course, in that case, knowing who to blame was going to be very cold comfort indeed.

FARSIDE STATION, CANNON CONTROL

The endless minutes slipped by, one by eternal one. Garrison paced back and forth across the small control room, and went repeatedly to the tiny observation bubble to look out, as if there would be anything different to see out there. Hofmeister sat brooding over the main command board, watching the health of the four-thousand-plus lasers that were all that mattered anymore.

"Fifteen minute, Herr Doctor Morrow," Hofmeister said quietly to Garrison. "We should force ourselves to eat something. It is a long and busy twelve hours we have ahead."

It was going to take a lot less than twelve hours, but Garrison wasn't going to tell Hofmeister that just now. "Yeah, you're right, Herr Hofmeister."

They found some long-store rations and choked them down without tasting them. The stuff could have been gourmet food, or flavorless glup. Garrison was in no state to know or care. For the thousandth time since he had moved from the station proper to Cannon Control, he called Ben at Sidebet. "How's she look, Ben?"

"Cornucopia is now just about at our local zenith, almost directly overhead and broadside to the Moon. She's getting darker by the minute, too, which means the robots are still stripping away the bagnet. There seems to be a lot of junk coming loose—we can pick up radar echoes from the debris cloud. *Dawn Treader* is well clear, and you should be able to see Cornucopia on your horizon any second now—"

"We have her!" Hofmeister cried excitedly.

"Commence firing," Garrison said at once, leaning eagerly over Hofmeister's shoulder.

Hofmeister threw the main switch.

Out on the great Cannon Field, the four thousand lasers had long ago been locked onto the point on the horizon where the asteroid would appear. Primed and ready for action, now was their moment. They fired as one, blasting invisible gigawatts of energy into the sky.

"Firing commenced, all systems is normal," Hofmeister announced.

Garrison closed his eyes and sagged back into a chair next to Hofmeister. This was it. This was the moment to which he had dedicated two years of his life. The stakes of this moment were higher, much higher than he had ever dreamed. There was no mere danger, no slight *chance* of harm to Earth to defend against. If he failed, Earth was dead.

"On target!" Ben called joyfully. "The damn thing just lit up bright red—and so did the whole debris field around it. You've got to tighten your focus."

"Yah, yah," Hofmeister muttered irritably. "We held initial focus wide to make sure we'd hit it. Now we got asteroid glowing bright red in sky, nice target to tighten focus on. Any better?"

"Much better," Ben said. "Cornucopia just got a lot brighter and the debris field is fading away."

"Concentrate fire on the forward end of the asteroid," Garrison ordered. "Focus on the end closest to the horizon."

"Why?" Hofmeister asked. "Why that end?"

"Because we'll get more bang for the buck concentrating fire and the god-damned bomb is at the *other* end of the asteroid. We don't want to take a chance on setting it off or starting a radioactive chain reaction," Ben replied.

Garrison tried not to look at Hofmeister. Ben's explanation was a little thin, to put it mildly. Would Hofmeister buy it?

"Okay, okay, redirecting fire," Hofmeister said wearily. "You fellows want I should focus down on initials some guy carve in rock?"

Garrison grinned. "No, just hold it steady there. Just hold it steady there and let's see what happens."

CORNUCOPIA

The asteroid was turned into a vision of Hell, a scene that Hieronymus Bosch would have sought out as a subject for one of his mad canvasses. The very stone was turned blood-red by laser light, and the forward end of the worldlet, the north pole where the *Dawn Treader* had docked, seethed with a lurid brightness as it absorbed the worst that the Farside Cannon could deliver. The docking complex and the asteroid's control station received the full brunt of the laser's wrath and were soon reduced to molten puddles of metal and sputtering plastic.

Further from the forward end, the spider-robots still scrabbled purposefully about the scarlet surface, their metallic bodies glinting and gleaming in the lurid light, relentlessly ripping up the support structure they themselves had laid down. One of them crept too close to the forward end and overheated. Its left front leg joints froze up, but still it limped forward over the hellish surface, grasping at the rough ground to hold itself down.

But the heat was starting to weaken the asteroid's surface. The spider wrapped a claw around a knob of rock that suddenly snapped off. The spider scrabbled frantically for another toehold, but the entire patch of surface was giving away, leaving it nothing to cling to. The asteroid's gravity could not hold the spider to the surface against the asteroid's spin, and the damaged robot drifted free of the surface, its legs still snapping spasmodically, trying to grab at a toehold that was no longer there. It drifted deeper into the most intense of the laser light.

And melted.

More and more fragments, and larger and larger ones, started to break off the forward end, and the core of the asteroid underlying the surface began to feel the heat. Long-trapped pockets of volatile chemicals melted or sublimated, expanding as they heated, forcing open cracks, shattering the surrounding rock.

The forward end of the asteroid began to glow a dull, oppressive, mottled red of its own, the glow visible even in the hell-red of the laser light.

The asteroid was close and easy to target, but even so Hofmeister's aim was remarkably good. While the temperature at the forward end of the asteroid shot upward, even a kilometer or two back the heating was quite moderate. The one surviving fusion engine, well aft of the nose, was barely warmed at all, and the aft end of the asteroid, where the braking bomb waited, remained at normal heat levels.

But the forward end was beginning to die. Boulder-sized fragments began to break off, only to remain trapped in the glare of the laser's wrath. The broken-off fragments could absorb far less heat, and began to heat up rapidly, glowing brick-red, cherry-red, incandescent-white before they vaporized altogether.

The relentless laser fire gnawed away at the forward end of the asteroid, tearing off bigger and bigger chunks of its substance.

Cornucopia was dying.

DAWN TREADER

It hurt to watch the flame-bright glow of Cornucopia's forward end, but Cathy was willing to endure it. It was the light of hope. The painfully intense glare seemed to be growing brighter with each moment that passed.

The *Treader* flew in formation with the asteroid at the prudent distance of one hundred kilometers. Even that would be far too close if a fragment blew off in just the right direction, or if Hofmeister's hand slipped on the targeting controller.

But the sight was too remarkable, too gaudy and unlikely a spectacle to even think of the danger.

Cathy watched the asteroid in fascination. To Cathy, the monstrous thing looked ridiculously like a huge, surreal cigar, one end glowing red as it burned. Even the cloud of debris and dust streaming off it resembled smoke.

And like a cigar, the asteroid was burning down from one end.

That was the whole idea. There was still a certain amount of orbit-changing power in the remaining fusion engine and the braking bomb, but not quite enough to do any good with a mass as big as Cornucopia.

If they couldn't increase the rocket power available,

they could reduce the amount of mass the rocket had to move. If they could just lower the perilune far enough, Earth might survive yet. The numbers were actually promising.

It all sounded good.

Now they just had to make it work.

PORT VIKING, MARS

McGillicutty watched in fascination as Earth seemed to go to war with itself. With the partial news blackouts, the censorship, the cryptic images gathered from Martian telescopes and terrestrial video transmission, it was hard, indeed impossible, to form a clear picture of what was happening. Now this asteroid seemed likely to crash into the planet. Incredible.

In a few weeks or months, the Settlers would have at least a fleet of armed merchantmen. McGillicutty was starting to wonder if they would be sent to attack Earth—or arrive as a rescue team to save a ruined world.

EARTH

They could see this new ruby-red light in the sky, so like the other one they had seen only a few days and a lifetime ago. But this time people did not look up in panic, but in fearful hope. The astronomers, the commentators, the reporters explained what it might mean, and people tried to believe them. Cornucopia, drawing ever nearer the Moon, shone bright against the night sky, glowing by the light of the unseen and mysterious Farside Cannon.

People looked up from their end-of-the-world prayers and orgies to see if the blood-red light truly offered hope.

CORNUCOPIA

Now the forward end of the asteroid's core passed a major threshold. Even there, the rock was now hotter than the melting point of ice, and many zones of subsurface strata were hot enough to boil water. Water and the other volatiles hissed and steamed out of every crevice, and steam pressure started to build in internal pockets. A rapid series of steam explosions broke two massive chunks off the forward end. The house-size rocks rebounded off each other and smashed back into the still rotating asteroid, breaking up larger fragments.

Soon the front end of the spinning asteroid was lost in a jostling cloud of its own wreckage. Debris particles of all sizes from molecules to boulders caromed off each other and into the front end of the asteroid, bashing off larger and larger pieces which in turn joined the cloud. Cornucopia was grinding itself to bits.

DAWN TREADER

It was time to try the fusion engine. Soon the stone to which it was mounted would start to crumble, and the engine might shear off as soon as it fired. The engine had received a complete and complex set of firing commands from the *Treader* while the ship was still docked to the control complex, and while the control complex still existed. Now all that was required to set it in motion was for the *Treader* to send a radio command to the engine's built-in control computer.

Cathy keyed in the comm link to Farside. Now they were in line-of-sight with Garrison, and no longer had to relay through Ben. "This is *Dawn Treader* requesting preplanned firing pause," she said. If the Cannon fired while they were maneuvering, the lasers would have a much tougher time tracking the asteroid—and also might start cooking the surviving fusion engine.

"Stand by, *Treader*," Garrison replied. "Shut down for two minutes, Hofmeister. They want to maneuver to clear away some of the debris. Okay, *Treader*, powering down. We will let you get clear and then direct fire on the debris during your burn."

The garish nimbus of light around the nose of the asteroid abruptly snapped off, leaving only the glow of radiating heat behind. Cathy nodded to the comm officer. "Do it."

The comm officer relayed in the command, and all hands watched for the fusion engine to fire. If it failed, all was in vain.

There was an endless, mind-wrecking pause of perhaps half a minute while the engine pressurized itself and powered up to fire—and then the fusion plume stabbed out into the darkness, momentarily blinding everyone aboard the *Treader* as the fire of dying atoms lanced out across space.

The engine bell swiveled back and forth crazily as the engine's controller tried to compensate both for the off-axis thrust and the asteroid's rotation. Like a huge parody of a child's toy fireworks, the fusion plume corkscrewed lazily through the sky, battering the asteroid drunkenly through the debris field. The rocket's thrust dislodged one of the last spider-robots and sent it tumbling off into space, its legs flailing wildly.

Huge chunks of rubble smashed into the asteroid, breaking off more of the weakened forward end. The engine burned on, finally forcing Cornucopia through the edge of the debris cloud. The fusion plume lanced through the rubble, vaporizing whatever rock fragments it touched.

"Farside, you are clear to fire on debris," Cathy said into her mike.

Instantly, the red glow of laser light snapped back on around the debris. This rubble was still on a collision course with Earth, and while none of the fragments were large enough to threaten a mass extinction, they could certainly cause serious damage. Jesus Moroz's skillful targeting program was able to spot the largest fragments and concentrate fire on them, rapidly reducing the already red-hot rocks to vapor.

And the asteroid plowed on, looping and pinwheeling wildly about the steady flame of the fusion engine. Cathy wished she could use the att rockets to clean up that wobble, but the att rockets had been designed to work in concert as a unit, and all the forward atts were of course long gone. Aside from the main fusion engine, they had no more control over the asteroid's attitude in space.

Cathy watched the chronometer. So far, five minutes of thirty-percent thrust. Cathy didn't want to try any heavier thrust than that, given all this poor old engine had been through. But in one way, the engine had it easy. A large fraction of Cornucopia's mass wasn't there anymore, and the fusion engine was making great progress moving the lighter load. Even so, it was not going to be enough to force the asteroid out of Earth intercept.

But that was not even what they were trying for anymore. Cathy had a different plan in mind.

Five minutes, six, seven of thrust, forcing the asteroid into a lower and lower orbit. Rubble was still breaking loose and streaming away from the crumbled asteroid. And then the fuel ran out, leaving Cornucopia a tumbling derelict. Cathy checked the revised orbit. It *might* be enough. It *had* to be enough. She thought of Earth, of cool green forests and bright sunlit days, of infinite beauty and babies and kittens, all doomed should they fail. It *had* to be enough.

"Farside, you may recommence fire on Cornucopia," she whispered into the mike. "The tumble is as bad as we thought it might be, but try and keep your fire directed at the forward end."

And the lurid firelight reignited around the tortured worldlet.

EARTH

The flame-bright light in the sky crept slowly toward the disk of the Moon as the world watched the silent, jewel-like radiance of Cornucopia's agony. Slowly, painfully, the splinter of sapphire moved closer to the first-quarter Moon.

At last it slipped behind the Sunlight edge of the lunar Nearside to be eclipsed by the satellite. The next act of the drama would be played out beyond Earth's view, and all eyes shifted to the darkened eastern limb of the Moon. From that direction, in a mere forty minutes, Earth would learn the news of her fate.

FARSIDE CANNON CONTROL

The hours were beginning to tell on both of them. Hofmeister's normally emaciated frame seemed to have shrivelled on him, and his usual greyish complexion had grown more ashen still from exhaustion and strain. His puckered, hollowed face, still wearing its accustomed, manic, meaningless grin, resembled nothing so much as a mummi-fied skull, the very image of death in life.

Garrison wondered if he looked much better. He felt as if he had aged a year today.

But it was over, nearly over. He had done all he could.

He allowed himself a moment of pride, knowing he had worked wonders.

Wearily, Garrison stepped through the short tunnel to the observation dome and looked, for the last time, on the incredible and frightful thing he had built. The endless ranks of laser units were still a sight to awe him. Such fantastic power!

More power than could be allowed to exist. He knew that now. Here, today, the Cannon was needed. But tomorrow? A weapon that could kill whole cities from across the Solar System? Tomorrow could have no place for such a nightmare.

If there were enough tomorrows left to matter. The odds still were that Earth would die.

Garrison looked in admiration at the glittering triumph of the Cannon and bade it farewell, then turned away back down the tunnel to the control room. There was one last job to do. Jesus Moroz had done one last bit of programming for Garrison before he left for Mare Moscoviense. Garrison sat in front of his control panel and carefully punched in a certain thirty-character code group. He stood up.

"Let's go, Herr Hofmeister," he said gently.

Hofmeister looked up at Garrison. "What do you mean, go? Where should we go? Why should we leave here?"

Garrison shut his eyes in infinite weariness. He knew what would happen, what Hofmeister would say—even that Hofmeister was probably armed. But the scene must be played out. "We have to leave because this place is not going to be here much longer. The *Bouncer* is ready to fly us to Moscoviense. The Cannon is on automatic, and the asteroid is not going to maneuver again." That was a lie, but a very small one. "We don't need to stay, and we will die if we do stay."

"No! There is no self-destruct device here!" Hofmeister protested. "You are lying! This is a trick to get me away from the Cannon!"

"It's no trick, Hofmeister. It's time to go."

Hofmeister leapt to his feet and a gun appeared in his hand. "You lie! You want to keep me from using the splendid tool I build. You think I build for *you*?" Hofmeister leveled the the pistol at Garrison's heart.

Garrison stared down the barrel of the gun, astonished by his own remarkable calm. Was he so tired and over-wrought that a man threatening to kill him raised no particular emotion? Or did his own death seem that insignificant in the face of the doom that faced Earth? "No, Hofmeister," he said steadily. "I don't think you built it for me. I've locked out manual control. But I doubt it will be much use to you, either. I'm going to leave now, and you're welcome to come or go." *And if I let you stay, I'm condemning you to death*, Garrison thought. *But I'm too tired to argue, and there just isn't time.*

Garrison turned his back on the gun and walked toward the airlock, wondering, in a sort of detached intellectual way, what it would feel like when the bullet struck his spine.

Only when the airlock door sealed behind him did any sort of reaction set in. He reached for the inner-lock controls with shaking fingers, felt his guts turn to liquid, felt the bile of fear rising in his throat. All the frights and dreads and nightmares, the deaths of billions, the destruction of a world, everything he had held at bay for so long suddenly welled up inside him.

With a shock, he understood. Up until now, he had not expected to live, and fear meant nothing to the dead. But Hofmeister had let him go, and if the *Bouncer* did its job, he would escape the Cannon. He was going to live, and fear had meaning once again. But he could not allow himself to feel it yet. Not yet. He must hold it all at bay a little longer.

Once the *Bouncer* was aloft it would be time enough to be incapacitated with terror.

CORNUCOPIA

The asteroid tumbled wildly across the sky, its forward half a blazing wreck. That end was a super-heated blob of molten rock, huge gobbets of the fiery stuff whirling off into space. The midsection was not yet melted, but glowered with a heat that promised it could not survive much longer.

Down below, Farside Cannon kept up the fire, blasting out a relentless onslaught of heat and light that went on and on.

Only the stern section was still solid, but even there the heat was starting to do its damage. At the aft end of the asteroid, inside its protection cocoon, temperature gauges on the braking bomb were starting to show an alarming rise in temperature. The bomb could not last much longer.

It was time to use it or lose it.

DAWN TREADER

Cathy watched the read-outs from the bomb, wondering how long she could dare to hold out. There were so many risks, so many unknowns, so many gambles on top of gambles that it was impossible to gauge.

But guessing right was her *job*. Back in Iceland, guessing where to set the drilling rig had seemed the challenge of a lifetime. Now that problem seemed like child's play. She had no data on the current mass of the asteroid, no figures on its structural integrity, no real way of knowing if the bomb would work, or how much heat it could take. At least she had the asteroid's tumbling worked out pretty well for the moment. She knew which way it was pointed from moment to moment. That was *something*.

She watched the radar display as the asteroid swept nearer and nearer the Moon's surface. It would get close—but would it be close enough? When would be the right moment? It would have to be soon, but *when*? There weren't any numbers.

She shook her head and gave up. This one, she would have to do by feel. And the time to do it was very close indeed. She reached out a finger and rested it over the detonation button.

Very soon indeed.

ABOARD THE BOUNCER

The engine fired, filling the cabin with a noise like a giant pressure cooker blowing off its steam, and the *Bouncer* leapt up into the sky. Garrison sat in the pilot's seat, flying blindly into a sky full of turmoil. Moroz's special code was supposed to shut down the defense system and completely lock out the manual control system. If the defense lasers were still running, or Hofmeister managed to break in and regain control, or if this damn windowless pogo stick's flight path managed to take it through the Cannon's beam on its own without such outside interference—well, then Garrison wouldn't live. long enough to know about it.

It didn't matter. The struggle was over. Now that he could afford the time for fear, he no longer felt it. If he had to die now, that was a little thing in the lives and deaths of worlds.

More at peace than he ever dreamed he would be, Garrison Morrow flew on to the Sea of Moscow.

DAWN TREADER

Cathy watched the radar screen, the visual display, the ground track, the temp gauges, the computer's obviously inaccurate mass estimates for the asteroid, her eyes flickering back and forth across the numbers and pictures, a thin film of sweat forming on her brow. Her breath came in shallow gasps when she remembered to breathe at all.

Now, she realized. It had to be *now*.

With the fate of Earth in the tip of her finger, she slammed home the detonator button.

CORNUCOPIA

The bomb exploded, slamming forward against the carefully designed cradle that was meant to cushion its force and direct it aft to provide forward thrust. For the first millisecond, that worked, and the entire asteroid was driven down toward the Moon at an acceleration of hundreds of gees. But the rock that held the cradle, the rock that shaped the nozzle structure, was half-melted. It could not support the cradle or absorb the force of the explosion.

The rock gave way and the directionalized force of the blast slammed the bomb cradle forward into the softened core of the asteroid.

By the third millisecond after detonation, the bomb cradle was engulfed in molten rock, and the shock front of the explosion was already ripping through to the surface of the asteroid.

Much of the blastwave channeled through the heat-weakened core to blast through the molten rock of the forward end. The front of the asteroid splashed outward toward the Moon's surface, a fire-rose that blossomed outward and swelled across the darkness.

The asteroid blew up, the force of its explosion driving the wreckage down toward Farside in a massive wall of shrapnel a hundred kilometers across, aimed as precisely as Garrison might have wished, directly at the Cannon. For the Settlers were right: the Cannon was too powerful to be tolerated.

Ignoring its own imminent doom, the Cannon still fired, blazing away at the hell-fire that streamed down from the sky, four thousand lasers trying to target an incoming skyful of wreckage.

The Cannon's death rained down from the sky, billions of shattered fragments of all sizes that blasted into the surface, riddling the Cannon field and all the laser units, wrecking Farside Station, a billion impacts churning up the ground. Hofmeister must have died then, when impact fragments found Cannon Control.

But it was not over. Behind the smaller stuff came more massive pieces of the asteroid, pieces the size of cars, houses, hillsides, apartment buildings, slamming down into the crater fields of Farside over a three-hundred-kilometer radius, each impact flinging up new debris that reimpacted a meter or five thousand kilometers away, or escaped the Moon altogether and flew off into orbit.

The ground shook, the Moon's skies filled with dust and ash, impact flashes flickered and flared across the landscape.

And where once Cornucopia had moved in orbit, now there was nothing but dust and rubble.

Earth did not know it yet, but she was going to live.

Chapter Thirty-One

OPERATION SIDEBET HQ

The lasers of Sidebet Array swung into action, tracking and firing on the asteroid debris and impact ejecta that streamed overhead.

A nice little side bet it was, Ben decided as he watched the lasers firing, targeting, and firing over and over again. Some junk would get through, yes, but not enough to cause a real disaster or even major headaches, except for any orbital facility that happened to be in the way. And most of them could handle a few impacts from dust and pebbles.

And dust and pebbles were all that was going to be left of an asteroid ten miles across. Sidebet had two days before the debris cloud would reach Earth. Two days to blast any threatening boulders. What would have killed a planet would instead be little more than a spectacular meteor shower.

Ben looked toward the east, where Farside Cannon had been until an hour ago. That had been some Cannon that Garrison had dreamed up.

But then he thought of the Station, the outpost in the middle of nowhere that had been his home for two years.

That was a loss. The Research Station, the Observatory. But in exchange for a planet? The Settlers had already cancelled their ultimatum. Maybe the war scare would be enough to send both sides back to the bargaining table.

The word from Central Colony—no, Central *City* they were calling it already—the word from there was interesting as well. The ground had scarcely stopped shaking after the Cornucopia-induced Moonquakes when Hillary Wu, of all people, had declared the Lunar Republic. One outpost lost in exchange for so much gained.

It was a fair bargain.

Much more than fair.

MARE MOSCOVIENSE

Dr. Garrison Morrow stood on the surface in a rumpled pressure suit, watching from a respectful distance as the *Dawn Treader* touched down. Two years of sorrow, hurt and betrayal, two years of loneliness all seemed to vanish of their own accord as the *Treader* touched the surface.

Two years ago Cathy had disappeared, and now she was back. That was all that mattered now. The *Treader* shut down her engines.

Garrison could wait no longer. He ran, full tilt, across the rough wilderness, arriving at the ship's hatch before it could even open.

She was the first down. He knew who it was, before he saw her face through her helmet's faceplate. He went to her, and two absurd, clumsy figures in oversized pressure suits flung their arms about each other in the jumbled wilderness of Mare Moscoviense.

They looked deep into each other's eyes across the thin space of vacuum that was all that now divided them, and unashamed tears shone on their faces. Soon enough, even that barrier would be gone.

"Oh, Garrison," Cathy said at last, in a voice choked with more emotion than she could name. "We *did* it! We stopped the damned asteroid."

"That we did, Cathy. That we did."

Suddenly she started crying in earnest. "Oh, Garrison, I'm sorry. I'm sorry for it all. I never wanted to hurt you, or ruin your work. I messed up everything. If I had—if I had only—"

"Easy now. Easy. It's all right," he said. "It's going to be all right." He wrapped his arms about her and rocked her back and forth. The future was certain to be interesting. He pulled back from their embrace just far enough to look in her eyes. "None of that matters here," he said.

"After all, this is the Moon."

THE END

THE ORBIT SCIENCE FICTION
YEARBOOK 2
The Best Short SF of the Year

Edited by David Garnett

Plus articles by

Brian Aldiss and John Clute

WORLDS OF TOMORROW

Rolling and tumbling from the typewriters of the world's best Science Fiction writers, here are twelve gems, as different as diamonds, emeralds and rubies, but with the flawless glitter that denotes the perfect artefact.

J. G. BALLARD, PAUL DI FILIPPO,
SHARON N. FARBER, STEVEN GOULD,
JAMES PATRICK KELLY, KATHE KOJA,
IAN McDONALD, JACK MESSA, RUDY RUCKER
& MARC LAIDLAW, HOWARD WALDROP,
IAN WATSON, ROGER ZELAZNY

The second volume of THE ORBIT SCIENCE FICTION YEARBOOK also feature articles on the best SF novels of 1988 and a review of the year in Science Fiction by BRIAN ALDISS, JOHN CLUTE and DAVID GARNETT.

"Absolutely first-rate . . ." *Arthur C. Clarke*

"The anthology to buy first . . ." *Interzone*

"By far the best anthology . . . a stunning collection" *The Independent*

FUTURA PUBLICATIONS
AN ORBIT BOOK
SCIENCE FICTION
0 7088 8316 8